Up to
No Good

Also by Carl Weber

Something on the Side
The First Lady
So You Call Yourself a Man
The Preacher's Son
Player Haters
Lookin' For Luv
Married Men
Baby Momma Drama
She Ain't the One (with Mary B. Morrison)

CARL WEBER

Up to No Good

KENSINGTON PUBLISHING CORP.
www.kensingtonbooks.com

DAFINA BOOKS are published by

Kensington Publishing Corp.
119 West 40th Street
New York, NY 10018

Copyright © 2010 by Carl Weber

All rights reserved. No part of this book may be reproduced in any form
or by any means without the prior written consent of the Publisher, ex-
cepting brief quotes used in reviews.

All Kensington titles, imprints, and distributed lines are available at special
quantity discounts for bulk purchases for sales promotion, premiums,
fund-raising, educational, or institutional use.

Special book excerpts or customized printings can also be created to fit
specific needs. For details, write or phone the office of the Kensington Special Sales Manager: Kensington Publishing Corp., 119 West 40th Street,
New York, NY, 10018. Attn. Special Sales Department. Phone: 1-800-
221-2647.

Dafina and the Dafina logo Reg. U.S. Pat. & TM Off.

ISBN-13: 978-0-7582-3179-6
ISBN-10: 0-7582-3179-2

First Hardcover Printing: February 2009
First Trade Paperback Printing: January 2010
10 9 8 7 6 5 4 3 2 1

Printed in the United States of America

This book is dedicated to *my friends of relation*.
My thanks for standing by me when others
knew the truth but wouldn't.
My loyalty and friendship is a bond we will share forever.

James

1

"So, are you going to take me back to your place, or are we going to make Benny rich by running up a ridiculous bar tab?" Crystal whispered seductively.

Her eyes traveled over my body, stopping a little below my belt as she took a sip of her drink. This was her way of letting me know that she was ready. The next move was mine, and her body language was begging me to make it. She lifted her head, her eyes meeting mine as she put her drink on the bar. I smiled, giving her my own once-over. I couldn't help but respond with a devilish grin as I placed my hand on the small of her back, high enough to be respectable but low enough to have an effect. She shuddered slightly under my touch, even though her face failed to give anything away.

We hadn't seen each other in almost a year, and probably wouldn't see each other for another one, unless our son Darnel's wife-to-be Keisha became pregnant in the next few months. Crystal had traveled back to New York from Richmond, Virginia, for Darnel's wedding, which was tomorrow night. We'd met at Benny's bar, one of our old neighborhood haunts, to catch up on old times after the rehearsal dinner.

"So?" she asked again, this time with a little more desperation in her voice. She wanted me. She wanted me bad. She wanted me to do what only I could do for her—satisfy that sexual itch that nobody else seemed able to reach. I know it sounds rather arrogant, but I'd been sleeping with this woman off and on for the better part of twenty-eight years, so I knew what she needed in the bedroom, just like she knew what I needed.

I glanced at her again. Even in a conservative pantsuit, she had a way of enticing me. Her face was a beautiful bronze color, highlighted by a beauty mark right above the left side of her lip. She'd gained a few pounds over the years, and her hair showed a hint of gray around the edges, but hell, whose didn't? Besides, truth be told, I liked a woman with some meat on her bones and some mileage on her engine. Experience meant a lot in life, especially in the bedroom.

She turned her head slightly, exposing a small tattoo with the letters *DB*, our son's initials, on the lower side of her neck. A memory of the way she cooed when I kissed her neck came to mind. Then I looked down at her chest, and the thought of her neck was quickly replaced with an image of her large, plump breasts and the silver-dollar nipples that rested atop them. My heart rate increased, and my breathing became heavier. It never mattered where I touched her; Crystal's body was so sexually in tune with mine that I didn't even have to take off my clothes to give her an orgasm. Oh, but when I did get undressed, she would return the favor like very few women I'd ever known. Having a child together bonded us, but it was the sex that kept us hungering for each other year after year.

She licked her lips, and my manhood sprang to life. I flicked my wrist so I could see the time on my watch. I was wondering if Crystal was planning on a quickie or one of our all-night marathons. I'd already canceled a date to meet with her, so an all-nighter with someone of her sexual prowess was fine by me. That, of course, left only one question.

"Where's your husband?" I asked, getting straight to the point.

Crystal looked annoyed by my question. Yes, she was married, going on five years now, and she definitely preferred that I didn't mention her husband when we were getting ready to get busy. We both knew that her marital status really wasn't a factor in all this anyway. We'd played this game before, Crystal and I, through countless boyfriends and two husbands. She didn't make any excuses for the fact that she was a woman who needed a man in her life. She always said that she would prefer it if that man were me, but after a while, she stopped holding her breath and moved on.

One thing was for sure, though: It didn't matter who she was with. If we saw each other or had the chance to talk on the phone, it was never a question of *if* we were going to get together, but rather when and where it would happen.

"He had to work third shift. He'll be here sometime early tomorrow morning." Crystal slid off her bar stool and folded her arms as if to say, "So, come on. We got time, but we ain't got all night." I knew her well, and she was not about to take no for an answer. And as good as she was looking, I wasn't about to give her an argument.

"Okay, but only if you're going to respect me in the morning," I teased.

She didn't laugh. Instead, she came back with, "Please. You my baby daddy. I ain't got to respect you." Unfortunately, I knew she wasn't joking, and her words stung like hell.

"You don't?"

"Hell no. Everybody knows you ain't shit, James. As much as I love our son, I should have never had a baby with you." She'd been using this same line on me since Darnel was a baby, and now here he was, a grown man getting ready to get married and have babies of his own. Jesus, I was getting old.

"Then why do you want me to take you home? Why do you keep sleeping with me after all these years? You tryin' to say you ain't got no love for me?"

"Please, James. You broke my heart more times than I care to remember and in more ways than I will ever forget. I'd be a fool if I still had love for you."

"If you ain't got love for me, then why are you trying to sleep with me?"

"Good dick is hard to come by," she said, like it was a simple fact of life that everyone understood. "And you've got some really good dick. Now, are you going to sit here and debate it, or are you gonna take me home and remind me why I rented a car and drove seven hours up here instead of waiting for my husband so we could drive together?"

I reached in my pocket and pulled out a twenty-dollar bill. I slapped it down on the bar, nodding my head.

"You know me. Last thing I want is for anyone to make a seven-hour trip in vain," I said with a laugh. The truth of her words could have deflated my desire for her, but I knew this was not an opportunity to waste on being overly sensitive or sentimental. Besides, I'd known this woman my entire adult life, and there wasn't a thing she could say that I hadn't heard at least a dozen times before. We were too far past that naïve stage to believe we'd ever be anything more than what we were today.

Crystal leaned in and kissed my full lips, then smiled as if I had just given her a large sum of money. The way she stared at me made my manhood grow, making it clear that I was the one about to hit the jackpot. In less than twenty minutes, we'd both be in my bed, as naked as the day we were born, making love like there was no tomorrow. And as it had always been between the two of us, there would be no tomorrow—only a here and now.

Five hours later, Crystal was snoring with a purpose, her back to my chest and her round hips and ass securely resting against my groin. I'd wake her up in about ten minutes for another round. She would have to leave after that in order to make it back to her hotel before her husband showed up. Part of me didn't want her to leave, because I was having such a good time. I always had a good time when Crystal and I got together.

I stared at her face as I stroked her sweaty hair. We'd gone at it for the better part of an hour—twice. The way she called out my name and told me that this would always be her dick was definitely good for the ego. It also told me that after all these years, no matter what she said, she was still in love with me.

Crystal had sacrificed most of her adult years chasing after me. We'd met right after high school. I was far from being faithful, but she was as close to a steady girlfriend as I had during those days.

She looked out for me when no one else would, sometimes even when it wasn't in her best interest. There wasn't anything Crystal Jackson wouldn't do for me. I knew that better than anyone on this earth, and the thing that haunted me the most was that she wanted only one thing in return: my love. But as much as I tried, I just couldn't give it to her the way she wanted it.

Like most women, she wanted to be a wife much more than a girlfriend. Don't get me wrong; I liked her, but I wasn't having no part of getting married. I was having too much fun with all the other women in my life. Crystal, on the other hand, wouldn't take no for an answer. As far as she was concerned, she was in love with me, and all I needed was a little coaxing to understand that I loved her too. She was so convinced of this that she got pregnant, hoping it would settle me down enough for us to get married. It didn't. All it really made me do was act the fool even more. It was something I wished could have been changed, but I still had no regrets. I'd had a good life, a fun life. Why would I mess it up by getting married?

"I'm sorry," I whispered.

"Huh?" She lifted her head. "What did you say?"

"Ah, nothing." I leaned over and kissed her cheek.

She rolled over to face me. "If you're gonna kiss me, kiss me right."

I smiled as I studied her face through the dim light that peeked between the curtains. She really was beautiful, and I'd never seen a woman age so well.

I pressed my lips against hers, and our kiss became passionate. My hands roamed her body hungrily. Just as she mounted me for another round, my bedroom door flew open and blinding light flooded the room.

Crystal dove under the covers to hide her nakedness.

"What the—" I shouted, squinting my eyes to adjust to the bright light as I saw what looked like a woman standing in my doorway. In that brief moment, my mind went into overdrive, trying to understand who had just broken into my house. It could have been one of any number of women I'd been seeing over the past few months—but most likely the one I had broken a date with to meet Crystal. But how the hell had she gotten into my house?

The woman yelled, "I knew you was here with her!" and suddenly I knew who the intruder was. This wasn't just any woman standing in my doorway. This was a woman I loved with all my heart, but when it came to me pursuing my love life, she could be described with only one word: *trouble*.

Darnel

2

"Well, tomorrow's the big day. You're really gonna go through with it, aren't you?"

I smiled, nodding my head at my best friend, Omar, as I slid my key into the door of my hotel room and pushed it open. We'd just left what was quite possibly the best bachelor party ever thrown, and we were both drunk. I plopped down on the first of two queen-sized beds while Omar stumbled toward the bathroom to relieve himself. I didn't know about Omar, but I was tired, both mentally and physically drained from preparing for my big day tomorrow and from celebrating my last night as a single man with my boys.

Omar, who was my best man, had gone all out, inviting all our friends, along with six of the wildest strippers I'd ever seen. They were more like erotic circus performers than strippers, with all the contortions and tricks they showed us. Add them to the top-shelf liquor our friend Reggie supplied and *Bam!* One hell of a bachelor party.

"You know, Dee," Omar slurred as he stood in the bathroom, "I never thought you'd really go through with it. I mean, I like Keisha and all, but . . ." He paused. I heard him say "Ahhhh," followed by the sound of him relieving himself.

"Man, will you close the door? Don't nobody wanna hear you peeing." I loved Omar like the brother I never had, but he could really be disgusting sometimes. Some might even call him repulsive.

"Don't get your panties in a bunch. I'm done now." He walked out of the bathroom with his zipper down and his pants hanging off his ass, exposing his plaid boxers. I didn't bother to remind him to wash his hands, because, like I said, he could be a little raw.

"So, what were you saying about me getting married? You didn't think I was gonna do it? Man, I been with that woman since I was fifteen years old. That pussy is bought and paid for. I ain't got no choice but to marry her." I tried to sound cool for Omar, but the truth was, I loved Keisha with all my heart.

"Yeah, I know that, and you been faithful to her since you was fifteen. But what I wanna know is, do you really want to die having been with only one woman?" His expression made it look as if he felt sorry for me. I hated that look.

"You act like me being faithful is a bad thing."

This conversation was nothing new to me. Omar and my boys had always thought me strange because of my faithfulness to Keisha. The way they saw it, a man was supposed to get as much experience as he could with as many women as were willing to give it up. But I viewed things differently. I had given my virginity and pledged my faithfulness to Keisha, and I wasn't about to hurt her by cheating with some woman who didn't mean anything to me. My father had done that to my mother. I grew up seeing how deeply it affected her life and saw the hurt in her eyes over and over again, so I vowed never to do that to the woman I loved. It just wasn't worth it to me.

"Nah, it ain't a bad thing," he conceded, "just unrealistic. Besides, with that chick Tia as her maid of honor, who knows what they're doing across the street at her bachelorette party." Omar sat down on the bed across from me with a strange look on his face—like he had something important to say but couldn't find the words. He was starting to piss me off. "Dee, I heard Tia hired male strippers for Keisha's bachelorette party. Who knows what Keisha could be—"

I cut him off right there. "Look, bro, Keisha ain't Tia, just like I'm not you! You got that?"

"You think our strippers had big titties? Can you imagine how big those male strippers' dicks are? Stretch that tight little pussy right on out."

Omar was my boy, but he was really pushing the limit tonight. "You're drunk, so I'm gonna ignore that. But, O, you better check yourself," I warned him.

He laughed, but I wanted him to understand that I was serious. The night before my wedding was not the time for him to be disrespecting my fiancée like this. I loved that woman more than I loved myself.

"I'm just saying . . . do you really think you're the only guy Keisha has ever been with?"

I stood up and pointed my finger in his face. "Best friend or not, don't come out your face like that about her again or I'll—"

"Or you'll what? Man, sit your ass down." He laughed. "What you gonna do, fight your best man for trying to get you some pussy the night of your bachelor party?" He shook his head.

I let out an aggravated sigh. "O, I don't know why you gotta disrespect me before my wedding."

He was still smiling, but he had stopped laughing. I think he could finally see that I was upset. "Yo, Dee, I'm sorry, man. I meant no disrespect, but—"

"You need to shut that drunk-ass mouth of yours, then."

"You right, I'm drunk," he admitted, still smiling at me. "And maybe I should be quiet. But just remember, drunk people usually tell the truth. So I'm telling you, Darnel, you need to get some ass before you get married. I could set it up like that." He snapped his fingers.

I was amazed at how persistent Omar was. He knew damn well that Keisha was my life, so he was wasting his time trying to convince me to cheat on her.

I lay down on the bed. "Can't do it, buddy. I'm a one-woman man."

"You wasn't such a one-woman man when that stripper was giving you that lap dance in the corner, were you?" Omar's smile widened. "I saw the way you was trying to hide your hard dick once she got off of you." He imitated my actions, crossing his arms casually over his lap.

I turned my head away so he wouldn't see my smirk. I had indeed been turned on by the honey-colored stripper who called herself Destiny. She had coaxed me into a lap dance when I thought everyone was watching the other strippers do tricks. I'd be lying if I said I didn't enjoy it. But that still didn't mean I wanted to have sex with her.

"You saw that, huh?" I said.

"Yeah, I saw it. So did half the other brothers in the room."

"Jesus Christ." I was so embarrassed.

"What's wrong with you? It was a fuckin' bachelor party, Dee. What? Your dick not supposed to get hard when a fine-ass naked woman sits on your lap? I'd be worried if it didn't." Omar smiled as he tried once again to tempt me to get laid by another woman on the night before my wedding. "You couldn't keep your eyes off that fine-ass honey the rest of the night, could you?"

"You just don't understand. Keisha is my soul mate. I'm not supposed to be attracted to any other woman that way. I made a promise, and I'm keeping it."

"No, you don't understand." Omar paced back and forth like a lawyer delivering a passionate closing argument. "I mean, I appreciate that being faithful shit, but you take it to another level. You need to have some fun, Dee."

I didn't have a chance to answer him, because his cell phone rang. He must have been expecting the call, because suddenly his eyes lit up and he looked really excited. He answered the phone in a hurry and took it into the bathroom. Unlike when he used the toilet before, this time he closed the door behind him.

He came out about five minutes later, smiling.

"Yo, I'm about to hook up with one of them strippers. Her friend Destiny asked about you. She wanted to know if you wanted to hang." He looked at me eagerly. "This is your last opportunity, man."

"Nah, you go. I'm gonna chill out right here and get some rest. I got a big day ahead of me."

"Whatever." Omar shook his head, looking very disappointed in me as he headed for the door. "If you change your mind, give me a call."

"I won't," I assured him.

Once he was gone, I pulled out my cell and dialed Keisha's number. She answered on the second ring with a sweet, "Hello." I loved her voice. I know it sounds corny, but it was like music to my ears. I can't even begin to explain how much I loved this woman.

"Hey, babe," I greeted her. I was lying on my side, remembering how beautiful she looked tonight at the rehearsal dinner. I couldn't wait to make her my wife.

"Hey, boo." She sounded excited to hear from me. "You still at the bachelor party?"

"Nah, I'm in the room, bored and lonely."

"Oh, my poor baby." She was using this cute little-girl voice. "Don't worry. After tomorrow, you don't ever have to be lonely again."

"I like the sound of that. So what you doing?"

"I'm about to leave the bar and go up to my room. Tia done found her some man."

"Figures," I replied. "Hey, want some company?"

"I'd love some . . . tomorrow night." She chuckled. "I know what you're up to, Mr. Black. You ain't gettin' none until after the wedding. Besides, you know it's bad luck to see the bride before the wedding."

Keisha had been holding out on me for the past three weeks. We shared an apartment together, but she'd been making me sleep in the guest room, telling me some crap about I'd appreciate it more if we waited until after the wedding. As horny as I was the past few days, I was deeply regretting the fact that I'd actually agreed to our mini-celibacy.

"Okay, okay. I guess I'll go see if I can find my other best friend."

"I just saw Omar and some woman leaving the hotel."

"It was probably that stripper he was going to meet."

"Maybe. Look, baby, I'm about to get in the elevator. If I lose the signal, I'll call you back."

"Nah, it's a'ight, babe. You go 'head. I'll see you in the morning. I love you, Mrs. Black."

"I love you, too, Mr. Black. Good night." I could hear her smiling through the phone. She loved it when I called her Mrs. Black.

"Night, babe." I hung up the phone, fiending for my woman. I just wanted to be near her. Hell, I would have settled for a kiss and a hug.

One long, lonely hour later, I found myself wishing that I had gone with Omar—not to have sex with that woman Destiny or anything, but just to get out of the room. I was so keyed up. When I first got to the room, I was dead tired, but after talking to Keisha, anxiety set in and I couldn't sleep. All I could do was think of her and the wedding. Was everything going to be all right? Were the limos going to pick us up on time? Was the reception going to be decorated the way we wanted? Was Omar going to get back from screwing that woman on time? Were my father and stepfather going to get along? There were so many things running through my mind.

Whenever I had nights like this, when I had too much on my mind, Keisha was always the one who could soothe me and help me fall asleep. If I could just get one kiss, I thought, I could make it through the night. One kiss was all I wanted. Never mind all that "bad luck to see the bride" stuff; I decided to go surprise my future wife.

I got out of bed, still feeling the effects of the alcohol. I wasn't as bad as when I had first got back to the room, but I was still drunk.

I staggered to the elevator, punched the DOWN button, and rode to the lobby. Fortunately, I wasn't so drunk that the lady at the front desk would give me a hard time. I told her that I had lost my key to the wedding suite. The truth was that Keisha was staying there alone tonight, and we would be there together after the wedding. But the desk clerk didn't need to know those details. As long as the name on my driver's license matched the name on the reservation, she was happy to give me a duplicate key card.

"Congratulations," she said with a smile.

"Thanks," I answered as I grabbed a handful of mints and headed back to the elevator. As I rode up to the twentieth floor, I popped a few mints in my mouth to mask the smell of alcohol on my breath. Keisha hated when I was drunk.

I couldn't wait to see her. Maybe if I played my cards right, I would get more than a kiss.

When I got to the suite, I slid the card in the door and walked into the living room. The lights were out, and I didn't see any reason to turn them on as I walked from the living room into the bedroom. There were enough bright city lights coming through the space between the curtains for me to see everything I needed to. And what I saw was my worst nightmare come true.

On the bed, lying naked on her stomach, was Keisha. Now, normally that wouldn't have been a bad thing, but lying on top of her was Omar. That's right, Omar. The same Omar who was supposed to be my best friend and the best man in my wedding tomorrow, the same Omar who had tried his damnedest to get me to cheat on Keisha, was now screwing her from behind. Oh, and was he having a good old time, too, pumping away like there was no tomorrow. Unfortunately for him, there would be no tomorrow, because I was going to kill him.

Like someone hit by lightning, anger struck me. I sobered up completely within a matter of seconds. Before I could think, I took three long steps across the room, grabbed the ceramic lamp off the night table, and smashed it as hard as I could into Omar's head. The lamp shattered as Omar rolled off Keisha, screaming in pain.

I turned my attention to Keisha, and for a moment, time stopped. It was like our entire relationship flashed before my eyes. I saw our first date, our first kiss, the first time we made love, the prom, our apartment, the day I proposed, the last time we made love, the rehearsal dinner earlier tonight, and now her lying in front of me. I don't know how my eyes must have looked, but Keisha began pleading, "Don't get crazy, Darnel. This is not what it seems."

I couldn't help myself. I slapped the shit outta her. "It's not? 'Cause it sure as hell seems like you fuckin' my best friend." I slapped her again, then turned to Omar.

"I'm sorry, man," Omar whimpered.

I looked down at his dick, and rage filled my entire being. "Motherfucker, you ain't even wearing a condom!"

I lunged at him and started whaling on his ass. I beat him fiercely, kicking him in the face and trying to stomp his fucking guts out.

"I thought you was my boy," I kept repeating with every punch I delivered. My blows fell into some kind of rhythmic pattern: Fist, fist, kick, kick. Fist, fist, kick, kick. "I thought you was my dog, and you gon' do me like this? Fuck my girl without a condom? I ain't even fucked her without a condom. Oh, hell naw. I'ma kill you!"

Omar never returned any blows. I guess he knew he was wrong, or else he was just too hurt to muster a defense. He covered his head the best he could, but I was relentless in my fury.

I could feel Keisha trying to pull me off. "Stop, Darnel! You're going to kill him!"

"Bitch! Get the fuck off, you fuckin' ho!" I was so full of adrenaline that I threw her across the room with barely any effort. Then I returned to Omar.

I couldn't stop beating O until I got all my venom out. I've never known such pure hate. And pain. Yes, I was in just as much pain as I'm sure Omar was. I wanted him to feel my agony, to know that what he did had crossed the boundaries of human decency. It reminded me of when I was a little boy and my mom would whoop me and say, "This hurts me just as much as it hurts you."

I saw Omar's nose gushing bright red blood, and his eyes were blackened and swollen. He was bleeding from his mouth. I think he was trying to say, "I'm sorry," but I didn't care. I already knew he was sorry. He was a sorry excuse for a friend and a man; that's what he was.

Keisha must have called security, because two men in blue uniforms came out of nowhere and pulled me off Omar. It took both of them to get me loose from him.

Finally, I relented and stopped kicking his ass. "Let me go. I'm cool."

Jamie

3

I slammed my foot on the brakes, cursing under my breath when I spotted his Lexus parked in the driveway. Behind it was one of those compact cars that car-rental companies have hundreds of. I had a good idea who had parked it there too.

I'd been calling his ass for the better part of two hours, both on his house phone and cell phone, but got no answer at either. Whenever that happened, it was pretty much guaranteed that he was with some woman. And now that I saw the cars in the driveway, I knew that they were in there, in his bed.

He is so fucking predictable.

I sighed and reached into the glove compartment for the set of keys to his house. I'd made them last month when he let me borrow his Lexus while my car was in the shop. I'd had my own set when I was living with him, but when I moved out a few months ago, he changed the locks so I wouldn't catch him in the act with one of his whores. I'm sure he thought he was being smart by taking my keys, but I guess he forgot: *Smarter* was my middle name.

Keys in hand, I got out of the car and headed up the walkway, checking the rear bumper of the car parked behind his for a rental-car sticker. Of course, you know there was a black-and-yellow Hertz sticker there, just as I suspected.

I was pissed. No, I was more than pissed. As much as I loved him, I just couldn't understand why he always had to sleep with her when she came to town. It was just so damn disrespectful. Not to mention the fact that she was such a damn slut for doing it. I mean, he was a man; men do this type of thing because they're dogs. But she was a woman. Didn't she have any shame? She was married, for Christ's sake!

I opened the door, then walked into the living room. Not much had changed since I had been there two nights ago. On the coffee table, however, were two empty champagne glasses and an open bottle of Cristal, which I assumed came from the liquor he kept down in the basement. That stash was supposed to be for special occasions. I guess getting some ass from her was considered a special occasion—never mind the fact that they'd probably done it a million times before. Well, no matter, because it was a special occasion I was gonna break up.

I picked up the bottle of Cristal and selected the glass that didn't have any lipstick marks on it. I poured myself some champagne. As I sipped, savoring the way the bubbles felt on my tongue, I contemplated whether I should act ghetto or ladylike when I confronted him. I could very easily run up the stairs and bum-rush his bedroom like a maniac, yelling and screaming like a fool. Or I could act like a lady and just holler up the stairs. That way they could get their shit together and come down so we could handle our business like adults.

I weighed my options for a few seconds, then came to a final conclusion: *Fuck that!* It was five o'clock in the morning, way too late to be a lady about any-damn-thing. I was going upstairs.

I finished my champagne with one gulp and headed for the stairs. When I got to his bedroom door, I could barely contain my anger at hearing the two of them rustling around on the bed. It sounded like I was about to catch them right in the act. As angry as it made me, I had to give him some credit. For a man his age, he sure had some stamina. I knew damn well they had been screwing all night long and were expecting to keep it going, but that wasn't about to happen.

I chuckled, wondering how long he would be able to keep it up once I entered the room. Well, I was about to find out. I took a deep breath, then reached for the doorknob. I threw open the door, stepped in, and flipped on the light.

There they were, doing exactly what I thought they'd be doing. She was on top but quickly retreated under the covers.

He, on the other hand, yelled at me and sat up. I knew he was angry, but I didn't give a damn at this point. Just the sight of her had angered me so much that I'd momentarily forgotten why I was there.

I walked toward the bed with a purpose, pointing my finger at her. "I knew you was here with her!"

His forehead creased and his jaw tightened as he glared at me like he was trying to burn a hole right through me. I'd seen this look from him before, and it was usually followed by an angry tirade.

"Jamie!" he yelled. "What the hell are you doing in my house?"

I froze right where I was standing. For the first time since I entered his house, I had serious second thoughts about how smart it had been to bust into his room.

"Ah . . . ah . . . Daddy, you wouldn't answer your phone," I stammered, "and . . ."

"And what?" he demanded.

I stared at my father, suddenly dumbstruck. I hadn't seen him this mad in years. Here I was, twenty-five years old, and I felt like I was sixteen going on twelve. Why the hell hadn't I just hollered up those stairs, or at least knocked on the bedroom door?

I glanced over at Crystal, my half brother Darnel's mother, who was now sitting up with a sheet wrapped around her upper body. This was all her fault. If that wench could keep her panties on, my father would have answered his phone and I wouldn't be in this predicament. What the hell did Daddy see in her anyway? Damn, I hated that wench.

"Don't look at her! She's got nothing to do with this, dammit. Now, what the hell are you doing here?" He actually seemed to be getting angrier.

I turned back to him, avoiding eye contact. Then, suddenly, my brain started working properly, and I remembered why I had come here in the first place.

"Darnel," I said, breaking my silence.

This time Crystal jumped in. "Darnel? What about him? Is he all right? There wasn't an accident, was there? Where's my baby now? He's not in the hospital, is he? Is he all right? He's not dead, is he?" She was talking so fast and asking so many questions that I could barely understand a word she was saying.

When I didn't answer quickly enough, she stood up from the bed and approached me, naked. "Where the hell is my son?"

My father stopped her from getting too close. Good move on his part. He'd probably noticed the way my fingers curled into fists as soon as she came near me. "Crystal, calm down and let her talk," he advised.

"I'm not gonna calm down. I wanna know what's going on with my son."

He glared at her and she became silent. Daddy's eyes had a way of talking to you. "What's going on with your brother, princess?" His voice had lost its edge, and the fact that he had called me by my pet name made me feel better.

"He's been trying to call you two all night. Daddy . . . Darnel's in jail."

Darnel

4

"Sign here and here and here." The corrections officer pointed to the places where he wanted my signature. I did as I was told, and then he handed me a brown paper bag that held my wallet, cell phone, keys, and court documents. He pointed toward a door at the other end of the corridor. "You wanna head down there."

"Thanks," I replied, then turned to walk toward the door.

"No problem, Black. And good luck to you. I think you can beat this case." He sounded sincere, and I knew it was probably because he felt sorry for me. Everyone in the Queens courthouse building had heard my nightmarish story by now. Most of the corrections and court officers were going out of their way to look out for me, doing things like giving me an extra bologna-and-cheese sandwich and a second cup of the watered-down Kool-Aid they fed us as we waited to see the judge. One CO even brought me to his office so I could call my sister when I was unable to reach my parents.

Yep, I'm sure they felt sorry for me. Who wouldn't feel sorry for a guy who caught his fiancée and his best friend screwing the night before his wedding? What man in his right mind wouldn't have tried to kill both of them?

I walked down the corridor, and another CO patted me on the back for encouragement, then let me out the door. My stomach immediately began to churn when I spotted my father standing next to my sister. Sitting on a bench across from them were my mother and my stepfather, Milton King. I'd seen them in court a few hours ago when the judge set bail, but I hadn't expected them all to be waiting for me, especially not my father. He'd always told me that if I ever got arrested, I was on my own.

When she saw me, my mother jumped up off the bench and grabbed me in a bear hug, like I'd just come home from war. It was obvious from the mascara streaks running down her face that she'd been crying. This didn't help the churning in my stomach, which had become more like the spin cycle on a washing machine, the result of a combination of anger, pain, and embarrassment.

When she finally let go, my mother's face was wet with tears. She stepped aside and my father approached.

"You okay?" He sounded genuinely concerned, but I knew it was just a matter of seconds before he started one of his high-and-mighty lectures about how I should have used some self-control. To hell with the fact that I was hurt and that two of the people I loved most in the world had just ripped out my heart.

"Yeah, I'm all right." I nodded, avoiding eye contact with him.

To my surprise, he wrapped his arms around me and hugged me as tightly as my mother had. Then he whispered, "I love you, son."

One of my eyebrows went up. *I love you, son?* Where the hell did that come from?

It took me a few seconds to respond, because we didn't have a kissy, huggy, I-love-you type of relationship. That had always been reserved for my sister, my father's unquestionable favorite. Our relationship, on the other hand, had been built on the fact that whatever he said, I did. I respected him as my father and my elder, but in truth, I didn't much care for him as a man.

It's funny, because as a kid, I thought he was the most wonderful, attentive father in the entire world. He never missed a Little League game or a school play. I can't remember a Sunday he didn't come by and pick me up for Sunday school. He even dressed up as Santa Claus for Christmas every year, up until I was eight. But none of that mattered when I realized he was a womanizing bastard who basically stole my mother's youth.

My mother loved him so much that she used to cry herself to sleep when he wouldn't answer his phone. Many a late night she'd throw me in the car so she could drive around, knocking on strange women's doors, looking for him. I think I was about ten when I realized what was really going on. That was about the time I found out that all the women who came by his house when I spent the night weren't really related to us. Before that, I just took my father's word for it when he referred to every female visitor as yet another auntie.

This was also around the time when I found out my parents weren't really married. Somehow, I'd always believed they were, even though we lived in separate homes—probably because he always seemed to be around. Things really kicked in when an older bully realized that calling me a bastard and my mother a whore would piss me off. I didn't even know what those words meant. But when I did find out, I asked my father to marry my mother, and he refused, giving me one of his lectures. This particular lecture was about sticks and stones and that nonsense about how words can never hurt you. I didn't give a damn what he said; words can hurt. I know they hurt me.

It took a long time and a lot of coaxing from my mother before I got over the fact that my father wouldn't marry her. Actually, I was still not really over it and probably never would be.

It was his treatment of my mom that made me so strong in my conviction to be faithful to Keisha. I didn't want to do to her what my father had done to my mom. But now, in retrospect, I realized I should have fucked everything that moved. If she had slept with my best friend, only the Lord knows who else she'd laid down with.

Although I appreciated my father's "I love you" gesture, I just couldn't bring myself to say it back to him, so instead I said, "Thanks for being here."

"You don't have to thank me, son." He released me from his embrace, moving over for my sister, Jamie.

"Hey, big bro." She gave me a quick hug and a kiss on the cheek. "I told you Daddy would take care of everything."

I loved my little sister despite how spoiled she was for a grown-ass woman. You name it, my father gave it to her. He even gave her a job in his real estate office, with a salary that probably made her the best-paid secretary in Queens. So, unlike me, Jamie believed my father could walk on water and do no wrong. As far as she was concerned, the sun rose and set because of him. Our views of our father couldn't have been more different.

After a few more words between Jamie and me, my stepfather extended his hand. I took it, pulling him in close. I liked Milton a lot. Not only was he genuinely a good man, but he also treated my mother the way she deserved to be treated—unlike my father, who'd always treated her like a last-minute booty call that would always be there.

Milton and my mother didn't live in New York. I had suggested several years ago that Milton move my mother somewhere far away when he told me he planned on asking her to marry him. My dad had a way of tricking my mother into bed. He'd helped her mess up quite a few good relationships and one marriage by screwing around with him. I knew that although my mother cared for Milton, he didn't stand a chance if my dad was anywhere nearby. My mother was addicted to James Black like he was a narcotic, and she would do anything and go through anybody, including me, to get some. Thank goodness my stepfather took my advice once they got married and transferred his job and my mother down to Richmond.

I felt a hand on my shoulder.

"I'm going over to the church. The bishop just called and said people are starting to arrive for the wedding. I think someone from our family needs to tell them the wedding is off." My father was like that, all about appearance and family reputation. He didn't want anyone at the church to think badly of us, especially since he was a big-time deacon there. Of course, everyone in the congregation knew he was the biggest whoremonger in the entire borough of Queens. But he still tried his best to keep the façade of a respectable family man.

My father glanced at his watch, then looked toward me. "I'm assuming the wedding is off?" he asked. A silent nod was my answer. "Crystal, you and Milton don't mind—"

"I'll go with you," I said quietly.

"You don't have to do this, son. I can handle it." I know he was trying to be helpful, but why couldn't he just do as I said this one time?

"I know, but it's not your responsibility. Those are my guests. I need to be the one to tell them."

"There's a chance Keisha and her family might be there." I could tell my father was reading my face to see if I still cared about her. Like Omar, he was one of those who had often suggested I sow my wild oats before I walked down the aisle. I wondered if he was feeling the urge to say "I told you so."

"I kind of hope she is there," my sister said with a smirk. "'Cause I will beat her ass and you'll have to bail me out next."

"Jamie!" my father snapped.

"Leave her be, James. 'Cause if she don't beat her ass, I will." My mother placed one hand on her hip and her arm around Jamie's neck. The two of them were displaying more attitude than a couple of street thugs. My father frowned, shaking his head as he glanced at me, then at Milton. I'm sure the three of us were thinking exactly the same thing: my problem had just become a family problem, and if we weren't careful, that church was gonna be turned out.

James

5

The ride to the church was solemn and felt much longer than the fifteen minutes it took. Both Darnel and Jamie rode with me, while Crystal and her husband followed behind us in his car. Regardless of what Crystal and Jamie had said at the courthouse, I don't think any of us were looking forward to facing our guests or Keisha's family—especially not Darnel, who was staring blankly out the window.

I glanced at him as I drove, admiring his smooth chocolate skin and handsome features. He was a good-looking young man who seemed to be wearing my face from my younger days. I tried to hide a prideful smile. I couldn't deny him even if I wanted to, but who would deny such a fine young man as his son? I just wished I could find the words to help him get past all this mess with Keisha. From the way he looked, I'm sure he felt like he had the weight of the entire world on his shoulders.

"Your mother's going to ask you to move to Richmond." My words interrupted our silence as we pulled into the church parking lot.

"I don't wanna move to Richmond," Darnel insisted. "I hate it down there."

I felt like I had just added another thousand pounds to the mental load he was already carrying. I had told Crystal this was going to be a problem. "Look, son, don't kill the messenger. I'm just giving you a heads-up." I pulled into a parking space about fifty yards from the church. "Your mother's a mother; she wants to protect you from yourself. You can understand that, can't you?"

"I'm not a baby, Dad. I'm a grown man. I don't need my mommy to protect me."

"You sure about that? 'Cause I've seen you suck your thumb." Jamie leaned forward as she teased her brother. Caught off guard by the remark, both Darnel and I turned our heads in the direction of the backseat.

"You need to stop it, Jamie!" I shouted. "You are way too old for this. What is wrong with you?" I gave her the eye, letting her know that we were going to have words later.

She sat back in her seat and folded her arms across her chest. I loved her to death, but she could be so childish at times.

"Sorry about that, son," I said, turning back to Darnel. "I don't think your sister had much sleep last night. I'm sure she could use a nap."

"She ain't the only one," he replied. "Look, like I was saying, I'm not a baby, Dad."

I placed my hand on his arm. "I agree, but you can't stay in that apartment with Keisha, can you?"

"No, but why do I have to move out? Why can't she move out? The lease is in both of our names. Besides, she's the one who cheated."

"She's also the one with order of protection against you," I reminded him.

"She didn't ask for that order of protection. My lawyer said that they issue them out to everyone in domestic cases."

I wondered if he was really trying to defend Keisha.

"That doesn't change the fact that if you violate it, they're going to revoke your bail and throw you in jail."

"So, what, am I supposed to be homeless? 'Cause I'm not moving to Richmond. God, I hate her!" With those words, he opened the door and placed one foot on the concrete. Before he got out of the car, I reached out and stopped him.

"Son, why don't you move in with me?" It wasn't my idea of Disneyland, but it was the right thing to do, asking him to come live with me. I'd just gotten Jamie out of the house not too long ago and, man, was I loving it. But this was my son, and as long as I had a roof, so would he. "Just until you get your head straight."

Darnel, who was usually so self-assured, suddenly looked a

little lost, like he'd been caught off guard. I couldn't blame him, I guess. I'd always been there for Darnel, but he'd never lived with me before, and he probably never expected I'd be making an offer like this, especially now that he was a grown man.

"Come on," I continued. "What do you say? You stay out of my way; I'll stay out of yours."

"What about Ma?"

"Don't worry about your mother. I'll talk to her."

"A'ight." Darnel agreed much more quickly than I would have expected. Poor kid must have really been hurting. With the decision of where he was going to live now made, he even looked relieved for a few seconds—until we stepped out of the car and started to walk toward the church.

Crystal and her husband joined us as we approached the door. The burden on Darnel was evident with every slow step he took, his shoulders slumped and his head hung low. I would have done anything to bear that weight for him, but it was doubtful he would let me, even if he could. I moved in front of him, hoping to somehow buffer him from what I knew was going to be devastating.

When I stepped inside the church, the photographer's camera flashing in my eyes almost blinded me. White orchids and Casablanca lilies decorated the church, and the pews on both sides were filled with family members, church members, and friends of the family. I'm sure most of them had already sensed something was wrong from the casual way we were dressed. Darnel looked a mess after spending the night in jail, and as soon as people got a glimpse of him, I heard the whispers starting among the guests.

I ignored them as best I could as I scanned the church. No sight of Keisha or her family. At least she had the good sense not to show up.

I led our small group down the aisle. We were greeted at the altar by my good friend and pastor, Bishop T. K. Wilson. I'd explained the situation to him earlier on the phone, and he'd promised not to say a word until we arrived.

I waited a few seconds for Darnel to say something as we stood in front and he turned to face the people in the pews. But he just stood and stared at them blankly, almost like he was looking right through them. For a second, I was worried he would break down in tears in front of everyone. I nudged him, but he barely even moved.

I looked at Crystal, and without me having to speak a word, she knew instinctively what to do. She took Darnel gently by the arm and pulled him close to her. I stepped in front of my family to give our guests the bad news.

"Good afternoon, everybody. I just want everyone to know that—" I stopped abruptly, realizing that I hadn't given any thought to what I would tell them. Darnel and I hadn't even discussed whether he wanted them to know the truth. Having everyone know that his fiancée cheated on him might be embarrassing to Darnel, and the last thing I wanted to do was cause that. I looked toward Darnel for some indication that it was okay for me to continue.

He seemed to snap out of his daze. "Wait, Dad," he said. "I'll handle this." Darnel stepped forward and spoke in a firm voice. I don't know where it came from so suddenly, but he had regained the strength that seemed to have been knocked out of him before. "I just want everyone to know there's not going to be a wedding today. The wedding is off—for good."

With that, Darnel stepped to the side atrium of the church. There was not even a moment of confused silence from the people in the pews. Sounds of shock and confusion escaped their mouths in an instant. Their questions echoed throughout the church, and though many of them were whispering to one another, the combination of so many voices was like a wave that could have knocked us over.

A few people looked at Darnel sympathetically, but I was surprised by the number of people who actually looked angry. Like this was all his fault.

"Where's Keisha?" someone from the bride's side shouted.

"This is bull!" another man shouted. "Why didn't somebody tell me this before I drove fourteen hours from North Carolina?"

"Fine time to tell me now. I just spent all this money on the wedding gift."

I felt like yelling at these fools, to tell them that their inconvenience was nothing compared to the pain my son was feeling, but then a loud, shrill voice from one of the side doors rose above the din, and all chatter ceased.

I turned to face Gloria Nichols, Keisha's mother, who had shouted, "Where is my daughter?" She did not look happy, to say the least. Behind her, her husband, LeRoi, looked equally irate.

I stepped forward when I saw Gloria, whose usual sophisticated façade had disappeared, heading for Darnel like she was ready to attack him. Her fists were raised. "Where's my baby? What have you done with my daughter?" she sputtered. Her husband was right on her heels.

"I didn't do anything to her, Mrs. Nichols," Darnel replied. "I swear."

I stepped between him and Gloria. She leaned in so close that I could feel the heat of her breath on my face.

"Where is my child, James Black?" Gloria bellowed.

I shrugged my shoulders. "I don't know, Gloria. And neither does my son."

She threw an angry glare in Darnel's direction. "I always knew you'd break her heart. What did you do to her, you bastard?"

Gloria's accusations shocked me, because she and her husband had always seemed to love Darnel. I think the stress of the wedding had gotten to all of us, and now with its cancellation, Gloria had reached her breaking point. Crystal, on the other hand, didn't share my sympathetic view of Gloria.

"Wait a minute, Miss Muckety-Muck. Who the hell are you callin' a bastard?" Crystal had left Darnel's side and was stomping her way toward us. She grabbed Gloria by the shoulder and spun her around so they were facing each other. The movement made Gloria's hat fall to the floor, and Crystal just kicked it out of her way. She got up in Gloria's face and pointed her finger inches from her nose. Then she started in on her tirade.

"I don't know who the hell you think you're talkin' to, but, sister, that's my flesh and blood over there, and I'll be damned if you gonna accuse *my* child of doing anything wrong. It was your trampy-ass daughter who broke *my* son's heart." There was a collective gasp from all parties watching. "And if anything, Darnel is too good for Keisha. How dare you call my child a bastard? What is that little whore you raised—a double bastard?"

For a moment, it looked like Gloria might haul off and slap Crystal, but just as quickly as she raised her fist, she lowered it back to her side and looked at her husband, then back at Crystal, with a bewildered expression. I didn't know what made her come to her senses like that, but I was glad that she did before any more orders of protection had to be issued.

"What is going on here?" LeRoi asked.

Crystal sounded smug when she said, "The reason Darnel is here and Keisha isn't is because she didn't have the nerve to show up after what she did to him."

"What are you talking about?" Gloria sounded close to tears.

"I guess ain't nobody told you that Darnel caught that slut of yours in bed with his best man last night, did they? Oh yeah, she's a real class act, that daughter of yours."

Gloria seemed to be at a loss for words as she turned toward her husband. I couldn't help but wonder if they'd had an inkling all along that their daughter was no angel. If someone had called my little girl a slut like that, I would have been all over them, but Gloria and LeRoi, while they looked sad, really didn't look shocked. The guests who had stayed around to witness the drama, however, did.

Gloria's tears flowed freely now as she leaned against her husband and sobbed. He tried his best to comfort her, but the two of them looked almost as upset as Darnel at this point.

Now that the Jerry Springer–like intensity of the episode between Gloria and Crystal was over, people had started whispering among themselves again. Slowly, they began rising from their seats and heading down the aisle toward the exit. I was sure that most of them would stand around outside and chew on this juicy piece of gossip for a while. I doubted it would make much difference to them, but I stood and made an announcement.

"I'd like to thank all of you for coming here today." Many people stopped and turned to look at me when I started speaking. "And I apologize for the unfortunate change of plans." Someone laughed at my choice of words, but I continued anyway, hoping my speech would deter some of the more vicious gossip. At the very least, I hoped people would have the decency to leave church grounds before they started talking, to spare Darnel from having to hear it all.

"I would like to thank you in advance for your support and your kind words. We know that you were here with the best of intentions and that you will keep these young people in your prayers."

A few people nodded their heads in a kind gesture of support, while others averted their eyes, looking like I had just read their minds and called them out on the enjoyment they were getting from someone else's heartbreak.

When I turned to face my family, I noticed that Darnel was exiting the church through a side door. I followed him to make sure he didn't go do anything foolish.

Jamie

6

By the time I arrived home, it was almost five in the afternoon. My hope was that my boyfriend, Louis, would be up to making me something to eat before I jumped in bed for some well-deserved rest. I'd been up since seven o'clock the previous morning, and the only reason I hadn't fallen out was because of all the drama that Darnel was going through. I'm not gonna lie; if he wasn't my brother, I would have enjoyed that scene at the church like I was watching a good soap opera. You know the kind where you don't want to look away because you might miss something good.

I really did feel bad for my brother, though. As if spending the night in jail weren't trouble enough, I know Darnel just wanted to shrivel up and die when we got to the church and he had to explain that the wedding was being canceled.

Keisha, of course, was nowhere to be found. She didn't even have the guts to let her people know what was going on, so Darnel had to tell them. She would get hers, though, when she ran into her mother and father. They had laid out a bundle of money on the wedding, flowers, and reception—most of which, I'm sure, was nonrefundable. I'd heard Darnel tell his mom that they had to take out a home equity loan to pay for it, so you know they were gonna want to knock her upside the head. Just wish I could be there to see it.

Oh, and on a personal note, I was gonna make sure that trifling wench gave me back my three hundred dollars for that ugly-ass purple bridesmaid's dress I had to buy.

I'll tell you, some women need to get their asses whipped just for sheer stupidity. What the hell kinda woman sleeps with her fiancé's best man the night before her wedding, especially when she's got a guy as fine as Darnel willing to marry her? Marrying the guy who took your virginity is like something straight out of a romance novel. Add in the fact that he's been faithful, loving, and true to you for ten years—oh, and let's not leave out the fact he's got a good J-O-B—and you've damn near got yourself Prince Charming. Keisha just didn't know that guys like Darnel only come around once in a lifetime.

Speaking of once-in-a-lifetime men, I had a damn good man myself in Louis. The second I walked in the house and closed the door, he greeted me with soft, passionate kisses that made me forget all about my hunger for food and ignited my hunger for him.

"Well, well, well, I think you missed me." I laughed as I ran my hands along his bare, muscular chest.

He didn't answer me with words but let his actions speak for him. He guided me until my back was against the door, moving his succulent kisses down to my neck. I let out a long moan when his tongue tickled my earlobe.

"Oh my God, that's the spot," I murmured, like he didn't know it. Louis always knew how to get me going, but more importantly, he knew how to keep me there.

He slid his hands under my skirt and pushed my panties down until I could step out of them. I wrapped my arms around his neck and kissed him passionately. He took hold of my ass, lifting me off the ground. I wrapped my legs around his thighs, pulling him in close until I felt his hard penis grinding into the triangle between my legs.

I closed my eyes. "Mmm, that feels so good." I kissed his lips, sucking on his tongue as it darted into my mouth. The pleasure I was feeling from his constant grinding was making me wet beyond belief. But I didn't just want to be wet; I wanted to explode, and grinding just wasn't going to do it.

Louis knew what I needed. He might not have been my first, but he was without question the best I'd ever had, especially when it came to oral sex. The only question now was how he would get there from the position we were in.

As if he had read my mind, his strong arms lifted my hundred-and-twenty-pound frame higher, like we were in some kind of sexual ballet. My body slid up the door while he kissed down my neck to my breasts, where he gave each of my nipples the proper attention they needed. When both my girls were standing at attention, he lifted me farther until my legs could rest on his shoulders. I braced my upper back against the door, and he held my thighs with his arms.

I barely gave him enough time to get himself set before I took hold of his head, guiding his face to my treasure chest.

"Oooo, la, la! That's it, baby. Keep doing it just like that and you gonna make me explode. Mmm, mmm, mmm, that's what I'm talkin' 'bout."

We'd never done anything like this before, and if I had given it any thought at the time, I probably would have made him put me down for fear of falling. But that's one of the reasons why I loved Louis so much. He was spontaneous, and ever since our first time together, he'd always known how to bring out the inner freak in me.

I'd met Louis in the craziest way about eight months ago on my way home from work. That night, I had worked late and caught the subway home. I usually don't do subways, but at that time, I was waiting for Daddy to buy me a new car. I'd had a Honda Accord I got for my college graduation but sold it to one of my exes for peanuts when I saw how cute I looked in Daddy's new Lexus. He was pissed off when he heard I sold my car, but I knew it was just a matter of time before the two of us went down to the dealership so that he could buy me a new car. I'm sure he thought he was teaching me a lesson, but Daddy always gave in eventually. So I was stuck taking the subway until then.

The night I met Louis, the subway was nearly empty where I got off the F train on Hillside and 154th Street. While I was coming out of the station, a hooded man swooped down, grabbed my purse, and started running. It happened so fast that at first I didn't know what had hit me. But because the purse was hooked up under my arm, the man pulled me down to the ground with the force of his impact and began dragging me. I heard the sound of my pantyhose ripping and felt the burning pain from my knees scraping against the cement.

"Let it go, bitch!" I'm not sure if it was his fist or his foot, but something hit my head hard.

"Help me! Please, help me!" I screamed, but no one came to my rescue.

"Shut up, bitch!" he barked, then hit me again.

He wound up dragging me to a nearby alley. He was infuriated because he thought I wasn't giving up the purse. But I didn't give a damn about the purse; he could have it. I just needed him to give me a chance to untangle the strap from my arm.

"Gimme the purse, bitch," he demanded, and then he did something unexpected: He dropped his end of the purse. I was confused for a split second, until I realized why he'd done it. That's when things became truly terrifying. He reached into his pocket, and I saw the glint of his knife. He raised it up high over his head, and I just knew I was getting ready to die over fifty dollars and a Coach bag.

Suddenly, this stranger dashed forward into the alley. "Put that fucking knife down!" the man yelled, then threw a series of punches at my attacker. It all happened in a matter of seconds, but it was truly like watching an action movie. I watched my protector hit my attacker with blow after blow. Stunned, my attacker released his grip on the knife, then staggered backward as my Good Samaritan picked it up.

"Get the fuck outta here!" he yelled.

The hooded man scuttled off down the alley, limping and holding his side.

"Are you okay?" the kind stranger asked as he lifted me up off the ground.

It took me a minute, but I finally said, trembling, "Yeah, I'm okay. Thank you." I looked down. My stockings were torn, my knees were all bloody, and my body felt like one big bruise. But I was alive.

"I was driving by and saw what happened. I'm sorry it took me so long, but I wasn't sure if it was . . . you know, domestic. I've seen women attack a brother for messing with their boyfriends, even if the brother was trying to save them."

Looking back on it now, I know it was probably a stupid thing for him to say. I mean, the man was dragging me down the sidewalk on my knees, for God's sake! But at the time, I was too grateful to be mad at his comment, so I didn't respond to it. Instead, I said, "We should call the police."

"Nah, police ain't gonna do nothing. That dude's long gone, and all they gonna have us do is waste the rest of the night filling out paperwork and looking at mug shots. I didn't even get a good look at his face. Did you?"

"No, I was too busy trying to get him to stop hitting mine."

"Don't worry about it. Trust me; the ass whipping I just put on him is gonna stay with him much longer than a couple of days at Rikers Island. I don't think he's going to be mugging anybody anytime soon." He picked up my purse and handed it to me. "Look, you sure you okay? Can I give you a ride home? Do you need to go to the hospital or anything?"

I wasn't sure if I could trust him, but since I was alone and he did just rescue me, I figured I could take a chance. And I felt even safer when he folded the knife up and threw it in a garbage can. The way he looked—all tall, dark, and handsome—he kind of reminded me of my father.

"I could use a ride home," I said. "I don't live far from here."

"Come on. My car's this way."

When we got to my house, we ended up sitting in his car talking for about two hours. It turned out he lived around the corner, about three blocks from me. We exchanged phone numbers, and a week later we went out to dinner at T.G.I. Friday's in Long Island. I was really digging him. We had chemistry, and he made me feel safe, something only my father and brother had done in the past. And now, eight months later, we were tighter than ever. Four months ago, I moved in. One day, I planned on marrying him.

Thirty minutes after I arrived home, Louis and I were lying naked on the living room floor, covered by the blanket I kept on the sofa for when we watched TV together. My head was resting on his shoulder while my fingers played with the small patch of hair on his chest. I'd gotten everything I wanted and more out of the past half hour. And from the way Louis was breathing and the satisfied grin on his face, I think he got what he was looking for too.

"So what happened with your brother?" Louis asked.

"Well, right now Darnel's facing felony assault charges. Possibly manslaughter if Omar doesn't pull through. My dad called the hospital, and they say he's in intensive care."

"Damn, he beat him like that? He really loved her ass."

"Please, you beat a man half to death over me."

"First off," Louis explained, "he had a knife, so I had to do what I did. Second, you wasn't my girl back then. I was just a Good Samaritan trying to save your life."

I slapped his chest, then rolled away from him, pretending to be offended. "So you wouldn't try to kill a man if you caught me sleeping with him?" I sucked my teeth. "I knew it. You don't love me like my brother loved Keisha."

"What?" He rolled on top of me, his eyes glued to mine. "Let's get something straight. Not only would I try to kill someone if I caught you in bed with him, but I'd finish the fuckin' job." I was shocked by his tone, because while I'd only been playing with him, he sounded completely serious. "I love you. Do we understand each other?"

He'd never spoken to me this way before, and something inside told me maybe I should be a little worried, but I wasn't. To tell the truth, I was turned on by the fact that someone loved me so much that he might kill another man.

"Do we understand each other?" he repeated.

I nodded my head, and he leaned down to kiss me. I opened my mouth and returned his passion, letting him slip between my legs so that he would know just how much I understood.

James

7

"Can I get some more sugar?" I asked the waitress in the twenty-four-hour diner as she set down a cup of coffee in front of me.

She put her hand on her hips and gave me a devilish smile. "Want me to put my finger in it? That'll be much sweeter," she flirted.

I smiled as I thought about just how easy this was. Sometimes, all I had to do was walk into a room and women were making moves on me. It's like I gave off some sort of scent—Man Who Loves Women cologne—and it got their juices flowing immediately.

"You don't want to go there with me," I told her, and I wasn't kidding. Just like any time a woman flirted with me, I got right to the point. I was always honest with women about my intentions, ever since I got busted lying to two women in high school. I wasn't trying to hurt nobody just to get laid, so I never hid the fact that I wasn't looking for a wife or even a girlfriend. I liked women—a variety of women—too much to give up my freedom.

The funny thing was, the truth got me much further than the lies I'd heard some men tell. Sure, some women walked away once they figured out I wasn't going to get on the husband track, but many others seemed to welcome the challenge. This waitress was in that group.

"Oh, and why don't I want to go there?" She hadn't moved to get my sugar. "Maybe it's the other way around and you don't want to go there with me."

"Is that right?" I flirted back. If a woman didn't turn and run once I set out my rules, then I figured it was game on.

"Yep. I'm like a drug. Some people get addicted to cigarettes, some to drugs, or gambling, or whatever. But any man who's ever had a taste of this ends up addicted to me."

I like a woman with confidence, and I must say, this one had my imagination running wild with the things I planned to do to her once we got past these preliminary games. The way she was eyeing me, I already knew where this conversation would end up—in my bedroom.

"Yeah, I can say the same thing about myself," I bragged. "I've never had a complaint department. Only satisfied customers."

She laughed.

"Oh, you think I'm kidding?" I said. The self-satisfied smirk stayed on her face, so I explained, "I'm just try'na tell you I got skills of my own, so I ain't one of those men you can whip it on and then I'll be ready to take it to the next level."

"Is that right?" she said, sounding doubtful.

"That's right. I got one level and that's that. I don't chase after women. I don't call. I'm just not a one-woman man."

"Well, you ain't had none of this yet," she argued. "Once you try some of my sugar, you're gonna change your tune."

I shook my head. "I doubt it. I have yet to meet a woman with paradise between her legs."

This woman was definitely excited by my challenge. I swear I saw her nipples harden through her uniform. I checked her name tag, which told me her name was Salli Reid. My eyes told me Salli Reid had it going on underneath that uniform. She might not have paradise between her legs, but I had no doubt it was still some treasure. She wasn't traditionally beautiful, but she had legs that went all the way up to an ass so perfect you could sit a cup of coffee on it and it would stay hot all day long. Then she had this tiny waist, which reminded me of one of those old-fashioned cartoons, and a nice firm rack that I'm sure kept her tips coming.

I was quite sure she was telling the truth when she said, "I got guys I knew in high school still try'na get another taste."

"Mmm-hmm," I answered, allowing my eyes to roam freely over her figure. "I'm sure you do. But that's not me, sweetheart."

She stared me straight in the eyes, clearly up for my challenge. "You get a taste of this and I ain't got to worry about you calling me." She took a napkin off my table and wrote on it. She slid it to me and said, "I get off in an hour. Call me." Then she finally went to get some sugar for my coffee—even though I wasn't even interested in my breakfast now that I had such a tasty dessert to look forward to.

Before Salli came back with the sugar packets, another sister walked by, switching her ass on the way to be seated at a table. She gave me a subtle nod to let me know she liked what she saw, but I wasn't interested. This sister looked a little too young for my tastes. In my experience, it was the young ones who got attached. I preferred women like Salli, a little more mature in years and in attitude and less likely to become a problem when I hit it and quit it. Actually, if I had my choice, I'd stick with married women. They were usually cool with one-night stands, because they already had their men at home to provide for all their other needs.

I wondered if Salli was married. When she came back with my sugar packets, I was happy to see that she was sporting a nice-sized diamond on her left hand. Yeah, this was gonna be fun.

"Here's my address. I'm going home now, so if you want to stop by after you get off . . . ," I said as I wrote the address on a napkin.

"I'll do that." Salli licked her lips and grinned at me as she stuffed the napkin into her bra. "Are you ready to order?"

"Nah. I think I'll skip breakfast. I got me a taste for something that's not on the menu here."

I got up, left a twenty-dollar tip on the table, and told her, "See you in an hour."

"Hey, Daddy."

When I got home to get the apartment ready for Salli's visit, I found Jamie in my kitchen, cleaning out the fridge. It wasn't enough that she had a live-in man and a full-time job at the real estate company I started in my late twenties; she still found the time to be up in my business and in my space. Because I loved her so much, I usually just let her behavior slide, but today was not the day. Salli had me worked up, and I was not about to miss an opportunity to get a piece of her.

"You got to go." I picked up Jamie's purse from the counter and slipped it on her shoulder.

"I'm not done." She motioned to the fridge.

"Oh, you're done. I got company coming."

"Who?" Jamie put her hand on her hip like I deserved her attitude.

"Jamie, you're not my keeper. Now, get out." I tried to hustle her to the door, but she stood her ground.

"Daddy, why are you messing with these skanks?"

"We both know that you think being your father is a full-time job, but **FYI**, I'm also a man."

"Oh, you're not about to give me that 'men have needs' speech. I have heard it all before, Daddy."

"Well, you're not listening anyway. Don't you have a man at home?"

"Why do you need these women?"

"Good-bye, Jamie." I had no intention of letting her mess up my game, but she had no intention of giving up that easily.

"It's not like you're a kid. You're too damn old to be sleeping with a different woman every night. What are you trying to prove?" Her voice kept getting louder, probably because she thought that was the best way to get me to give in. On any other subject, I might have, but when it came to me and my sex life, I had never let my daughter influence my choices, and I wasn't about to start now. I pulled out my biggest weapon—her spending habits.

"Jamie, go home or go to work so you can stop sending me your credit card bills."

"Fine." She rolled her eyes, knowing she was defeated. "But you are still getting old, and sleeping around won't make you any younger!" she yelled before storming out of the house.

I raced up to my room, changed the sheets, lit some candles and incense, and jumped in the shower. Salli would be here shortly, and I wanted to make sure I was clean and ready for all the dirty fun I planned to have.

Salli showed up a while later, still dressed in her uniform. I invited her in and slid her sweater off her shoulders.

"You feel a little tense," I said. "I ran you a bath. Would you like to go relax in the tub for a while?"

"You don't waste any time, do you?"

"Why should I? I told you what I was all about, didn't I?"

"Yeah, you sure did," she said with a smirk.

I took a step and pressed up against her, close enough that she could feel my body heat—and my package pressing against her backside. Her shoulders relaxed ever so slightly, and I figured things were ready to get started. That's why she surprised me when she said, "I shouldn't be doing this," and took a step away from me.

"Oh, so you're all talk?" I challenged.

"No."

"Then what's the problem?" I glanced down at her ring finger. "I promise I won't tell anyone."

Her right hand instinctively covered her left to conceal the wedding ring. "That's not it. I do what I want anyway."

I seriously doubted that was true. There was no way a man with a wife as fine as Salli would willingly share her.

"Then what is it? You scared of this?" I asked with a glance down at my erection, which was straining to get out of my pants at this point. "It's okay if you just realized you're in over your head. You wouldn't be the first woman."

"Oh, you think you're all that?" I saw the sassiness coming back to her. What a relief. I was starting to think she was going to be more work than she was worth.

"I don't think anything; I know it. Now, I let you know who I am, and if you can't handle it, then let me walk you to the door."

I moved toward the hallway, but instead of following me, she tossed her bag down on a chair and kicked off her shoes.

"Lead the way. As long as you recognize that this isn't something you're gonna want just once."

"Yeah, once is usually enough." I took her hand and led her up the stairs to my bedroom.

"Are you ready to be satisfied?" I breathed close to her ear. She nodded, and I sat her down on the bed and started to massage her feet.

I kissed her legs, working my way up. Once I reached the top, I slid her pantyhose off and nibbled the inside of her thighs. She whimpered, a combination of pleasure and anticipation. I could have brought her to orgasm right away, but I wanted to savor our time together, so I stood her up and led her into the bathroom.

"I'm going to take care of you," I whispered, staring into her eyes.

I loved the way her ass was straining against the fabric of her uniform. Lord have mercy, this sister had the kind of body I loved, everything in the right place, and I couldn't wait for her to let go and get loose.

"Why don't I help you out of this uniform so you can get in the tub?"

She gladly obliged, and in no time, I was caressing her smooth, creamy skin with scented oil while she bathed.

When she got out of the tub, I toweled her off, massaging her butt cheeks, the insides of her thighs, her stomach, and her breasts. I had Salli hollering my name before I even got undressed. I took off my clothes, lay her on the bed, and let my tongue take care of all her needs.

Salli had the kind of orgasm that let me know somebody was not handling his business at home. This was a woman in need. Once I slid on a condom and entered her, she let me know just how much she needed what I had to offer. She grabbed my ass, smashing me deeper inside of her, and screamed at me to give her more, harder, faster.

We went at it for nearly an hour in every imaginable position. Salli had at least four orgasms before I finally exploded into the condom. She flopped back onto the mattress looking completely satisfied and gazed up at me in a way that made my radar go up. I felt good, too, but I wasn't about to lie down next to her and cuddle. That was never part of the deal.

"You got to get up. I have to go to work." I threw my robe on, collected her clothing, and handed it to her.

"Damn, that's kind of cold." She rolled her eyes.

"No, just real. I told you this wasn't gonna be some big romance. You said you could handle it," I reminded her.

Reluctantly, she got up and began to dress. After a minute, she regained some of her confidence and told me, "I can handle it. You're gonna be the one calling me for seconds."

I didn't bother to correct her. She'd been pretty good in bed, so I saw no need to hurt her feelings. She'd get the message loud and clear when she never heard from me again. I'd just have to find a new twenty-four-hour diner to have breakfast at.

"Thank you." I walked her to the door, trying not to appear like I was hustling her out, although that's exactly what I was doing.

I'm sure she was switching her ass all the way to her car, but I didn't even bother to watch. As soon as I got my rocks off, you could twirl around naked and I'd barely notice. It's just the way I was, and I made no apology for it, especially since I never played like I was any different.

I jumped in the shower, then dressed and headed to the office, my body relaxed and ready for work.

Darnel

8

Two weeks after my wedding fiasco, I was sitting in my dad's living room, drinking Grey Goose from the bottle and "trying" to watch TV. I say trying because my father was getting his late-night exercise, and the way his "workout partner" was crying out, I could barely hear myself think. She was so loud that I almost felt embarrassed for her, but then again, this wasn't the first woman who had snuck over here after ten for a booty call since I'd moved in with my dad. This one was by far the loudest, though.

What I didn't understand was how my father never got caught up in any drama, because he sure enough had himself one hell of a middle-aged harem. Tonight it was some woman who taught Bible study at the church, but what they were doing up there sure wasn't godly.

Speaking of ungodly, I lifted the bottle and took a long, hard swig of the vodka. I swished the liquor around in my mouth, closing my eyes and savoring it, until an image of Keisha appeared in front of me. I wasn't quite drunk yet, but I was definitely on my way. I'd been drinking pretty heavily lately, but it still wasn't taking away the pain of what Keisha and Omar had done to me.

I know this sounds crazy, especially after what went down between her and Omar two weeks ago, but I missed Keisha. Don't get me wrong; I hated her, but in some distorted, sick way, I missed her too. It was as if a piece of me was missing from my life, and deep down, I knew it was her. Now I knew why so many couples got back together after one of them got caught cheating. God, was I ever going to stop loving her? I swallowed the liquor and opened my eyes to erase the image of her face. I felt so alone.

I heard through the grapevine that Keisha had taken our honeymoon tickets and gone on vacation. Can you believe that crap? That heifer had a lot of nerve sitting out on some sandy Jamaican beach, drinking fruity cocktails out of coconut shells after her treacherous behavior had destroyed my life. I knew she was back now, because I'd scoped out her car outside her job this afternoon, but she still hadn't shown her face, not even around her own family.

Rumor had it that Omar had gone down to Jamaica with her, but then my boy Charles told me that Omar hadn't been released from the hospital until a few days ago. It seems I'd given him quite the ass whipping. My lawyer said I was lucky I hadn't been charged with attempted murder.

A couple of my friends said he wanted to see me so he could apologize, but I still couldn't forgive him. Not in a million years. I couldn't even think of him without seeing an image of him riding my woman and enjoying every moment. How was I ever supposed to forgive the man who helped rip my life apart while calling me a friend? A best friend.

I kept thinking, What if I hadn't gone up to her room that night? What if I had married her, totally in the dark about her cheating? What if she'd gotten pregnant? What if . . . ? I had too many unanswered questions. I lifted the bottle again. Yeah, I was a brother needing all the liquid tranquilizer that I could find, even though no amount of drinking took the edge off the pain of my broken heart.

After one more swig from the bottle, I decided to do something I knew would end up coming back to haunt me. Nevertheless, it was something my heart was telling me I had to do if I was ever going to get any answers to my questions. I picked up the phone and dialed Keisha's number. I know—stupid, right?

"Hello?" Keisha sounded shocked. I'm sure she had recognized my cell phone number on her caller ID. "Darnel? Is that you?"

I thought about hanging up. I couldn't make myself speak, but I sure knew what I wanted to say. I wanted to tell her how much I hated her, how she was a slut and was going to burn in hell for what she'd done to me. I just didn't have the guts.

"I . . . I just wanna know . . ." My voice was timid and hesitant, and I hated myself for sounding so weak. "I just wanna know why."

"Why what, Darnel?" Her tone was not confrontational, but her question angered me nonetheless. I couldn't believe she was acting like she didn't know what I was talking about. Like this whole thing was some figment of my imagination.

Suddenly I found my strength. I exploded, my voice pure bass now. "Why the hell did you do me like that?"

As I waited for her to respond, I could hear quiet whimpers on the other end of the phone. Why she was crying was beyond me. I was the one who should be crying. I was the one who was done wrong.

"I'm sorry, Darnel," she managed to speak through her sobs. If she were anyone else, I might have felt sorry for her.

"Naw, you ain't. You ain't sorry about shit."

"Yes, I am. Please, baby, please forgive me. I made a mistake."

"A mistake? That wasn't a mistake. That was Omar. That was my best friend." I tried not to cry, but I was so angry that I couldn't hold back the tears.

"If I could do it all over again . . ."

It was too late for regrets as far as I was concerned. "I hate you! Do you hear me? I hate your ass."

Her sobs became louder. When she was finally able to speak, she said, "I know. But I still love you."

I wanted to spew more venom at her, but her words and the sincerity in her voice sent me back to the past ten years of our relationship. I was so glad I was on the phone, because I did not want her to read my true feelings in my body language. I didn't want her to know what I was thinking: *I still love you too.* The only thing that stopped me from saying it out loud was that I hated her just as much as I loved her.

"Darnel, it was a mistake, a big mistake."

I allowed my pain to banish the sentimental feelings I'd had a moment ago. "Oh, I see. Omar's dick just mistakenly fell into your pussy. That kinda crap happens all the time. What the hell am I pissed off about?" I asked sarcastically.

"I was drunk. I know it was stupid. I wasn't trying to hurt you."

"You weren't? That wasn't some dude you met in a bar. That was Omar. You fucked Omar, my boy."

"I know, and I'm sorry. I'm not perfect like you, Darnel. Real people make mistakes. Can't you just forgive me? I'll do anything to make it up to you."

"I just want to know one thing."

"What's that?"

"Why?" We were back to the original question. "I wanna know why you did it."

It took her quite a while to speak up, and even then she still didn't have an answer. "I don't know, Darnel. I'm just stupid. Maybe I should just kill myself."

"That's not funny." I had never known Keisha to play games like this, but she was obviously not the person I once thought she was. Now she had sunk low enough to fake suicidal thoughts just to gain my sympathy.

"I'm not laughing," she insisted. "Everyone hates me. You hate me. Your family hates me. My mother and father hate me. I don't have any reason to live."

"Like I do? I'm the one who should be killing myself. But it has to be about you, doesn't it, Keisha? Well, then, fuck it. Go 'head and kill yourself." I had decided to call her bluff, but she wasn't about to back down.

"You know what?" she responded. "Bye, Darnel. See you next lifetime."

I stared at my cell in disbelief. The screen read CALL DISCONNECTED. She had actually hung up on me. Was she really going to go through with it? I know what I'd said, but the last thing I wanted her to do was commit suicide. I hit the TALK button to redial her number.

"Hello." Her voice was quiet, and she was still crying.

"We need to talk in person. I'm coming over," I said in a tone that meant no was not an option.

She sounded drained. "I'll see you when you get here."

I disconnected the call, unsure of what I was feeling. Would she really try to kill herself? I didn't think so, but I had to make sure, because my conscience couldn't handle something like that.

Besides, if I was really being honest with myself, I wanted to see her again. I considered the idea that maybe she had lied about attempting suicide, knowing that it would get me to come to her place. Maybe she wanted to see me as much as I was now realizing I wanted to see her. I loved this woman, and as crazy as that sounds, in the back of my mind, I was wondering if there was any way to make this work.

I allowed my mind to wander, to imagine a scenario for when I showed up at her place. In my brief fantasy, our reconciliation was quick and passionate. Within minutes, I was imagining the two of us naked, limbs intertwined as we made love.

Even in this inebriated state, I knew this was foul. This was sick. How could I even want to touch her again? But I just had to—

My father interrupted my fantasy when he came into the living room wearing a burgundy silk smoking jacket and matching pajama bottoms, like some black Hugh Hefner or something. But I wasn't mad at him. I guess if I had some woman screaming at the top of her lungs like a damn fool, I'd be strutting too.

Without a word, he reached over to the coffee table and picked up the half-empty Grey Goose bottle and examined it. He frowned, shook his head, and then placed the bottle back on the table. The way his face hardened told me he was disgusted with me. My father drank socially, but he definitely wasn't the kind of guy who would finish off half a bottle of vodka sitting alone in his house. Neither was I, until I caught Keisha and Omar together.

"Is the pussy that good that you'd violate an order of protection?" It took a moment for my alcohol-soaked brain to understand what he was telling me: He'd heard my conversation with Keisha. At least he'd heard part of it. Damn, I did not want him to know I was going over there. My lack of response opened the door for him to lecture me.

"She's not worth your freedom, Darnel," he continued. "Don't let this woman ruin your life. You need to stay your behind home."

"I have to talk to her."

"You don't have to do anything but stay black and die," he said in a no-nonsense tone.

"Dad, you don't understand," I protested. Part of me knew

how stupid I was being, but no matter how wrong she'd done me, I couldn't control the way I felt. She had taken up residence in my heart a long time ago.

"You're right; I don't. But don't be stupid. Anything you need to say to her can be said over the telephone."

He was right and I knew it, but the image of me and Keisha making love had lit a fire in my soul, and I had to be near her, had to be able to touch her. A phone call just wouldn't do it. Of course, I couldn't admit this to my father, so I used Keisha's suicide ploy to try getting him off my back.

"She told me she's going to kill herself. I can't have that on my conscience."

He laughed. "If I had a hundred dollars for every woman who told me she was going to kill herself, I'd be rich." My father sat down next to me. "She said that because she wanted you to come over. You're giving her what she wants. She knows you still love her."

"She's right. I do love her. I was going to marry her, remember?"

"I do, and I know you were deeply in love."

"Oh yeah? What would you know about love?"

"Still won't give me a break, huh?"

"Nope. I love you, but you could have married my mother. No woman has ever loved you like she does."

Usually this topic caused a fight between me and my father, which would end with him telling me to mind my own business. But this time, maybe because he was feeling sorry for me, he took my criticism like a man.

"I can't argue with you on that," he told me. "She loved me more than I deserve. And I care about your mother, son. Your mother was, and is, a beautiful woman. But it takes a strong man to love a good woman."

"What do you mean by that?"

"You have to be a risk-taker to be in love. Love always opens you up to being hurt, and there are some hurts you never get over." I could tell by my dad's tone that he knew how I felt. I didn't think he'd ever been hurt the way Keisha had done to me—he was more likely to be the one cheating, not the one cheated on. But even if he'd never felt it himself, he definitely had sympathy for me. This wasn't his usual cool and calm spiel, when he was giving advice he'd never take.

For a while, we sat quietly, commiserating together, I guess.

I thought about it, flipping back and forth the pros and cons of taking this step. In the end, I knew that I still had to see Keisha. I just had to.

"I'm going over to Mark's house." I made up the lie to avoid any more lectures from Dad, but he was old school, and he'd already told the lies I was still dreaming up. I had to give him credit for staying out of it and letting me make my own decisions.

"Yeah, all right. Whatever. You can lie to me all you want, but you can't lie to yourself." My father waved his hand in dismissal, shook his head, and walked toward the kitchen. He obviously knew I was headed to Keisha's, but at least he didn't try to stop me.

Jamie

9

I slammed down the telephone, pissed off at Daddy for two reasons. Number one, he had one of his playthings over at the house, and number two, he hadn't stopped Darnel from running over to Keisha's house. He was so weak-minded, that brother of mine. Okay, maybe not exactly weak, but how about kindhearted? He was just too damn kindhearted and trusting.

Darnel wasn't like me or Daddy; we were naturally suspicious, and it took a while for us to trust anyone outside of our family circle. You can ask my boo, Louis, about that. It took us almost five months of being together before I felt like I could trust him with my heart. But Darnel, he always took everyone at face value, trusting their word to be their bond. He just couldn't believe shit stank. And everyone from his friends to his fiancée took his kindness for weakness.

"So, is everything okay?" Louis asked. He was sitting up in the bed, watching TV, probably waiting for me to finish my eleven o'clock call to Daddy. We hadn't done anything in a couple of days, so I'm sure he was waiting up to get some. Shoot, I could use a little stress reduction myself, but only after I got this off my chest.

"Daddy said Darnel's gone over to Keisha's."

Louis rubbed his forehead. "What the hell's he thinking about?"

"I don't know. I think we're going to have to find him a woman."

"Oh no, you don't. We're not going to find him anything. That's you. I'm not in the matchmaking business," he said seriously.

"Oh, come on, baby." I snuggled up next to him. "Don't you want to see my brother happy?"

"Of course I do. That's why I'm staying the hell out of his personal life." Before I could find the right thing to say, he changed the subject. "So what's your pops up to?"

"Would you believe he's got some woman over at the house?"

Louis chuckled. "I'm not surprised. Your pops always got someone over at the house."

I rolled my eyes at him something fierce. "That's not funny, Louis."

"I'm not laughing, Jamie. But you need to cut your pops some slack. You're grown. The man's gotta have a life too."

"Yeah, well, he don't need to waste his time on those gold diggers and whores. He's too old for that. I got a good mind to go over there."

"What, you expect him to play bingo with the senior citizens? The man just turned forty-eight years old, not ninety-eight. Damn, why can't you give him a break?"

"He ain't gotta play bingo. He just needs to slow down. You don't understand, Louis. These women ain't got nothing good for my daddy."

This time, Louis rolled his eyes. "No woman has anything good for your father as far as you're concerned."

"You got that right."

He shook his head. "You know, baby, your obsession with your father's life is not healthy."

I pulled away from him and sat up in the bed. "Obsession? What the hell do you mean by that? Are you trying to say me and my daddy are doing something?" I pointed my finger in his face, daring him to accuse me of something sick like that. I would knock his ass out if he did.

"No!" he said, sounding just as offended as I was. "Damn, baby. You're touchy tonight. I'm just saying you're a daddy's girl, that's all."

I didn't answer, because he was right. I was a daddy's girl. But don't pass judgment until you hear my story.

You see, I didn't even find out that James Black was my daddy until I was ten. Apparently, my mother had been tipping around with him while she was married to Chester, the man who had raised me as his daughter. Chester was an ex-military man, and he raised me and my three older brothers—or rather the boys who turned out to be my half brothers—with plenty of rules and regulations. I always respected him, but I can't say I was ever one of those little girls who worshipped her father.

Anyhow, when I was ten, my mother confided in me that James Black was my biological father, and she took me to see him on the sly. To this day, I wonder why she opened up that can of worms by introducing me to Daddy. Maybe she was feeling guilty about keeping the truth from me. I guess she figured that at ten, I was old enough to understand and smart enough to keep her secret. Or perhaps it had something to do with the fact that she and Daddy had started screwing again behind Chester's back. Now, I can't prove that, but they sure went in his room for a lot of so-called talks when I visited.

That withstanding, she couldn't have predicted in a million years the bond that would form between me and Daddy. He was so nice to me, and I thought he was so handsome. We hit it off from the start. Even though I had just met him, it was obvious that we were cut from the same cloth. We shared the same sense of humor and loved the same foods. We even liked the same cartoons. Where Chester was strict and distant with us kids, Daddy would get right down on the floor and play with my dolls with me. Not to mention the fact that I was wearing his face. I *loved* my real daddy. I loved Chester, too, but there was no denying that Daddy was a much warmer man, and the connection between us was deep.

My mother saw how happy it made me to visit my father, so she brought me to see him as often as she could sneak away from Chester. Little did she know that this would eventually spell disaster for her.

One day, when I was about twelve, I was playing with my brothers when Chester came into the room and snatched the toy right out of my hand. My brothers and I had left the kitchen a mess after we fixed ourselves a snack, but apparently he thought I was the only one who should be responsible for cleaning up. Chester ordered me to wash the dishes but said nothing to the boys. He always treated me like I was Cinder-fuckin'-ella or something, and I was fed up.

"I don't have to do what you tell me to do," I said, standing in the middle of the living room as my brothers watched in confused silence. "You ain't my real daddy. James Black's my daddy," I informed him.

From the look of shock on his face, I may as well have hit him with a baseball bat. His expression gradually transformed from shock to pain. When I think back on it, I realize that was the moment when he wrapped his head around the facts and knew that I was telling the truth. But someone like Chester was not about to show weakness in front of his boys, so he turned his pain into rage and took it out on me by trying to beat the black off of me.

Afterward, all hell broke loose between him and my moms. I thought for sure that because I'd let this twelve-year-old secret out of the bag, they would get a divorce. As I lay in bed still aching from the beating I'd received, that idea didn't sound too bad to me anyway. However, my mom smoothed his feathers, probably in the bedroom, and the whole incident was put to rest with my mother's words: "It's nothing I can do about it. We have four kids. It happened."

They stayed together, but there was still plenty of tension in the air. My brothers were mad at me for starting the whole thing, and my mother reminded me just about every day that I had broken my promise to keep her little secret. And Chester, he couldn't even stand to see my face. In his eyes, I had become a living symbol of his wife's infidelity.

It didn't help matters that we went to the same church as Daddy, so Chester had to see Daddy every Sunday. He started complaining to my mother that every time he looked at me, he saw James Black's face, and it was driving him crazy. Not to mention the fact that my mom had the audacity to name me Jamie, after James. It was one thing to know his wife cheated; it was clearly another to live with the proof of that affair.

My mother did what she thought she had to do to save her marriage. The next thing I knew, my ass was hauled off to stay with my daddy. As far as I was concerned, she had sacrificed me for the sake of her husband and her sons. I suffered the ultimate punishment for an affair that she'd had.

She tried for a while to visit me at Daddy's house, but it wasn't long before the frequency of the visits dropped to almost never.

No doubt Chester was giving her hell every time he knew she was coming around James's place, and I wasn't making her time with me very pleasant either. As a preteen girl who felt abandoned by her, I didn't have much love to show my mother.

She'd try to tell me funny stories about my brothers, but I didn't want to hear it. Ever since the day I'd told the secret, they made my life as uncomfortable as possible. They stopped calling me by my name and referred to me as "Mama's little mistake." Not long after I moved in with him, Daddy introduced me to Darnel, and although he didn't live with us, Darnel and I were tight— tighter than I'd ever been with my other brothers. So anything my mother had to say about the boys fell on deaf ears. By the time my mother told me that she and Chester and the boys were moving out of state, I think it was probably a relief for everyone involved. I hardly ever spoke to my mother after she moved.

I ended up living with Daddy from the age of twelve until just a few months ago, when I moved in with Louis. In all those years, Daddy never complained. He gave me all the love a young woman could ever want, including teaching me about hygiene and, believe it or not, shopping for my first bra. Women came and went— some of them, including Darnel's mother, even seemed to think they had a shot at becoming Mrs. James Black—but Daddy remained devoted first and foremost to me, and that was just the way I liked it. To say I'm a daddy's girl is an understatement. He was my best friend, and I would see to it that no one ever broke that bond.

"You know how I feel about my daddy. That's not the issue," I told Louis.

"Well, what is the issue? Your father's an adult. You're trying to hold him too tight."

"He may be grown, but he's got a family to worry about. He's all Darnel and I really have."

"So what is this here that me and you have?" Louis looked at me pointedly, waiting for my reply.

"You don't understand because . . ." I fell silent before I said something that could hurt Louis.

Louis had told me about his childhood, so different from mine. He was raised in an orphanage in Iowa, and he had no family to speak of. He seemed to be like Adam—as if he just came into the world with no father or mother, and he didn't need anyone except me. I loved him for his devotion to me, but it was also a point of contention between us, because he found it impossible to understand how I could love my father so much. We had already had several confrontations over Louis feeling that I was too into my family, which meant he took second place in my world. He would never understand, I decided, and it wasn't worth the fight.

We sat there, staring at each other, trying to avoid an argument. Luckily for me, Louis's cell rang before our tense silence escalated into angry words. But that didn't stop me from catching an attitude when I glanced at the clock and realized how late it was.

"Who the hell is calling you at this time of night?"

Louis just gave me a blank look, like I was stupid to even be acting suspicious, but I didn't care. I'd learned many things from my father, including never assume that your mate isn't cheating. As much as I loved my father, I knew he was a womanizer, and he had made fools of half the women in Queens, a good number of them married to husbands who had no clue. My motto had become "Ask the right questions now so you don't have to pack your bags later."

Louis knew that I had this jealous streak in me, so he answered my question to avoid another fight. "I don't know. Probably work."

His answer made me even more skeptical. Louis worked as a manager at a used-car dealership on Hillside Avenue, so he constantly got calls about problems, but never at this time of night. Something told me this wasn't a work call. I watched him walk over to his dresser and pick up his cell phone, and I wondered if he would have the nerve to take the call in front of me.

"Hello."

I was satisfied that it couldn't be anything to worry about, because he didn't make a move to leave the room when he answered. I leaned back against the pillows and relaxed for a moment, but my relief was short-lived. He listened intently for a few seconds, then said, "I understand. Friday's fine," then disappeared into the bathroom, where he finished his call.

He wasn't in there long, but by the time he came out, I was

ready to pounce. "So, who was that?" I asked before he could even get back into bed.

"Oh, that was work. They want me to go outta town on Friday."

I felt my stomach clench. I was sure he was lying. His job never sent him out of town.

"To where?" I asked coldly.

"Somewhere in Pennsylvania. I'm supposed to go to a dealer auction and look for this BMW my boss promised a customer."

Why was he trying to play me? He was about to make me flip on him.

"So, that was your boss?" I made no effort to hide the skepticism in my voice. I got out of bed and started to walk toward his dresser, where he'd placed his phone. "And he wants you to go to Pennsylvania Friday?"

"Yeah, why? You don't believe me?"

I picked up his phone and hit the necessary keys to find the last call received. "Hell no, I don't believe you." I fully expected him to jump out of bed and try to stop me, but I was close enough to the bathroom to make a quick dash. Before he had a chance to pull the covers back, I'd have the door locked, talking to whatever hooker had just called him.

"Boo, you don't have to do this. I was gonna ask you if you wanted to go," he said with a hint of amusement in his voice.

Oh, so he thinks this is funny, huh? I could feel my blood pressure rise at least five points. Damn, I really thought he was different than other men.

"Stop lying, Louis, and tell me who was on the phone," I said as I hit the TALK button to redial the last number.

He sat up in bed and folded his arms. "Guess we're going to find out." He was trying to act cool and in control, but I knew he had to be scared.

"I guess we are," I said with a smirk. I put the phone to my ear, fully expecting to hear a woman answer the phone. That's why I nearly dropped the cell when I heard a familiar voice—a male voice.

"Hello?" Louis's boss repeated for the third time.

I disconnected the call. Knowing that Louis's boss had probably seen the number on his caller ID, I could only hope that he wouldn't call back now. If Louis was mad enough, he might just embarrass me by telling his boss why I'd called. But neither of those things happened—his boss never called back, and Louis wasn't mad.

He got out of bed and wrapped his arms around me. "You don't have anything to worry about," he said. "I'm not like your father. If anything, I'm more like your brother. And I love your ass enough to forgive you, but you gotta stop being so suspicious, 'cause I ain't got nothing to hide from you." He kissed my forehead, then released me from his hug.

Before I could begin to apologize or try to explain myself, he stepped into the bathroom again and closed the door. When I heard the shower running, I eased my clothes off and pushed open the bathroom door. I had some serious making up to do.

Darnel

10

"Oh my God!"

Thump!

I couldn't tell if Keisha was screaming from pleasure or from pain. What I did know was that every time I slammed my dick inside her, her head banged up against the wall with a loud *thump*! I know it sounds horrible, but in some warped way, I found pleasure in this and picked up the pace between strokes. I have to admit, part of me wanted to see her head go right through the wall.

"Oh my God!" *Thump! Thump! Clunk!* "Oh my God!" *Thump! Clunk! Thump!*

When I drove over to see Keisha, I had been worried about the state I would find her in, but I gave some thought to what my father had said. Maybe she really was bluffing when she said she wanted to kill herself. I mean, this was a woman who would stoop low enough to sleep with my best friend, so it wouldn't be much of a stretch to tell a lie for sympathy now. By the time I got to her place, I was so full of mixed emotions—love, hate, anger, and desire—I didn't even really know how I would react to seeing Keisha. What I wanted to do was cuss her out, call her every name in the book except her own. But when she opened the door, her eyes were full of tears, and in that split second, my heart just melted and love suppressed all those other emotions. And I hated myself for it.

"I'm so sorry, Darnel," she cried over and over as we sat on the couch together. She was pulling out all the stops—shaking her head, wringing her hands, and rocking back and forth. Yes, my father had warned me, and I knew I wasn't supposed to, but the next thing I knew, she was in my arms and I was comforting her. Can you believe it? She was the one who had made a complete ass out of me, and here I was reassuring her. What the hell was the world coming to? What the hell was wrong with me? The familiar scent of her perfume and the warmth of her body made me not even care about the answers to those questions.

Before I knew it, I was kissing Keisha deeply, and in a matter of seconds, we were all over each other, undressing like our clothes were on fire, right there on the living room floor. I'd never felt so drawn to anyone. The whole thing was like some scene out of a movie, except that beneath all the passion lurked my pain and anger, and it only took a few words from her to bring it all back to the surface.

"I have to go in the bedroom and get a condom," I whispered.

"Don't worry about a condom," she said breathlessly. "Just put it in."

Just put it in.

Without warning, my mind filled with the image of Omar on top of my future wife, and she was whispering those urgent words to him, not me. Keisha and I had always used condoms, because she didn't want to get pregnant before we were married. But hearing her say I didn't need a condom now forced a memory to the forefront of my mind—Omar had not been wearing a condom when I caught them in the act. Had she told him to "just put it in"? Why the hell had she been so reckless with him when she had always preached safety to me, even when I begged her to let me go raw? The thought wounded and infuriated me, and I did just as she told me; I put it in—or more accurately, I slammed it in, over and over.

Again, my mind was overloaded with conflicting emotions. I was hurt; I was angry; I was confused; and surprisingly, I was more turned on than I'd ever been. It was as if a lightbulb went off, and I was seeing her as a different person. I imagined her as some sort of nymphomaniac, carelessly giving away what was supposed to be mine and mine alone. She seemed more sexy, more exciting, more thrilling to me. She was a completely different woman. Instead of the innocent girl whose virginity had been mine, she was now someone I needed to conquer. And hopefully my conquest would prove, not only to her but also to myself, that I was better than Omar. I was better than he could ever be.

I pushed all thoughts and images out of my mind and gave in to my own body's demands. While I had always made love to her, treating her delicately, never wanting to cause her any pain, this time I felt differently. I was rough with her, as if I wanted to punish her body for its sins. I didn't want to remember the tender love we used to share. Instead, I wanted to bang her like some nameless woman I would forget as soon as it was over. I wanted to be like my father and satisfy my own needs. So I told myself that instead of this being the woman I loved, she was nothing more than some prime piece of ass there for the taking.

Keisha tried to pull me close, to stare into my eyes, but I didn't want to look at her. I turned my head and kept pounding away. She grabbed my face between her hands, forcing me to see that familiar look in her eyes. I recognized it and knew she was about to climax. A few more strokes and then I climaxed with her, spraying her womb with my seed for the very first time. It was the most awesome sensation I'd ever felt.

As we lay together on the living room floor, it didn't take long before the glow wore off and the whole situation felt cheap and dirty. It had just hit me. Omar wasn't sleeping behind me; I was sleeping behind him.

I glanced over at her face. She was lying on her back, smiling, but where she had looked exciting and exotic just minutes earlier, now she looked used up and old—not at all like the pure woman I had wanted to marry and love forever.

"That was incredible," Keisha whispered to me. She rolled on top of me, and I felt her firm breasts pressing against my chest.

Incredible, she'd said. Was that what incredible was now—me trying to bang her so hard that her head made an impression in the wall? I nudged her off me and turned away from her cuddling arms.

"What's the matter, baby?"

I stared at a spot on the wall, refusing to look at her as I spoke. "Did you ever think about AIDS?"

"What?"

"When you was with Omar. You didn't use a condom, did you?" I rolled toward her, staring in her face.

"Baby, don't start, please. We were having such a good time."

"I didn't start this, Keisha. You did."

"I told you I was sorry."

"Sometimes sorry ain't good enough. Do you know how many women Omar has been with?"

She tried to touch me, but I pushed her hand away and got up off the floor to find my clothes. It was time to get out of there.

"Baby, please come back here." She sat up, and when I looked back at her, I saw the tears glistening in her eyes. This time, I didn't want to comfort her. She deserved to cry.

"How could you do that to me, Keisha?"

"I'm sorry, Darnel. You have to believe me." Tears rolled down her cheeks now. She came near me as I was sliding on my pants.

"How do you expect me to believe you? We were supposed to be together forever. I'm supposed to forget that crap happened?"

She reached for my belt as if to stop me from getting dressed. I suppose if we stayed screwing all the time, we'd never have to deal with the reality of what she'd done to our relationship, but I couldn't do what she wanted. I couldn't just pretend that everything was back to normal. I shoved her hand away, then collapsed onto the couch, my head in my hands.

"But I love you."

"You sure got a funny way of showing it."

"Darnel, it wasn't like that. It was a mistake. The biggest mistake of my life. You have to give me another chance. You are my life." By this point, she was on her knees on the floor in front of me. How many times had I seen her in this position before, using her mouth to make me feel like the only man on earth? But now she wasn't giving me pleasure; she was begging, and it seemed so wrong, almost perverse.

"Please don't leave me." Her body shook as she reached out and took my hand, tears streaming down her face. Suddenly, all the anger and rage I had evaporated. As messed up as this was, I wasn't sure I could walk away, no matter how much she'd hurt me. There was no denying it; I was deeply in love with her.

"I need to know something."

"Anything." She looked up at me through red-rimmed eyes.

"Was this the first time?"

She nodded her head slowly. "Yes, it was the first and only time."

I felt my pain give way just the slightest bit. Maybe I could come to understand her mistake, and we could work our way through this. There was one thing for sure: I didn't want to live my life without her.

"Do you still want to be my wife? Do you still want to marry me?"

She pulled herself up off the floor and sat next to me on the couch. Holding my hands in hers, she answered, "Yes, Darnel. I still want to marry you. I love you more than anything in the world. What about you? Do you still want to marry me?"

I let go of her hand and stood up, looking down at her. "No," I said in my most sincere voice. I shook my head. "No, I don't want to marry you." I started walking toward the door. "I'm not even sure why I just fucked you."

I left, feeling good about myself for the first time since I'd seen her and Omar together.

Jamie

11

For the third week in a row, Louis had to drive up to Pennsylvania for work, but this time I decided to stay home. I swear there is nothing more aggravating than going to a luxury car auction when you ain't got luxury car money. Besides, I had only gone to Pennsylvania the first time to make sure Louis was really going to work. His boss had been on the phone that night I flipped out, but for all I knew, he was just covering for Louis. Once I was satisfied that Louis was indeed attending that boring-ass auction, I had no desire to go to another one. So I sent him on his way and made plans to cook dinner and spend a little time with Daddy.

I was sitting at Daddy's kitchen table cutting potatoes when Darnel walked into the kitchen, then left abruptly without saying a word. I'm sure he was hoping I hadn't noticed him. Why do men always think they're so sneaky when we women are five steps ahead of them?

"Darnel!" I called his name to assure him that he'd been busted.

I knew exactly why he'd hauled ass out of the kitchen that way. He was afraid I was going to give him a hard time about talking to Keisha. And he was right. I'd been holding on to a few choice words for my brother ever since Daddy had told me Darnel went to see her.

When he stepped back into the kitchen, the sheepish look on his face told me that they had done more than talk. The thought of my brother getting back into bed with Keisha after what she'd done to him really disappointed me. Why was it that Darnel was the one who got hurt, but he seemed to be the least mad about it? I just couldn't see myself forgiving someone for doing what she did. I really hated that wench for what she'd done to my brother.

I stopped chopping and set the knife down on the table. "Hey, where you been? I been calling you all week."

"I don't know. I just been busy." He shrugged his shoulders and tried to look casual as he sat down across from me. "Mostly looking for an apartment. I gotta get outta this place."

"Whatever. Don't try and change the subject. You been screwin' that piece of shit ho Keisha again, haven't you?"

"No, I haven't." His eyes darted around the room, making contact with everything but me. Well, that was a start, I thought. At least he still had enough pride to deny it. But he wasn't getting off that easy.

"You lyin'. Daddy told me you went over there."

"Well, 'Daddy' needs to mind his own business. That's why I need to find my own place."

Oh no, he didn't! "We *are* his business," I reminded him. "I can't believe you slept with her. Did you forget she slept with your best friend?"

He winced. My words had struck a nerve, but he still wasn't willing to get mad the way I thought he should. "Jamie, just let it go, a'ight?"

"No, it's not all right. You're my brother, and as long as you are, I'm gonna tell you when you're being stupid."

"Jamie, you're my sister, not my momma, okay? I can handle my own life. I got this."

As much as I didn't like his momma, I almost wished she was there at that moment. Someone needed to knock some sense into this boy. And trifling-ass Crystal was just the woman to do it.

"You gonna let that woman play you, aren't you?"

"Ain't nobody gonna play me." His words were meant to convince me, but the look on his face told me that he hadn't even convinced himself. I almost felt sorry for him. My poor brother was so whipped, he couldn't stop loving that woman even if he wanted to. Damn, I wish I knew her secret.

Then an idea came to me. If it was all about the booty, then maybe all Darnel needed was someone else to offer him something better. I'd given up on that idea when Louis shot it down a while back, but now that I thought about it, I knew someone who would be perfect for the job.

"Darnel, look, I'm sorry. I just hate what she's trying to do to you. You deserve better."

I got no response. Keisha had messed his head up to the point where he had no idea how special he was. But I was determined to help my brother regain his self-esteem and his pride.

"Listen, why don't you let me introduce you to one of my friends?"

"No, thanks."

"Please. Just give it a try. I've got this friend Sandra who is perfect for you."

Still no response.

"How about I bring her to Daddy's Memorial Day barbeque? If you got somebody by then, it's not going to matter."

"Like I said before, no thanks. I'm good."

"No strings attached." I wasn't going to give up.

"Do you understand what *no* means?" He stood up and headed toward the door, but I followed and stopped him before he could leave the kitchen.

"Yeah, I know what it means, but when was the last time you can remember me letting someone tell me no about anything?"

He rolled his eyes and leaned against the doorframe. "Never."

"Exactly. Now, you're gonna say yes sooner or later, 'cause I'm gonna bug you 'til you do, so you might as well say it now."

"Okay," he finally relented. "But no strings attached."

I clapped my hands and gave him a peck on the cheek. "Good. So that's settled. Now, don't go nowhere, 'cause I'm making dinner tonight," I said as I returned to the table to get back to work on the potatoes.

"Cool," he answered, sounding relieved to be off the hot seat. "What time is Louis getting here?"

"He's not. He had to work in Pennsylvania, but he'll be home tomorrow night."

"Really? That's strange, then."

I stopped chopping again and looked at Darnel. He had a puzzled look on his face. "Why is that strange? There are plenty of car dealerships in New York that get their used cars from Pennsylvania auctions."

"No, that's not what I meant. I thought I saw Louis in Manhattan today."

"It couldn't have been him," I said. "He left last night for the auction."

Darnel looked truly confused. "Well, your man must have a twin, then, 'cause I could swear that was him I saw. Then again, maybe I'm wrong, 'cause this dude was dressed in a suit, and you know I ain't never seen Louis wearing nothing but some jeans and a polo shirt."

"Well, did you say anything to this mystery man?"

"Nah, I didn't have a chance to actually talk to him. He was on the other side of the street, but I swear he was a dead ringer for Louis."

"You know what they say—everybody's got a twin." I don't know why, but I was getting a little annoyed. I mean, I knew my man was working in another state, so why was Darnel trying to make me think otherwise? Shoot, I had enough problems controlling my jealous nature as it was, and I sure didn't need Darnel planting any seeds in my mind. Ever since I went off on Louis about the late-night phone call from his boss, I'd been trying to keep myself in check.

"Look," I said, changing the subject before my imagination could start running wild. "Don't let her hurt you again."

"Call me when dinner's ready," he said, then practically ran out of the room to stop me from saying anything else. The conversation was over for now, but let me find out he was still messing with that ho, I would definitely have more to say about the subject.

On the way home from Daddy's, I called Louis's cell phone to check in. We usually spoke several times a day, but I hadn't heard from him at all since early in the morning. I missed the sound of his voice.

Unfortunately, I only heard a recording of his voice as the call went straight to his voice mail. I figured maybe his boss had taken him out to dinner. He had been working really hard, putting in lots of hours, and it was obviously paying off. He was the only one his boss had taken to the auction with him two weeks in a row, and now he was probably being rewarded with a nice dinner. Who knows? Maybe he'd even be promoted to a senior management position if things kept up like this. I was so proud of Louis.

I left a short message on his voice mail before getting out of my car and heading into the house. I was pretty wiped out from cooking dinner and cleaning up the kitchen. Daddy and Darnel loved it whenever I cooked for them, but that didn't mean either one ever offered to help with the dishes afterward. I shook my head and smiled, remembering how the two of them were already snoring in front of the TV by the time I finished putting away the last of the pots and pans. They were lucky I loved them so much.

Exhausted, I headed straight to the bedroom and changed into my nightshirt. I opened the closet to put my dirty clothes in the hamper, and that's when it hit me like a ton of bricks. Louis's suit—the one I bought him to wear at Darnel's wedding and the only one he owned—was not hanging in its usual place in the closet. Ever since the day I bought it, that suit had never left this spot.

I shuffled through the rest of Louis's things, trying to convince myself that Louis had simply moved the suit to a new spot. But the sudden sick feeling in my stomach told me what my heart already knew—the suit was not there. And just like that, my suspicious nature kicked back into overdrive.

I was waiting at the door early the next afternoon when Louis stuck his key in the lock. I snatched it open to find him in his regular sagging jeans and white T-shirt, grinning like he had just stepped out to the store for a gallon of milk instead of stepping out for something—or someone—else. It was the same stupid grin I'd seen my father give to so many women, fooling them into believing he was faithful when in fact he had three or four other chicks on the side. Well, I was not gonna be that kind of fool for Louis. And the bouquet of flowers he handed me was just another trick I'd seen my father use a million times before.

"Thanks." I kept my voice as calm as I could. I wasn't going to go off this time; I was going to let him hang himself with his lies.

He put down his suitcase and reached out his arms for a hug.

I gave him a weak embrace and stepped back quickly. "So, how was Pennsylvania?"

"It was good, baby, but I missed you."

I felt my hand twitch, like it had a mind of its own and wanted to slap him right now. He missed me. Yeah, right. He didn't miss shit while he was all up in some other woman.

"I called you. You didn't return my call," I said, still trying to keep my tone neutral. It wasn't easy, considering the adrenaline racing through my system.

"Oh yeah, I forgot to bring my charger," he lied again.

"Really?" I glanced toward his pocket, where he usually kept his phone. A look passed over his face, and it was clear he knew where this conversation was headed.

He sighed as he pulled his phone out of his pocket and handed it to me. "Here. Check it for yourself. It's dead."

I looked at the phone, and sure enough, the screen was blank. But that didn't mean he was off the hook.

"Dead phone, huh? How convenient. Did you two plan that in advance?"

"Jamie, what the hell are you talking about? I was so damn busy at those auctions that I wouldn't have had time to plan anything even if I'd wanted to." Then he added sarcastically, "Would you like to call my boss and ask him?"

Oh, hell no. I wasn't gonna fall for that again. His damn boss was probably in on the whole scheme anyway. You know how men can be, always ready to provide an alibi for their boys.

"So, what's with the suit?" I asked, pointing toward the corner, where he'd set his suitcase.

"What do you mean, what's with the suit?"

"You brought it, didn't you?" Ha! He was busted now. Let him try to lie his way out of this one.

"Yeah, I brought it. What'd you do, X-ray my suitcase before I left or something?"

"No, but I know it's not in your closet, so it must be in that suitcase," I said, doing my best imitation of a prosecuting attorney revealing the final piece of damning evidence. But Louis proved to be a tougher witness than I'd expected. He was still trying to defend himself.

"Yeah, I brought my suit, but so what? My boss told me he

was gonna take me to that Italian restaurant you and I saw near the hotel, and it's not exactly the kind of place I could wear khakis and a polo shirt."

I remembered the restaurant. Louis's boss had pointed it out to us and told us what great food they had there. And I did notice a few people walking into the restaurant dressed in more formal clothes. This place was no Olive Garden. But the fact that we had seen it together two weeks before just meant that Louis had filed the information away to use it as part of his alibi. I guess he figured if he could cloak his lies in enough details, I would believe him.

In the short amount of time that I stood silent, formulating my next question, Louis tried to flip the script on me, just like all men do when they're caught.

"Girl, why you trippin'?"

I finally just came out with it. "Darnel saw you in the city yesterday."

I don't know what I expected to see on his face—fear, guilt, maybe even regret. But I couldn't see anything, because he turned his back on me and went toward his suitcase. I watched impatiently as he dug into the pocket on the front. I was itching for a fight now. But then he pulled out a pile of papers.

"Here." He shoved the stack of receipts into my hands.

I was almost afraid to look down at them, because I already sensed my whole case had just been lost. In the pile was a hotel bill with a small room service charge, definitely less than what breakfast for two would cost. There was a receipt from Starbucks, again an order for one. I looked at the toll receipt that confirmed he had been driving on the New Jersey Turnpike. I didn't need to look any further. There was no way Louis had been in the city.

"Would you like to see the matchbook from the Italian restaurant?" he asked angrily.

I reached for his hand. "Baby, I—"

"Don't, okay?" He pulled away. "I'm not gonna live like this. You hear me? I'm not gonna do it."

Before I could even start an apology, he had picked up his suitcase and headed to the bedroom. The sound of the slamming door told me that I was not welcome to join him this time.

Jamie

12

"Hey, Jamie. How you doing, Louis?" Sandra slipped into the backseat behind Louis, then leaned forward to kiss us both on the cheek.

I smiled as Louis put the car in gear, pulling away from Sandra's apartment complex. I couldn't wait to get to Daddy's house, because my girl Sandra was about to break Keisha's hold on my brother. There was no way he was going to be able to resist Sandra's charm, smarts, and exotic good looks, not to mention her dynamite figure. She was tailor-made for my brother. Heck, she was even into sports, and he was a sports fanatic. She was the type of woman who could accompany a man to a black-tie affair one day, then hang out and play hoops and drink beer with him and his friends the next.

I turned sideways so I could see both her and Louis from my seat. "Girl, look at you. You look so cute."

Sandra was wearing a pair of tight jeans and a red Baby Phat shirt that showed just enough of her assets. She didn't have them spilling out in a distasteful, ho-ish fashion like some of the sisters I knew, which is why I thought she might make a perfect fit with Darnel. She managed the health club where I worked out, and over time, we'd talked, which eventually led to us hanging out.

Men were always fawning over Sandra, because she was absolutely gorgeous—half-Korean, half-black, with a body even I was jealous of. She looked like a young Kimora Lee Simmons.

Men at the gym kept sweating her for her number, but she made it clear that she don't shit where she eats, and since the gym provided her livelihood, the brothas didn't have a chance. Besides, from everything I could tell, Sandra was into the more sophisticated, professional guys like my brother. Her previous boyfriend was a stockbroker. Now, that preference did make me think she might have some gold-digger tendencies, but I wasn't too worried about it. It wasn't like I was looking for her to have no long-term relationship with my brother. I just wanted him to get a taste of someone other than Keisha so he could move on with his life.

"I hope I'm not dressed too casual," she said.

"Girl, please. Look at me. I got on jeans too. We're just going over to my daddy's for a barbeque, so you can meet my brother."

Sandra smiled, leaning forward so that her head was between the two front seats. "So, tell me about this brother of yours."

"Well, like I told you at the gym, he's fine, so you ain't got to worry about that."

"Oh, I could tell that from his picture. But what kind of man is he? 'Cause I'm looking for a man, not a boy. Lord knows I've met enough of them."

"Then, girl, you're going to the right place. And I'm not just saying this 'cause he's my brother. He's a good guy—fine, hard-working, and he treats a woman like a queen. Aside from Louis, he's one of the only good ones left."

"I hope so, Jamie, 'cause I'm sick of wasting my time."

"Trust me, girl. His last girlfriend didn't know how to appreciate him, 'cause she was a lame-ass snake." I hadn't bothered telling Sandra all the sordid details about Keisha and Darnel and Omar. She was cool and all, but I didn't want to take any chances. I mean, what if she heard the whole story and decided my brother was damaged goods? "But I know you two are gonna hit it off," I assured her.

"With all the losers I've met, it would be a miracle to actually meet someone who is who he says he is. Most of the ones I meet are such liars and have so much drama," Sandra complained.

"Well, not Darnel. Ain't that right, Louis?" I asked, trying to include him in the conversation. The silence made me glance over at Louis, who seemed to be ignoring me. He was still mad at me after I accused him of not going to Pennsylvania. "Louis?"

"I told you before we left home, don't bring me into this, Jamie. I'm just the driver. If your brother was looking to find someone to date, don't you think he could do it without your help? It's not like there's a shortage of women in New York."

"But he does have my help, because that's the kind of sister I am. I love Darnel, and I don't see anything wrong with setting him up with someone who would appreciate him." Maybe because Louis didn't have any family, he didn't understand that I would do anything to see my brother happy. "Besides," I argued, "he told me it was all right."

"Yeah, almost two weeks ago," he mumbled.

"What did you say?" I wished he would repeat that in front of Sandra and embarrass me.

"Nothin'. I just think you should stay out of it," he added. "I'm not saying you won't get along with him, Sandra. I just think Jamie should stay out of it."

"I understand, Louis. It's not like we're going out on a date. She's just introducing us."

Louis was always hating on the way I got involved with my family, but hey, it wasn't my issue. If I listened to him and stayed out of it, my brother would just continue to chase after that stupid bitch. But I knew what was best for Darnel, even if he didn't. There was one thing guaranteed to get Darnel's mind off Keisha—the present I planned to deliver to him on a silver platter.

"Maybe you should call your brother and warn him I'm coming," Sandra offered.

"Girl, don't trip on Louis. I got this."

Louis's jaw tightened, and I knew he was upset. I hated it when he was mad at me. I slid my hand over onto his lap, giving him a reminder of the fun we'd had earlier. He might have still been upset about the whole Pennsylvania thing, but that never stopped Louis from wanting to get some of my good stuff. I gave him a little squeeze to let him know that I was not finished with him, and his facial expression relaxed just a bit.

"Did I tell you that Darnel has an MBA? He got a good J.O.B. too."

Louis removed my hand from his lap. Damn, he could be so stubborn sometimes. But then again, I guess he would say the same thing about me.

"Gotta love a man with a job these days," Sandra said with a smile. "Especially if it's one that pays well."

I turned around and high-fived my girl, paying no attention to Louis's funky mood. "And did I tell you he used to run track? You two should run together."

"Yeah, I love to run around Flushing Meadow Park," Sandra added just as we pulled up to Daddy's house.

I was surprised there wasn't an unfamiliar car parked in the driveway. My father usually had some woman inviting herself over. He didn't have any one type; they were mostly women from the church who knew how to stir a little something in the pots. Of course, it was still early enough for one of his latest fans to show up with a pie or a cake in hand, fawning all over him like he was the judge in the Miss Past-Your-Prime contest and she was hoping to win the big prize—him.

I carried some of the groceries to the door and used my key to let us all in, letting Louis grab the case of beer. Sandra carried the bottle of Bordeaux she'd brought. Mmm-hmm, I thought, Darnel had better be thanking me for convincing a banger like Sandra that he was worth a shot.

"Hey, Daddy." I smiled as we walked out the back door and onto the deck. "This is Sandra."

Daddy offered his hand to her; then he shot me a look. He knew me too damn well to think I had just casually invited some friend over. Even when I lived with my father, I wasn't great about sharing his company, so friends were rarely over. Plus, Sandra was fine and smart, and exactly opposite of that loser Keisha. I gave my father a dazzling don't-mess-this-up smile. He and Louis exchanged looks as if to say, "Women!" but I didn't care, because I always knew what was good for the men in my life, even if they didn't.

Daddy was lighting the grill, talking to Louis and Sandra as I prepped dinner in the kitchen.

"You want some help?" My girl came over to the table, where I was slicing the cucumber for the salad. I was about to hand her a knife to cut the carrots when Darnel came into the kitchen, dressed like he was expecting company.

I hadn't seen my brother in a couple of weeks, and thankfully he had pulled his stuff back up a few notches. After canceling the wedding, he'd been looking a little rough, but clearly that phase had passed. I just hoped Daddy was wrong and it wasn't because he was sleeping with Keisha again. He was sporting a LeBron James Cleveland Cavaliers jersey over a red T-shirt, jeans, and some new sneakers. Even I had to admit he looked fine.

I glanced at Sandra and saw the unmistakable look of appreciation on her face. She definitely liked what she saw.

"Darnel, this is my friend Sandra. Could you get her a cocktail?" I threw them together quick before he got all weird on me. Since his fiasco, something was going on with my brother, but he didn't let me close enough to figure it out. Fortunately, that mother of his did have the good sense to teach him how to treat a woman.

"Sure, what would you like?"

"Do you mind if I see what you have first?" She gave him this smile that could have changed the world. The next thing I knew, they were off into the house. My plan was moving along much more easily than I expected. I rushed my preparations and started putting the food on the table so I wouldn't miss anything.

"Darnel, did I tell you that Sandra is the manager of my gym?" I said while we were eating dinner. I was hoping to give him a conversation starter, since there were too many silences between them as far as I was concerned.

"Oh, cool," he mumbled between bites.

"She's increased membership almost fifty percent."

"I just like being able to offer people something that they really need," Sandra commented.

"Darnel is the top salesperson at his insurance company," I threw in there to keep it moving, since Darnel wasn't making much of an effort.

"People need insurance. Especially with all the natural disasters," Sandra added.

"Yeah, like the one right here." Louis pointed to me, laughing.

"Yeah, our Jamie is something," Daddy added, but I could hear his fatherly pride. Besides, I didn't mind being the target of their teasing for a while if it would loosen up Darnel. But he didn't even seem to notice half of what was going on around him. He just sat at the table, constantly checking his phone.

"Darnel, Sandra just won a five K race out in Long Island," I said, trying to pry Darnel away from the phone.

"Oh, cool." He barely looked up when he answered.

"Darnel went to school on a track scholarship. He almost made the Olympics."

"Naw, I barely made tenth place at the trials." Darnel was finally participating in the conversation, but only to make himself sound less than the superman I was trying to present him as. Damn, did he always have to tell the truth? That boy had to learn how to stretch things if he wanted to start getting any quality women.

"That's still pretty good. Most people don't even get invited to the trials," Sandra offered as a compliment to Darnel.

"He could have gotten a basketball scholarship," I added.

"Really? What position?" Sandra asked. "That's my game."

"I played forward," Darnel answered.

"So did I. I played forward for Delaware State."

"Yeah, we're big B-ball fans around here," Daddy added.

"Almost all of us." Louis didn't have a thing for sports, which was fine with me. It meant I'd never be one of those sports widows.

"I love the Lakers," Sandra shouted out enthusiastically, like she had spent some time cheering for the team.

"You mean the Fakers?" She had finally gotten Darnel's attention.

"Hey, hey, don't talk about my team. You gonna make me get my number twenty-four jersey and wipe the floor with you," Daddy threatened Darnel playfully.

"Kobe is lame," Darnel shot back.

"What?" Both Sandra and Daddy spoke at the same time.

"It's all about LeBron James," Darnel hollered, gesturing proudly toward his jersey. But Sandra and Daddy pounced on him with names and facts and figures.

Daddy started. "We gonna see who's the sucker team this Sunday, 'cause the Lakers are going to kick the Cavaliers' asses this weekend."

"Puhleease! In your dreams." Darnel was getting jazzed. He and Daddy had always bonded over sports. *Finally, something to put some life into this conversation,* I thought with relief.

"We already got fifty on it," Darnel said to Daddy. "Why don't we make that a hundred?"

"Can I get in on this?" Sandra asked.

"Sure. You can take the other fifty," Daddy offered eagerly.

"Don't matter who's in it as long as I get paid," Darnel said, laughing. I noticed that he'd finally put his phone back into his pocket.

"Keep laughing now. You're not going to be laughing when my Lakers spank that butt." Sandra looked like she was as much into basketball as they were. She knew how to work her thing, and I wasn't mad at her. "Now I can't wait to watch that game."

"You two should watch the game together." I threw it out there innocently enough. "I mean, you both are going to watch it anyway. It's not a problem, right, Darnel?" I had him on the spot. He'd never be rude to a friend of mine, and I knew he wasn't about to start now.

"Well, I was supposed to watch the game with the old man, since we got money on it and all." Darnel glanced at Daddy. I couldn't tell if he was hoping Daddy would rescue him from this setup, but it wasn't happening. Daddy disliked Keisha as much as I did.

"A Lakers fan is always welcome in my house," Daddy said. "Besides, I'm sure she's going to want her money as soon as the game's over. As do I." He smiled confidently as if the game were in the bag.

Darnel waved his hand at Daddy. "Okay, so I'll see you two Sunday. Bring cash. I don't take checks."

As everyone at the table erupted into laughter over the friendly bet, Darnel's phone rang, and he jumped up from the table. "Excuse me a minute."

I was sure that it was Keisha on the phone, but at the moment, I didn't even care. Now that Darnel and Sandra had plans to get together again next weekend, I knew that Keisha's days with my brother were numbered.

James

13

As I sat in my living room having a drink, I thought about the barbecue I'd had with my kids. Once again, Jamie had accomplished what she did best—she manipulated the situation. Don't ask me how Jamie made it happen, but Darnel, who was still preoccupied with Keisha, ended up driving Sandra home. Despite the fact that it was the result of my daughter's meddling, I actually thought this was a good thing. Someone needed to do something to take Darnel's mind off Keisha, and I was starting to doubt that anyone would be able to. Then Sandra showed up, and maybe meeting her would push Darnel in the right direction—away from Keisha.

I was hopeful that it would work out between Darnel and Sandra, even if only temporarily. Darnel's ego needed a little boost. Sandra seemed to be a nice enough girl, and there was no doubt that she was a looker. Hell, if this was twenty years ago, who knows? I might have given my son a run for his money. The sad thing was that if this really were a competition between the two of us, I'd come out the winner. Darnel had been so damn devoted to Keisha that it was like all other women were invisible to him. He sure didn't know how to play the game. I just hoped he didn't blow it with Sandra, because she was definitely showing signs of interest.

The doorbell snapped me out of my thoughts. I walked to the front door, wondering who might be stopping by. It probably wasn't one of the kids, because both Jamie and Darnel had keys to my house—which, by the way, was something I hoped to change as soon as Darnel found his own place. Between Jamie barging in while I was in bed with Crystal and Darnel moping around every day, I was more than ready to fly solo again. I loved my kids, but their constant presence was starting to interfere with my social life, and I wasn't gonna have that.

In the short time after Jamie moved out, I had enjoyed the luxury of having the whole place to myself. I could let a woman into my home and take her right there on the living room couch if I wanted to. With Darnel around, that had become impossible.

As I realized now that he was out with Sandra and might be gone for a while, I hoped that the person at the door was someone of the female persuasion coming to call for a night of pleasure. If so, she would be right on time.

When I opened the door, I saw that there was indeed a woman, but I didn't know why she was there, because she didn't usually stop by unannounced like this, especially since she lived in another state.

"Hello, James," Crystal said as she pushed past me and made her way inside.

Although I was confused, she was a welcome surprise.

As I closed the door, I peeked outside and noticed that there was no car parked in my driveway. It was safe to assume she had parked a few blocks away. After the way Jamie had busted in on us last time, Crystal wouldn't want to take any chances. She was smart that way about her creeping. Back when she was living in Queens, she tipped around with me all the time, but her first husband, Joe, never caught her. In fact, Crystal was so slick that Joe probably never would have suspected a thing if Darnel hadn't spilled the beans.

Even though I was his father, Darnel never wanted me and his mother to be together once he figured out I didn't intend to marry her. I can't say I blamed him, though. He wanted to see his mother with a fully committed man, something I never pretended I could be. The problem was that no matter how hard he tried, he would never be able to change the sexual chemistry between me and Crystal.

After all these years, the attraction was still powerful. Crystal had her hands all over me before I could even ask her, "What are you doing here?"

"Milton's brother passed away, so we came up to make arrangements," she answered between kisses on my neck.

"Where's your husband?" I asked, though the answer never seemed to matter. Wherever Milton was, Crystal always found a way to see me whenever they came to New York.

"He's with his family. I told him I was going to see Darnel." She placed my hands on her breasts, and I gladly massaged them.

"Where's Darnel?" She quickly glanced around the room; then her eyes came to rest on my crotch.

"What are you trying to do to me, girl?" I teased her like I'd done when we were young.

"Where is he?"

"He's not here." I looked into Crystal's eyes and saw the desire burning there. "So, what's up? You trying to go upstairs?"

"You so bad," Crystal joked, like that wasn't on her mind in the first place. She was standing so close to me that I could smell her Trésor perfume wafting in my nose. And like two dance partners who'd always done the same familiar tango, we wound up in bed together.

After a couple of lustful rounds in bed, I sat back and enjoyed the view while Crystal put on her bra and slid her underwear up her legs. This whole scene was customary for us: an hour or two of passion, then Crystal getting dressed and us parting ways, both knowing that it wouldn't be the last time we made love. But this time, Crystal decided to flip the script.

"I'm thinking about leaving my husband and moving back to New York."

Oh Lord, not this, I thought. We hadn't visited this subject together in quite a long time. After all these years, I thought that Crystal finally understood where she stood with me—I loved her, but I was not *in love* with her. She was one of the best bed partners I'd ever had, but there was something missing, something that prevented me from taking our relationship to a higher level. There had always been something missing.

The truth was, there was something missing with every woman I'd ever met. But it was just like the old saying, "It's not you; it's me." I had known some fabulous, sexy women in my life—plenty of them went on to make wonderful wives for other men—but I'd never met any woman who made me want to hand in my player card. It just wasn't in my genetic makeup, I guess, but whatever it was, I had explained it to Crystal plenty of times, so I had no idea why she was bringing it up again.

"I thought you said you and Milton have a good life."

"We do. But that doesn't mean I'm happy." She came over and sat on the bed. "I spent one night with you last month and two hours tonight, and I felt more passion than I've felt with that man in all the years we been married."

"So come up more often," I suggested, hoping that would be enough to satisfy her. "Let's plan some secret getaways. But you don't have to leave him."

Crystal sighed. "You just don't understand, do you? I'm still in love with you, James. I'm just going through the motions with him. I almost can't stand for him to put his hands on me anymore."

When she looked at me, I saw that her eyes were glistening with tears. I wished like hell that I could make her feel better, but I would never be the man she wanted. I hated these conversations.

"I'm not asking you to marry me," she said sadly. "I'm just asking you to let me be your woman."

I held her hand and said, "You know how things are with us, Crystal. I'm not gonna change, so you really oughta try to make it work with Milton. He seems like a good enough guy. He really loves you."

"In other words, I'm good enough to be a booty call but not good enough to be your woman," she said, pulling her hand away.

"You know you're more than that, Crystal. You're the mother of my only son. A good mother. You raised Darnel to be a good man, and I can't ask for more than that."

"But, Darnel aside, how do you feel about me as a woman?"

"You're a good woman. If I had half a brain, I would have married you years ago."

"I'm a good woman," she said sadly, "but evidently not good enough."

I knew I was hurting her, and I hated to do it, but I had never lied to Crystal about where we stood, and I wasn't about to start now. "It's just that I have never been the marrying type. I told you that when we met, and my story has never changed."

"You don't have to marry me, James. I'm just looking for you to make a commitment to me. You're not getting any younger, and neither am I. Sure, you can still sling it, but the Viagra days aren't far away."

"You sure know how to hurt a brother." I laughed to deflect the sting of her comment, but the idea of using Viagra was chilling. I had always been a vibrant man and planned to be for years to come. Sure, I had been noticing that I got a little more winded lately during sex, but there was no problem with the important equipment.

"It's not funny, James. I'd always envisioned us growing old together, sitting on the porch, rocking in our chairs, waiting for Darnel to bring our grandchildren by."

It was a nice image—for someone who was a romantic. But it bothered me, because all it really meant was that it didn't matter how honest I'd been with her all these years. She still held it in her head that someday I would change my mind.

"I just want to be a part of your life," she said.

"We will always be in each other's lives, Crystal. We do have a son together, you know."

"Yeah, but Darnel's grown, and he never really wanted us together anyway, so you can stop making excuses. This isn't about Darnel, and it isn't about Jamie either. It's about you and me and whether you love me enough to have a committed relationship." She wiped away a few tears.

I stayed silent, because I knew I couldn't give her the answer she wanted to hear.

"Let me ask you a question," she said. "Do you want to die alone?"

"Where did that question come from?"

"Just answer me."

"I never really gave it much thought," I replied honestly.

"You should. It's not something I recommend. I watched my father go through it, and I can tell you that men aren't meant to die alone."

"Well, I'm not planning on going anytime soon," I joked, this whole conversation making me very uncomfortable. I wasn't used to having such a serious conversation with a woman.

"You know what?" Crystal said with a sigh. "Never mind. I can see you're not ready for this conversation. But trust me—one day you're gonna feel your age, and you're gonna need me. I just can't promise I'll still be waiting around for you."

With that, she stood up and finished getting dressed, then left without another word. I wondered if she was serious and if that might possibly have been the last time we would ever have sex. But the more I thought about it, the more I came up with one answer: Crystal and I would always end up sleeping together.

Darnel

14

I ran my hand down her back and along the smooth curves of her round buttocks as she slept next to me. I'd done it, I thought. I'd finally slept with a woman other than Keisha. Less than thirty minutes ago, I had been making love to Whitney Johnson, the one woman Keisha hated most in the entire world. I know my sister thought I'd end up sleeping with her friend Sandra, but as nice as she was, I just didn't feel any chemistry, not to mention the fact that I hated being forced into anything. I still planned on watching the game with Sandra, but there was no chance that Jamie's matchmaking attempt would work out. Whitney, on the other hand, I did have chemistry with, if only because Keisha hated her.

Whitney and Keisha had quite a history. We had all gone to college together at VCU, and Keisha had hated Whitney from the first time she caught her checking me out in line at the dining hall during our freshman year. Whitney tried a few times to get my attention, but it hadn't worked. Even as fine as Whitney was, I never had any interest in her that way. I was just too wrapped up in Keisha. You know, all that one-woman-man crap I'd been preaching the last ten years.

Keisha didn't care how faithful I was, though. The only thing that mattered to her was that Whitney was disrespecting her by trying to get with me.

Whitney thought the whole thing was funny and even got some of her sorority sisters in on the act, spreading rumors that Whitney and I had hooked up one weekend when Keisha went home for a cousin's birthday party. After quite a bit of work on my part, I was able to convince Keisha that it had never happened, but from that point on, it was war between her and Whitney.

Things finally came to a head when Whitney forced Keisha to drop pledge line for the Delta Sigma Theta sorority. That was quite embarrassing for Keisha, considering she was a double legacy, with both her mother and grandmother being Deltas. Keisha and Whitney ended up in a fistfight at a frat party one night, and the way Keisha walked away with a handful of Whitney's weave became a campus legend.

There was an uneasy truce between them after that, and they managed to keep away from each other until Whitney's graduation the year before ours. But every once in a while, Whitney's name would come up in a conversation, and it was obvious that Keisha still hated her passionately. I hadn't seen or spoken to Whitney since graduation, nor had I ever felt the need. But when I saw her walk into a bar in Queens where I was once again trying to drown my sorrows, it felt like fate.

Keisha and I had been arguing on and off on the phone ever since the night I had gone to her place, then left her in tears. Every time I spoke to her, it was like ripping the scab off an old wound. Hearing her voice made me feel like crap, because any time she said something cute or endearing, I would wonder, Did she say those same types of things to Omar once? I couldn't stop the pain in my heart, no matter how much alcohol I consumed. This particular night, I almost went over to her place again, knowing that if I did, we'd end up screwing. But somehow, fate made me stop off at the bar for a drink first.

I knew that even though I still loved her, cutting Keisha loose would be the best thing for me. That's why the timing couldn't have been more perfect. If I could get with Whitney, it might take my mind off Keisha and help me move on. The thought of some closure put a smile on my face as Whitney approached me.

It turned out that Whitney was just as happy to see me, having just ended a long-term relationship herself a few months ago. This was one of those "right place at the right time" meetings, and it took only a few martinis before Whitney was bare-ass naked, riding me in the queen-sized bed in her apartment.

This was the kind of behavior that would make my father

proud, I thought as I rewound the entire thirty-five-minute sexual act through my mind. We'd done everything under the sun,
but, unfortunately, I still didn't know what the hype was all about,
sexing someone you didn't care about. Pussy was pussy to me,
I'd decided. It was warm and wet, and the more you moved your
dick in it, the sooner you'd come. I could have masturbated to
do that. Whitney could have been Halle Berry, Mariah Carey, or
Beyoncé, and it wouldn't have mattered. To me, she didn't feel
like anything more than a sperm receptacle, because she didn't
mean anything to me.

I never just came when I was with Keisha. Every single orgasm was like a new high for me, and that included the time
I tried to knock her head through the wall. She just did things
to me.

All of a sudden, I felt dirtier than the last time I'd slept with
Keisha, and I hurt. I hurt bad, and it was all Keisha's fault. We
should have been happily married by now, and I never would
have been in the bar in the first place to end up having meaning-
less sex with a woman I didn't give a crap about. If only Keisha
had kept her damn legs closed . . .

I wanted the pain in my heart to go away, but more than that,
I wanted Keisha to feel what I did. I doubted she had any idea
how badly she had wounded me, but I decided I would try to
make her understand.

Trying not to wake Whitney, I slipped out from under the
covers and picked up my pants off the floor. I slid on my pants,
found my cell phone in the pocket, and dialed Keisha's number
as I headed into the living room. Keisha answered on the first
ring, like she'd been waiting for me to call.

"Hey, baby, I'm so glad you called. I miss you so much." The
cheerfulness in her voice was so contrary to my own anger that it
felt like a slap in my face.

"What are you doing?" I asked her, refusing to acknowledge
that I missed her too.

"Why? What are you doing? You want to come over? You
want some of this?"

"Not in this lifetime."

There was a beat of silence before she asked cautiously, "Uh . . .
what's wrong, Darnel?"

"You want to know what I been doing?" I asked.

"Uh, yeah, I guess so . . . ," she said, drawing out her words to emphasize her confusion.

I delivered my news with malicious satisfaction. "I just fucked Whitney."

Again, there was silence on the other end as she processed my words.

"Did you just say what I think you did?"

"I sure did."

"No, you didn't, because I thought you said—"

"Yeah, I did. I said I fucked Whitney Johnson. I fucked her, and it was daaaaaaamn good."

In my fantasy of this moment, I imagined her bursting into tears right about now, so I was completely caught off guard when she laughed. "Okay, Darnel. You had me going there for a minute. Look, I know you're hurt about what I—" She stopped herself. I guess she figured it would be wise if she didn't speak about her act of betrayal. So I spoke it for her.

"Yeah, I'm still hurt about how you *fucked my best friend*! But that's why I was all up in Whitney's pussy tonight. Trust me—she made me feel much better."

"Darnel, come on. You're lying. You wouldn't do that just to hurt me, would you?" she asked, as if I didn't have every right to seek some revenge for what she'd done.

"Uh, yeah, I would do that, and I did. You want me to wake her up and put her on the phone to prove it to you?"

This time, there was no hesitation before she answered. "Yeah, put her ass on the phone, 'cause I will kill that bitch! Do you hear me? I will kill her ass!" From the level of her rage, I knew there was no reason to wake Whitney. Keisha believed that I'd fucked Whitney, and it was like a knife in her heart.

I laughed. "I know the feeling. I felt the same way when I saw Omar's dick up your ass."

"I can't believe you would fuck that bitch! She's been trying to get with you ever since we were in college."

"Well, now she got me," I said with some satisfaction. "And now you know how it feels."

She slowed her roll a little as my reason for sleeping with Whitney sunk in. She sighed and then said, "So, now we're even. Does that make you feel better?"

"No," I said, though I hated to admit it. My true feelings came pouring out. "I thought it would, but it didn't. I just wish this whole thing had never happened. I just wish you had loved me the way I loved you." I was starting to get choked up. "We're supposed to be man and wife right now, Keisha. All I ever wanted to do was love you. Why couldn't you love me?"

"I do love you, Darnel," she said, her voice sounding full of genuine regret. "I don't care if you're screwin' a hundred women; I'm still going to love you. I'm always going to love you."

"What do you know about love, Keisha?" I spit the words at her, wanting them to hurt her as much as she'd hurt me. But I think I finally understood that they never would. She could never truly know what she'd done to me, any more than we could ever go back and undo the past.

"I know I messed up, and if you give me another chance, I won't ever do it again."

"But why did you do it in the first place?" I asked. "How do I know you won't do it again if I don't even understand why it happened the first time?"

"I already told you I don't know."

"That's not good enough this time. We're on the phone, Keisha, and you can't kiss me and fuck me and avoid talking about it. So either you tell me why it happened, or I'm hanging up this phone and I swear you will never hear from me again."

"You sure you want to know?" she asked.

"Yes. Stop stalling and just tell me why you broke my heart, 'cause I really can't take this anymore."

"Okay . . ." It took her a while to speak again, and then she finally gave me an explanation for the events that changed my life. "I was drunk, and I was down at the bar with my girls. Omar came in talking about how I was making a mistake getting married without sleeping with at least one other man."

Omar had used the same argument to try to convince me to sleep with the stripper that night. I just wasn't that stupid. Shit, was it possible he had been planning the whole thing? Maybe he wanted me to sleep with the stripper so I'd be occupied while he went to seduce my fiancée. It was possible, I decided, but he still couldn't have succeeded without a willing participant, so Keisha was not innocent by any stretch of the imagination.

"But why him?" I asked.

"Darnel, please, I just want to forget that night."

"Bye, Keisha."

"No, wait!" she yelled. "Don't hang up."

"Why not? You don't want to tell me the truth. I told you what I need, and if you can't give it to me, then we ain't got nothin' to talk about."

"Promise you won't get mad."

It was not a promise I wanted to make, but I needed to hear the explanation if I had any hope of ever getting past this, with or without Keisha. "I won't get mad."

"Okay, he was flirting with me. I was drunk. My girl was whispering to me about how big the bulge in his pants was."

This was killing me to hear, but I let her keep talking.

"It was all just drunken flirting until he told me you were screwing some stripper whore upstairs."

"He what?"

Her voice was quiet, almost apologetic. "He said you were getting laid upstairs."

"And you believed him? What the hell is wrong with you?"

"You promised you wouldn't get mad," she said, crying now.

"Fuck what I promised! Why didn't you just come up to my room and find out? Shit, Keisha, it wouldn't have taken that much to find out the truth."

"I don't know, Darnel. I was drunk, I was pissed off, and when I said I was going up there to kick your ass, Omar calmed me down and convinced me to stay in the bar. Told me you had to get it out of your system and that I needed to do the same."

I could picture the scenario. It was starting to sound like Omar really had set this whole thing up. I was still furious with Keisha for falling for it as easily as she did, but, I thought hopefully, maybe she'd learned her lesson and something like this would never happen again.

"Was that the only time?"

"I swear, Darnel. You can give me a lie-detector test."

She sounded sincere, and I wanted desperately to believe her, but in the back of my mind, there was this nagging feeling that I couldn't take her word for it. I would definitely have to do some investigating of my own before I was satisfied that I knew the whole truth. But in the end, I had to admit to myself that I loved her enough to give this a try. Maybe if I found out that their affair was deeper, I could still learn to forgive, even if I would never totally forget.

"I just want to marry you and spend my life making you happy. You will never have to worry about this happening again," she said.

She still wanted to marry me. My heart leapt a little at the thought, because I sure as hell still had feelings for her.

"Keisha, I don't know . . ."

"What don't you know? You love me, don't you?"

"Yes," I answered without hesitation. "Yes, I love you."

"So, do you want to marry me or not?"

"It's not that simple."

"Why not? We love each other. What else matters?"

"You hurt me."

"I know, baby, and I promise I'll never do it again."

"And then there's my family."

"What about them?"

"My family hates you, Keisha. They're not going to accept this. You didn't just hurt me. They got hurt too."

"Are we supposed to let them dictate our lives? I love you, baby, and you love me. I want to spend the rest of my life with you."

I still felt the same way about her. After everything that had happened, I could still imagine myself spending the rest of my life with this woman.

"You promise me that you will never, ever be unfaithful?"

"Darnel, I promise. You are the only man I ever want to be with. I will never make that mistake again."

"Then let's do it." As I said this, I felt a relief in my body like I had been holding my breath for weeks. Even with all the pain she had put me through, I still knew that making love to her, holding her in my arms, and taking care of her, was worth more than a thousand one-night stands with girls like Whitney.

"We're going to get married?" she asked excitedly.

"Yes."

"When?"

"Tonight. Fuck it. Let's fly to Vegas."

"Really?" she squealed. "Oh my God, Darnel, I love you! Why don't you come over? I'll look for flights online."

And that's when reality hit me.

"I can't."

"What?"

"I can't leave the state."

"Why not?"

"Court. I can't leave the state until I go to court on those assault charges."

Her voice was shaky, like she was about to start crying again.

"To hell with the court. How are they going to know? You don't have to go back to court for at least a month. Baby, I want to marry you."

"I wanna marry you too. But I've got to do the right thing. We'll go to Vegas and get married right after I get these charges taken care of."

"Darnel, we're gonna get through this."

"I know we are," I answered. Now that I knew Omar had planned to seduce my fiancée, I was glad for every punch I'd landed on his face. Having to go to court was a small price to pay, and I had faith that in the end, I would be found not guilty. Karma is a bitch, and Omar had plenty of it coming to him for what he'd done.

"We're meant to be together, Keisha. Nothing's gonna change that. I promise you that when this case is over, we are getting married."

"What about your family?" she asked, obviously scared of what their reaction would be. And I can't say I blamed her. Both Jamie and my mom would hurt any woman who even looked at me wrong. But I wasn't a kid anymore.

"Keisha, you are my family." If there was a choice between them and her, I was going to choose Keisha.

"Then don't you think you should come home to Mama?" she teased.

"I'll be right there."

I hung up the phone and went back to Whitney's room to find the rest of my clothes. She woke up when I sat on the bed to put on my shoes.

"You ready to go another round?" she purred at me.

"I got to go." I leaned forward to stand up, but she stopped me, placing a hand on my chest.

"Maybe I can change your mind about that." She lowered the

sheet to reveal her perfect breasts. As good as she looked to me, I just couldn't get excited.

"I'm in love with another woman," I confessed, getting up and heading for the door. "I think we both know who I'm talking about. I'm sorry, but I got to go home."

Jamie

15

"Get out! Get the fuck out my house!"

At first I thought Louis didn't really mean it, but when he repeated himself at the top of his lungs, I became a believer. Damn, what was he flipping out about anyway? All I did was ask him nicely whose blond hair was on his jacket. Well, maybe I wasn't quite that nice about it, but what woman would be? I mean, I knew for damn sure that it wasn't mine, so it was only natural for me to wonder who had been so close to my man that her hair ended up on his clothing. And it was real hair, not that synthetic stuff they use on them cheap weaves. Some sister spent a lot of money on that hair.

"Louis, calm down, baby." I tried to keep my voice quiet, even though I wanted to go off on him for getting mad at me. He was the one who came home with incriminating evidence on his jacket, not me. I had every right to ask him about the hair. Still, I really didn't want to fight with him, so all I could do now was try to ease the situation.

"I wasn't accusing you of anything, baby. I was just asking a question."

"Bullshit! You asked me about the damn hair because you always think I'm doing something, Jamie. Living with you is like being under a damn microscope all the time, and I've had enough of this shit. I want your ass out." He pointed at the door.

Damn, he was standing his ground on this one. Either this temper tantrum was a calculated act to take the heat off himself, or he was honestly sick of me. The thought of Louis actually breaking up with me was too much to handle, and I started to cry. "Louis, please don't do this. Give me another chance. I promise I won't accuse you of cheating anymore."

Louis didn't budge. "It's not going to work this time, Jamie. I just can't take your jealousy."

"I don't mean to be so jealous. It's just . . ." I paused to wipe away my tears. When I glanced at him, he was still frowning. This confused me a little, because I was used to my tears getting me some sympathy. The expression on Louis's face only made the tears fall faster now. "You don't understand."

"You're right. I don't understand."

I had no idea why he was so angry. What was wrong with a woman trying to protect her relationship? As far as I was concerned, only a stupid woman wouldn't have asked the question. How could he be threatening to kick me out when any reasonable woman would have done the same thing?

"Louis, please don't do this. It's not my fault that I'm a jealous person. You know my history. You know the way I watched my father mistreat women. I have a hard time trusting any man because of him."

"Yeah, well, I don't deserve to be punished for your father's actions."

"You're right. I know that." I tried to reach out and touch him, but he stepped back.

"I'll go to counseling. I'll do whatever it takes. Just don't leave me. Please."

We stood silently and stared at each other for a long time before he finally shook his head and said, "I don't know why I'm doing this, but you can stay."

I wanted to jump into his arms, but he kept them crossed firmly over his chest. "But that don't mean you're off the hook, Jamie. You need to stop this shit. If it happens again, you can just move back over to your dad's house, since that's where you seem to want to be all the time anyhow."

I wiped away the last of my tears as I watched him head for the bedroom. He closed the door, and I knew I'd be sleeping on the couch tonight.

I cried myself to sleep that night but woke in the morning with hope renewed. You can't keep a good woman down, I decided. Louis had been pissed at me, but I was determined to get our relationship back on track. I kind of liked it when he showed me who was boss, which surprised me. I don't know, maybe I did need to see a counselor. I mean, my father had always had a huge influence on me, and now it seemed like I enjoyed it when Louis put me in my place. Maybe I was attracted to father figures. But whatever it was, I was impressed by Louis's strength and determination the night before. It just convinced me even more that I needed him in my life, and I would do whatever it took to keep him.

Louis had already left for work when I got up. The fact that he hadn't said good-bye meant he was probably still mad, but I wasn't worried. I knew just how to smooth things over.

I called Daddy and told him I wouldn't be coming to work; then I got dressed and headed to the mall. In Victoria's Secret, I bought a sexy negligee; then I went to an expensive organic market and purchased olive oil, garlic, saffron rice, lobster, and crab legs—everything I needed to go into paella, Louis's favorite dish.

When he arrived home that night, Louis still didn't have much to say. He just plopped down on the couch and watched TV until dinner was ready. I was a little concerned at this point, because he'd never given me the silent treatment for such a long time. But once we sat at the table and he tasted the paella, his shoulders seemed to relax and his eyes looked a little less guarded. After his third helping, he looked enough like his old self that I figured it was safe to talk.

"You like?" I asked.

"Yes, I like. It was very good," Louis complimented me, unbuckling his belt and running his hand over his stuffed belly. "But you're still not off the hook for last night."

Damn, he was going to make this harder than I thought.

"I'm not trying to be off the hook. I know I was wrong," I said, even though I really didn't think I was wrong, and no one would ever convince me I was. "I just don't want to lose you, Louis. I've never been in love with a man like you before. I don't want that taken away from me the way it was taken away from my brother."

He let out a frustrated sigh. "I'm not Keisha . . . and I'm not your daddy either. If you can't start trusting me, we're never gonna make it."

I got out of my chair and walked around the table. I sat on his lap and asked, "Do you still love me?"

"I never stopped."

He allowed me to lean in for a kiss, and as soon as our lips met, I felt so much better.

"Louis, let's never fight again."

"I'll do my best. But it would help if you could stop being so jealous."

"I promise." I kissed him again, glad that this ordeal was finally coming to an end. "Hey, let's go watch that movie you rented last night."

"Sure."

We poured ourselves two glasses of wine and walked to the living room arm in arm. I now knew why people could be such fools for love. This man had my nose wide open. I had never felt so loved now that he took me back in his arms. Louis was no longer mad at me. If I died right now, I would be happy.

I put on *Training Day,* a movie we both loved and had rented several times before. We'd watched it so many times that we could quote lines together. As we cuddled on the couch and became engrossed in the movie, Louis got this contented look on his face. I felt like we were vibing again.

"I can see how Denzel got the Academy Award for this part," Louis commented when the movie was over. "This role went totally against the type of characters he usually plays."

"Yeah, he was one dirty cop . . . Do you think there are real cops who are that dirty?" I asked.

He sipped on his glass of wine and grunted. "I'm sure some cops are worse than the ones portrayed in this movie. People can be really good at concealing the parts of themselves they don't want the world to see."

Then he let me know that all conversation was over, and I didn't mind one bit. He pulled me into his arms, and we began kissing passionately. After all the stress from our fight, I knew this was going to be some amazing make-up sex. I felt Louis's erection through his pants, but I didn't want to rush into anything. I liked this foreplay. The more we prolonged it, the better the sex would be.

Some twenty minutes later, I was just about ready. Louis was sucking on my breasts and I was in seventh heaven.

Suddenly, his cell phone chirped, letting us know he had a text message. He picked it up, glanced at it, and then put it back down as if it were nothing. He slid my panties down and stroked my thighs gently. I let out a moan and said, "Make love to me, baby. I want to feel you inside me now."

He reached for the waistband of his boxers, but then backed up off me and stood up. "Damn," he cursed.

"What is it?"

"I'm out of condoms."

It took all my strength not to say we could do it without a condom. I was so horny, I was almost willing to roll the dice on getting pregnant.

"Are you sure?" I asked. "You don't have one in your wallet or something?"

"No." He shook his head, looking as disappointed as I felt. "I gotta run to the store and get some."

"All right," I said with a sigh. I hated to wait, but now that we had made up, I didn't want to start complaining. "Hurry back, baby. I'll wait right here for you." I spread my legs to give him a better view of what he could have when he got back.

He licked his lips and took a deep breath, looking like he was tempted to dive in headfirst. "Damn, girl. You gonna make a brother go to the store with his stuff all hard, ain't you?"

I gave him a wicked smile. "You know that's right. Now hurry up and get the condoms so you can come back and take care of me."

Louis put his clothes on quickly and headed out.

As soon as he closed the door behind him, I heard a familiar chirp. I looked down at the floor, where I saw his cell phone. He must have received another text. Louis usually kept his phone in his pants, so he never left the house without it. But when he checked that text earlier, he probably placed it on the floor and didn't notice it when he rushed out.

The phone beeped once, indicating there was an unread message, and it was like a switch went off in my head. Suddenly, I had to know who was texting him. It was probably nothing important, because otherwise he would have reacted differently after the first text. But I couldn't change my suspicious nature overnight, so I did what came naturally to me: I picked up the phone to read the texts.

The one that had just come in was from a number I didn't recognize, and it read CALL ME! The one that had come while we
were getting busy was from the same number. It read WE NEED TO
TALK. Who the hell were these from?

Now my curiosity had the best of me. I went to get a notepad
so I could write down the number. I know I'd told Louis I would
stop accusing him of cheating, but I didn't ever say I'd stop sus-
pecting, did I? I would just keep the number in a safe place and
call it the next day while he was at work.

Just as I sat on the couch and copied the number, I heard the
front door opening. I quickly closed the phone and dropped it
on the floor, then stuffed the notepad between the couch cush-
ions.

"Hey, baby, that was fast," I said, hoping I didn't sound nervous.

"Yeah, I just came back for this," he said, bending down to
pick up his phone off the floor.

"Oh . . . okay. Hurry back, baby," I said, just as I had before,
except this time, my words were hollow. I was no longer turned
on. I felt like we were back at square one.

When he left again, my woman's intuition kicked in. I was no
longer certain that Louis was going to get condoms just because
he didn't want me to get pregnant. Something told me that
maybe the trip to the store was a convenient excuse to get out of
the house to call the mystery texter.

I ran up the stairs and checked the nightstand by our bed, and
sure enough, there was a box of condoms in there. There was
only one condom left, so for a moment, I gave Louis the benefit
of the doubt. It was possible that he forgot he had one more. But
my skeptical side reminded me that it was also possible he was
really going out to call someone.

My dilemma was this: After I'd promised him I would stop
being so jealous, I couldn't exactly confront him now. If I brought
up the issue of cheating again, I would have to present him with
concrete proof. Anything less and he'd kick me out on my ass.
Plus, I wanted the proof for myself. I loved Louis enough that I
didn't want to break up with him unless I was absolutely certain
he was cheating. From this point on, I would be searching for
real evidence, but doing it carefully, keeping my investigation
under the radar.

James

16

Man, there was something about a Sunday afternoon game that always got my adrenaline going. Yeah, I was the kind of man who worshiped at the altar of sports, and I'm not talking golf or tennis. I mean real mannish sports, watching athletes give one hundred and ten percent. You got to love everything about the game of basketball.

I was sitting in front of my seventy-two-inch plasma TV complete with surround sound, waiting for the game. I had my snacks and my brew, and I was dressed in my number twenty-four purple-and-gold jersey, ready to cheer on my boy Kobe.

Sister Patricia, one of the lovely ladies from church, had stopped by earlier with a spread of fried chicken, collard greens, mashed potatoes, gravy, and some homemade biscuits. The good ladies of the church knew how to make sure a man got his needs met, which always made me say an extra "Amen" on Sunday.

Of course, I had to politely lead Patricia out of here, because I didn't want anything to distract me from my game. The last thing on that woman's mind was cheering for the Lakers. So, after I enjoyed her cooking, I gave her a little something to remember me by and quickly sent her on her way. Luckily, she had the good sense to leave without putting up a fight. Any woman who knew me knew she was wasting her time trying to get my attention while the Lakers were playing.

The game was about to start, so for me, life was perfect. All I needed now was that son of mine so I'd have someone to talk trash to as the Lakers whooped some tail. When the doorbell rang, I figured he had forgotten his keys again. I guess I couldn't expect him to have his head screwed on straight when he had just had the rug pulled out from under him.

"Hi, Mr. Black." I was surprised to see that friend of Jamie's smiling up at me. What was her name again? She was loaded down with a pizza box and a six pack of beer. I might have rushed her away from the door if it weren't for the fact that she was wearing a Lakers jersey identical to mine. That's when I remembered that Jamie had managed to plan a sort-of date for this girl and Darnel.

"Oh, hi. Uh . . ."

"Sandra," she reminded me.

"Right, Sandra. Uh, Darnel's not here yet."

"He's not? Are you expecting him soon? We made plans to watch the game together, remember?"

I stepped aside to let her in. "Come on in. He's not home yet, but I'm sure he'll be here soon."

Her hopeful face fell. Poor thing wasn't seasoned enough to play it off. Older women would know how to do that in a second.

"That's okay. Could I just call a cab? I got dropped off."

"If you want. But the game is coming on now, and since you had the good taste to dress appropriately, why don't you just come in and watch with me until he gets here?" I took the six-pack from her and led her toward the couch.

"Are you sure?" She couldn't hide her embarrassment. She was a good-looking girl, and it probably wasn't every day that a man forgot a date with her.

"What kind of pizza you got in there?" I asked playfully, trying to make her feel more at ease. I felt bad that my son had put her in this position.

"Half pepperoni and half sausage and peppers."

She seemed to relax as we sat together and ate the pizza. After a while, I called Darnel, but his phone went straight to voice mail. It didn't take a genius to figure out why he forgot Sandra or where he was spending the day. I wasn't happy about it, but there was nothing I could do. That boy had to learn to handle his business. I wasn't the kind of father to tell his children how to live, because there are some lessons you have to learn yourself. I just hoped that girl didn't hurt him any more than she had already.

*   *   *

Two hours later, we sat on the edge of the sofa, waiting to see how this tied game would play out. Darnel was still a no-show. I would have to school that boy about leaving a woman waiting. But in spite of being stood up, Sandra got over her initial awkwardness and seemed to enjoy watching the game with me.

"No!" Sandra jumped up when Gasou missed a three-pointer at the foul line. We were sweating this game out like slaves in the summertime heat. Last thing I wanted was to hear from my friends for the next month about the Cavaliers beating the Lakers.

"Oh my God, oh my God!" she screamed as Kobe stole the ball from LeBron James and made a helluva three-pointer just before the bell. Pandemonium broke out on the court and in my living room as we screamed and shouted, hollering like fools.

After a few moments of high fives and victory dances in front of my couch, Sandra must have realized what she was doing and felt a little silly.

"Um, I guess Darnel's not coming, huh?" she said, breaking the celebratory mood. I shook my head, disappointed for her. "Can I use your phone now to call for a ride?"

We were having such a good time I almost forgot I wasn't the one who'd invited her over. Most women were only into sports to keep a man interested, but I could tell B-ball was really her thing.

"Hey, I'll drive you home," I offered.

"No, that's okay. I don't want to make you go out of your way."

"It ain't no thing. I'm looking forward to flossing this jersey all over Queens." I laughed.

On the drive to Jackson Heights, I found out Sandra was the top salesperson at the gym where she worked.

"But I really want to sell real estate," she admitted.

"Really? I been try'na get Jamie to get her license for years, but the girl is lazy. I told her she could make a lot more money as a salesperson than my office manager. 'Course, she's not worrying about money as long as she can stick her hand in my pocket." As much as I tried to sound annoyed, I could never be mad at Jamie.

"Are you kidding? That would be my dream. When I was in

high school, I wanted to be an architect, but my dad died, and we just didn't have the money, so it didn't happen."

"How old were you?" I usually assumed all young women were just like Jamie—a little spoiled and definitely self-centered—but Sandra was more serious, and now I knew why.

"Sixteen when my dad died."

I changed the subject to something brighter. "Sorry to hear that. Wanna get something to eat? Go over to T.G.I. Friday's over on Queens Boulevard and rock our number twenty-fours?" I asked with a laugh.

"Really?" She seemed genuinely surprised that I was being so nice to her. When I looked back over at Sandra, I saw something I had missed earlier—interest. It's not that I had never dated a woman younger than myself, but in general, I ruled them out. They were way more trouble than they were worth—too hormonal, not to mention that ticking time bomb called a biological clock, ready to rear its ugly head at any moment. Women in my age group were definitely the way to go. They were generally through with baby fever and were getting their children up out of the way—or, even better, their children were already gone.

I was too damn old to deal with the drama, no matter how fine a specimen Sandra was. Yeah, there were just some things you don't do, especially when the woman in question is a friend of your daughter. Now, that would be more drama than anyone could deal with. If I thought Jamie was jealous of the many women in my life now, I could only imagine how she would react to someone her own age, friend or not.

I could feel Sandra looking at me, and I tried to give her my best fatherly smile.

My phone rang. I looked down at the caller ID. Speak of the devil; it was Jamie calling. Did this girl have ESP or something?

"Daddy, did Sandra show up?"

"Yeah, but your brother didn't. I called him twice, but he didn't pick up the phone."

It didn't surprise me that Jamie called to follow up on Darnel. She couldn't stay out of either of our love lives, no matter how much I warned her.

"Daddy, he is such a fool. Girls like Sandra don't come around every day. Where was he?"

"Darnel is grown, and I am not his keeper." I had to keep myself from screaming at her sometimes.

"Well, was Sandra disappointed?"

I glanced at Sandra before I answered. She was checking me out with a look in her eyes that said she had probably forgotten all about Darnel by now.

"Sandra's right here. She waited around for Darnel and ended up watching the game with me. I was taking her home, but we decided to stop and get a bite to eat first. You want to meet us?" I knew Sandra wouldn't get any ideas about this being a date if Jamie came along.

"Oh, Daddy, I can't. Louis is mad at me about something, but you're the best. And when you talk to Darnel, tell him to call me, 'cause I'm pissed."

I disconnected the call and told Sandra, "She said she can't come."

Sandra's smile let me know that she didn't mind that Jamie wouldn't be joining us.

Darnel

17

I watched Keisha drive by on her way to work at exactly 8:45 A.M., just like she did every Monday morning. I was parked about two blocks away from her place, crouched down low in my truck so she wouldn't see me when she passed.

Two minutes later, I was headed toward the apartment. I took a nervous breath as I put my key in the door. I knew I shouldn't be doing what I was about to do, but I needed some answers to the questions that had been tormenting me ever since the night I caught her and Omar together.

Although everything probably seemed fine to Keisha, I was slowly dying inside, and my uncertainty was getting worse. She'd told me that it had only happened that one time with Omar, but doubt kept creeping into my mind. Sometimes when we were together, I thought I saw a look pass over her face, and I'd wonder if she was hiding something. Maybe she was day-dreaming about some other guy, or worse, maybe she was day-dreaming about sex with Omar.

If we were ever going to be truly happy, if our relationship stood any chance of surviving her infidelity, then I needed to get past my doubts. I loved the hell out of Keisha, but this was no way to have a relationship. Once I knew unequivocally that it had happened only once and that there were no others before Omar, then nothing else would matter—and that included my family. Once I knew that my woman was really my woman, then it was us against the world.

The night before, an idea had finally come to me about how to get the answers I needed without starting another fight with

Keisha. It meant betraying her trust, but at this point, the only other option was to end the relationship, because I couldn't keep living this way.

I'd spent the afternoon with Keisha but had promised my father I'd watch the game with him and Sandra that night. I was headed out the door to go to his house when Keisha started kissing on my neck, telling me she was horny. Well, one thing led to another, and the next thing I knew, she was bent over the kitchen table and we were making love doggy style. I mean, we were going at it like two deranged animals. Ever since our wedding fiasco, we'd had plenty of wild sessions like this. It was something we hadn't really done in the past, and although the passion turned me on, even this change in our lovemaking set off some sort of alarm in the back of my mind. This rough, wild sex really seemed to excite Keisha. What bothered me most was that it was exactly how she and Omar had been doing it when I caught them. Keisha had been so into it that night that she hadn't even realized I was in the room until I bashed Omar's head with the lamp.

Nothing was easy for me anymore. Everything left me wondering if I was missing some sort of clue, like maybe Keisha was making a fool out of me and I just hadn't figured it out yet. Then again, maybe I was just paranoid. Whichever one it was, I had to find out the truth.

It didn't help my uneasiness when her phone rang in the middle of our lovemaking last night. I was so deep into what Keisha and I were doing that I might have been able to ignore the phone, except that it was a ring tone I'd never heard before. Shit, she hadn't even given me my own ring tone.

I slowed down my strokes.

"Don't stop," she demanded as she held on to both sides of the kitchen table. "Please, baby, don't stop. I'm about to come."

But I did stop. I stopped when I heard the beeping sound her phone made when someone left a message. I wasn't sure what was going on, but something just didn't feel right. The mood was totally lost. At this point, I was so distracted that I couldn't keep my erection. I pulled out and sat in a chair at the kitchen table.

"What's the matter?" she asked, and not very nicely. Before this whole mess, nothing would have stopped me from finishing the act with my girl.

I shrugged my shoulders, unable to put all my feelings into words.

"Dammit," Keisha cursed under her breath. "I'll be right back." She turned around and left the kitchen. When I heard the bathroom door shut, I grabbed her phone off the kitchen counter and anxiously pushed the buttons to display the number of the missed call.

The screen displayed PRIVATE, which meant the caller had blocked the phone number. Well, I tried to reason, maybe that was why the ring tone was different. I knew plenty of people who refused to answer calls from blocked numbers. But then again, maybe the unfamiliar ring tone meant Keisha had assigned a "special" tone to some other dude. I put down the phone and tapped my forehead lightly against the countertop, wishing I could shake loose the suspicions that wouldn't leave me. God, I never used to think like this. Why couldn't my mind just go back to prerehearsal dinner thoughts?

When Keisha came back into the kitchen, she had lost a little of her attitude and reminded me sweetly that we still had some unfinished business to take care of. I made a halfhearted attempt to get her off using my tongue, since I was sure I wouldn't be able to get it up again. As she reached her final, screaming peak, the answer to my problems finally hit me. I said my good-byes late that night knowing that I would be back the next day to search for Keisha's diary.

So that's how I found myself skipping work and letting myself into my woman's apartment. First, I went through the nightstand where she used to keep her diary, but it wasn't there. She'd kept her diary in this same place for all the years I'd known her. If I wasn't sure she was keeping secrets before, I was now. You move something from the place it's been for years and that's gonna raise a red flag.

I started digging deeper, checking under the bed, in the closet, in shoe boxes. Hell, I even looked in her Tampax box in the bathroom. I searched through her jackets in the closet, thinking I might find some receipts or a phone number scribbled on a slip of paper. But I didn't see anything. I was starting to think my plan was a bust, but then it hit me: the strongbox where she kept her valuables. It had to be there.

"What the fuck are you doing?"

I hadn't heard Keisha come in, but there she stood, hands on hips and breathing fire.

"I'm looking for your diary." It didn't make any sense to lie, especially since this whole thing was about lying. I turned to face her.

"What do you want that for?"

"I wanna know the truth. I wanna know if that was the only time you were with Omar."

"I told you the truth."

"Well, I wanna see for myself. If I'm wrong, I'll be the first to apologize."

"What are you trying to say, that I'm lying?" She looked pissed, like I'd betrayed her instead of it being the other way around.

"I'm not trying to say anything until I see that diary."

"Sometimes when you go looking for shit, you'll find shit. Didn't your momma tell you that?"

"So is that it? Am I going to find something if I read your diary?"

"This is stupid, Darnel." She avoided the question, which only made me more suspicious. "Aren't you supposed to be at work? I knew you was up to something when I passed your car. Did you really think I wouldn't recognize your truck?"

"Aren't *you* supposed to be at work?" I countered. "Unless you came home to meet someone for a booty call."

She waved her hand at me. "You're acting crazy, Darnel."

"You think? My woman slept with my best friend on the night before our wedding, and I'm acting crazy?" Keisha turned away and started to walk out of the room. "Don't you walk away from me," I said sternly.

I reached out and took hold of her wrist. She tried to pull away, but I was possessed or something, because I didn't loosen my grip at all.

"Get off of me, Darnel." Her voice sounded angry, but I could tell she was scared.

"I wanna know what's in that diary!" I screamed, no longer in control of my emotions. "Tell me!"

"Get your hands off me, Darnel!"

"Tell me!" I pulled back my other hand, not even realizing it was balled into a fist.

"So you gonna get all nigga on me and we gonna go through this violent shit again, just like that night at the hotel, aren't we?" She turned to face me, jutting out her chin defiantly, daring me to hit her. My hand dropped as if someone had just placed a heavy weight into it.

"So what was it? Did Omar have a bigger dick than me?" I spit the words at her like a weapon meant to destroy anything left between us. I just didn't care anymore. An image of them going at it was permanently seared on my brain, and I couldn't be held responsible for the things it made me do.

"Darnel, stop!"

Unfortunately, I was past the point of letting up. I had to know, and I wasn't thinking about the cost.

"Did he fuck you better than me? Did you like sucking his dick more?" I screamed at her. "Did you even think about the fact that you would just be another notch on his player's belt? I bet you liked feeling like a whore!"

She stood in front of me, tears falling, but I didn't give a shit. She deserved worse.

"This is stupid." She had the nerve to turn like she was walking away.

"What is? Finding out my woman is a cheap tramp? Is that what you're calling stupid?"

"I'm not gonna let you treat me like shit."

"Just tell me the truth!" I yelled at the top of my lungs.

"You can't handle the truth." I saw this blazing fire in her eyes, and it was on.

"Don't tell me what I can handle, Keisha. You screwed up our lives, and now you owe me the truth."

"Fine." She swiped away the tears from her cheeks and stood in a defensive posture, glaring at me. "You want to know the truth? Just remember you asked."

I raised my eyebrows and crossed my arms, waiting for her to speak.

She huffed like I was inconveniencing her, but when she figured out I wasn't backing down, she dropped her bomb on me. "The truth is, Omar fucked me like I was a woman—not like some precious object he was afraid of breaking. I wanted to know what it was like to have someone put it on me. Dammit, Darnel, I wanted to get slayed, just one time."

I'd always treated Keisha gently—I made love to her instead of just screwing her. I thought that was something any woman would appreciate. As if it weren't painful enough to find out I was wrong, she kept throwing more words at me, and they hit like daggers in my heart.

"And, yes, he did have a bigger dick, and he wasn't afraid to use it. And guess what? I could handle it. I liked it."

"That's because you're a whore." I looked around for something heavy to pick up. I wanted to throw something at her, maim her, slap that smirk off her face. "You're a damn whore and I hate you!"

"Get out! You can't talk to me like that." She headed toward the front door. I followed behind her, still attacking her with my questions.

"So who else you been screwing? You don't think I really believe that Omar's the only dick you fell on, do you? I don't even know who you are anymore."

She stopped in front of the door and turned to face me. "Neither do I. I just know that there are some things in life that can't be fixed, and maybe this is one of those things."

Her statement stunned me silent for a moment. I thought everything had gone back to normal for Keisha, but now she was telling me that she thought the same thing I'd been thinking—that maybe our relationship was truly beyond repair.

"I just wish I could stop loving you," I told her, and it was the truth. What was it going to take to be able to walk away from her?

"Maybe love just isn't enough to get from where we are to where we want to go."

"And where is that?" I wanted to hear it from her, because I was so confused at this point, I didn't really know what I wanted or where I wanted us to go.

"I don't know, Darnel, but I think we need to let this go."

"What?"

"I have to let it go."

Out of nowhere, my eyes filled with tears. "Is there someone else?"

"Darnel, this isn't working. Maybe one day it will, but that day isn't today."

"Just let me read the diary," I said, feeling desperate. As angry as I was, I'd never really allowed myself to imagine life without Keisha. Now she was forcing me to, and I wasn't ready. "Put it all on the table and we'll just deal with it."

Keisha opened the front door. "My diary is my personal thoughts and feelings. No one gets to read it until I'm buried and gone."

"Buried and gone, huh? That can be arranged," I threatened, surprising myself as much as her with my sudden aggression. I would never hurt her, but why wouldn't she just do what I needed her to so we could get back to our old selves? "Now, give me the damn diary."

"You wanna know what can be arranged?" she spat back, the look of surprise and shock glued to her face. "What can be arranged is your ass going back to jail for violating an order of protection. Now, get the fuck out my house before I call the cops."

For now, she had delivered the knockout punch, and the fight was over. I did as I was told and walked out of the apartment. But one day, she was going to pay.

James

18

"Boy, what are you doing? Clean this place up. I didn't leave my house like this." I was fire funky hot when I returned home from church service and a quick visit with one of my lady friends. It was only one o'clock in the afternoon, and my house smelled like a distillery. Darnel had emptied countless beer cans, and liquor bottles were scattered all over the place.

I coughed as I fanned the alcohol fumes away from my face. "What the hell is wrong with you?" I yelled, but he just stared into space.

I walked over and cut off the CD player, which had been play-ing another sad, old-school love song, the kind he'd been listen-ing to constantly. I took a good look at my son. He'd now sunken to a new low.

"You've got court tomorrow. You need to get your stuff to-gether."

"Leave me alone. I don't give a damn about going to court. My life is already ruined. I just wish God would end it, for Christ's sake."

His despondent tone took me off guard, and I softened my de-meanor. This was more than just Darnel feeling sorry for himself. This was a genuine depression, and he didn't need me attacking him right now. "Don't talk like that, son. You have a lot to live for."

Darnel waved his hand lethargically. His eyes were glazed and vacant-looking. I really didn't like that stare in his eyes. I hated to admit it, but it was almost a deranged look, like he'd had some type of breakdown or something.

I pushed that thought out of my head. No, this was my son, who would never hurt a fly . . . or himself. He'd always been a gentle person. He was just going through a rough patch.

"Listen, this is all gonna pass, son."

He sat back in his chair. "You don't understand. I just feel so stupid. How do I go on?" Darnel stared down at his hands, then pulled his balled fists up to his forehead. "Everybody knows."

"No, they don't. And if they do, so what? You just got to take it one day at a time." I tried to touch his shoulder in comfort, but he jerked away from me.

"That's easier said than done. She may be a whore, at best a bitch, but I still love her. I know I sound like a fool, but I do."

"You know, like that old song by the Spinners goes, 'it takes a fool to learn that love don't love nobody.'"

"I never knew what that song meant, and I don't care what it means. Maybe, then, I'm just a fool. All I know is I still love Keisha."

I didn't know what to say that would make a difference. I could talk 'til my teeth fell out, but I couldn't make his heart stop loving that woman. I made a lame attempt to redirect his thoughts. "You need to get up and keep moving on with your life. In the meantime, why don't you go take out Sandra—that girl your sister introduced you to?"

"Why? So she can tell Jamie all my personal business? No thanks."

I tried to sound casual as I said, "Why don't you give her a call? Ask her out to lunch. My treat."

Darnel just shrugged. "I've talked to her. She seemed a little too high maintenance for me." Then he added with a little too much attitude in his voice, "If she's so nice, why don't you have lunch with her? I don't need you to set me up with anyone, and I don't need Jamie's help either."

"Son, we all need someone's help at some time."

"Not me. I don't need anyone's help. Not unless you got a gun and you let me borrow it so I can shoot both Keisha and Omar in the head."

"Darnel!" I'd heard a lot of shocking things in my lifetime, but never anything like this out of my own son's mouth. "Don't talk like that."

"So I guess you can't help me," he said, and it didn't sound like a joke.

The next thing I knew, he stomped out of the house, slamming the door behind him. I heard his tires screech out of the driveway, and I cringed, shaking my head.

Lord, help him, I prayed.

After I calmed down, I decided to clean up the living room and freshen up a bit. I threw out the empty beer cans and liquor bottles and sprayed air freshener.

I thought about what an old woman told me when I was young: "A woman is like a trolley car. There'll be another one along shortly." I wished it were that simple for Darnel. I'd been around long enough to know that the old woman's wisdom was correct. When one woman isn't worthy of your love, another one who's ten times better will always come along sooner or later. But Darnel was too inexperienced to know this. He'd just had his heart ripped out by the first and only woman he'd ever loved, and he couldn't see past that to believe that sometime down the line, the right woman would walk into his life and make him forget all about Keisha.

Until he met the one who would take her place, what could I do for his broken heart? It killed me to see him in this kind of pain. He was still struggling to understand how Keisha could do him like that. I wanted to tell him, "You just can't love that hard, son." I guess he was like his mother in that respect, pouring his heart into a losing proposition.

As I put the finishing touches on my now clean living room, I heard the doorbell ring. I opened the door to find Sandra standing there. I tried not to notice how sexy she looked, young woman or not; I couldn't help but to admire her sexy top, which clung to her perky breasts without being too risqué, and some curve-hugging jeans that accentuated her hips perfectly.

"Hey, Sandra. I'm sorry to tell you, but you missed Darnel again." I hadn't gotten on Darnel the last time he stood her up, but this was getting ridiculous. I was going to have to talk to him this time—or so I thought, until Sandra let me know that wasn't her reason for stopping by.

She shrugged her shoulders with a coy smile. "That's okay, 'cause to tell you the truth, I didn't come to see him. I came to see you."

"Me? Why?"

She took a deep breath and straightened her shoulders, like she was trying to gather the courage to say something. "Mr. Black . . . I mean, James, would you like to go to the Lakers–Nets basketball game with me tonight?" She extended her hand with two tickets.

Did she just ask me out on a date?

She stood looking at me expectantly, and before I had time to remind myself of all the reasons why I shouldn't be going out with a woman young enough to be my daughter, I heard myself saying, "Sure."

I walked around to open the car door for Sandra, who slid into the passenger's seat, giving me a look of pure availability.

James, you don't want to go there. You do not want to go there, I repeated to myself like a mantra.

This girl knew exactly what she was working with. Unlike a lot of women, she showed, just enough to let me know everything was where it should be. Each time I glanced to the side, I could see her giving me her full attention.

Finally, I pulled into a parking garage near the Meadowlands. I turned my attention to her and got to the heart of the matter. "What's this all about anyway?" I held up the two tickets she'd bought.

"It's tickets to the game." She gave me a look that was both innocent and devilish at the same time. "What does it look like?"

"So . . . ," I started, hoping to give her one more chance to tell me this was not a date. "Is this your way of thanking me for that game and dinner? Because you didn't have to do this."

"I like you." She stared straight into my eyes, not blinking or turning away.

"Yeah, but I mean, these couldn't have come cheap." Again, I showed her the tickets. "They're floor seats."

"Maybe we'll sit near Jay-Z." Sandra leaned closer so that I could smell her Creed perfume, a light, woodsy scent.

"Yeah, but . . . wouldn't you have preferred to go to the game with Darnel?"

I kept trying to offer her excuses to back out before we started something we would both regret, but she didn't want to go that way.

"No, it's you I wanted to go to the game with," she said very frankly.

"Why?"

"Because I like you."

"I like you, too, but—"

"No, James, you don't understand. I like you . . . like, romantically." And there it was. She had put all her cards on the table, and now I didn't have a clue what to do. I was not trying to go there with her, but she was making it so damn hard to resist. The way she was staring at me, I think if I wanted to, I could have done her right there in the car.

"I'm not a one-woman man," I told her, just as I'd done to all the women who had come before her.

Usually, I explained this to a woman once I knew we were heading toward the sex zone, but this time I was hoping it would be like a repellent, and Sandra would realize this was just a schoolgirl crush. Of course, she wasn't looking like any schoolgirl that I knew. She was up to no good.

The reason I'd been doing all right with women my whole life was that I knew what situations to avoid, and this one was waving a big red flag. It was a *Lost in Space,* "Danger, Will Robinson" type of moment, and I wasn't trying to go against my instincts.

"I'm not a one-woman man," I repeated.

"Not yet." She held my gaze, a tiny smile curving up the corners of her mouth. Her confidence was damn sexy.

I decided to take another tack with her, because as sexy as she was, I was afraid I felt my resolve weakening. For God's sake, I kept reminding myself, this was my daughter's friend. She couldn't be older than twenty-three, twenty-four.

I made sure that there wasn't a hint of flirtation in my voice when I told her, "I'm serious."

"So am I." Her smile grew wider.

"I'm not kidding." Again, I was trying to sound stern and fatherly, but despite my best efforts, she made me laugh.

"Me either." She threw it right back at me, refusing to break away.

"You're something else." I shook my head, but instead of being embarrassed or shy, she nodded in agreement.

"Scared?" she taunted me.

"No, I'm just try'na stop you from doing something you'll regret."

"I'm not afraid of you." Her whole body swelled up, looking even more ripe and luscious.

"You should be. I'm old enough to be your father." No man over forty likes to think of himself in those terms, but sometimes you don't have a choice. This was definitely one of those times.

"But you're not my father. I have a daddy, and you don't remind me of him at all." She burst out in laughter at the look of frustration on my face. Everything about her was so tempting, but for once, I was committed to doing the right thing.

"You need to date men your own age."

"I don't like men my own age. Men my age are still trying to find out who they are. I always date older men. They're more intelligent and confident, they know who they are, and they usually know how to sling it."

"But men your age have their whole lives ahead of them. They want the same things you want." Never before had I found myself in a situation like this, actually trying to convince a woman that she *didn't* want to get with me.

"How do you know they want the same things as me? Maybe they just want to get laid."

I felt like telling her that maybe that's all any man wants, no matter what his age.

"I'm not into a man who doesn't know where he's going yet or where his next paycheck is coming from."

"Oh, so it's like that? You're just looking for an older brother with some money in the bank?" In a way, I would have been relieved if she said yes. If she was just looking for a sugar daddy, it would have made it easier for me to cast her aside.

"My father always treated me like a princess, and I like a man who's able to do that. I'm not a gold digger, but I'm not interested in going to IHOP for dinner on every date or going Dutch at the movies. I want a real man who knows how to take care of a woman. What's so wrong with that?"

"Nothing, I suppose."

She did have a point. When I thought back to my life at twenty, I was a mess. My money was funny, and I kept changing careers, trying to find out exactly what I wanted to be. I couldn't be mad at a woman who knew what she wanted.

Our conversation was going in circles, with neither of us conceding, and it was nearing game time, so I unlocked the doors and we got out. As we followed the crowd into the stadium, she slipped her hand into mine with a look of pure satisfaction on her face. I didn't remove my hand from hers. *Yeah, I might be in some kind of trouble with this one.*

Sandra looked damn cute in her Lakers cap as we drove home. Not only did the Lakers win, but I was also surprised by what a good time we had together. She was fun, smart, and not afraid of me, even when she should have been. Against my better judgment, I was now envisioning the things I could do to her tight, young body—things that might satisfy my growing lust for her. But if my instincts were right, doing those things would most likely lead to this impressionable young thing becoming the ultimate pain in my ass. However, I was so horny that I couldn't wait to tear that ass up. When I got finished with her tonight, she was probably going to end up being a stalker.

We rolled up to her place, and I got a parking spot right up front, which was always a good sign. I unhooked my seat belt, taking in what I was about to explore. I was glad I'd just bought a brand-new pack of condoms—not that I'd planned on using them with her, of course. But since I had them, no sense in letting them go to waste. As fine as she was, I might just use them all.

"Want me to come up?" I reached for the door handle.

She leaned across the seat, close to me.

"Soon enough." She placed a hand on my face, pulling my mouth toward hers. Her lips were soft and moist, and although I'd been kissed by hundreds of women, the sensual way she slipped her tongue into my mouth was like nothing I'd ever experienced before. Our kiss lasted a full five seconds, and by the time it was over, I felt as if my entire body was on fire. I can honestly tell you I thought I'd been kissed by the best, but that was before Sandra kissed me.

She pulled away when I went in for more. She stepped out of the car as I sat there, my head still spinning from our first kiss. That's when I knew I had to have her. I absolutely had to.

"I'll walk you to the door."

"No, I can make it." She giggled and flashed a beautiful smile. "Thanks for a wonderful night."

"My pleasure."

"It will be soon." She giggled again. "Oh, and you might wanna do something about that when you get home." She pointed at the lump in my pants, then turned and walked toward her building.

I removed a napkin from my glove compartment and wiped the sweat from my forehead. We hadn't even done anything and I was perspiring! I had to sit in the car for a few minutes to slow my breathing back down to a normal rate. This girl had me practically panting like a dog.

I realized that I wasn't too far from a friend's house. Once Sandra was safely inside her building, I opened my cell and scrolled through my contacts list until I found the number I was looking for.

"Teresa, hey, it's James. I'm in your neighborhood, and I wondered if you wanted some company. . . . You do? . . . See you in five."

She wasn't anything close to Sandra, but beggars can't be choosers when you got a hard dick.

Jamie

19

I slipped the piece of paper out of my wallet and looked at the phone number I had copied off Louis's phone. I had been holding on to it for a couple of days, but all I could do was stare at it. I damn sure wanted to dial it, but if I was wrong and Louis found out, it would be the end of us. No, I had to find another way to get some answers.

I slipped the paper back in my wallet when my dad's office door opened and this young couple came out with him, smiling from ear to ear. Dad had been working with them for a while, so I knew their story. The wife couldn't have been much older than me, but she wore a huge rock on her finger, and her husband looked at her like she was his reason for living. They were at the real estate office because they had put in an offer to buy their first home, and the seller agreed to the amount. Soon, these two young lovebirds would become homeowners.

Her husband gently placed his arm around the woman's waist and pulled her in for a kiss. Daddy patted him on the back. The whole scene was so cozy I wanted to scream with jealousy. I wanted to be the one standing there with Louis as we bought our first home. I wanted to have a diamond sparkling on my finger and become Mrs. Louis Kennedy. Instead, I was watching these happy newlyweds as I wondered if my man was up to no good.

I looked on as my father led the couple outside. He always took a big sale out to lunch or dinner, so I knew he wouldn't come back for a while. I picked up the office phone to save my cell phone minutes.

"Hello?" Aunt Winnie's voice sounded all deep and smoldering. She was a young forty and the only person on my mother's side of the family who I spoke to. She was also searching for a husband before her biological clock stopped.

"Hey, Auntie. What, you expecting some man to call?" I joked, but seriously, she was sounding like a bitch in heat. She had to find herself a man, I thought.

"Nah, I'm just tired."

Yeah, probably tired of being without a man, I thought.

"What's up?" she asked.

"Nothing." I lied because I wasn't used to spilling my business with women. I'd always been able to talk to Daddy or Darnel, although lately, they'd both been pretty much MIA.

So, if I had to call someone, it was Aunt Winnie. She was the closest I'd ever come to having a real female friend. Growing up, I saw sisters, cousins, coworkers, and best friends stab each other in the back to get some of my daddy, so I'd always practiced caution when it came to women. I trusted Aunt Winnie more than most, because she and I thought alike; neither of us gave a damn about petty competition or chasing behind losers. We wanted to be with men who respected us and treated us as well as our fathers did.

Yeah, I might as well let her in on my problems, I decided. "Well, it's not really nothing."

"What happened?"

"I think Louis is cheating on me."

"No! Jamie, Louis worships you." I know she was trying to make me feel better, but I'd seen enough women fooled before to know that sometimes things weren't always as they seemed.

"That don't mean he ain't messing around on me."

"But what makes you think he's cheating?"

"'Cause he got a penis."

"Jamie!" I don't know why she sounded so shocked.

"It's true. Auntie, I just got this feeling. Something's not right."

"Have you asked him?"

"I can't confront him. I love Louis. I don't want him to think I don't trust him." Of course, I left out the part about how I'd already accused him and been wrong, and if I did it again, he'd be gone.

"But you can't keep driving yourself crazy thinking he's cheating. You have to know."

"I know! I just don't know what to do."

"What makes you think he's cheating? Do you have any proof?"

"He keeps getting these text messages, and I saw this number come up on his cell, and it was from Detroit. Louis has been traveling a lot more lately. What if he's seeing someone there?"

"You gonna drive yourself crazy. Have you searched the house for clues?"

"Sort of."

"Well, I don't know what 'sort of' means, Jamie, but if it was me, I'd be turning over mattresses and shit to find evidence."

By the time I hung up with Aunt Winnie, I decided to leave the office. I forwarded the phones to voice mail. Maybe Daddy wasn't coming back to the office today anyway. He'd said something about going to a doctor's appointment to get a prescription for the cough he'd developed. I didn't care even if he was coming back. I had more important things to do than answer telephones—like find out if my man was messing around on me.

Once I got home, I checked the house for any signs that Louis was creepin'. I went through all his pockets, checked in his clothes drawers, and riffled through receipts, but I came up empty-handed. I spent about two hours searching our place before I just gave up. If he was doing anything, then he was damn good, because he sure wasn't leaving any evidence.

I decided to take my mind off things by doing a little housework. We'd had a good weekend together, and I hadn't gotten around to doing any laundry. I dragged the hamper down to the basement, thinking that the four or five loads would keep me busy for a while.

I put the first load in the washing machine, and when I bent down to pick up the detergent bottle off the floor, I saw something I'd never noticed before. Louis kept some things stored under the stairway. I'd never paid attention to it, thinking it was all junk, but with my suspicions raised, everything was a possible clue. The black briefcase that sat in front of a box marked OLD CLOTHES looked like it was just begging for me to examine it.

I picked up the briefcase, eager to see what was inside, but was quickly disappointed when I saw that it had a combination lock. It took about thirty failed attempts at guessing the combination before I got pissed. By then, I was tempted to just throw the stupid thing against the wall to try breaking it open. I went in search of the bolt cutters but stopped myself before I actually cut anything off. What if the briefcase was full of insignificant papers and a bunch of stuff that had nothing to do with nothing? How in the world would I explain that one to Louis? I already knew Louis wouldn't appreciate me going through his stuff. If I damaged it in the process, he'd be even more pissed, and I wasn't willing to risk it.

After a little thought, I came up with plan B. Living with Daddy, I learned to be smart about finding my way into things. He was constantly hiding naked pictures, letters, sex toys, and anything else he didn't want me to find, but I always did. I rushed to the hardware store and bought one of those tiny screwdrivers.

Back at the house, I carefully unscrewed the hinges.

"Shit!" I broke a nail with the last screw, but it finally came off.

Inside the briefcase, I found a stack of papers and letters bound with a rubber band. I set them to the side and opened a second compartment, where I found more papers. I pulled them out and shuffled through them, finding a Detroit driver's license with Louis's picture. Louis had told me he was from Atlanta; he'd never said anything about living in Detroit. As I inspected the license, I noticed something even more puzzling. It was issued to someone named Rashid Jensen.

I sat down on the floor, my heart beating out of my chest.

I picked up the stack of letters and flipped off the rubber band. The letters were addressed to a Mr. and Mrs. Jensen. A wave of nausea hit me.

I had just seen a TV documentary about this brother who was married to three women—one in Georgia, one in Virginia, and one in North Carolina. He got arrested for polygamy when two of the wives found out about each other. They put his ass in jail.

Was that it? I wondered as I fought the urge to throw up. Is that why something just hadn't felt right to me? Did Louis have another family?

I ran upstairs and got that piece of paper out of my purse. I blocked my number and dialed.

"Hello?" a woman answered, and my heart sank. "Is anybody there?"

I hung up the phone and sat back in shock.

Darnel

20

As I stepped outside onto the courthouse steps, my parents and Jamie were still jumping up and down, celebrating because the assault charges against me had been dropped.

My dad moved toward me. "Now, be careful, son. God is giving you a second chance," he warned.

"Thank the Lord for making my son a free man," my mother shouted, tears glistening in her eyes. It was almost funny to me, because she'd never been a particularly religious person, but now she looked about ready to drop down on her knees right then and there.

"Hey, Darnel! Can I speak to you for a minute?"

I turned around and saw Omar standing in the courthouse doorway. As he hobbled outside on crutches, I gave him a look meant to squash any expectation of us ever talking again. Now, if he wanted to go toe-to-toe, I was ready to give him another beat down, send him into a wheelchair, or worse, but as far as talking, I didn't have anything to say to him.

"I ain't got nothing to say to you, man."

"We need to talk." Omar came closer, like he didn't care that I was breathing fire. I was about to ask him if he had some kind of death wish when my dad put a strong hand on my shoulder. I knew he was trying to calm me down because he didn't want his only son to spend any more time behind bars. He held his other hand out in a gesture meant to stop Omar from coming any closer.

"I'm cool," I told my father, not because it was true, but because I didn't want to worry him any more than I already had.

"We need to talk." Omar just kept coming with his lame-ass line.

"No, we don't. I ain't got nothing to say to you," I hissed, trying to keep my cool since I was standing in front of the courthouse and within range of the police.

"After all we been through, it's like that?"

This motherfucker was coming too close to being slammed down on the concrete.

"What? I must have heard you wrong, 'cause you sound like I'm the one who fucked *your* fiancée and not the other way around. I don't owe you anything!"

"Just one minute. Please."

"I ain't got nothin' for you, man."

"Maybe I got something for you. Don't you want to hear the truth? Don't you wanna know why?" He kept pressing, and I had had enough. I stepped to him, ready to take that crutch and put it up his ass.

"Oh, so now you gonna give me the truth? All those years you been like my brother, and now you gonna give me the truth? I almost walked down the aisle with the stench of your dick on my woman. How is that for truth?"

"Darnel!" my father shouted. "It's not worth the trouble. Just hear the man out so we can get out of here."

A policeman standing in the doorway came outside, giving us his full attention. I took a step back from Omar, because it was the only way to stop myself from going upside his head.

"What you got to say to me that I didn't already see?" Deep down, I really did want some answers.

"It ain't worth ending our friendship over no girl."

We walked away from my family so they couldn't hear our conversation.

"This wasn't just no girl. It was my woman. . . . I love her." I started to turn away, but his next words stopped me in my tracks.

"So do I."

"What the hell are you talking about?"

"I love Keisha, too, Darnel." As long as I'd known Omar, I could always tell when he was messing with me and when he was laying down the truth. And as much as I wanted to blow this off, something in his expression struck a nerve and wouldn't let me just dismiss this.

"What do you mean you love her?"

"I wanted her to be my woman, but she wanted to be with you." He tried to back away. I studied his face.

"You're serious, aren't you?" I pulled back my fist, ready to jack him up. Omar raised his crutch to block me.

"Darnel, I didn't mean to hurt you. I love you like the brother I never had."

"You got a funny way of showing it." By this time, I was trying to hold back tears. "So how long has this been going on?"

"Since high school, but that night you caught us was supposed to be the last time."

"You're lying. There's no way you could have been doing it that long without me knowing. Keisha would never do that to me."

"You don't know Keisha, Darnel. You don't know her at all. I wasn't the only one."

"You fuckin' liar. You want me to believe that I don't know the woman I had planned to spend my life with? No, what you want me to think is that she was fuckin' everybody else so that I don't have to focus on you stabbing me in the back. But it was you she was screwin'. It wasn't some other bitch-ass nigga I caught with his dick shoved inside my woman. That was you. Don't try and put that shit on nobody else. Your ass was the one who was foul."

"Yeah, I fucked up."

"You think?"

"It don't matter what you think about me, Darnel, but you needed to know the truth."

"You a dirty dog and a liar. You used your A game to seduce my girl and to take advantage of her naïveté. Isn't that the big truth?"

"Man, you're gonna find out one way or another. The truth always comes out."

"Fuck you, Omar."

"I'm not lying to you."

"You ain't shit."

"I may not be, but at least I'm not the one lying to you now."

I would have punched him in the face, but I could see my dad at the bottom of the steps, watching me, and the cop with his hand on his billy club, ready to pounce. I turned and walked away before I did some serious damage.

"I wasn't the only one, Darnel," Omar repeated as I stepped off.

I wish I could forget this conversation had ever taken place, but now that it had, Omar's accusations were something I was going to look into.

James
21

One month. It had been one month to the day since Sandra and I went to the Lakers–Nets game, since that night when she sent my world into a spin by doing something no other woman in recent memory had done—she shut me down sexually. But even though she still hadn't given me any, somehow or another we'd ended up seeing or talking to each other every day since then. We'd gone out a few times, and whenever I knew Darnel wasn't going to be around, we spent time at my place and a few evenings at hers, but we never made it to the bedroom. This night, we had stayed in to watch a game on TV and were snuggled up together on my couch.

At first I was spending so much time with her just because I felt I had a challenge to conquer. All I really wanted to do was get between her legs and show her who was in charge. But as time went on and one sexless date became ten and so on, I realized I wasn't in it for the sex anymore. I was in it because I really liked her. With most of my women, we bypassed all the formalities and just jumped into bed, but with Sandra, we were doing all sorts of romantic things that I found myself actually enjoying. I looked forward to our daily conversations and our picnic lunches and romantic dinners.

As corny as it sounds, Sandra made me feel alive, and that in itself was very confusing, because I'd never needed any woman to make me feel good about myself. Usually, as long as I got her to take off her clothes for me, I felt great. But this was different. We'd spend hours just hanging out, and she could get me to talk about things that I hadn't thought about in years. She was funny,

UP TO NO GOOD

easygoing, and smart, and the combination had me "open," as my daughter would say.

"You comfortable?" Sandra stroked the top of my head as I lay on her lap, watching a movie. We had watched the game, and now we were into a Lifetime flick. Me, watching a Lifetime movie. Everything about that was foreign. Any other time, I would have been showing a sister the door if we had made it this far into the night and still had our clothes on. I dug this woman in a way I hadn't planned to. I mean, sure, it would be nice to enjoy her body, but I was amazed that I was lying here with her and sex wasn't my only mission. In fact, at that moment, it wasn't my mission at all.

"I'm relaxed." I smiled up at her. She had these dimples that made her look even more beautiful.

Sandra leaned down and kissed me, and it wasn't no quick peck on the lips. It was passionate, like the one she gave me the night of our first date. I loved those kisses, but if we weren't going to do anything, I didn't want to go down that road. I'd taken my share of cold showers behind Sandra's give-a-brother-blue-balls kisses, and I was not in the mood to take one so early. I pulled away gently.

"Don't stop. I really like you, James."

"Me too," I said as I sat up and faced her.

"And I want you." She gave me another killer smile, all intense and self-assured.

I hesitated, hoping like hell she wasn't just teasing me this time. "You do?"

She nodded, placing her hand in mine. When she pulled it away, she left behind a condom. I stared at it, letting the realization of what we were about to do sink in. I'd been waiting for this moment for a month, but for some reason, I was still hesitant, which was sure not like me. What in the world was this woman doing to me?

"Are you sure? I need you to be sure."

She didn't speak. She just slid from the couch down onto the rug, her knees on the floor; then she leaned over and slid her tongue into my mouth, and damn if I didn't feel myself start to loosen up.

Next thing I knew, Sandra had unbuckled my belt. Once she

got my pants off, she started kissing my inner thighs. I instantly hardened in anticipation, but instead of putting me in her mouth, she tasted every inch surrounding my member.

When I was fully erect, she stopped and stood up. I watched as she untied the sides of her leopard-print wrap dress and sensuously removed it, letting it drop to the floor.

"Damn," I managed to mutter, though her beauty left me almost speechless.

I was so used to dating women my own age that I had forgotten what a body unaffected by age or childbirth looked like. Now, don't get me wrong; I have always preferred a woman with some miles on her, but this was something else. I hadn't seen a figure like this in years, except on visits to a titty bar, which was usually a "look but don't touch" situation. Sandra definitely wasn't the kind of woman you'd find turning on a pole for tips. Her body was nearly perfect, and her standing there offering it to me made me feel like the luckiest man on the planet at that moment. Before now, I'd thought my days of being in the presence of this kind of beauty were long over.

"You sure?" I asked again.

"I've never been surer of anything in my life. Make love to me, James."

The next morning, I was whistling my rendition of Ray Charles's "Georgia on My Mind" as I whisked eggs in a ceramic bowl. I make a mean omelet, if I do say so myself. I mixed in mushrooms, tomatoes, and black olives. While the eggs were cooking, I poured a glass of orange juice and buttered the toast. When everything was done, I put my best china and crystal goblet on a tray, placed a rose by the plate, then climbed the stairs to my bedroom.

Sandra was still sound asleep. I couldn't remember the last time I'd let a woman spend the whole night and then woken up happy to see her still there. But Sandra was a beautiful vision, looking almost angelic all curled up under the covers. Her face wore the contented look of a woman well satisfied. *Yeah, the old man still has it,* I thought proudly.

I have to admit, though, that Sandra kept up with me every step of the way and even showed me a few new tricks. At one point, she had to stop and let me catch my breath. I was still getting over some kind of bronchitis, and her wild acrobatics in bed sent me into a coughing spell. She had a brother screaming by the time she finished with me. Maybe it was because she was young and flexible, but she let me flip her around and bend her like a pretzel for what seemed like eternity, until we were both panting and sweating. Yeah, she might have made me wait for it, but it was well worth it. She made me feel like a young man again.

"Wake up, sleepyhead." I carried the breakfast tray over to my king-sized bed.

Sandra slowly roused herself, rubbing her fists into her eyeballs. "What time is it?"

"Time for breakfast."

"Is this for me?"

I nodded. "Yes."

"You're so sweet."

"No, you deserve it. I've done a lot of things in my life, but that was . . . wooo!"

"It was." She flashed a smile. "So you don't want me to leave?"

"You're not going nowhere."

"You're not going to kick me out like you kick the other women out your bed, are you?"

I thought I was being playful, but her response made me realize I couldn't joke about certain things with her. She knew my daughter, which meant she knew about my reputation for loving 'em and leaving 'em.

"No way. Never," I assured her. "Here." I picked up her fork. "Let me feed you."

As I watched her enjoy her breakfast, I thought about how quickly she'd gone from a self-assured vixen in bed to a young woman unsure if she had just been used. Unlike some of the older women I'd dealt with, who had become so hardened and cynical that they didn't care if it was all about the sex, Sandra still had an innocence about her that made me want to wrap her in my arms and protect her heart. Life hadn't knocked that starry glow of hope out of her eyes yet, and I was going to try like hell not to be the one who did it.

"You know I meant what I said last night," I told her.

She stopped eating and looked at me sweetly. "You did?"

"Yes." I stroked her soft hair and then ran my hand along the smooth skin on her face. "There's something very special about you. Something that just makes me want to be around you. Makes me want to be a better man. But I'm not gonna lie. You're wife material, and I'm not looking for a wife."

"Not yet, you're not. But who knows what the future holds? I'm just glad that you're letting me stay." Her eyes sparkled with sudden tears. Now, I wasn't about to cry or anything, but I was feeling pretty emotional myself. This woman had gotten into places in my heart that I didn't even know existed.

Sandra wrapped her arms around my neck and pulled me in for another one of those kisses that I felt all the way down to my toes. The breakfast tray was pushed to the side, and I was ready to be deep inside of her again.

That's when my cell phone beeped, alerting me that I had a text. Sandra stopped kissing me, and from the look in her eyes, I could tell that her imagination was getting the best of her. I'm sure she was wondering which of my "recreational partners" was texting me for a booty call this morning.

She wasn't necessarily right, though. For all I knew, the text was from a client. Any other time, I would have ignored it until we were finished in the bedroom. But she had put enough distance between our bodies now that I knew her mood was ruined.

I decided to put her mind at ease by looking at the text. If it was from a client, no problem. And even if it was from another woman, I still had a solution. I was so into Sandra that I would reply to any woman with a text that said I was no longer interested. Sandra could read my text and see that I was serious about not hurting her, and then we could get back to making love.

Unfortunately, the text fit neither of those scenarios. It was from Jamie, and it read I'M AT THE FRONT DOOR AND MY KEY WON'T WORK! WHERE ARE YOU?

"Damn it," I cursed under my breath.

"What's the matter?" The way Sandra's eyes darted around the room, I could tell she was already thinking of the worst-case scenario and was preparing to grab her clothes and leave. But in this case, her leaving would be the worst thing. We'd both be in deep shit if Jamie saw her leaving my house this early in the morning. How the hell would we explain that?

"Jamie is at the front door."

"She is?" Sandra had a look of panic on her face. We'd never discussed keeping our budding relationship a secret from Jamie. There was no need to talk about it, because we both knew Jamie well enough to know that telling her was out of the question.

"Should I go?" she asked, making a move to get out of the bed.

"No!" I put my hand on her shoulder and pushed her back a little harder than I should have. "Sorry. But you gotta stay here until she's gone. I'll go talk to her, and you keep quiet up here, okay?"

I threw on some sweats and a T-shirt and headed to the door, trying to think of the quickest excuse to get rid of Jamie.

I peeked through the peephole and groaned. She had that crazy, self-righteous, "I'm going to run your business" look in her eyes. I decided my best line of defense was to not let her get even a foot inside. As determined as she looked, she might just head straight for my bedroom, and then Sandra and I would both have to deal with her wrath.

"What, Jamie? I'm busy right now," I yelled through the door.

"Daddy, let me in! My key won't work."

"It's not supposed to. I changed the locks again."

"What? Why?"

"Because this is my house and I wanted to."

She started pounding and jiggling the doorknob like that was going to get her in. "Daddy! What is wrong with you? Just open the door!"

I cracked the door slightly but left my body pressed against it so she couldn't open it farther. "You have a home, Jamie. I don't have a key there, do I?"

"Yeah, but . . . but does Darnel have a key?" She seemed confused that I hadn't just opened the door and welcomed her in. Usually by this point I would have given in to her tantrum. Shoot, I thought, lots of things about me were changing since I met Sandra.

"Nope. He doesn't have a key either. Darnel moved out. He found his own place. Haven't you talked to your brother lately?"

"I've been busy. Louis and I are having some problems. That's why I came over."

For a second, she almost got me. I hated to see my little girl as sad as she looked, and I was close to letting her in so I could talk to her about what was going on between her and Louis. But in the blink of an eye, she lost that look and was back to interrogating.

"Daddy, who's in there? Why won't you let me in?"

"I've got company. I told you about coming over here unannounced."

"It's Crystal, isn't it? She done snuck away from her husband again, didn't she?" She gave me a disgusted look. "What do you see in that woman?"

"Look, Jamie, I'll give you a call later, but I've got some things going on right now, okay?"

"Oh, so you gon' tell me you won't let me, your youngest child, your baby, in your house?" Now she was giving me her best attitude, with hands on hips, lips poked out, and head tilted to the side.

I felt my blood pressure rising, but I was not in the mood for a long, drawn-out fight. Not when I had Sandra waiting in my bed upstairs. "Jamie, you're a grown woman. Now go home and handle your own business with your own man."

"You wrong, Daddy, but that's all right," she said, and then offered her final word before walking away. "I'm leaving now, but I'm gonna find out what's going on with all this sneaking around you've been doing."

"Do whatever you have to, baby, but do it from your house, okay?"

I closed the door and locked it, quite sure that she meant every word she'd said. If this thing between me and Sandra became anything more involved, we had a tough road ahead of us.

Jamie

22

I stepped into Punta Rojo, a tasty Columbian restaurant on Hillside Avenue and walked past the hostess to the back, where Sandra was sitting in a booth. She was half eating, half playing with a salad, and if looks could kill, I would have been as dead as they come when she looked up from it.

She was annoyed because I was a full thirty minutes late for lunch, but I just couldn't get out the door. Every time I got up from my desk, the phone rang or someone walked into the office. Usually, I would just say to hell with it and forward the phones to our service, but Daddy was trying to rush me out the door, which only made me take my own sweet time. I had a feeling he had a lunch date with this mystery woman he was seeing, and I was dying to know who was this heifer who was brainwashing him lately. I stuck around in the office as long as I could before Daddy finally shoved me out. From the look on Sandra's face, it still wasn't soon enough.

"Is your watch set on CP time or what?" She rolled her eyes playfully. "You know some of us only have an hour for lunch. Not all of us work for our rich daddies."

"Jealous?" I teased as I slid into the booth across from her.

"Actually, I am. You know how I feel about real estate. I'd love to have your job."

"Well, it's not up for grabs, so forget it."

I'd only seen Sandra a few times since the night I tried to fix her up with my brother. She looked good, working some gold highlights and a new shade of lipstick. Truth is, she kinda glowed. If I didn't know better, I'd think she'd gotten some recently.

"I got this. It's on me today. I owe you for try'na set you up with my brother anyway. Did he ever call you?"

"Yeah, he left me a message apologizing. Said something about him and his ex were getting back together."

I pantomimed a gagging motion. The thought of Darnel wasting his time with Keisha made me sick to my stomach.

Sandra just shrugged. "You know, story of my life. That's why I don't fool with these young dudes."

"Sorry, girl. I really thought it was gonna work out. Trust me, it's his loss." My brother was a damn fool for passing on someone like Sandra. Where else was he going to find someone with a good job and a great body who knew how to respect herself? He sure as hell wasn't gonna find it if he kept messing with that skank. Sandra wasn't like Keisha or the rest of these tramps I saw chasing after Darnel and my father. She had class. Why couldn't my father or my brother choose someone like her?

"That's a'ight," she said. "I'm seeing someone."

"And you kept it from me?" I pretended to be offended, but really, I knew I was just as much to blame. We weren't best friends or anything, but we did try to get together at least a few times a month to catch up on gossip and talk about the men—or sometimes the lack of men—in our lives. I'd been so busy worrying about what Louis was up to lately that I hadn't checked in with her the way I usually did.

"Yeah, I'm just seeing how it goes for now. But, gurrrl, I think he's definitely a keeper."

"That's it? I want to know everything. Is he fine? Is the sex great? Does he have a job? College graduate?"

"I don't want to jinx it by talking about it," she said, looking everywhere but straight at me. "I just got my fingers crossed on this one."

"No, no, no, no. That's not how we do it. You gotta give me some details, girl. How long you been wanting to meet someone, and now that you have, you don't want to talk about it?"

"Jamie, I'm sorry. It's just that I'm superstitious. I don't wanna mess it up."

I had never known her to be so closemouthed about a man, but whatever. I was dealing with enough of my own drama. "At least answer this: Is he a brother?"

"Yes!" Sandra laughed. "And I will tell you that I haven't had this much fun with a man in a long time."

"Really? Well, the sex must be great, 'cause you got that look," I teased her.

"What look?" Sandra blushed.

"That I'm-being-fucked-really-good look."

"Who, me?" She pointed at herself with a sly smirk. "Why would you say that?"

"Yes, you. And you know why I'm saying it. Now, is he packing or what? Come on, girl. Give up some details."

"Let's just say I don't kiss and tell. But I'm sure if you had your chance, you'd want a man just like him." The way she was looking at me said this man must be the bomb.

"I know that's right. He really must be something."

We high-fived and laughed. If Sandra wanted to be superstitious and silly about this dude, then she could go ahead. I just hoped for her sake he was worth all the fuss.

"Long as he's treating you good."

"Good? Girl, it's better than good. I haven't had to open my wallet once since I met him."

Sandra always did have expensive tastes, so whoever this mystery man was, he'd better have a fat bank account if he wanted her to stick around.

"Sounds like he meets all your requirements," I said.

"Yeah, he's pretty amazing." She got this dreamy look in her eyes for a second, then said, "But enough about me. What's up with you?"

"My life is crap right now."

"Why? What's wrong?"

"God, where do I start? First of all, my father is seeing some wench."

"So what's the problem?"

I wanted to ask her, "Are you for real?" She had heard me talk about my father enough times to know that I never liked anyone he dated. Most times, she would nod her head and bash the bitches right along with me, but today she tried to play it off like she had no idea about my history with my father's women. I didn't know what her problem was today. But instead of jumping on her, I explained my point.

"He's been acting strange. I mean, he's doing shit that's not like him at all."

"Really? Like what?"

"Like I went over to his house last week and he was in the garage, bench-pressing."

"So?"

"My daddy doesn't press weights. He ain't got to impress nobody. You should hear him. He be all huffing and puffing and shit," I said with a laugh.

"Yeah, but that doesn't mean anything. Maybe he's just try'na get in shape."

"No, I know my father better than anyone, and trust me, he's seeing some new skank. I tried to make him dinner, and he told me no and then ate some damn Lean Cuisine! I've never seen him eat frozen food. He don't even like leftovers."

"Yeah, but that still doesn't prove anything. Maybe he's really trying to get it together, you know, for his health. Black men have to worry about high blood pressure, diabetes, high cholesterol—"

"Yeah, well, you don't know my dad, 'cause he don't worry about shit. His favorite exercise is sex."

"Jamie!" Sandra looked shocked.

I was starting to wonder if the person sitting across from me was some kind of body double, because the Sandra I knew was never this uptight. Give the girl a little dick and all of a sudden she acts like a nun!

"I don't know why you sitting there with your mouth all open. It's the truth."

"I'm just saying. That's your father. Don't talk about him like that. I've met the man. He ain't that bad."

"Okay, you're right, but I'm mad at him right now," I said with a pout. "Plus, I saw a motorcycle magazine at his house. A damn motorcycle magazine! Has he lost his mind? Now he's thinking about buying a motorcycle."

"I think motorcycles are sexy."

"Yeah, it's sexy with a man you would date, not my old-ass daddy."

She took a sip of her drink. "He's not that old, is he?"

"Sandra, he's my dad. Of course he's old. Ain't your father old?"

Shit. I suddenly felt really bad when I saw the look on Sandra's face. I forgot her father was dead. "I'm so sorry, Sandra. I forgot."

She shrugged and stared down at the napkin in her lap.

"It's just that these women come sniffing after my dad like his penis is the Holy Grail or some shit. He's still doing Darnel's mother, for God's sake! That woman's been after him for damn near thirty years now. Can't she see that it's just not happening?"

"They're seeing each other?" She had a weird look on her face, but I figured it was because she was still upset about me mentioning her father.

"Not really seeing each other. It's more like a booty-call thing. She's married, but whenever she comes to town, they sleep together. It's disgusting."

Her eyebrows scrunched up and met in the middle of her forehead. She was wearing a huge frown. I knew how she felt, though. It was disgusting to think of my father and old-ass Crystal getting busy together.

I picked up the menu and glanced at it. "And now there's some new ho try'na get into his life."

"Maybe he wants to settle down," Sandra suggested. "You ever think he's tired of being alone?"

"Please. He ain't never been alone. He's got me and Darnel. Besides, I can't tell you how many women have come through that place. He's like a sex machine or something."

"Well, maybe this time it'll be different."

"Doubtful. Whoever this new chick is, he's gonna be really into her for five minutes, and as soon as she tries to have a real relationship, he'll kick her to the curb. It never fails."

"Well, if you're so sure that he's gonna get rid of her eventually, then what are you worrying about?" Her tone was a little too snippy for me. She sure had some kinda problem today. I might not be having lunch with her again anytime soon. I thought she was my friend, not my damn social worker.

"What is so wrong with me watching my father's back to keep all these gold diggers away from him?" I asked. "My father has a lot of money, Sandra."

"I know."

"What do you mean, you know? Don't be counting my father's money, Sandra."

She laughed. "Stop trippin', Jamie. I've been to his house with you, remember? You can't be on welfare to own that."

"I'm sorry. Maybe I am trippin'. I just don't know what to do."

"Well, for starters, he's a grown man, and he can take care of himself. He did right by you and raised you all by himself. Maybe it's time you let him have a life of his own."

"You sound like Louis."

"Maybe Louis is right."

"Please don't talk to me about Louis."

"Why? What's going on with you and Louis?"

As much as I didn't like airing my relationship troubles outside my family, I went ahead and did it this time. Daddy and Darnel had both been too preoccupied to talk to me lately, and Aunt Winnie hadn't done anything but make matters worse by convincing me to search Louis's house. Besides, Sandra looked as relieved as I did to be changing the subject. For some reason, talking about my father seemed to have both of us worked up today.

"Let's just say me and Louis are having some trust issues right about now."

"You were doing fine last we talked."

"Well, a lot can happen in a short period of time."

"You got that right," she said with another weird look on her face. Before I could even wonder what it meant, she asked, "So, what's changed?"

"Louis is cheating on me. He has another family somewhere in Detroit."

She sat back in her chair. "What! Does your father know about this? He'll kill Louis."

"That's what I've been trying to tell him. But this chick, whoever she is, has Daddy's nose wide open." And we were right back at square one with our conversation. I was ready to get the check and bolt before I'd even ordered my food. Between Louis and Daddy, I didn't know who had me going through the motions more, but I sure as hell needed to regain control of the situation with both of them.

Darnel

23

"Dammit!" I tried to turn my key, but it wouldn't budge.

Apparently, Keisha had changed the locks. I knew we'd had a fight the last time I was there, but this made no sense. She didn't mean what she'd said about moving on. She couldn't have. Or could she? Either way, it didn't matter, 'cause I was not about to let her end things this way. Not without me knowing the truth. Omar's words outside the courthouse were eating me alive, and I had to get into this apartment and find that diary before the stress of not knowing killed me.

I wondered if Keisha had tried to take my name off the lease too. Even if she had, though, she couldn't. I'd already checked, and no one could remove another person's name from the lease. So technically, I had the right to be in there—which is what I was prepared to tell the cops if they came around while I was trying to get in.

I went around the back to see if the windows were open. When I was living with her, Keisha was always forgetting to close and lock them. We'd had plenty of arguments about it. I was always reminding her how unsafe it was. But now it made my day to see that she'd left them open once again.

I pulled down the fire escape and hoisted myself up onto the bars. One of the neighbors was peeking out her window and looked like she was about to say something.

"Hey, Ms. Williams." I waved and gave her a big smile. "Forgot my key."

Thankfully, she nodded and closed her blinds. For a second there, I thought I was gonna be busted before I even made it inside. I climbed up to the second-floor window and let myself in, feeling triumphant. Did Keisha really think something like changing the locks would stop me? No way. I was a man on a mission.

Once inside, I went straight for the bedroom closet, hoping to find the strongbox. Last time I was there, Keisha busted me before I could look inside the box, but I was pretty sure the diary would be in there, since I'd searched just about everywhere else. I put in the combination, and voilà, the box opened! There was the diary that I just knew would hold the answers to all the questions that had been plaguing me.

Had I been smart about it, I would have stuffed the diary in my back pocket and left the apartment, but I couldn't wait to open the book and read the truth.

I sat down on the bed, eager to read, but I'll be damned if I didn't hear the front door opening before I even cracked open the diary. All those justifications about being on the lease left my head as I searched for a hiding place. If Keisha entered the bedroom, she would catch me red-handed with her diary, and based on what she'd said to me last time I was here, there was a good chance she'd call the cops. I didn't want to be no punk, but with the order of protection lifted not too long ago, I couldn't take a risk. I slipped under the bed with the diary still in my hand and my body drenched in sweat.

"Hey." I heard her on her cell phone as she entered the bedroom. "Yeah, that sounds good. Let me throw on something cute and I'll meet you there."

I could see her kicking off her shoes and removing her clothes. Damn, even her calves looked sexy. But the bigger issue in my mind at the moment was who the hell was on the phone that had her in such a big hurry to put on something cute and meet them. Omar had better not be stepping to her again—not unless he wanted me to finish that whoop-ass I put on him.

Keisha stripped down and went into the bathroom, and I heard her turn on the shower. I waited another minute, and as soon as I heard the shower curtain sliding shut, I got the hell out from under the bed.

"Ouch!" It took a moment for me to realize it was my own voice I heard shouting out. I had stabbed myself with a belt buckle that was lying on the floor.

I heard the shower curtain sliding open immediately. Damn! She heard me. I sprinted to the open window and threw myself onto the fire escape, but I couldn't get the damn ladder to unhook. I had no choice but to jump, because there was no way I was going to stick around long enough for Keisha to call the cops.

There wasn't a damn thing there to break my fall, and the shit hurt. But there was no time to stop and check for cuts and bruises. I had to get out of there before Keisha came out of the bathroom and saw me. I limped around to the front, got in my car, and drove like a bat out of hell.

The whole ride home, I thought about the diary, which I had shoved under the front seat. I kept imagining scenarios where I was pulled over, the car was searched, and the diary was confiscated. I pictured myself going to jail for breaking and entering. The thoughts had me so distracted that a few times I swerved out of my lane and nearly had an accident. I gripped the wheel tighter and slowed down to the speed limit, determined to make it home in one piece. There was no way I was going to crash or get pulled over before I had the chance to read what Keisha had written in that diary.

I knew that whatever was in there could quite possibly be more painful than the fall I'd just taken off the fire escape. What if Omar was telling the truth and the book contained every dirty detail of her affairs? Would I be able to live with that? How could I be with a woman for years, live with her, and plan to spend the rest of my life with her and not know who she really was?

Or what if I had stolen her diary only to find out that the night I caught her and Omar really was the only time she had ever stepped out on me? I thought I would be able to forgive her, but what if seeing the details in black and white sent me over the top? Then I would lose Keisha for sure, and I didn't know if that would be worth it.

My mind was in overdrive, thinking of all the things that could be in that book. I was sick to my stomach by the time I drove down the block and parked in front of my apartment. I took the book out from under the seat and got out of the car, giving a quick look over my shoulder. As nervous as I was, I half expected to see a cop car pulling around the corner, coming to arrest me.

Even though I lived alone, I didn't feel safe reading the diary until I was in my bedroom with the door locked. I'd been interrupted twice trying to read the information on these pages, and this time, I was determined to finish what I'd started.

From the first page, I was already starting to wish I could turn back the hands of time and put the book back, unopened, right where I found it. It read like one of those sordid chick-lit novels. Keisha's very own *Sex and the City*.

"Oh, hell naw!" I yelled out when I got to a page describing how she gave a blow job to one of my boys. It was after a basketball game sophomore year in high school. She wasn't even going down on *me* then!

There were two stars next to the dude's name. What the heck did that mean?

"I hate that nigger." I threw the book across the room after I read about her letting this punk-ass player screw her in his car after he took her out for ice cream. Ice cream? I introduced her ass to sushi. I brought her flowers and candy. I treated her like a princess, and here she was letting some guy slip it to her in the backseat of his car after a trip to Carvel. Ain't that a bitch!

As much as it hurt, I picked up the book and continued reading. I couldn't stop. Something wouldn't let me pull away from the painful truth on those pages. Now I had the answers I'd been looking for, and it hurt like hell to know that Omar wasn't lying when he'd said he wasn't the only one—not by a long shot.

The further I read, the more names I saw, all of them listed as Keisha's past sexual partners. Next to every dude's name were stars, ranging from one to five. I figured out that it was some sort of fucked-up rating system Keisha had devised so she could classify everyone by how good they were in bed.

One entry was about a dude she met in a club, who got four stars next to his name: *I went out dancing with the girls and wound up in bed with this guy who works at the car wash. Every time I go in there now, he takes my ticket and gives me a free upgrade. I guess you can say we're even. I don't know why I'm doing this, because I love Darnel so much.*

Every entry I read was like plunging a knife in my heart, as it described in graphic detail what she did with each guy and how much, or how little, she enjoyed it. The worst part was that between each descriptive entry, there were passages about how much she loved me and how she couldn't imagine loving anyone else. How sick is that? She called what we had love, yet she was doing just about every brother on campus.

As if all of this didn't hurt enough already, I came to the page that cut me the deepest. There it was, in Keisha's own handwriting: *Omar is the best sex I have ever had. He does things to my body I can't describe. I didn't realize how good sex could be. He makes me feel like a real woman. I love Darnel, but he can't hold it down like Omar. I wish I didn't need one man to love and another to fuck the shit out of me.*

I wanted to rip the pages right out of the book, to destroy any evidence of her words. But it was too late; I'd already seen it, and the truth would be burned into my consciousness forever—there, next to Omar's name, were ten stars and a little caption that read, *Omar gets ten stars because he's ten times better than anyone I've ever been with.*

Like some sort of masochist, I flipped through the pages to find my own rating. I couldn't help it. I had to know how I rated against my ex-best friend.

Two measly stars. That was all Keisha had given me. Oh, she had written over and over in the diary about how much she loved me, but none of that mattered. The only thing I cared about was that she gave me a two-star rating, while Omar, my best friend, received ten.

I wanted to go over and bang the shit out of Keisha just to show her that she was wrong about me; I didn't need to make love to her like she was some precious jewel. Obviously, she preferred to be treated like some piece of shit anyway.

The more I read about Omar, the more I realized that everything Keisha had told me about the night before our wedding was a lie. She had been messing with him for a long time. Apparently, he was like a drug to her, based on these lines:

I can't seem to stay away from Omar. He keeps telling me he loves me, he knows I don't feel the same way, but he doesn't seem to care as long as I keep sleeping with him. I know I should leave him alone, but the sex is just addicting. I feel like I need a fix at least two or three times a week.

I hated that Omar had been right, but he'd also been the one taking up the most space in these pages. Apparently, the two of them got busy whenever they could find the time. How many times had Omar said he had to go and get with this girl or that one when it was probably my girl? Now I wished I had done some more serious damage to him that night at the hotel—the kind that would make it impossible for him to ever fuck anybody else again.

The last entry in the diary was written the morning before I caught her and Omar together.

I'm getting married, so it's the last time I'm going to have sex with anyone other than Darnel. I want our marriage to last and to be honest, so from this point on, I will be faithful. I'm going to get my last piece of Omar, and after that, I'm going to forget all about great sex and just love Darnel. I don't need my world to be rocked by sex. I have love, and I am marrying the man I love.

So that's it. The last time I'll ever need to write about my sex-capades in this book. From now on, it'll be all about me and my husband, Darnel.

I slammed the book shut, struggling to process what I had just read. How the hell did she think she could go from screwing multiple dudes on the side to being faithful? Especially since she seemed to think I was so boring in bed. I hate to say it, but it hurt so much that I felt like crying.

Everything I'd read told me that I had no idea who Keisha really was. She sure as hell wasn't the woman I thought I knew, who pledged her heart to me when she gave me her virginity. . . . Shit! I couldn't even be sure if that was real now. I thought my first time was her first time, too, but now who knew? She might have been screwing for years before that.

I felt like someone had punched me in the gut, and there was no way to recover. I wanted to throw up, to punch something, to scream, but the only thing I could do was sit there, wondering who Keisha was screwing at that exact moment.

James

24

Sandra speared a piece of cheesecake onto her fork, then leaned across the table to feed it to me. I opened my mouth, savoring the dessert. It tasted almost as good as she did.

We were nestled away for lunch at Louie's, a quaint seafood restaurant in Port Washington, Long Island, which was far enough away from the prying eyes of nosy neighbors or my meddling daughter. The lights were low, the background music was soothing, and the smell of gourmet seafood dishes made the place feel nice and homey. It was nothing like Red Lobster, where we might get some decent seafood, but we'd be surrounded by hundreds of other diners, with all the noise and confusion that brings. Louie's was an out-of-the-way place with only a small crowd. It was a good place to be with someone special, and that's what Sandra was fast becoming—someone very, very special.

"Pinch me, will you?" I whispered, still unable to believe that I was uttering such a corny romantic line without being the least bit embarrassed.

"Why?" She dug her fork into her dessert to feed me again.

"I don't know. I just want to make sure I'm not dreaming." I parted my lips, and she slid the fork into my mouth.

"What do you mean by that?" Sandra gave me a penetrating gaze.

"I just can't believe I'm here with you. We've been seeing each other every day, and—"

"And what?" she teased. "You can't believe you're not bored with me yet?"

I playfully swatted her forearm. "Very funny. No, I'm just trying to say that I really enjoy your company. I'm so comfortable around you; I feel like we've known each other a long time."

"It's only been two months."

"I know, but it seems like it's been years. I'm having all these feelings for you. What the heck is that all about?" I asked sincerely, since I had never really felt this way with any woman before her. I suppose it was weird for me to be asking, since I was older and should have had more experience with relationships. But mine was a different type of experience, which consisted mostly of one-night stands and booty calls. This emotional stuff was unfamiliar to me.

"I guess I just have that effect on men," Sandra said with a confident smile.

"Yeah, but I'm forty-eight years old. No woman is supposed to have this kind of influence over me."

"You know, James, just because you've always been the player in control doesn't mean you're above falling for someone. Why don't you just relax and enjoy it?"

"Oh, trust me, I am enjoying it. It's just that it's all pretty new to me."

I didn't tell her that it was also quite unplanned. Once I decided to sleep with this much younger woman, I had intended to make Sandra a booty call. No way had I planned on courting her, spending almost every day with her on dates or just chilling together in my house. As I got to know her, I found myself having more fun than I'd had in a long time. Maybe it was because she made me take the time to get to know her before she went to bed with me. Or maybe we just had that kind of connection. I didn't know which it was, but I was amazed by the bond I felt with her in such a short time.

"Well, I'm glad you're enjoying yourself," Sandra joked.

The date would have been perfect if the conversation had ended right there, but unfortunately, she turned serious. "Maybe someday you'll enjoy yourself enough to take me somewhere in Queens."

That caught me off guard. I had been taking her to places where we wouldn't run into someone we knew, because as much as I was enjoying her company, I wasn't ready to announce it to the world. There would be too much hell to pay from jealous exes and, even worse, from Jamie. I didn't think Sandra had caught on to what I was doing, but obviously I was wrong.

I tried to play dumb. "You don't like the places I take you?"

"Of course I do," she said. "But let's not pretend I don't know why you choose the places you do."

"What are you trying to get at, Sandra?" I asked, not ready to admit that I'd been busted.

"I can't keep doing this."

"What?" Was she breaking up with me? My voice cracked when I asked the question, so no matter how much I wanted to play it cool and act like I'd be fine if she left me that night, my body gave away my true feelings. It shocked me to realize that I'd be devastated if we broke up. Was this the way so many women had felt when I dumped them?

"Well, unless this is going to be a serious relationship, I'm not going to continue seeing you after tonight."

"Why not?"

"You know how much I like you, James."

I nodded. "I like you too."

"Actually, I think I might be in love with you."

"Then what's the problem?" I asked, trying to remain calm even though my heart started racing when she said she might love me. I'd never heard a woman say that before and not have me wanting to bolt from the room. Now I think I was happy to hear it. The problem was that even if she might love me, something was making her unhappy.

"I don't like sneaking around like I'm some married man's mistress. We're both single, so why are we tipping around? Are you just afraid you'll lose your player status if your other women see you with me?"

"No!" I said loudly enough that a few other diners turned to stare at me. I lowered my voice and said, "How can you ask me that?"

"Let's not pretend like I don't know all about your history with women. Jamie is my friend, you know."

"Oh, trust me, I know that. She's the biggest reason I'm still keeping what we have a secret. But how could you think it's about other women? I've been with you every single day since we got together. When exactly do you think I've had time to see anyone else?" This was kind of pissing me off. For the first time in my life, I had been monogamous for more than a few days, yet I was still having to defend myself.

"I'm not going to argue that point with you, James. I think I have every right to worry that you still want to see other women on the side, considering your track record. Besides, how else am I supposed to feel when you act like you're scared to take me anywhere near home?"

"I thought we both understood that Jamie would make this difficult for us."

She frowned. "She's already made it difficult for me. Do you have any idea how I felt having to sit with her at lunch and listen to her talk about her father's new mystery woman like I was a piece of trash?"

"I'm sorry. I didn't know." Sandra hadn't told me about this, but I knew Jamie well enough that I could imagine the things she had said and how they must have hurt Sandra.

"Well, it sucked, and I don't want to go through that again. If we're going to be together, we'll have to deal with her sooner or later, so we might as well just get it over with now."

This was tearing me apart. All these years, I'd never had to choose between Jamie and some woman, because no woman had ever meant enough to me. If Jamie ever made things difficult enough that the woman wanted to walk, I just let her go. But this time, I didn't want to lose Sandra.

"Just give me a little more time, okay? This is all new to me." I reached for her hand, but she pulled hers away.

"I'm a good catch, you know, but I can't wait around forever. I'm young, and I'm not going to sit here and waste my youth with you if this isn't a true, committed relationship. I want the world to know we're a couple. I can't spend my life worrying that some other woman—whether it's an ex or Jamie—could come between us at any time."

I stared at her blankly. I had been so unprepared for this whole conversation that I was literally speechless now.

"So what's it going to be? Do you want me to be your woman or not?"

I couldn't get my brain out of first gear. Finally, the only thing I managed to say was, "Excuse me." I needed some time to think.

"I've got to go to the restroom. We'll pick this up when I get back."

I'm sure she knew I didn't have to go to the bathroom, but she didn't protest. "Sure, we'll finish when you get back." She reached up and took my hand. "But, James, we *will* finish this conversation."

I walked around a corner and down a hall, into the bar area. I was headed to the men's room on the opposite side of the bar, until something stopped me dead in my tracks. Louis was sitting in a booth in the corner. The woman he was with had her back to me, but even without seeing her face, I knew it wasn't Jamie, because the woman with Louis had blond hair. What the hell was going on tonight? First Sandra sprang the "commitment speech" on me, and now I caught my daughter's boyfriend out with another woman. This was more than I wanted to deal with.

For a moment, I thought about finding the exit and bolting. That would be the easiest way to avoid all the drama that was threatening to unfold. But leaving now would put an end to what I had with Sandra, and I wasn't ready to do that. So, I had a choice to make. Did I turn around and head back to my table before I really had time to think, or did I go to the men's room, which meant having to walk right past Louis and his cheating ass?

Sandra had to come first, I decided. I had to deal with our issues, and then later I would find a way to tell Louis that I knew what was up. I mean, sure, we men need a little variety in our sex lives now and then—after all, I had been the king of players for most of my life—but this was my daughter's man, and he was gonna have to play by a different set of rules. I wasn't about to let him break her heart.

Louis was leaning in close to the blonde; they looked like they were whispering sweet nothings to each other. This pissed me off, but at the same time, it was convenient, because Louis was too busy with her to even notice me.

I moved quickly across the room and made it to the men's room without being spotted. Inside the bathroom, I stood in front of the mirror and checked out my reflection. I wasn't a bad-looking guy, but the gray hair at my temples and the laugh lines forming around my eyes reminded me that I was no spring chicken anymore. Sure, I could still get plenty of women, but were they really what I wanted? Sandra was special; she was smart and funny and sexy as hell. Women like her didn't come around every day, and I would be a fool to let her get away.

I stood there for a while, considering the idea of my life without her versus my life with her. It was more appealing by far to imagine myself with her. The more I thought about it, the more I realized I didn't want to go back to the way it was before we got together. The idea of sleeping with a different woman every night of the week no longer seemed like the ultimate lifestyle to me. I couldn't even remember half those women's names once they walked out the door. But I was getting to know Sandra on a much deeper level, and I liked the way that felt. I was enjoying every moment I spent with her, and I didn't want it to end. With a sudden shock, a question came to my mind: *Is this what love feels like?*

Whether or not it was love, I knew one thing for sure: I had to do whatever it took to keep Sandra. That meant dealing with Jamie, of course, but maybe this would be the best thing for her. It was time for her to grow up and cut the strings anyway.

I left the restroom on a mission. I was ready to go tell Sandra that I wanted a committed relationship too. Hell, I would even burn my little black book if she asked me to.

I was so determined to get back to the table and deliver my news that I didn't notice Louis coming toward the men's room until I practically ran into him.

"Excu—Oh shit! James!" Louis exclaimed before he could stop the words from coming out of his mouth.

"Louis. Funny meeting you here. What are you doing all the way out on Long Island?" I asked, making no effort to conceal the suspicion in my voice.

"Oh . . . just working, you know." He made a lame attempt at sounding nonchalant, but I could see the tension in his face.

"Really? Working at Louie's, huh?" I asked, turning to look at the blonde, who had clearly been watching us but quickly looked away when she saw me checking her out. If that wasn't a guilty move, I don't know what is.

Louis saw me watching her, but he still tried to play it off. "Oh yeah, that's Jeannette. She's one of our best clients."

"And she just happens to be out here with you for lunch, huh?"

"Yeah, we, uh, had to go over to a dealership in Glen Cove to check out this used Mercedes AMG. She's been asking us to get her one for a while, and I finally found one out here on Long Island."

"Well, aren't you a conscientious salesman," I said sarcastically. "And lucky for her Glen Cove is right around the corner from this romantic little restaurant, huh?"

Louis was so nervous that sweat was dripping down his forehead. He might have been fooling Jamie, but now he was trying to lie to the master of sneaking around, and I think he was figuring out just how busted he was. All he could say was, "Yeah, lucky."

"Hmmm . . . maybe you could bring Jamie here someday, Louis. What do you think about that? Good idea, right?"

He nodded, looking scared.

"Yeah, it's a good idea, because we both know that my little girl deserves only the best, don't we?"

He nodded again.

"So we understand each other, right?"

"Yes, sir." He looked like he was about to pee on himself.

"Good. Because if my little girl gets hurt, it's not gonna be pretty for you, Louis. I'm very good friends with the man who owns that dealership you work at. I actually sold him his house. We understand each other?"

He nodded. "I won't hurt her, James. I love Jamie."

"I'm glad to hear that. So whatever you got going on with Goldilocks over there, get it out of your system in a hurry. I won't tell Jamie this time, but if I even think you might be stepping out on my little girl again, you won't be *able* to love her, because I will rip your fuckin' heart out your chest. You got that?"

I walked away to the sound of him stuttering some sort of response.

"You were gone quite a while," Sandra said when I got back to the table. "Everything okay?"

"Oh yeah. Just ran into someone in the bar that I had to talk to for a minute."

Luckily, she didn't press for details. She probably figured I was lying anyway, just to stall for time.

"So, did you think about what I said?" she asked.

"I did."

"And?"

"And I think you're a very special woman." I took her hand.

"And?"

Part of me was still not ready to deal with this and wished she'd never brought it up. But the expectant way she was staring at me now told me she wasn't leaving this table without an answer.

"Sandra, just give me two weeks. That's all I'm asking. I've gotta figure out a way to tell my kids." It was the best I could give her. I was still too scared to give her a wholehearted "yes." I really did need to think about how to tell them, but I was also buying myself a little more time to get used to the whole idea of being in a committed relationship.

She nodded. "I understand. But you should understand this: If you don't make a decision in two weeks, I will."

Jamie

25

"Baby, I'm gonna miss the hell out of you."

Louis pulled the covers back, kissing me on each breast as he stood next to our bed. I wriggled lower so that our lips met.

Things had been good between us recently, much better than should have been expected considering what I found in the briefcase in the basement. He hadn't given me one reason to be jealous, not one suspicious phone call or text, so part of me had pushed the contents of the briefcase to the back of my mind. That was the part of me that wanted things between me and Louis to work out. I loved him so much, and I really wanted to believe that he wasn't doing anything behind my back. So when things were good, I just went with the flow.

Now, the other part of me was still working on a plan. I could have just confronted Louis about the driver's license, but I knew that wouldn't be enough. Even if he was busted, he would act just like any other man and come up with an innocent story, like it was an old fake ID or something. And me, loving him the way I did, might believe any flimsy excuse just because I wanted it to be true. So, no, I wasn't gonna give him a chance to lie to me. I would hold on to what I knew—that Louis got texts from a strange woman that made him run out of the house when we were about to get busy, and he had ID from Detroit, where he'd never mentioned living—until I knew for sure what it all meant. Then, if I discovered that he did indeed have another family or a whorish lifestyle, I'd hit him over the head with it so hard it would knock him on his ass.

In the meantime, I kept quiet about things and enjoyed all the good loving Louis gave me. He'd been really attentive lately. The night before, he took me to Louie's, a romantic seafood restaurant in Long Island. The food was delicious, and the service was great—he must have slipped the waiter some money or something, because I swear they treated us like we were regulars. This morning, he was getting ready to go away for a few days. This was his first business trip in a while, and I wanted to give him a little going-away present.

Our kiss became passionate. I slid my hand up his thigh, reaching for his penis as I attempted to seduce him back into bed.

"Uh-uh, no can do." He backed out of my reach, shaking his head.

"Um, are you sure about that?" I asked, looking down at his stiff member, which told me something different.

"I've got to get going."

"But he wants to play. And so do I." I rubbed my hands over my erect nipples, where he'd been kissing just moments earlier. "Besides, you started this."

"I know. I'm sorry." He placed the covers back on top of me.

I kicked them off and got into my best centerfold pose. I dared him to walk away as I rolled over onto my stomach, arched my back, and turned so he could see all that I offered.

"Fuck!" He licked his lips, enjoying the view, and I hoped he was on the verge of doing something he knew he shouldn't.

"No, fuck me," I teased. He stepped closer and ran his hand over my ass. I reached up and began to stroke his dick.

"Babe," he whined, glancing at the clock. "You gonna make me late."

"No, I'm going to make you very late," I promised as I lowered my lips onto his penis. I was ready to swallow him whole, and for a second I thought he was going to relax and let me do what I did best. But before I could really get going, he pulled himself out—and I wasn't happy about it.

"You know I want to . . ."

"So do it." I took a lick and he moaned.

"Mmm, this isn't fair."

I gave him another lick.

"Please, baby, I can't."

I stopped, holding him in my hand and looking up at him. "Yes, you can."

"Really, I can't. I have to go by the shop, and then I gotta get on the road."

"You expect me to believe you can go three whole days without getting some?" I pouted. It wasn't often that Louis turned down one of my patented blow jobs, and my radar was kicking in. Something wasn't right.

"It's only three days. Besides, I got some last night. And as good as you were, that should hold me a hell of a lot longer than three days." He laughed and kissed me on the cheek.

What straight man in his right mind turns down oral sex, no matter how much he got the night before? I was about to ask him that, but he darted into the bathroom almost like he was running away. I heard the shower running; I assumed it was a cold one.

I wasn't used to Louis resisting me, and I wasn't liking it at all. Hell, we were still in that honeymoon stage, or at least we should have been, yet here I was practically throwing myself at him, and he was more interested in getting to work on time. This was not a good sign.

I'd seen my daddy turn down offers from some fine women over the years, and it usually meant only one thing: He had someone else offering something better. This one time, a lady from the church showed up, looking ready to get busy on the front stoop before Daddy even invited her inside. The fool had no idea I was sitting in the living room watching TV and saw the whole thing. She was rubbing all over my father's chest, whispering in his ear, no doubt telling him all the nasty things she wanted to do to him. You should have seen the look on her face when Daddy basically said, "No, thanks," and sent her on her way. Even I was a little shocked that he was telling her to leave, because this was one beautiful woman. But, of course, thirty minutes later, someone even hotter showed up, and it was obvious from the way he greeted her that he had been expecting her visit. He gave me money to take the bus to the mall, and then he escorted contestant number two back to his bedroom. So, with experience like that under my belt, I knew that it was never a good sign when a man turned down sex.

I headed to the bathroom, determined to give Louis one more chance to make me think differently. I climbed into the shower behind him.

"Can you pass me the soap?"

Louis handed me the soap, but he didn't seem interested in me being in there with him, naked, slippery, and ready for action. He picked up the shampoo and lathered up his hair. I slipped my hands between his legs and massaged him until he started to grow. The whole time, he just finished washing his hair and rinsing the soap bubbles off.

"Jamie, I got to go." He moved my hand away, did a final rinse, and stepped out of the shower, leaving me in there feeling like a fool.

A few minutes later, as I watched him get dressed, I said, "Hey, why don't I go with you?"

If he had nothing to hide, there was no reason I couldn't go with him. His answer didn't help ease my worries one bit.

"I got so much work to do, you'd be lonely. Besides, that crappy motel I'm staying at is no place for a bona fide princess. You'd hate it."

"No, I wouldn't."

"Jamie, you think Red Lobster is slumming it. There ain't no way you'd enjoy it."

"I could deal with it."

"But I don't want you to 'deal with it.' Besides, I'll be home before you know it. Three days isn't a long time."

"I don't like being away from you even for a day."

"Don't you have a hair appointment tomorrow anyway?"

I'd had a standing appointment for the past five years and he knew it, but he also knew I didn't let it hold me hostage. My hairdresser would always fit me in another day if I had to reschedule. Besides, what man in his right mind cares about a woman's hair anyway? This was some bullshit excuse.

"Please," I whined. "I'd much rather go with you."

"Next time, honey." I kept pushing, and he kept refusing. We were at a standstill. "We'll go away as soon as this is over."

"As soon as what's over?"

"Just all this work." He kissed me gently on the lips and walked toward the door. Why did I keep getting the feeling that as soon as he didn't like where the conversation was going, he would just run away? It was time for me to get serious about finding some answers.

As soon as Louis's car pulled out of the driveway, I opened my computer. Thank God for the information superhighway. I went to one of those search engines where you can type in a person's name and get their vital information, like addresses, phone numbers, and any known relatives. If he was telling me the truth, then a search on Louis would reveal no known relatives.

What I discovered after putting his name into several different search engines was that not only did he have no known relatives, but also Louis Kennedy of Jamaica, Queens, had only one known address—the one we were living at together. There were no records of him ever having lived anywhere else. I checked the names of a few other people, including myself and Darnel, to test my theory: Anyone who has ever had a credit card statement or a phone bill mailed to them will have that address show up on their search records. Most people move a few times in their lives, and their records will show at least a few different addresses. This was true for me and my brother, as well as for my father and Crystal, but not for Louis. Basically, this search engine made it look like Louis didn't even exist before he moved into Jamaica, Queens. What the hell was going on?

I typed in a search for Rashid Jensen. I had an inkling of what I would find, and my stomach was in knots as I pushed ENTER. Just as I had feared, there were in fact records of a Rashid Jensen in Detroit.

I typed in my credit card number and paid to get the information on Rashid Jensen. And there it was in black and white: the same address that was on the driver's license in the basement and a phone number to go with it.

With shaking hands, I dialed the number. I don't know what I expected to hear, but best-case scenario would have been a recording saying the number had been disconnected. That's not at all what I got.

"Hello?" It was a woman's voice, with lots of talking and laughing in the background, like she had a full house.

It took me a moment to get my thoughts together to ask, "Um, do you know a Rashid Jensen?"

I heard the woman say, "Somebody's calling for Rashid," in a muffled voice, like she'd placed a hand over the receiver. The background noise became silent.

She spoke to me again. "Yeah, I know him. Why? Who is this?"

She had the nerve to ask me that! Who the hell was she? "This is his woman, that's who this is!" I shouted to make sure she knew that I wasn't just some ho on the side. If anyone was on the side, it was her.

"His woman?" She sounded surprised. Again, there was some muffled talking to the other people in the room with her, but I couldn't make out what she said this time. "So you live with him?" she asked when she came back on the line.

"Yes, I live with him. He sleeps with me every night." *Take that, bitch. You the ho, not me.*

"You don't live in Detroit, do you?" she asked.

"No, *we* live in Jamaica." I made sure to emphasize the we.

Again she started talking to the other people. Why did she need to keep conferencing with them? Did they share one damn brain or something? "Jamaica, Queens, or the island of Jamaica?"

"Do I sound like I'm from the islands? We live in Jamaica, Queens."

This time when she relayed my answer to her people, I heard lots of chattering in the background. For some reason, this news was really exciting them. I was starting to get a little leery of this woman and her crew. She was asking too many questions, and it dawned on me that she didn't seem to be upset in the least that I said I was Louis's woman. If she was his wife or something, she sure wasn't acting like it.

"So who are you to him?" I asked. "And how do you know him?"

"It's a long story, but I was planning on coming to New York in the next few days. Why don't we get together so I can explain it to you?" she offered, like we'd go to lunch and be all civil and shit. Didn't she realize this was my man we were talking about?

"I can come to your house if you like," she said when I didn't answer. "What's your address?"

She must have thought I was some kinda stupid. Why the hell would I tell her where I lived so she could come over here and do God knows what? She might not have seemed jealous right now, but maybe that was all just an act. For all I knew, she wanted my address so she could come over here and beat my ass.

I hung up the phone, glad that I had blocked my number. I was hoping that the phone call would give me some answers, but I felt even more confused than before. Was this Rashid person the man I knew as Louis, or was it some kind of crazy coincidence that Louis had an ID with that name on it? And this woman in Detroit said she knew Rashid Jensen, but I didn't get a description from her, so I couldn't even be sure we were talking about the same man. Something treacherous was going on, but I still didn't quite know what it was. All I knew was if it turned out that the man I loved was a bigger womanizer than my father, Louis's ass was gonna be sorry he ever met me.

Darnel

26

I checked my rearview mirror, then glanced at my watch before I turned the corner to drive down Keisha's block. It was 8:45, and there she was, like clockwork, standing next to her car. She was looking fine as hell in a hot-pink top and a tight skirt, but the frustration on her face didn't do her beauty any justice. The way she was shaking her head told me she was not having a very good start to her day. I almost—and I do say almost—felt sorry for her as I pulled up next to her car.

I rolled down my window and asked, "Everything a'ight?"

She sucked her teeth and glared at me. "I'm not a fool, Darnel. I know you did this."

"Huh? Did what?" I bit the inside of my cheek to suppress a smile.

She pointed at her front driver's side tire. "You let the air out of my tire."

"What are you talking about? I just got here."

"You are such a fucking liar, you know that?"

"You need to stop trippin', Keisha. I was just on my way to work. I didn't do anything to your tire."

"Yeah, right. This is a little out of the way for you, isn't it?"

"Nope. I just moved to the other side of Baisly Park, so I guess we'll be seeing a lot of each other, won't we, neighbor?" I flashed a smile and put my car back into DRIVE. "Good luck with that tire. I know how you hate to be late for work."

I pulled off slowly and started counting backward: "Three . . . two . . ." And before I got to one, she shouted, "Darnel, wait!" I put my foot on the brake and waited for her to jog up to my car. She leaned in the passenger's side window.

"My boss is going to be mad if I'm late again. Can you—"

"How about if I give you a lift? That tire's gonna have to wait."

She glanced around the block as if looking for a better option than the one I'd just offered. But it wasn't like a tow truck was going to come down this street anytime soon, and she'd always been too damn cheap to pay for AAA membership, so riding with me was her only choice if she wanted to keep her job. I had her right where I wanted her. Since she'd stopped answering my phone calls, I felt like I had no other way to get her to talk to me.

"Oh, all right." She went back to get her purse, then returned, looking like she dreaded every step.

When she got in, the scent of her perfume filled my car. It was something new and light, and it smelled kind of fruity. It wasn't the scent I was used to, but on Keisha, anything smelled good to me. Once again, I realized how much I loved this girl, even if I hated her.

As I pulled away from the curb, Keisha sat silently and glared out the window. She was leaning as far away from me as she could possibly get. I tried to reach out and touch her shoulder, but she jerked it away from me.

"Why are you so tense, Keisha? You should be happy I was driving by this morning, or else you never would have made it to work on time."

She looked at me and rolled her eyes. "Please. You think I don't know you planned this whole thing?"

"I still don't know why you're accusing me of doing something to your car," I said with mock innocence. I was so furious about what I'd read in her diary that I didn't really give a shit if she knew I'd messed up her tire.

"I'm accusing you because no one else would do some shit like that to me."

"But why would I do something like that? I love you, Keisha."

"I don't know why you'd do it, but for some sick reason, you did. Just like you broke into my apartment."

Damn! Now, that one I did care if she knew about. The last thing I needed was some more charges against me. I pressed her for details.

"What? Someone broke into your apartment? When?" I did a pretty good job of sounding shocked, if I do say so myself.

"You know when," she said, folding her arms across her chest and giving me an evil glare.

"No, Keisha, I don't. Was anything taken?"

She turned her head away and looked out the window as she answered. "You know what's missing."

I ignored her comment. "So, did you get a locksmith to come fix your locks?" I asked.

"They weren't broken."

"Wait. So, the locks weren't broken. . . . How do you know someone broke in?" Things were looking better for me by the second.

Her shoulders sagged in defeat. "I just do. I was in the shower, and I heard a voice."

"And did you see anyone?"

"No. I ain't stupid. I wasn't about to get out the shower and go investigate. What if it was some rapist or something?"

"Exactly! How could you say it was me? It was probably just some crack head looking for shit to steal, and he heard you in the shower and took off." My suggestion wouldn't be too hard to believe, considering Keisha didn't live in the safest of neighborhoods.

Keisha shrugged her shoulders. It wasn't an apology for accusing me, but at least she no longer seemed sure that I was the one in her apartment.

"Did you leave your windows open or something?" I asked. She nodded.

"You know . . . if I was living there, you'd be safer."

This finally got her to turn and look at me. "Darnel, don't."

"Don't what?"

"Don't do this to yourself. Just let it be."

"Why? Can't I worry about the woman I gave the best years of my life to?"

She frowned. "Yeah, sure, you can worry about my safety, but we both know that's not what this is about."

"Then what is it about?"

"I told you we can't be together right now. Maybe someday, but not now. It's just not working."

"It can work," I protested. Believe it or not, I truly did feel like we could work things out. I'd read Keisha's diary from cover to cover, and I knew about every dude she'd ever fucked—or at least the ones up to that night with Omar. But even after all the pain she'd caused, I finally realized I would never stop loving her. No matter what she had done in the past, I wanted to believe that we could start over again: she would confess the truth to me, I would forgive her, and she would remain faithful from now on.

"No, it can't work, because you can't seem to forgive the past, and truthfully, I just want to get on with my life."

"Oh, so it's like that, huh?"

"Darnel, don't. Please don't start this."

We had arrived at the parking lot at her job, and she reached for the door handle to get out of the car. I grabbed her wrist tightly.

"You're not going anywhere, Keisha."

Rather than struggle against my grip, she leaned back against the seat and cut her eyes at me. "Look, we had some good times, Darnel, and I'll always love you. You were my first love. But—"

"But what? You got a new love now? Omar? Or maybe Mark?" I asked, throwing out one of the names I'd read in her diary.

She gave me a look that said, *"How the hell did you know about Mark?"*

"That's right. I know about Mark. I know about a lot of things."

"Whatever. You shouldn't believe everything people tell you," she said, playing it pretty cool for someone who was so close to having all her dirty little secrets thrown in her face.

"If you say so," I answered. "So you're still sticking with your story that Omar was the only one, huh?"

"Look, I'm not gonna go there with you. I made a mistake with Omar, but maybe it's best that it happened this way. Maybe it just wasn't meant to be between you and me. Have you ever thought about that?"

"Oh yeah, I've thought about it," I said honestly. "But I believe we were meant to be together. In spite of everything you've done to me, I still love you. I wanna make this work."

I looked at her for a reaction, but she sat staring at me and said nothing.

"Let's go to dinner tonight and talk about this some more," I suggested.

"I can't. I have something to do."

I was getting tired of her negative responses to everything I said. Why did she have to make it so damn hard when all I wanted to do was love her? Well, if she wanted to make this difficult, I was through being nice.

"Oh, you have something to do. Another date? Who you screwing tonight—my dad? Lord knows he's screwed everything else in my life."

Her eyes welled up with tears. "How can you say that?"

I laughed. "I'm just telling the truth. You're a fuckin' whore, aren't you? And so is he."

Keisha pulled her hand back as if to slap me.

"I swear to God, I'll smack you right back," I warned.

She lurched forward like she was going to hit me anyway, but then she dropped her hand to the door handle.

"Look, can't you see I love you?" I said, not wanting her to leave the car mad.

Before she could respond, a big dude was tapping on the driver's side window. I rolled it down and glared at him. "What the heck you want?"

He looked right past me and asked Keisha, "Are you okay?"

"Mmm-hmm," she answered quietly, wiping away the tears that had fallen down her cheek.

The guy didn't move away fast enough for me, so I looked at him and said, "Oh, are you screwing her too?"

He gave me a disgusted look and told Keisha, "I'll wait inside the lobby for you." Then he told me, "I'll be watching through the window, and I won't hesitate to call security if I see you touch her."

When he walked away, I turned to Keisha. "We going to dinner tonight, or what?"

"No, we're not." She pulled the handle and climbed out of the car.

"Well, then that flat tire is just the beginning," I said under my breath.

"What did you say?" she asked, leaning down to speak to me through the passenger's side window. "You're crazy, Darnel."

I turned and smiled at her. "Only because you made me this way. And trust me, you haven't seen crazy yet."

James

27

I liked to smell good for my lady, so I dabbed on just the right amount of cologne. Some people put on so much "smell-good" that it actually smells bad and works like a repellent. I preferred my scent to be subtle so that a woman had to get close to get a real deep whiff. Something about a woman inhaling at my neck always made me happy.

I pulled my belt through my jeans, slipped on my leather jacket, and I was good to go. I smiled as I caught a glimpse of myself in the mirror. Not bad for a man in his forties. Hell, why be modest? I took good care of my body, and I looked better than most of these young brothers out there. If I could just get rid of this cough I'd had lately, I would be straight.

The doorbell rang, and as I went to answer it, I felt an excitement building in my body. Sandra and I were going out to the Hamptons on my new motorcycle, and I couldn't wait to see what she was wearing. Last time we went riding, she wore the sexiest leather outfit. She always managed to outdo herself, even when she wore jeans and a T-shirt.

I opened the door, smiling from ear to ear, but it wasn't Sandra who greeted me. It was Crystal, and my smile fell right away.

"What's the matter? Aren't you happy to see me?"

"Sure, I'm always happy to see you, Crystal." Normally, that would have been true, but not today, not when Sandra was due to arrive at any moment. "I just wasn't expecting you."

"Really?" She gave me that flirty look that had always shot straight to my groin. Thank God I was wearing loose-fitting jeans, because this time it didn't work, and I was as surprised as she would have been if she knew.

"Well, after that last conversation, I wasn't expecting this. Once I told you I couldn't commit to a relationship, I kind of figured it was over between us."

"It'll never be over between us, James."

She took a step closer, and it made me feel a little uncomfortable, something I'd never experienced with Crystal. It was like my body was telling me it was time to stop messing with her. This blew my mind. After all these years, I had absolutely no desire to take what Crystal was offering. If this was true, I realized, then I was ready to commit to a relationship with Sandra—which was a good thing, since I'd already told her as much. I still hadn't told my kids, but I had talked to Sandra about how and when I would do it, and there was no turning back now. As weird as it felt to say it, Sandra was my woman, and even with Crystal standing before me, I had no regrets about the decision I'd made.

Crystal slipped her hand onto my arm in what felt like possessiveness, and I had to step back to separate her hand from my body. She reached for me again, and I avoided her.

"What's wrong with you?"

"I just wasn't expecting you to come over here today."

She took a step closer and I moved back.

"What the hell is going on, James? You got somebody over here?" She tried to look past me into the house.

"No. Nobody's in the house, but somebody is coming over."

"Well, then I suggest you let her know that your plans have changed."

"I don't think so, Crystal."

She eyed me with surprise. "Why not?"

"Look, I don't want to hurt you, but I'm in a relationship." This was the first time I'd said it out loud to anyone, and it didn't feel so bad. Yeah, I had definitely made the right decision. Sandra was the one.

"A what?" Her voice was close to a scream.

"A relationship. I'm in a committed relationship."

"Well, that's just fuckin' great. What the hell have I been try'na get you into for the last thirty years?" Crystal looked ready to attack me, something she'd tried once. When we were in our twenties, she caught me with a friend of hers and went ape-shit, but I was young and dumb. Older and wiser now, I knew things had consequences, which was why I was trying to get her out of here before Sandra showed up and a fight broke out.

"It didn't work out that way between us."

"'Cause you said you weren't the type to settle down. You told me how many times, James, that you never wanted to tie yourself to one woman?"

"I know what I said."

"So you were lying?"

"No, I wasn't lying. I didn't know that I would ever want to be in a relationship with anyone, so all those times, I wasn't lying. I just didn't know what the future held for me. This was the last thing I expected."

"So it's okay to use me all the time as your sex partner, but I'm not good enough to be in a relationship with?"

"Those are your words, not mine."

"Well here's some more words for you: You could fuck me, make a baby with me, and spend almost thirty years having random sex with me, but I'm not girlfriend or wife material?"

"Crystal, you're married, so clearly you are wife material. And I love my son and am grateful to you for having him, but I never asked you to get pregnant."

"Well, I didn't get pregnant by myself."

"I know you didn't."

"So now you saying what? I tricked you into having Darnel?"

"Didn't you? You thought it would make me settle down."

We'd had this same discussion years ago. I did believe that Crystal got pregnant on purpose, but after a while I didn't care, because Darnel was a great kid regardless of why or how he was conceived. But now Crystal was trying to accuse me of playing her all these years, which just wasn't fair.

"I did not get pregnant on purpose," she insisted.

"It doesn't matter now. You're a good woman, and you been good to me."

"But—"

"But I never asked you for more than I was willing to give."

"But I asked you, James. I asked you to get married and to raise our child together."

"That's all in the past."

"No, some things don't stay in the past. I gave you almost thirty years of love, and you know I was always waiting for you to settle down."

"You're married."

"And if you asked me to leave my husband for you, I would."

"He's a good man, Crystal. He loves you."

"Fuck you, James Black. You messed up my entire life. I spent my entire adult life waiting for you to grow up, and when you do, it's for another woman. Ain't that a bitch!"

"Crystal, I do love you."

"Yeah, just not in that way," she said, sounding like the words tasted bad in her mouth. "We're like brother and sister, except with a bit of incest on the side." She laughed, but not like she thought it was funny.

"Go home to your husband."

"So it's like that?"

Her breasts were heaving up and down like she was trying not to blow her top, but that air had to come out some way. It was only a matter of time before she exploded. I just hoped I could get rid of her before it happened in front of my house.

"Go home to your husband. Remember him? He's the man you married, not me," I said impatiently. To tell you the truth, I was getting tired of her pushing this issue. Why did she always seem to go deaf every time I told her something she didn't want to hear?

"Yeah, I married someone else, but whose fault is that? You know how it feels to wait all these years for a man to love you the way you deserve, and then you find out it's not that he can't but that he don't want to?"

"It's not that simple."

"Can you stand there and tell me that you ever really tried to love me the way I deserve?" Her eyes were glistening with tears now.

"Love doesn't happen just because you want it to or because it's good for you. It happens when you least expect it to, and there is nothing you can do about it."

She was starting to look like she was running out of arguments, and that might have been the end of it, if Sandra hadn't chosen that moment to pull up in a cab. Crystal saw the look of excitement and dread on my face and turned to see Sandra approaching the house.

"I guess you couldn't handle a woman, huh, James? She's a goddamned baby." Crystal reached out, and before I could react, she slapped me hard across the face. Then she turned and stomped toward Sandra. "You can have his ass! Maybe he can help you with your training wheels," she hissed as she passed Sandra and got into her car. Her tires squealed as she raced down the street.

"What was that?" Sandra asked when she approached me.

"That was Darnel's mother."

"Oh . . ." A look of recognition crossed her face. I'm sure Jamie had told her plenty of stories about my ongoing affair with Darnel's mother, and none of them were complimentary toward Crystal. "She didn't look too happy."

"I just told her I was in a committed relationship."

Sandra's eyes lit up. She leaned in and gave me a long, wet kiss. "So this means we're really gonna do this thing, huh?" she said happily.

"Yup. Next step is for you to come to church with me this weekend. What do you think?"

She jumped into my arms and hugged me tight. "Come inside and let me show you just how happy that makes me, Mr. James Black."

Darnel

28

Call me crazy . . . I'll show her crazy!

My living room looked like somebody had tossed the place looking for drugs, but that wasn't what happened. I was looking for something else, and to me, it would bring much more satisfaction than any amount of drugs. After I left Keisha at work, I raced home and spent the next three hours searching through my things, including boxes I hadn't yet unpacked from my move.

What I was searching for would be the nail in the coffin for Keisha's antics. She acted like she could behave any way she wanted, and as long as she continued to proclaim her innocence, no one but her would have to know the truth. But now that I'd read the diary, the cat was out of the bag, and I was going to make sure plenty of other people got to see the real Keisha. Like my father's friend Bishop Wilson always liked to say, "What's done in the dark will soon come to light."

I dug through some stackable plastic boxes I had stored under my bed, full of important papers and mementos I didn't want to lose. Bingo! I spotted the manila envelope I was looking for. I opened it and pulled out a stack of photos. Now, these weren't the kind of pictures you put in a frame and display in your living room. No, these pictures weren't meant to be viewed by everyone.

Keisha had always liked me to take pictures of her while we were making love. I don't remember if the first time was my idea or hers, but once she got a taste of being in front of the camera, she was like a porn star, always wanting me to bring the camera into the bedroom. I think it kinda turned her on, because she knew how sexy she looked. And it damn sure turned me on. Whenever she was away and I missed her, I would pull out those photos and let my imagination run wild.

I flipped through the photos and admired the gorgeous body that I'd once thought was all for me. I came across a snapshot of Keisha spread eagle with her hand between her legs, massaging her kitty kat. She had this gleam in her eyes like she knew exactly how bad she was being and was totally down for whatever. There wasn't anything shy about her—unfortunately, I knew that now more than ever. She was a straight-up freak.

I kept flipping through the stack, looking for my favorite, a photo of Keisha in some stripper heels and a thong. In it, she was bent over doggy style, her face turned up in a flirty way. But the picture wasn't there. In fact, there were a few of the more memorable ones missing. Was it possible that Keisha had given them to some of her other dudes? Yeah, I thought, it was possible, because once we moved in together, I basically put the pictures in an envelope in my closet and left them alone. Why look at pictures when I had the real thing in front of me? Keisha could have very easily taken a few and shared them without me ever noticing they were gone.

Just the thought of her sharing herself with so many other dudes sickened me. How could she do that to me—to us? I felt the sudden urge to call her. Maybe she'd be ready to explain herself, and then we could avoid all the ugliness that was sure to ensue if I used these pictures the way I was planning to. This phone call would be her last chance.

"Hey, we really need to talk," I said when she answered her phone.

"I ain't got shit to say to you," she yelled into the receiver.

"I'm telling you right now, if you don't talk to me, you *will* regret it."

"Leave me the fuck alone!" She ended the call.

Okay, if that's how she wanted to play it, then game on! Now she better be ready to play hardball, because that seemed to be the only way I was going to get through to her. This wasn't all about inflicting pain, though. Yes, I wanted to teach her a lesson, but in the end, everything was designed to bring us back together.

I went to my computer with the stack of pictures and logged onto MySpace. I was going to let Keisha's family and friends in on her little secret. By the time I was through, everyone would know what a freak she was. Then, once they ostracized her, she'd see that I was the only person who loved her enough to forgive her for her past. This might hurt her now, but in the end, it would bring her right back where she belonged—with me.

I'd never spent much time on the Internet, but Keisha sure did. She was a MySpace freak, always on there doing God knows what with her cyber-buddies. I never understood the obsession. It used to bug me that she needed to be in constant contact with anonymous people all over the world, like her life with me wasn't enough to keep her satisfied. Now I knew my feelings were justified, and I figured she'd probably been using MySpace to chat with some of the other brothers she was screwing.

I opened up Keisha's MySpace page and scrolled down to her list of friends. Damn! She had almost two thousand names on the list. How can one person have that many friends—at least the real kind, who will have your back when you truly need them? Half the names on Keisha's list were dudes with pictures of themselves, chests bulging with muscles, wearing nothing but some tight-ass underwear. If I had looked at her page a year ago, maybe I would have put a stop to it then and avoided a whole lot of this shit.

But I hadn't, so now I was forced to take action in another way. I clicked my way around the Web site for a while until I learned how to create a page of my own and how to invite friends to it. I created a page using the screen name "Sex Addict"; then I took all the naked pictures and scanned them into my computer. The page I created for Keisha was now covered with her porno shots for everyone to enjoy. Underneath a group of photos, I typed: **Like what you see? Let's arrange a date.** I added Keisha's e-mail address and her home, cell, and work phone numbers.

I knew MySpace wouldn't allow the site to stay up for long because of the nude photos, so I had to work fast. I figured out how to send an invitation to every one of Keisha's MySpace friends, asking them to view the page.

That should have been enough to satisfy me, considering how many cyber-friends she had, but I wasn't through yet. I wanted to make sure that her page was viewed by her real, live friends, not just her MySpace friends, who were probably just as freaky as her. I created a new e-mail address; then I went to the Web site for her job and found the employee contact page. I e-mailed all of her coworkers and any of Keisha's friends who I had addresses for. When I hit SEND, I felt good, like I had dropped a bomb that was sure to hit its target, and hit hard.

Call me crazy. I'll show her crazy.

"Ma'am, you can't go in there!"

The next day, I heard Bonita, my new secretary, yelling at someone. Before I could get up to check out the situation, my office door flew open and Keisha stormed in, looking ready to fly across my desk and hit me. Her hair was crazy all over her head, and her makeup was smudged.

"How could you do this to me?" She was screaming at the top of her lungs.

"Excuse me?" I had to force myself not to smile with satisfaction, because my little MySpace page had apparently hit her even harder than I expected. She looked tore up from the floor up.

"Those pictures on MySpace!"

"What are you talking about?" I asked as I walked toward the door. I didn't want her closing it, because I needed Bonita to be a witness to all of this. I didn't need Keisha trying to flip the script on me by accusing me of doing something to her behind closed doors.

"Those were the pictures you took of me! Why would you put them on the Internet? Why are you trying to humiliate me?" She struggled to ask the questions, because she was practically hyperventilating at this point.

"Keisha, what are you talking about?" I looked up and saw Bonita standing just where I wanted her, in the doorway, watching everything and looking nervous.

"Look, you've got to keep it together," I told Keisha. "I know you're having a hard time with the breakup, but you can't bring our personal stuff into my workplace."

"Mr. Black, I'm going to call security," Bonita said.

I nodded my approval. Keisha turned toward her, looking evil, and Bonita bolted back to her desk to make the phone call.

"Call security on him, bitch!" Keisha yelled after her. "He's the one who's crazy." Then she turned back to me and hissed, "I hate you, Darnel. I fucking hate you."

"So I guess that means we're not having dinner tonight, huh?" I said with a smirk.

"Dinner? You gotta be fuckin' kidding me!" She threw her hands in the air, and that's when I noticed she was holding copies of her nude photos. She had actually printed that shit out!

I laughed out loud, and she marched over and slapped me hard across the face. That's when the security guard raced into the room and grabbed her.

"He's stalking me! He's stalking me!" she yelled as she was being led away.

Mission accomplished.

Jamie

29

Sandra and I were parked near the entrance ramp to the Long Island Expressway, waiting for Louis to pass by. He was supposedly going on another one of his business trips out of town, but I needed to see with my own eyes where he was really heading. As we sat in the compact car I'd rented from Budget, I half expected that we'd end up following him to the airport. He told me he was driving to Pennsylvania, but maybe all these trips were excuses to travel to Detroit to see the mystery woman I'd talked to on the phone.

I still wasn't sure what to think about that woman, though. She hadn't seemed upset when I'd told her I was Louis's woman, and after the call, I saw no change in Louis. If he was screwing this woman, I would have expected her to call him and go off, and then he would have started acting funny around me. But he seemed like himself, so either he was a damn good actor, or there was some other explanation for the Detroit connection. Either way, I needed to gather more information before I confronted him, which was why Sandra and I were sitting here like two secret agents, me in a big hat and sunglasses, and Sandra with her long hair pulled back tight and hidden under her Lakers cap.

When I asked Sandra if she wanted to come along on my mission, I wasn't quite sure why I was doing it. I normally didn't like to share my issues with other women, because I didn't want to become the subject of anyone else's gossip. But depending on what I found out after following Louis, having Sandra with me might turn out to be helpful. If he tried to deny that it was him I saw, like he did when Darnel said he saw him in the city, then

Sandra would be my witness. If I lost my mind and tried to beat his ass, she could stop me so I wouldn't end up in jail like my brother did. And if, God forbid, I broke down and got all emotional in front of her, she could be my shoulder to cry on. I didn't want that to happen, because I usually only shared my true feelings with my loved ones. But this spy mission was not exactly the kind of thing I could have convinced Daddy or Darnel to participate in, so Sandra would have to do.

"I really appreciate you doing this with me," I told her as we sat and waited.

"No problem. I didn't have nothing to do until I see my man later tonight anyway."

"Oh yeah, your mystery lover. How's that going?"

"We're good." She blushed.

"That's it? Just good? I mean, you get this sappy look on your face whenever you mention this brother. You really look like you're in love."

She turned to me with a big smile on her face, almost like she looked relieved to be saying, "I am in love." I had no idea why this was such a big deal for her to tell me. It wasn't like she'd never told me before that she was into somebody.

"Well, that's nice. So, do you think he might be the one?"

"I don't know. We're not at that point. I haven't even met his kids yet."

"He has kids? How many?"

"Two."

"And an ex-wife?"

"No. He's never been married."

"Two kids and never been married? That don't sound too good. Is he at least a part of the kids' lives? You don't need to be dating a deadbeat dad or nothing."

"Oh no," she said, looking at me seriously. "He takes good care of his kids. He loves them very much."

"How come he hasn't introduced you to them yet?"

"Um, it's complicated."

"What's that supposed to mean?" I asked.

"Just that it's complicated."

She was starting to look uncomfortable, so I dropped it. I didn't know who this man was, but he sure had my girl acting all funny.

One minute she's smiling, gushing about Mr. Wonderful, and the next minute she's looking kinda nervous.

"He's taking me to church this weekend and planning on introducing me to his family soon," she said after a long silence.

"Make sure you put yourself on your best behavior. You know how family can be, especially kids. I mean, look at me with my father. Lord knows I never made it easy for any of the women he brought around."

She let out something that sounded like laughter, but there was no smile on her face. In fact, she looked kinda tense.

"Sorry. I didn't mean to scare you or nothing. I'm sure it will be fine. You know how to carry yourself. They'll love you."

"I hope so. I'm still nervous, though."

"Girl, you have no reason to be nervous. Anybody would be glad to have you in their family. If my knucklehead brother had any sense, he would have dated you himself."

"There he go, there he go!" Sandra suddenly squealed, pointing out the window at Louis's car as it sped by, then stopped at a red light up ahead.

I started my car, put my foot to the pedal, and pulled into traffic a few cars behind Louis. My adrenaline was pumping, and my heart was racing. I was scared that Louis would spot me tailing him, but I was equally nervous that he wouldn't, and then I would find out something about him that would break my heart.

As the light turned green, Sandra reminded me to stay two or three cars behind Louis. She didn't need to tell me. It wasn't hard to stay far back, since Louis accelerated to damn near eighty miles an hour once he entered the expressway. He was weaving in and out of lanes like it was nothing, and I had to struggle to keep him in sight. Damn, I always knew he drove fast, but this was ridiculous!

At one point, he was far enough ahead that I lost sight of him as he went around the bend. By the time we reached the curve, I was so excited to see his car up ahead again that I didn't notice the police car sitting on the side of the road, pointing a radar gun at all the cars passing by.

"Oh damn!" I said, tapping my brakes to slow down but knowing that it was already too late. Apparently Louis had managed to slow down enough to make it past the cop without getting pulled over. But when I looked down at my speedometer, I realized I had only managed to slow down to seventy by the time I passed the radar gun. That was definitely fast enough to earn me a hefty speeding fine.

In my rearview mirror, I watched the officer get into his car, and within seconds, he was behind me, his flashing lights signaling me to pull over. I had no choice. I wanted to know where the hell Louis was going, but not enough to risk a high-speed chase with the cops. Turning on my signal and moving over to park on the shoulder, I turned to Sandra and said, "Well, girl, get ready to get your flirt on and see if we can talk this guy out of giving me a ticket."

She gave me a nod. I looked out my windshield at the cars passing by, knowing that Louis was miles away by now. All I could think was there had to be a better way.

James

30

A couple of days after my confrontation with Crystal, Sandra and I stayed up all night talking. She let me get a lot of the past off my chest, and I didn't sense any judgment or distance from her. I told her things about myself that I had never told any other woman. I'm not just talking about the number or kinds of women I'd been with. I mean, I talked about everything, starting with Crystal and the birth of my son, and working my way forward and back. And all that talking led to a conversation about the one person who had impacted my life more than anyone else—my mother.

Sandra helped me open up about the day my mother walked out of my life for good, something I had spent forty years trying to forget. She had always been a little flaky, dropping me with my grandparents, coming home late, forgetting parent-teacher days, but she had always shown up eventually. If she had a boyfriend, she'd get caught out there for the first few weeks and forget she had a son, but sooner or later she'd come back to my grandparents' house, always reminding me that I was the only man in her life who mattered.

Shortly before my seventh birthday, the new guy she was seeing told her he wanted to marry her. For a while I thought that was great news; I'd have a dad soon. But then I overheard my grandparents talking about what a shame it was that this man didn't want to raise another man's kid. It hurt to know that he didn't want me, but I figured Mom would just leave him alone and come back to get me from Grandma and Grandpa soon.

She promised to come by on the day of my seventh birthday,

so I packed my bags, certain that she was taking me with her this time. I waited up way past the hour my grandparents sent me to bed, but she didn't show. She never came back.

My grandparents raised me from that point on, and we never discussed my mother or what she'd done to me. It was like she'd never existed. I know they thought they were doing the right thing by avoiding the subject, but not dealing with my feelings helped turn me into the man I had become. I shut myself off emotionally, vowing never to love another woman. It was the only way I knew how to protect myself. And until Sandra came along, I'd done a pretty good job of keeping up the wall around my heart.

Sandra was the first woman I wasn't running away from. To the contrary, I couldn't get enough of her, and it was scaring me. That was why I was headed into First Jamaica Ministries, to get some advice from Bishop T. K. Wilson.

"Is he in?" I walked into the church offices and smiled at Alison, Bishop Wilson's secretary, as I approached her desk. Normally she gave people a hard time when they dropped by unannounced to see her boss, but not me, because of my closeness with him and the new First Lady. Bishop Wilson was actually my best friend.

When I entered his office, he was on the phone but finished his call quickly when I stood in front of his desk.

"Well, look what the cat dragged in," he said with a grin, getting up from behind his large desk so that we could embrace.

"How you doin', T. K.? How's Monique?" I asked, referring to his wife. He had faced some opposition from church members when he chose to marry Monique, but the two of them were truly in love. I could see the depth of his feelings all over his face whenever he talked about her.

"We're both good. How you doing? How's your health?" We let go of our embrace and took a seat, him behind his desk and me in the chair in front of it.

"Well, I'm still trying to get rid of that cough, but otherwise I'm okay."

"Have you been to the doctor?"

"Yeah. He wants to run some tests just to rule out a few things."

T. K. leaned forward, looking genuinely concerned. "What do they think it is?"

"They're not sure yet. They did an X-ray and thought it might be a touch of pneumonia, but the antibiotics don't seem to be working, so the doctor wants to check things out."

"What kind of tests?"

"It's called a needle biopsy."

He cringed at the word *needle,* just like I had when the doctor told me about it at my last visit.

"Is there anything I can do?"

"I'm sure it's gonna turn out to be nothing, but a few prayers on my behalf couldn't hurt," I answered.

"Well, you already knew I was gonna do that, but if you need anything else, just let me know."

"I will," I said, suddenly wanting to change the subject. I didn't exactly enjoy thinking about my upcoming biopsy and the possible diagnosis. "That was a good sermon you gave Sunday."

He looked surprised. "You were here? 'Cause I sure didn't see you."

"I was here. I slipped out the back when the service was over. There are a few of the sisters I'm trying to avoid."

"I see. Another one of your love triangles gone wrong?" He didn't try to hide the disapproval in his eyes. He might have been my friend, but T. K. was still a man of God, and he'd always made it very clear to me that my womanizing was a character flaw that disappointed him.

As I stared at my friend and pastor, I just couldn't find the words I wanted to say. I wanted to explain how I'd cut off all the women I'd been seeing, many of them members of T. K.'s congregation. Part of the reason I had been avoiding the church was because a few of them weren't so happy about my change. I also wanted to tell him about the catalyst for my actions—about how I felt about Sandra, but the words just wouldn't come out. I think I was afraid he would laugh at me. He'd known me long enough and watched me juggle enough women that it would be hard for him to believe I was actually falling for someone.

"Is something wrong, James? You okay?"

I stood up. "Look, T. K., never mind. I shouldn't have come here. I don't want to bother you with this. You're a busy man. We can talk another time."

I took a step toward the door.

"James, sit down." His voice was deep and commanding.

I turned and did what I was told. Nobody went against Bishop Wilson when he was using his preacher's voice.

"We've been through a lot, you and me. You know you can talk to me about anything. So talk." He sat back in his chair.

I sighed, knowing there was no turning back now. "I know this is going to sound crazy coming from me, but, T. K. . . . Bishop, I think I'm in love." I lowered my head. Speaking the words out loud to another person took more out of me than I'd expected. Well, I thought, at least I'd had a chance to practice in front of my friend before I had to tell my kids.

He sat up in his chair. "You think you're in love?" He looked like he was smirking. I was sure he wanted to laugh.

"I know, crazy, right? James Black love-struck. But it's true."

"Wow. Now, that I wasn't expecting." He sat back and rested his arms across his stomach. "Although I did always warn you that it would happen to you someday, didn't I?"

I cracked a smile. "Yeah, I guess you did."

"I love it when I'm right."

"I know you do," I joked.

"Does she make you happy?"

"Yeah, she makes me happy. Happier than I've ever been." I looked up at the plaques adorning his office walls as I thought about all the wonderful things that drew me to Sandra. "T. K., I don't even think about other women. I wake up thinking about only her. There aren't enough words to describe how she makes me feel."

"You don't have to explain it. I've been there," he said with a laugh. "So I guess you really are in love."

"Yep, I'm in love."

"Well, that's a wonderful thing." He nodded in support. "Being in love is a gift from God."

"I guess. But it's not that simple."

"Oh, Lord, please don't tell me she's married."

I wanted to be offended by his assumption, but how could I? I'd earned my own reputation by spending plenty of time with other men's wives in the past. T. K. had delivered more than a few sermons on the issue of adultery over the years, and I'm sure many of them were written with me in mind.

"No, she's single."

He breathed an audible sigh of relief.

"But she is the same age as my daughter. They're friends."

"I see. You never make things easy, do you?"

"No, I guess not."

"Is she in love with you?"

"Yes."

He thought for a moment before he spoke. "Well, James, if you're both in love, then I can't really see a problem. Sometimes love happens in unexpected ways, but I always say you should follow your heart. If God has brought love to you after all these years, don't turn your back on it just because of an age difference."

"I'm just afraid that people will think I'm some type of dirty old man. I mean, it's not that I haven't been with younger women before, but never with somebody young enough to be my daughter."

"Well, you're probably going to get a few stares at first, but people will get used to it. Deacon Gifts's wife is twenty years younger than he is, and no one seems bothered by their marriage."

I wanted to point out that in spite of her youth, Deacon Gifts's wife looked older than he did, but I kept my mouth shut.

"So what does Jamie think about this? Must be nice for her to have her friend around."

This was the part I was dreading most. "I haven't told the kids yet. You know how Jamie can be when it comes to the women in my life."

"Oh my . . . So, exactly when do you plan on telling them?"

"After church this Sunday."

"James, do me a favor. Make that a priority. The longer you wait, the harder it's going to be. It's never good to keep secrets from family members. In the meantime, I'll be prepared to counsel Jamie, 'cause, my friend, she's not going to take this very well."

"You don't have to tell me that. That's why I haven't said anything yet. I just don't know how to approach it without upsetting her."

"I don't know if there is a way to tell her without at least some amount of difficulty, James. But you'll think of the best way, and then you'll do what you know is right. Don't keep this a secret any longer. It's not good for Jamie, and it's not good for your new relationship either."

"I know. And I'm going to take care of it soon."

"Good. Glad to hear it. I'm happy for you, James."

"Even though she's so young?"

"Love is one of the great mysteries. You can spend your entire life looking for it or running from it, but the Lord will give it to you in His perfect way in His perfect time. This is a joyous occasion, my friend. I look forward to seeing you two in church on Sunday."

"Thanks, T. K."

"Thank you, James. I am always grateful to hear of God's work in action."

I took a deep breath, pushed the button to close the sunroof, and clicked the locks open on my Lexus. "Well, we're here."

This was the moment. We were in the church parking lot, and there was no turning back now. We were finally going public with our affair—well, I guess it wasn't exactly an affair, since we were both single, but it did feel like a forbidden romance. I mean, in this church alone, I was sure we were about to encounter at least a dozen women who did not approve of our relationship, whether because of Sandra's age or because she was taking me off the list of eligible bachelors. I felt a little bad bringing Sandra into the lion's den for our first appearance as a couple, but she'd assured me she could handle anything these women had to dish out.

The scent of Red by Giorgio Beverly Hills, Sandra's fragrance for the day, filled my nose as I clambered out of my car and strolled around to help her out. She was looking exquisite in a white suit I'd bought for her on one of our frequent trips to the mall. Not that she wasn't sexy in her tight jeans and form-fitting dresses, but she really cleaned up well. I was sporting my white Armani suit, and together we sure made a handsome couple.

As soon as I opened Sandra's door and she stuck one of her muscular legs out, we got our first dose of the reactions to come. Althea Jones, one of my exes, pivoted her head around on her neck like Linda Blair in *The Exorcist* when she saw us. She stared through the window of her beat-up Buick, which was parked next to us.

What the heck is going on? was written all over her face.

I know Sandra saw Althea out of the corner of her eye, but she ignored her as she took my arm and we walked toward the church. We wove our way through the groups of people still milling around the parking lot. Plenty of them stopped their conversations and did double takes as we neared them, as if they couldn't believe what they were seeing. I had been a member of this church for a long time, and I'm quite sure no one could remember a time when I had shown up to a Sunday service with a woman proudly on my arm. I felt their eyes on our backs as we took long strides past them to the entrance.

Bishop Wilson was getting into the welcoming part of his service when we walked in. He glanced up and gave us a warm smile, and I smiled back nervously. Sandra actually seemed to be handling the attention better than I was, but that was probably because she hadn't slept with half the women in the room. She couldn't really imagine what they were whispering as we passed by, but I could—all too well.

We sat down in the middle of the church, and I stared straight ahead. I didn't want to make eye contact with anyone or see the malicious expressions that I was sure some of the women were wearing. Oh, if I could be a fly on the wall after service today, I was sure I'd hear plenty of un-Christian comments being shared among some of the more jealous sisters from my past.

As the service progressed, I relaxed a little and actually allowed my eyes to wander around the congregation. The sad thing was that almost everywhere I looked, I saw a woman who I'd been intimate with at one time or another. For the first time in my life, I felt ashamed of my promiscuous behavior. Maybe loving Sandra had me looking at all women through different eyes and realizing that they deserved much more respect than I'd ever shown them. I wished I could erase some of the things I'd done with different women, particularly those for whom I'd never felt anything. My body felt heavy with regret.

I accepted the angry glares coming from some of the women as penance for my past misdeeds. One by one, they craned their necks around or stole glances in our direction, then rolled their eyes at Sandra and me, pushing their noses up in the air for emphasis. Amazingly, Sandra seemed unfazed by all of it. She let their unfriendly expressions roll right off her and just kept listening to Bishop Wilson's sermon with a serene smile on her face. She must have sensed my uneasiness, because every once in a while, she reached out and squeezed my hand or rubbed my back in a supportive gesture.

As for me, I couldn't tell you one word that the bishop preached. I couldn't concentrate on the service because of all the accusing eyes on me. Whoever said people could hurt you without lifting a finger ain't never lied. I imagined the angry looks as bullets being shot at me from all over the church. And that saying about hell hath no greater fury than a woman scorned, oh, I had no doubt now that it was the truth.

When church was finally dismissed and the last "Amen" was uttered, I got up and took Sandra's hand. I was headed for the back door in a hurry, but I didn't get far before someone stopped us.

"You never showed up for dinner the last time I invited you," said Sister Jessica. She was a homely sister who used to be my Sunday meal ticket. At least I'd never slept with her.

"Good to see you," said Monica Jones, venom dripping off of each word she spat at me. I'd had a short fling with her.

"Yeah, long time no see," Aurora Williams said, her lips curled up in disgust. A piece of spit flew between her teeth and landed in my right eye.

I was wiping my eye when Brother Hayes came up to me, grinning like a Cheshire cat. "How you doing, man?" He gave me a firm handshake, but he wasn't looking at me. He couldn't take his eyes off Sandra. "You lookin' good, James."

"I'm glad you could make it to service today, Deacon Black." Deacon Howard's eyes drank in Sandra's figure also.

"That's a beautiful woman you're with," commented Marvin Rivers.

Sandra accepted his compliment graciously.

The attention was becoming overwhelming. Between the women who wanted to kill me and the men who wanted to be me, Sandra and I couldn't get close to the exit. Fortunately, Bishop Wilson approached us, and the others, especially the jealous women, took the hint and backed off.

"Brother Black, so good to see you." A broad smile lit up his face. "And who is this beautiful lady you've brought with you today?"

I introduced Sandra to Bishop Wilson. He extended his hand and shook hers. "I've heard a lot of good things about you," he said.

Sandra broke into a brilliant smile. "Bishop, I've heard wonderful things about you, and your sermon was so moving."

"Thank you. I'm glad you enjoyed it. Do you have a church home?" he asked as he helped guide us toward the exit.

"Actually, I don't. After your sermon today, I was thinking I'd like to join your church."

As we stepped outside, I stood back and watched how Sandra engaged Bishop Wilson in conversation, promising to return next Sunday and even expressing interest in volunteering in some of the church's community service projects.

I was so proud of the way she handled herself, not once allowing anyone to intimidate her or shake her confidence. She was an amazing woman, and in spite of our age difference, we were meant to be together. We'd cleared our first hurdle as a couple and came out without a scratch. Now came the hard part—convincing my daughter to accept us.

Darnel

31

It had just turned dark when I drove past Keisha's apartment Sunday night. It pissed me off to think of it that way, as her place. To me, it would always be our place, and if I had anything to say, it would be our place again, once I convinced this hard-headed woman that I was the only one who would accept her with all her flaws. Keisha was damaged goods, but I still wanted us to work things out and be together. As soon as she realized that I loved her in a way that none of these other dudes ever could, she would stop messing with them and come back to me.

When I looked up at the windows, I saw that the lights were off, but Keisha's car was parked out front. It was too early for her to be sleeping, so I wondered if maybe she was up there with someone, and if so, who. Was it Omar, or some other fool I knew? She seemed to have a taste for my friends. I wanted to get out of the car, climb the fire escape, and peek in the window, but it was dinnertime, and most of the neighbors were home, so that wouldn't work.

I called her on her home phone, but she didn't answer, even though I had dialed *67 to hide my cell phone number. It was possible she just wasn't home. Maybe someone had picked her up or she had walked somewhere nearby in the neighborhood. I so wanted to climb that fire escape to see if she was in there. I sat in my car for a while and considered taking the risk, but then I remembered the night I'd spent in jail and decided it wasn't worth it.

I drove over to a couple of restaurants and neighborhood bars we used to frequent, pretending to check out the menu for take-out while scanning the room for Keisha. But she wasn't at any of our haunts. Where could she be? The thought of her being in that apartment with some man was tearing at my soul.

I dialed her at home again, and the answering machine picked up. Shit! Where the hell was she? It was driving me crazy. Desperate for some type of clue, I punched in the code to retrieve the messages from the machine. Instead of playing back messages, the automated system kept recording. Obviously, she'd changed the code. This just pissed me off even more. Why would Keisha change the answering machine code unless she had something to hide?

I was determined to find out exactly what she didn't want me to know. I called her answering machine over and over, each time trying a new code. I punched in her birthday, my birthday, her mother's birthday, our anniversary, and Valentine's Day. None of them worked, but I refused to give up. I was on a mission. After everything I'd read in her diary, I didn't see how she could have any more secrets left to hide, but obviously she did.

Finally, I punched in Omar's birthday, and bingo, the messages began to play. There is no way to truly describe how furious this made me. Omar's goddamn birthday was her code, like he was her man or something! I wished he was there right now so I could bash his head in.

I sat in my car and listened to Keisha's messages. I could feel my body tense up when the first voice I heard was a man. But it wound up being a bill collector, which made me smile. Yeah, she couldn't handle her lifestyle without my help, could she? Keisha liked to shop and go out to fancy restaurants at least once a week. She was probably missing a brother for real now. Maybe I could use her financial situation to my advantage later. She was being stubborn, but once she got desperate enough for some help with her bills, she'd have to come crawling back to me. Her parents damn sure weren't going to help her out after they already lost so much money on our wedding.

Speaking of her parents, the next call was from her mama, and she sounded hot, telling Keisha how upset her father was that she hadn't been returning their calls. It seems that after the shame they suffered on our wedding day, her parents weren't too happy with her. Her mama said they were still waiting for her to come by to discuss how she planned on helping them pay off all the debt they owed to the catering hall and the florist. Yeah, if she didn't get her act together real soon, I was going to have to pay her parents a visit. Maybe we could put our heads together and come up with a way to make Keisha behave.

So now I had two more ideas for how to get the upper hand in this situation. I was feeling good. Then I skipped ahead to the next message and heard some Barry White–sounding motherfucker that pissed me off so bad I nearly put my hand through the windshield.

"Keish. Mmm-mm-mm. Last night was da bomb, girl. You made a brother bust a nut for days. I'm just glad you got over that loser Darnel and let a real man get at you. Lookin' forward to doin' it again. Holla at your boy."

Halfway through the message I recognized the voice.

"Trey? She fucked my boy Trey?"

Trey and Angela were a couple that Keisha and I hung out with all the time. Angela and Keisha grew up together, and they were supposed to be tight. Angela had been one of Keisha's bridesmaids before the wedding was canceled. I got to know Trey when we started hanging out as couples, and he wasn't a close friend like Omar or nothing, but we were cool. He damn sure wasn't supposed to be fuckin' my girl! And I was sure that Angela wouldn't be too happy either if she knew that Keisha was messing with her husband.

Truthfully, I never would have suspected Trey of screwing around on Angela. It wasn't like he couldn't get plenty of sex at home. Angela had always been the beauty that most of the guys in the neighborhood lusted after. Her parents were from Ethiopia, so she had those angular cheekbones, long straight hair, perky breasts, thin legs, and a big ol' ass. And from what Trey told me, she was addicted to sex. He swore he had to hit it five or six times a week or she would be complaining. Not too many men would have the bad sense to cheat on her.

But Trey's message left no doubt in my mind that he was that stupid, and so was Keisha. I guess those MySpace photos hadn't been enough to make Keisha understand my point of view. I wasn't playing with her ass. I'd been made a fool of once, and here she was screwing around with another one of my boys. The first time, Omar was the one who felt the pain. This time, pay-back was about to be a bitch for Keisha.

I pulled back onto the road, headed for Trey and Angela's house. This shit was about to get real ugly.

Angela answered the door, looking surprised to see me. I hadn't talked to either one of them since the day before my wedding, and I had no idea what lies Keisha had told about me since then.

She gave me that look I got whenever I went to church nowa-days or ran into any of Keisha's friends: sort of a cross between "I'm so sorry" and "Damn, ain't you a big fool." It dawned on me that as one of Keisha's close friends, Angela probably had some idea of what Keisha had been doing behind my back all these years. Little did she know that she really should have been concerned about what her man was doing behind her back.

"Trey ain't home."

"Good. I need to talk to you anyway."

"About what? I don't want to get in the middle of this thing with you and Keisha. She's been my friend a long time, and I don't have nothing to say to you about her."

You will in a second, I thought.

"I just need you to listen to something." I pulled my cell phone out of my pocket.

"Darnel, it don't matter. I want to stay out of your business with Keisha."

"That would be nice, except this is your business too." I turned on the speakerphone on my cell and then dialed Keisha's num-ber.

Angela stood there impatiently with her hands on her hips. When she heard Keisha's outgoing message, she opened her mouth to protest, but I put up a hand to stop her. I punched in Omar's birthday, then skipped over the first two messages. It looked like Angela's knees almost gave out on her when she heard Trey's deep voice coming through the speaker.

"Oh my God. Is that who I think it is?" she asked when the message ended and I hung up the phone. "Is that real, or are you just playing games?"

"I wish it was a game, but it's as real as that night I caught your girl screwing Omar."

I know it sounds coldhearted, but I had to suppress a smirk. She was all cocky when she first opened the door, talking about too bad for me but she wasn't gonna talk about her friend Keisha. Now she knew how much it hurt. I felt a little sorry for her, but you know what they say: Misery loves company, and now Angela and I had plenty in common. Unfortunately, she wasn't ready to believe it just yet.

"Wait a minute. The message says it was left today, which means they would have been together last night. But that's not possible."

"Why not?"

"'Cause he came home and had sex with me."

"Was he home all night?"

"No, he came in around two, but if he was sexing Keisha, he wouldn't have come home and had sex with me."

"Well, I guess he had a two-in-one night," I suggested sarcastically. This dumb chick didn't get it. She was being played just like me, yet she didn't want to see what was right before her eyes. "You gonna tell me there's no way at all that he could have done her, taken a shower at her place, and then come home to you for round two?"

She didn't answer me right away. She was probably considering the possibility. When she spoke, it became obvious that she'd decided it was true.

"I'm gonna kill Trey! Then I'm gonna shove his balls down that ho's throat."

I was glad to see we were finally on the same page. With Angela pissed at Keisha, she might become very useful to me.

"I'm really sorry I had to be the one to tell you about this. It's just that you know what I went through, and I don't like to see anybody else get stabbed in the back by a friend the way I did."

She nodded her understanding.

"How could they do this? I knew she wasn't faithful to you, and she was always talking about this guy and that guy, but to do this to me? She coulda had a whole bunch of dick, but Trey? I was her friend."

She had just admitted that she knew Keisha had been cheating on me, and she hadn't done shit to stop her. I wanted to curse her ass out, but really, there was no need. The information I'd just brought to her hurt way more than anything I could have ever said.

Angela really looked devastated. I knew exactly how she felt. I wondered if she wanted to beat Keisha the way I'd done to Omar.

"Angela, I'm sorry . . ." I put a hand on her shoulder.

"No, they're the ones who are gonna be sorry when I get through with them. I'm gonna kick him in the nuts and make it impossible for him to even think about sex. That muthafucker!"

I figured it was time for me to get my ass out of there. She was getting pretty agitated, and besides, I'd done all the work I needed to do here. I was quite sure she would come up with some plan that would make Keisha's life a living hell.

"I'm gonna go. Call me if you want to talk." I gave her a pat on the shoulder and turned to leave.

"Wait! Where you going, Darnel?" Her voice had suddenly transformed from an angry growl to a soft purr.

I stopped and looked at her.

"Maybe you and I need to fuck."

"Excuse me?"

"Trey and Keisha need to know exactly what it feels like." She moved closer to me, opening up her robe to expose her naked body.

Her body was slamming, and it was there for the taking. All I needed to do was say yes. But I couldn't. I reached out and closed her robe.

"I can't."

"Why not?" She looked like she'd never been turned down before.

"I just . . . We're friends, and you're only saying it because you're angry." I tried to reason with her.

"Damn right, I'm angry, and I want angry sex. She don't give a fuck about you, Darnel. You were the good guy she was marrying after screwing a whole lot of bad boys behind your back."

"I'm not like Keisha. You're beautiful, don't get me wrong, but I can't stick my dick somewhere just to get revenge. I tried that; it didn't work."

"So that's it? You just punk up like some pussy?" She sucked her teeth. "No wonder she always needed to mess around."

That was a low blow. In a lot of ways, I could see why Angela and Keisha got along together. They were both triflin' as far as I was concerned.

"Look, I'm sorry if you're pissed off, but like I said, screwing somebody just to be screwing doesn't work for me."

"You know what, Darnel? Something must be wrong with you. Most men *prefer* screwing just to screw. And sometimes women need it too." She pulled her robe back to expose her body again. This crazy woman really thought she was gonna change my mind.

"Well, I'm not most men."

"Well, then get the hell outta here, 'cause right now I got to go and find myself some revenge dick."

Angela slammed the door in my face, but I wasn't even a little bit upset, because I had accomplished what I came for. I knew she wasn't about to let Keisha get away with screwing her man. She would make Keisha pay for sure.

Jamie

32

Sundays had always been church days in our house when I lived with Daddy. We'd get up in the morning, have a big breakfast, and go to church until the early afternoon. Daddy never missed a Sunday. He was a deacon, and his best friend was the pastor, so he attended faithfully every weekend, no matter what he might have been doing the night before. I loved going to church with Daddy, even as a teenager, because it was like a social event. With my father's status as the pastor's good friend, I felt like a mini-celebrity.

But since I'd started dating Louis, who wasn't a church person at all, I'd been neglecting my Sunday ritual. I have to admit I did miss Bishop Wilson's sermons, but more than anything, I missed the gossip. I tried to stay in the loop by talking on the phone with people who I knew had attended and could fill me in on all the juicy stuff. This was just harmless fun as far as I was concerned. But this one Sunday, I got a taste of what it felt like to be the subject of the gossip—or at least related to the subject.

My phone rang at about one o'clock, the time that the late service normally ended.

"Girl, where you been hiding?" Monica damn near took my ear off with her loud voice. Her father and Daddy were both deacons, so we kinda grew up together. Monica and I were never close friends or anything, though, so I knew that if she was calling, it was because something interesting went down during today's service. And, yes, I was dying to know.

"What's up, Mo?"

"I don't know. You tell me. That's why I'm callin'."

I could just see her chubby face rolling around her neck. Monica was one of those women who said just as much with her hands and her facial expressions as she did with her mouth.

"Girl, what are you talkin' about?"

"Your daddy."

"My daddy? What about him?"

"I seen your daddy at church today."

"Yeah, and? He's there every Sunday, Mo." I know she didn't call me for this nonsense, especially when I had Louis standing near the stove, motioning for me to get off the phone. We had woken up late, and I was supposed to be in the middle of making breakfast, which I had been doing before the phone rang.

"Okay, Louis," I whispered. "I'm coming."

"Yeah," Mo said. "I know he goes to church every Sunday, but who was the jailbait on his arm?"

Jailbait? What the hell was she talking about? My father had done a lot of scandalous shit in his days, but I'd never known him to date anyone who could be considered jailbait. And no matter who he was fooling around with, he always kept that shit separate from his church life. My father never had anyone on his arm, except maybe some lady he was escorting to her seat. Maybe Monica was just playing with me.

"You know my daddy. That was probably just one of his friends," I said nonchalantly.

"Ha!" She let out a laugh. "She was a lot of things, girl, but I promise you she wasn't no friend. Not the way he was escorting her around like she was the Queen of England or something."

She laughed again. I laughed along with her, but I wasn't quite sure why. Her story was starting to make me uneasy, because Monica was usually pretty accurate with her gossip. If she was saying my daddy had a woman on his arm during service, there was a chance it was true. I couldn't wait to hang up the phone and call Daddy to find out what was going on.

"Trust me, Mo. It was nothin'," I said, hoping to end the conversation and get her off the phone. But she just kept going.

"So you cool with that?"

If what she told me was true, she knew damn well I wouldn't be okay with it. Since when had I ever been okay with any of my father's women?

"What'd she look like?" I couldn't help myself. I knew I was basically gossiping about my own father at this point, but it was necessary if I was going to get all the facts I needed before confronting him.

"She had real good hair, not no weave, with a nice wave pattern. And slanted eyes, almost like she was mixed with Chinese or something."

I pulled the phone from my ear, staring at it as the pieces started to fall into place. Sandra never did seem too upset about the fact that Darnel wasn't interested in her, because she found herself a new man pretty fast. And then there was that night she went out to dinner with my father after they watched a game together. It had seemed innocent enough then, since Darnel had stood her up, but now I felt a little sick as I wondered if that was the night she got her claws into my daddy. Finally, I flashed back to the day Sandra told me she was going to church this weekend with her mystery man. And now here was Monica telling me that a young half-Asian-looking girl was on my father's arm at church. That was too much of a coincidence; it had to be her.

"Oh my God, that bitch!" I mumbled to myself.

"You there? Jamie, you there?" I could hear Monica even though the phone wasn't on my ear.

"Yeah, I'm here." I picked the phone back up. "Mo, was the woman with my father about our age?" I already knew what her answer was going to be.

"Yeah, and, girl, even in that suit she was wearing you could tell she had a body."

I hated to admit it, but Sandra did have the kind of body that turned heads—and now she was using it to cast her spell over my father. What could be worse?

"Girl, your daddy's the talk of the church."

"So, were they standing close?" I asked, trying to hold on to some small hope that there was another explanation for this. Maybe Daddy and Sandra had struck up a friendship, you know, like a father-daughter type of thing, and he was just trying to get her into church.

I knew I was grasping at straws with that scenario, and Monica proved me right when she said, "Standing close? Girl, I couldn't tell where one ended and the other began. She was holding on to him for dear life."

"Oh, really?" *What she should be doing is holding on to that pumpkin head of hers before I knock it off,* I thought.

I glanced up at Louis, and since I wasn't standing over a hot stove cooking our meal, he didn't seem happy. But with news like this, neither was I. Monica's conversation had ruined any appetite I had. Still, I had promised Louis a big meal of crab cakes and eggs, so it was time to get off the phone.

"Yeah," Mo continued, "and let me tell you about the bangin' suit she was wearing. The two of them both had on white, and—"

"Mo, we're about to eat, so let me holler back at you later." I slipped the phone closed before she could get in any more comments.

Louis must have seen the expression on my face and known something was wrong, because instead of nagging me about the food, he came closer and asked, "Everything all right?"

"I'm going to kill her ass."

He took a step back. "Who?"

"Sandra."

"Sandra? Why?"

"Get this—she's screwin' my father."

"Nah!" He seemed surprised, but in typical guy fashion, he looked like he would have been impressed with my father's catch if I weren't standing in front of him. "You sure?"

"He took her to church. Do you know how embarrassing that is?"

"Well, maybe they're just friends."

Louis was using the same rationale that I'd tried on Monica, but now it just sounded stupid. "We're talking about James Black here, Louis. Be for real. He's slept with half the female congregation, for God's sake. Why would he need to bring a 'friend' to church with him?"

"I don't know. Does it really matter?"

"Of course it matters! It means he was trying to let everyone know he's unavailable!"

"Is that really a bad thing? Maybe your father is finally ready to settle down after all these years. You should be glad if he's found someone he cares about enough to bring her to church."

"Uh-uh," I protested. "That dirty heifer knows exactly what she's doing. Trust me; she is not the one for him."

"Honey, your father is a grown man," Louis said, just like he did every time I tried to vent about my father's dating habits with him.

"My father is a man who thinks with his dick!"

"Maybe he really likes her."

"He doesn't know her. I know her, and she's a gold-digging tramp. I'm gonna pull out all her hair! How dare she do this to me?"

"To you? Come on, she's your friend. And how is her dating your father a problem? She seems like a nice enough girl."

"That ho deliberately set out to get my father. She's after his money."

"You ever think maybe she really likes him?"

"Oh, please. She really likes his bank account."

I headed toward the bedroom, pulled out my clothes, and got dressed in a hurry. I was going over to Daddy's house to handle this.

"You are not leaving," Louis said sternly.

"I have to put a stop to this!"

"It's their business, Jamie."

"Well, I'm about to make it mine." I picked up my keys. "I'll be back in a while."

"Jamie!" I heard him calling after me as I walked out the door, but there was no stopping me now.

I was hot as I pulled out of the driveway and drove toward my father's place. There was no way I would allow Sandra to keep her hooks in my father, because I knew there was no way she really cared about him. If she did, she would have understood how close Daddy and I were, and she would have come to me in the beginning. Not that she needed my permission to date my father, but out of respect, she should have said something. I gave her the opportunity early on when I asked about her mystery lover, but no, like a lying tramp, she refused to give me any details while she snuck behind my back and started seeing Daddy.

I couldn't wait until I got to Daddy's house to speak my mind.

When I got there, I would deal with him, but in the meantime, I wanted to talk to Sandra. I put on my Bluetooth and dialed her cell phone number.

"Hello?" Sandra sounded all cheery, like she'd just gotten some. Of course, I thought. I should have known she would still be with him if they'd left church not too long ago. I felt like throwing up. It took everything I had not to curse her ass out yet. That would come in due time, but I didn't want to alert them or they might leave the house before I had time to get there.

"Hey, girl." I tried to sound as upbeat as possible.

"Hey, Jamie." She said my name as if she wanted someone else in the room to know I was on the phone. That wench really thought she was slick.

"What's up, girl?" she asked.

"Nothing. I was just riding. I'm out over by your house, and I was gonna stop by. What you doing?"

"Oh, girl, I'm not even home. I'm over at my man's house."

I wanted to punch something the way she said "my man" all romantic and shit.

"That's right. You two go to church today?"

"Yeah. It was nice. What about you? You go to church?" This chick was trying to be funny. She knew damn well I hadn't gone to church. If I had, she'd be picking her teeth up off the floor.

"So, did you get to meet his people yet?"

"No, not yet, but soon."

"Girl, what you waiting for? You really like him, don't you?" I asked as I pulled up to the curb in front of Daddy's place.

"Yeah, but we want the timing to be right."

"No time like the present. You never know. You might meet one of them today." I was really struggling to keep the sarcasm out of my voice now. "Hey, Sandra. Let me ask you a question."

"Sure. Anything."

"Well, this question's a little personal."

"You can ask me anything, girl. There's no secrets between us."

I wrapped my fingers tight around the steering wheel, wishing it were her neck. I took a deep breath. "No secrets? Okay. Here goes: Sandra, are you screwing my father?"

There was a distinct pause before she asked, "What would make you think that?"

"Oh, I don't know. Maybe 'cause I can see you through the front window of his house."

"Oh shit! James!" I saw her peering through the curtain, pointing at my car.

When Daddy came into view, I just lost it. I jumped out of the car and raced to the front door.

Daddy pulled open the door and stepped outside, his body like a road block to the entrance.

"Jamie, that's far enough for right now."

"Let me by, Daddy. I'm gonna kick her half-Korean ass."

He put his hand out like a stop sign. "You're not getting in my house unless we're going to talk about this like adults. And you're not acting like one now."

"How am I acting, Daddy? Like I just got betrayed by my friend and my father? This is worse than what Darnel went through with Keisha!"

"I didn't want you to find out this way."

"What way did you want me to find out? How could you do this to me?"

"I'm sorry."

"Sorry I caught you?"

"I didn't intend it to happen, but it did."

"She's a tramp, Daddy, nothing but a gold-digging whore."

"Jamie, she's one of your closest friends."

"Newsflash, Dad: a close friend doesn't seduce your father behind your back."

"It wasn't like that," he insisted.

"So she hasn't been lying to me all this time? And you haven't been lying to me?"

"We have to get past this."

"I'm never getting past this. I hate her."

"If you can't, then we're going to have a problem, because I love her."

Did he just say he loves her? This just kept getting worse.

"Daddy, you and I will never have a problem, but me and Sandra? Our friendship is over, and we will always have a problem."

"Then I'm sorry, Jamie, but you can't be here." He turned and placed a hand on the door knob. "When you're ready to act like an adult, then you can give me a call and come by to talk. Other than that, I'll see you at work." And then he did something I would not have expected in a million years: he went back inside and closed the door in my face.

Darnel

33

"I hope you're enjoying your sushi," I whispered into my cell phone to Keisha. "But I thought you didn't like Japanese food."

From where I was sitting in my car on the second-tier parking lot, I had a perfect view of Keisha and her date sitting inside the sushi restaurant. Earlier, I had followed them from her apartment, careful to trail them by half a block so they never saw me. Lucky for me, they went to a restaurant with large picture windows, and they were seated at a table right in my line of sight.

I had sat in my car and fumed for a while as they ordered their food and chatted. It was torture watching how relaxed she looked, laughing and giving him flirtatious smiles and patting his hand. And that dress she wore—dude was practically getting a free peep show as low cut as it was. I had planned on just watching and taking some video to use against her later, but I couldn't stand it anymore after I watched that fool feed Keisha a piece of sushi with his fingers. She ate it like she was performing a sex act. I swear, she licked that brother's fingers, no doubt letting him get a preview of what she would be doing with her tongue later.

That's when I picked up my phone and called her.

"Darnel? How'd you know where I'm at?" I watched her jump up from the table and leave her date. Now she was no longer in view, but I could hear the panic in her voice. The guy she was with was no Prince Charming; he didn't even bother to follow her to see if she was all right.

"I can see you," I told her in my best imitation of a horror-movie voice.

"Where are you?"

"I'm in the same place you're at."

As I spoke to her, I took a few more pictures of the guy at the table. Whoever he was, he probably had a wife or a girlfriend. Once I found her, I'd be sure to share my photos with her.

"Why are you doing this to me?"

"Hmm, you think you slick. Think you can be with any man you want. But I ain't having it." I clicked off my phone.

I watched her head back to the table and start talking to her date, who had finished half the order of sushi while she was gone. She was gesticulating wildly, waving her cell phone in the air, a panicked expression on her face.

As Keisha and her date started looking nervously around them to see if I was seated somewhere nearby, I thought back to some of the more romantic dinner dates Keisha and I had been on over the years. For a moment, I felt nostalgic. I really loved doing those things with her: eating under the stars, finger-feeding each other, playing footsie under the table. Yeah, this had been our foreplay. We had a way of looking at each other that was our silent language when we were ready to get busy. But now that was all over—or so Keisha thought.

I went from the warm-fuzzy feeling of reminiscing about the past to straight rage. How did Keisha think she was going to end it with me and pick up with some other guy—or should I say other guys—just like that? It's like we never even happened. What about all our dreams to have children and build a life together? Didn't that count for something?

Everything Keisha knew about pleasing a man, I taught her: how to cook my meals, how to run my bathwater, and how to wash my back. At one time, I thought I was the one who taught her how to make love so a man would never want to leave her. Keisha had a muscle inside her that would drive a man out of his ever-loving mind. Shit, look what it had done to me. Now she thought I was going to let her give all that good lovin' to someone else? Was she crazy? I invested too many years in her to let her go this easily.

In the restaurant, I saw Keisha handing her phone to her date. He punched a few buttons, and then my phone began to ring. I flipped it open.

"Yo."

"Man, you better stop bothering her."

"Brother, you better watch yourself or that bitch gonna give you a disease like she did me. You know she got herpes, right?" I lied. "You think I'm trippin' for no reason? She's burning, dude. Ask anyone." Then I hung up.

He said a few things to Keisha at the table, and then I watched them leave the restaurant, their meal unfinished.

Good. Now, that's what I'm talking about. I pumped my fist in the air, feeling victorious. But I also knew the show wasn't over yet. I leaned forward in my car to enjoy the scene that was about to unfold before me.

I watched brotherman hand the valet his ticket and wait in front of the restaurant with Keisha. Finally, the valet pulled up with his Range Rover.

Keisha's date's face changed as soon as he got a good look at his ride. His eyes flew wide open, and he looked absolutely livid. Just reading his lips, I knew he was screaming, "What the fuck?"

He started shouting and cursing his behind off. He stalked around the car, looking at the deep key scratches running down both sides. In a flurry of motion, he began stomping; then he grabbed the valet attendant, who was a small man, by the collar. I could tell the valet was pleading with him, telling him he didn't know what had happened to his truck.

Meanwhile, Keisha was jumping up and down, screaming for her date to stop. She tried to pull him off the valet, but her date just kept shaking the little guy up and down like a rag doll. Keisha looked totally distraught.

I was laughing my ass off. What a mess!

Two bouncers raced out of the restaurant and pulled the date off the valet. "Oh, this gets better," I said out loud.

For a moment, it looked like the bouncers were going to hold him there until the police came, but they let him go after he calmed down and started talking to them. Keisha joined the conversation, probably telling them all about my phone call. Pretty soon, even the valet attendant looked like he felt bad for Keisha's date. As she spoke, they checked out the scratches, shaking their heads and glancing around them. I was sure they were looking for me, like I'd be stupid enough to lurk in nearby bushes or something.

I was laughing so hard, tears were rolling down my face. Maybe Keisha had finally learned her lesson.

Jamie

34

"Hell yeah. I'm getting a device. I'm gonna track that Negro everywhere he goes. Somebody gonna be a sucker, but it damn sure ain't gonna be me." I laughed out loud to myself before clicking on the BUY arrow.

After my failed attempt at following Louis, I'd done some research and learned that GPS devices were not only affordable, but wireless and battery operated. Hell, I could even put it on my father's credit card and call it a business expense, 'cause as far as I was concerned, I meant business. Daddy wouldn't mind paying anyway; he wouldn't want some man taking advantage of his daughter. Besides, he was too busy screwing my so-called friend these days to even notice.

If I ever caught Louis, I could just imagine the look he'd have on his face, trying to explain to my daddy that he was innocent. But his words would fall on deaf ears. My father had probably invented most of the excuses, so there was no way he'd be fooled by any lie Louis could come up with. In fact, if my father wasn't so wrapped up with his new woman, I could have talked to him about all the evidence I'd found, and he'd probably already have the whole thing solved for me.

I was so busy daydreaming about Daddy leaving Sandra and coming to my rescue that I didn't hear the front door of the real estate office open. I only looked up when I noticed a shadow. Standing in front of my desk, staring at me, was that skanky ho Keisha.

Her face looked pretty much the same, and she had lost some weight, but her wardrobe had completely changed. I guess now that the wedding was off, she'd decided to let her true inner ho come out. She used to wear "good-girl clothes" from Gap and Abercrombie, but now it looked like girlfriend had hit the straight-up tramp rack at Forever 21. Her breasts were all but spilling out of some tight polyester knit top, and her booty was hugged up in some stretch jeans that were so tight you could see every dimple in her ass. What my brother ever saw in this hooker, I have no idea. She sure didn't look like nobody's wife. This wench was no more than a booty-call girl all the way.

"I'm here to see your father." She tried to act all serious, like I was supposed to step out of the way and lead her to Daddy's office.

I gave her a disinterested look and took a sip of my Starbucks caramel macchiato. "He's not here. He's at a doctor's appointment." I turned back to my computer to complete my Internet order.

"Look, I need to see him. Your brother Darnel done lost his mind."

Oh, I know she didn't just come in here talking about my family! I shot her a nasty look.

"He's stalking me!" She tripped all dramatic like I gave a damn.

"Look, your cheap ass deserves whatever you get." I stood up so we were at eye level. "Now, if you don't mind, I got work to do, so why don't you carry your ass on out of here."

"If y'all can't stop Darnel from acting crazy, I'm gonna have to call the police." Maybe she thought she could bully me into listening to her crap about my brother, but I called her bluff.

I grabbed the phone off the cradle. "Here. Use my phone. Call the cops; call whoever. Just don't think you're gonna come in here and tell me about my brother when you're the nasty-ass ho who screwed his best friend."

She flinched a little, and I could tell my words had hurt. "You don't understand. Darnel has lost his mind. He followed me to a restaurant and spied on me while I was having dinner with a friend."

"Please. How the hell you know he was spying on you?"

"He called my phone while we were eating and told me he was watching."

I have to admit, if she was telling the truth, it did concern me a little bit. What the hell was Darnel watching her for? But then again, maybe it was no big deal. I mean, it wasn't really any different than me following Louis the other day, was it? Except that Louis and I were a couple, and I was trying to figure out what the hell was going on with my relationship. It isn't stalking if you're in a relationship with the person, but Keisha was no longer Darnel's woman. Was he really stalking this girl?

Oh hell, even if he was, I wasn't about to do anything to help her ass.

"Keisha, why are you telling me this?"

She didn't answer my question but instead kept ranting and raving. "He keyed my friend's car outside the restaurant."

"Hmmm, and did this 'friend' happen to be male?" I asked sarcastically.

It slowed her roll, but only for a second. "Yeah, he was male, but so what? That don't give Darnel any right to ruin the man's Range Rover."

"First of all, I don't know that he did anything to your friend's Range Rover. Secondly, my brother might be a little jealous. So what? Not too long ago, you were supposed to be walking down the aisle with him. You broke his heart. Far as I'm concerned, that gives him the right to be a little jealous."

"A little jealous! He got my answering machine code and broke up a close friendship of mine by using a message he heard."

"Shoot, there must have been something in that message that your friend didn't like. I can probably guess what that was about."

Again, I stunned her silent for a second. Keisha knew I didn't like her, but I think she still expected me to react differently to the things she was telling me. If she were anyone else, I might have had more sympathy, but this woman wasn't getting a drop of it from me.

"He sent naked pictures of me to all my friends."

I sat back down, because this chick wasn't worth me standing. "Why were you stupid enough to let a man take naked pictures of you in the first place?" Like I said, no sympathy from me.

She shed a few tears, but knowing her, they were probably fake. "He's crazy, Jamie. You gotta believe me."

"Keisha, you reap what you sow, and your ass deserves a whole lot worse."

"He's going to jail if he keeps this up. Is that what you want?"

"I want you to stay the fuck away from my brother."

"But I'm not the one stalking him!"

"You must be doing something . . . waving that skank ass up in his face. I don't care if Darnel sits on your front steps and tells everybody who passes what a nasty, lying tramp you are. You ruined my brother's life, so you deserve whatever the hell he decides is proper repayment for the pain you caused him."

"You don't get it, Jamie. It isn't some revenge thing he's doing. It's sick *Fatal Attraction* shit. It's not funny and it's not just mean. It's crazy."

"Bitch, you're crazy. Crazy if you think that my brother doesn't deserve somebody a whole lot better than you."

"So you don't give a damn if Darnel goes to jail? The stuff he's doing is scary. He's not dealing with a full deck, and if you won't listen, then I'll just wait and talk to your father."

"My father knows what a ho you are. He ain't gonna believe a damn thing you say."

"This ain't about what happened before the wedding. You and your father don't have to like me. But you have to do something about Darnel. Your brother ain't right, Jamie."

I was getting tired of hearing her talk about my brother. "Yeah, well, neither are you." I got up again and stepped from around my desk.

"You're gonna be sorry you didn't listen to me. This could end up tragic."

"Get outta my office or it's gonna really end up tragic—for you! My family don't want nothing to do with you. Go find some other fool to marry you, you tramp."

Keisha stomped out of the office, slamming the door behind her.

I almost got up and ran after her to punch her in the face, but I didn't have time for that shit. I had to finish searching this Web site to see if there was any more spy equipment I could order.

Hmm . . . maybe a wiretapping device would come in handy. I wonder if they work on cell phones.

James

35

"Well, Doc, what's the word?" I asked, trying to sound casual even though my heart was pounding in my chest. I'd had the needle biopsy performed and was back in the doctor's office to get the results. Before the test, he had described a few of the possible things they might find, some of which could simply be cleared up with the right prescription. Others were much more serious. Of course, I was hoping it was one of the more minor things, but when he spoke, he delivered the worst possible news.

"James, you've got cancer."

Those four words struck as much terror in my heart as if a missile had gone straight through me, but as I looked at Dr. Martin, my general physician of the last twenty years, I could respect his direct approach. Although his bedside manner wasn't the most tactful, I could always count on him to give it to me straight. Anyway, how could you sugarcoat this type of news?

I swallowed hard and looked directly into Dr. Martin's eyes. He was sitting behind his mahogany desk. "How far advanced is it?"

The doctor handed me a written report. "Well, you have what we call Stage One-B lung cancer."

I glanced down at the medical report, unable to focus on all the unfamiliar terms on the page. I put the report back in the envelope and slipped it into my jacket pocket. "What does Stage One-B mean?"

"There are four stages of cancer. Stage One-B means your tumor is still relatively small, but it's begun to grow into the inner lining of your lung. It doesn't look like it's spread anywhere else."

My stomach twisted as I imagined something growing in my lungs, eating me from the inside. "Is it treatable?"

"Yes, we're lucky to have caught it at an early stage. Many people wait too long or don't show symptoms, so we don't find it until it's too late."

"So . . ." I paused, almost unable to ask the question because I was so afraid of the answer. "So, I still have a chance?"

"James, there are no guarantees, but we have better treatments now than ever before. At this stage, it's very possible to beat this. I have every hope that you will live to a ripe old age."

I felt my body relax slightly. I trusted Dr. Martin, and if he was saying I had a good chance, then I believed him.

"So what do we do now?" I asked.

"I'll refer you to an oncologist, and he'll probably want to get you started on radiation and chemotherapy as soon as possible to see if we can shrink the tumor that way."

"Wait a minute. Doesn't that stuff make you sick and make your hair fall out?"

"Yes, but it can also save your life. This isn't the time to be vain."

He was right, of course, but considering I was in love with a much younger woman, I didn't exactly like the idea of harsh treatments that would probably make me age overnight. Sandra shouldn't have to walk down the street with a man who looked old enough to be her grandfather, for God's sake.

"Well, what about surgery?"

"The risks are much greater. If we cut you open, there is always the possibility of introducing infection into your chest cavity, which would only make things more complicated."

He didn't have to explain any further. As soon as he said "cut you open," surgery stopped sounding like a good solution to me anyway. Besides, Sandra always said she didn't care about my age. I was sure she'd support me through this no matter what I looked like. Yeah, I thought, I could probably rock a bald look.

"Well, if I was gonna get cancer anyway, I guess I could've kept smoking," I said, trying to lighten my mood and ease my fears.

"No, you needed to quit." Dr. Martin's voice remained grim. "How long has it been since you quit?"

"I quit three or four years ago."

"That's good. This could have been worse if you were still a heavy smoker."

I couldn't imagine much worse than the diagnosis he'd just given me, but I'm sure he'd had to tell other patients there was no hope. At least there were treatments they could try for me.

He opened a drawer in his desk and pulled out a business card, which he handed to me. "This is one of the best oncologists in New York. I want you to give his office a call and make an appointment. I'll have all of your test results faxed over to his office so he can get you started with treatments as soon as possible."

I took the card and put it in my pocket with the envelope I'd shoved in there before. Then I stood up and shook his hand. "Well, Dr. Martin, let me go home and digest this."

After I left the doctor's office, I walked to my car like a zombie, climbed in, and just sat there. I was too numb to drive. Without warning, the doctor's words hit me all over again.

I have cancer. Oh shit.

I grabbed the steering wheel, put my head down on it, and cried like a baby, something I hadn't done in years. I'd never felt so vulnerable, so out of control. My shoulders heaved up and down as I sobbed. Finally, when I had no more tears left in me, I pulled myself together and wiped my eyes.

Now I had to try to think rationally about this situation. I started up the car and decided to go for a drive before I went home.

Questions repeated over and over in my head like a broken record: God, why me? Why now, when I'd finally found the right woman? Was this punishment for all those years of womanizing? If I had ever worried about a disease taking me down, it was AIDS. But since they discovered the virus, I'd been careful to protect myself with condoms, so I just assumed I'd live to be an old man. Cancer had never crossed my mind.

Why hadn't I stopped smoking sooner? I picked up the habit when I was a teenager, so I'd been poisoning my lungs for almost thirty years before I quit. Jamie used to beg me to give it up, but I couldn't help it. I truly enjoyed smoking and even got into cigars once in a while. I saw no reason to quit until I started noticing that I was getting short of breath sometimes, and I developed a cough that never quite went away completely. Now I regretted every last smoke I'd ever had, but it was too late.

I could only hope and pray that the treatments Dr. Martin talked about would work. He said he was sending me to one of the best specialists. But even the best doctors were wrong sometimes. What if the radiation didn't work? What if my cancer got worse and spread?

I thought about my family and what would happen if I died. My kids were grown, but they still needed me. Jamie was only twenty-five, practically still a child as far as I was concerned. And I'd been spoiling her ever since she came to live with me at the age of twelve, so there was no doubt she needed someone to take care of her. Louis seemed like a good man, kind of reminded me of myself when I first started my own business. Maybe someday they would get married as long as he'd gotten the blonde out of his system, but their relationship was still too new for me to feel sure that he was the right one to take care of my baby.

And then there was Darnel. He was going through so many changes over his breakup with Keisha, and I wanted to be there to help him through it any way I could. I still had regrets about his childhood; I knew he resented the way I treated his mother, and I felt like I still needed time to make it up to him. I loved that boy, and before I left this world, I wanted to make sure he understood just how much.

Thinking about Darnel, my mind went to his mother. Crystal was a good woman. She had loved me for thirty years, and I knew I hadn't taken good care of her heart. I would always love her as the mother of my son, but I couldn't take back all those years she'd wanted a commitment I couldn't give her. Hell, with my new diagnosis, maybe in the end she was better off that she didn't end up stuck with me.

My thoughts went to the woman who had only recently gotten me to change my ways and commit. Sandra. How was she going to take this? Would she feel stuck? She said she didn't care about our age difference, but I was pretty sure she didn't expect me to go and get seriously ill. I didn't want to become a burden to her.

And that's when I found my resolve. I would not become a

burden to anyone, I decided. I would fight this cancer with everything in me, and I would come out the winner. I would do everything the doctors told me to, and then some. I would go on the Internet and research complementary therapies to help me through the chemotherapy, and I would visit the health food store and start taking better care of my whole body. Between Darnel and Jamie and Sandra, I had people who needed me, people who loved me, and I was not going to let them down. I was not going to die.

I picked up my phone and called Sandra.

"Hey, honey," she answered. "Are you on your way home?"

"Yeah, I'll be there soon."

"How was your doctor's appointment?" She thought I had just gone for a regular checkup. I hadn't told her about the biopsy, because I'd been hoping the doctor would tell me nothing was seriously wrong. At some point soon, I would have to tell her the truth, but today, I just wanted to go home, hold her in my arms, and make love to her.

"It was fine. Everything is going to be just fine."

Jamie

36

"And the worst part about all this mess is that these two have been sneaking around up under my nose. They didn't even have the human decency to come clean with me." I paced up and down the floor in our bedroom, pounding one fist into the other palm to release some of my frustration.

Louis grunted indifferently.

"Louis, do you hear me?"

I looked back at him. His eyes were glazed over with disinterest. He was looping his tie as he stood in front of the mirror. For the first time, I noticed he was wearing a black suit, a new one. This was the second time in a month that he'd dressed up, but I was too riled up to visit that issue right now.

"You know, I can't believe this shit."

Louis still gave me no response. I spun around on my heel and stared at him. Was he deaf or something? I had been ranting for at least a half hour, while he dressed in silence. In fact, I'd been ranting for the past two weeks about Daddy and Sandra being together, and every time, Louis acted like I wasn't even speaking.

"Louis!"

Finally, he turned to me and sighed, saying, "You can't believe what, Jamie?"

I threw my hands up in frustration. "Have you heard a word I've been saying to you?"

"Yes, Jamie, I've heard every word you've said, but I don't know what you want me to say. Your father is a grown man, and no matter how mad it makes you, he is free to be with whoever he wants."

Well, Louis would sure never win any awards for sensitivity. Couldn't he see I needed him to agree with me? I wanted him to take me in his arms and say, "Everything is going to be all right, baby." But he just wouldn't. He seemed bothered just by the effort it took to finally answer me. Here I was, trying to tell this fool about my daddy and Sandra and how she would ruin his life, and Louis went ahead getting dressed calmly, like I was discussing the weather and *he* had the weight of the world on *his* shoulders.

"First of all, I can't believe what my daddy is doing with Sandra. Why doesn't he realize how wrong and sick this whole thing is?"

"Why is it sick? I thought you liked Sandra."

"I *did* like her, when I thought she was interested in my brother. But now I can't stand her sneaky ass. She's just a gold digger trying to get my daddy's money." My voice rose an octave.

"How do you know she's after his money?"

"Please. I've known her long enough to know that she's always about the money when it comes to her men."

"Really? Then why were you trying to set her up with your brother?"

He had a point there, but I wasn't about to admit that to him. "Shut up, Louis."

"Gladly. But you're the one who was screaming at me to talk to you about this." He turned back to the mirror and buttoned his suit coat.

"This is serious, Louis. She is not good enough for my father."

"Excuse me, but you don't think any woman is good enough for your father." Louis started heading for the bedroom door.

"So what? Don't you understand that I'm only trying to think of what's best for him? What's wrong with watching my father's back?"

He stopped in the doorway and turned to face me. "Like I've told you before, your father is a grown man. He's allowed to make his own mistakes, and I think you need to stay out of it."

"See, this is what I've been talking about." I stepped up and invaded his space. "When I come to you all stressed out, needing a little support from my man, what do you do? You shut me down. You don't listen."

Louis cleared his throat and pursed his lips, looking like he had to stop himself from cursing me out or pushing me back up off him. "Look, I've got to be at a meeting in the next half hour, and I'm running late, so I have to go. We'll pick this conversation up when I get back."

"Why you got to go now?" I snatched the car keys out of his hands, putting them behind my back. "And why you wearing a suit?"

"Give me my keys back, Jamie." He reached for them, but I dropped them into my bra.

"Stop playing with me, Jamie. Believe it or not, I've got problems, too, but you don't ever see me in here whining to you about my shit, do you?"

"Oh, so now I'm whining?"

"Jamie, I don't have time for this right now."

The next thing I knew, Louis pinned my arms behind me, reached into my bra, and took his keys back. "I've got things to take care of right now. Like I said, we'll pick up this conversation when I get back."

He was in too much of a hurry to get out of here, as far as I was concerned. But that's all right. I had something for him. The moment he left, I was gonna be on that computer, tracking his ass. The equipment I ordered had finally arrived. I'd attached the tracking device to the underside of his car, and I couldn't wait to start trying it out.

"By the way, where did you say you were going again?" I asked as he headed down the hall.

"I told you I've got a meeting at work." Louis gazed down at his wristwatch. "And you have me running late."

"If you're just going to work, then why are you wearing a suit?" I followed Louis down the stairs. "You don't even have that type of job."

"I have a business meeting," he said, standing by the front door.

"Is that right, Rashid?"

"Yes, that's ri—" He stopped speaking midsentence, and his mouth was still hanging open. I swear that if he weren't a black man, I would have seen all the color draining from his face. He was cold busted, and he almost lost his composure for a minute there. But he pulled himself together pretty quick.

"I don't know why you just called me by another man's name, but trust me, you getting into something you really don't want to get into. So please, don't go there."

"So is your name Rashid or Louis?"

"You just don't get it, do you?"

"Get what?"

"There are some things you're just better off not knowing, Jamie."

"What the heck are you talking about?" I shouted.

He shook his head. "We'll talk about this when I get home." He put his hand on the doorknob.

"I just want to know who you screwing!" I spat out.

Louis turned around and looked at me, but he remained calm. His voice was deadly quiet when he spoke. "Jamie, I know you don't want to believe this, but I'm not screwing anyone but you."

"Oh yeah? Well, you damn sure coulda fooled me the way you been acting lately."

"I've gotta go. Like I said, we'll talk about this when I get home."

"Talk to me now or I won't be here when you get back," I warned. At first it was just a threat to stop him from walking out that door, but suddenly, I realized that I actually meant it. I had reached my breaking point. Between the stress of my father's new relationship and the constant fear that Louis was cheating on me, I couldn't take it anymore. Either he was going to show some loyalty and stay home with me now, or I was leaving.

"Well, if you really want to leave, then maybe that's for the best." His decision broke my heart. "I just want you to know that I love you, Jamie. And I always will."

Louis closed the door behind him. I picked up my keys and threw them at the closed door, knocking the wind chime on the back of it to the floor. The noise it made echoed throughout the hallway.

I was done, and so were we.

I walked over to the phone and dialed.

"Daddy, I need to come home. Louis and I had a big fight, and I told him I'm leaving."

My father didn't ask any questions, which is what I loved about him. We might have been fighting about his latest woman, but he was always there to come to my rescue when I needed him.

"If that's what you need to do, then come on home, baby."

"Thank you, Daddy. I love you."

"I love you too. But, Jamie . . ."

"Yes?"

"Just one thing: if you can't get along with Sandra, you might as well stay right where you are."

Out of the frying pan and into the fire. I'd be escaping my problems with Louis but would be forced to tolerate Sandra. Really, at this point, I had no choice.

"I'll be nice, Daddy. I promise."

Darnel

37

I pulled up to the curb in front of the Nichols's house like I'd done hundreds of times in the past. During that time, it had been just as much my home as my dad's or mom's places were. I always felt comfortable in that house.

Perhaps it was because the Nichols treated me like the son they never had. Don't get me wrong; they had a son, but let's just say he found his calling in the bottom of a gin bottle. So I was the son they'd wished for: educated, well mannered, and career-minded, not to mention the most important fact of all—I treated their daughter like a princess.

Too bad Keisha still hadn't learned to appreciate me as much as her parents had. She was making me work pretty damn hard to get our relationship back on track, but I had faith that eventually she'd see things my way and drop all these other guys so we could be together again.

I got out of my car and headed up the walkway, where I was greeted by Keisha's mom. She was standing at the front door, smiling from ear to ear. Considering the words she'd had for me when I told them the wedding was canceled, I was relieved that she seemed to be back to her old self.

"Darnel! Oh my God, baby, how are you?" Gloria Nichols swept me into a bear hug, her huge breasts smashing against me.

"How are you, Mrs. Nichols?"

"Mrs. Nichols, my behind. I know you didn't just insult me like that, Darnel. I am always gonna be Momma to you."

I smiled. When Keisha and I got engaged, her parents asked me right away to start calling them Momma and Pop.

"All right, Momma."

Gloria smiled as she took my hand and led me into the house. "I been wanting to call you. I just didn't know what to say."

"Don't worry about it, Momma." I placed my arm around her and we hugged again. "I understand. This has been hard on all of us."

We sat down on armchairs in the living room, and Gloria just kept smiling at me.

"It's so good to see you. Pop is out right now, but I wish he was here. He'd be so happy to see you. He talks about you all the time."

"I miss him too," I said. "Maybe I'll call him for a round of golf."

"Oh, I'm sure he would love that." She just kept smiling at me as if I were a lost child and she'd finally found me. "So what brings you by?"

"Did you think I would forget your anniversary? Thirty years today, isn't it?"

"I can't believe you remembered!" Gloria was grinning again.

"Don't I always remember?"

"Yeah, you always were thoughtful like that," she said, suddenly losing her smile. "You're one of the good guys. I really wish things could have turned out different for you and Keisha. It would have been a beautiful wedding. . . ."

This was good. She'd already brought the conversation right where I wanted it to be, and I hadn't even been there five minutes yet.

"Speaking of the wedding, there's another reason I came by."

"What is it?"

I pulled an envelope out of my coat pocket and handed it to her.

"What's this?" she asked, looking down at it.

"Well, I know that you and Pop went into a lot of debt for our wedding. It's not your fault that it didn't happen, so you shouldn't take the entire hit."

I watched her open it, and the look of surprise on her face was well worth it. Ultimately, this was all part of my plan to get

Keisha back, but I honestly did like her parents, so being able to make Gloria happy was an added bonus.

"Oh my God, Darnel. This is eight thousand dollars. We can't take this. We can't take eight thousand dollars from you."

"I thought I was going to need it for a down payment on a house, but it doesn't look like there's going to be a house. So please, Momma, let me do this for you. You and Pop have been good to me." If my plan worked and Keisha and I did eventually want to buy a house together, I still had another fifteen thousand saved up. I liked her parents, but I wasn't stupid enough to give them everything.

"Okay," Gloria agreed with no further argument. She got out of her seat to hug and kiss me.

After she sat back down and took a moment to get over her excitement, she asked, "So, how you doing, honey?"

"I'm all right. But I'm not going to lie. I still can't believe Keisha did this to me."

She shook her head sadly. "I don't know what happened. I mean, I've heard things, but I'm not really sure what happened. And Keisha won't tell me anything."

What was she supposed to tell them, that she was a whore?

"Maybe she's right, Momma. You really don't want to know what's going on. Trust me; the truth ain't pretty." I stood up like I was preparing to leave, but she gave me a look that said *You're not going anywhere until I get some answers.*

"Darnel, I want to know."

"Are you sure? 'Cause I'm telling you, it's pretty hurtful stuff."

"I'm sure."

"All right, but after you read this, just remember that in spite of everything that's happened, I love your daughter." I handed her Keisha's diary.

"What's this?"

"It's the truth. Some of it might be hard to read, but I'm going to be right here."

She opened the book, looked at the first page, and asked, "Is this Keisha's handwriting?"

I nodded. "I highlighted some of the important parts." Thank

God she didn't ask how I had gotten a hold of her daughter's diary.

An hour later, we heard the front door open and then a pair of stilettos clackety-clacking quickly through the house. We looked up to see Keisha standing in the doorway to the living room. I knew she'd be stopping by after work to visit her parents on their anniversary. She was getting so predictable.

"What are you doing here?" she shouted.

I smiled and nodded toward her mother, who was slowly closing the diary.

"Oh no." Keisha didn't take her eyes off the diary, but I could still see the fear in them.

"Darnel, you son of a bitch."

Suddenly, Gloria screamed, "I know I raised you better than this!" She marched over to Keisha, raised her hand in the air, and, with full force, slapped her daughter across the face. It left a bright red handprint.

Keisha burst into tears. "Momma!"

"Don't you *Momma* me, Keisha. You should be ashamed of yourself."

"He's the one who did this." Keisha pointed at me, then lunged, but Gloria inserted her large body between us.

"He's the one who wrote this?" Gloria waved the diary toward Keisha. "Do I look like a fool? I know your handwriting, girl. I can't believe I raised you to be so nasty."

"Momma, you don't understand. This is just Darnel's way of trying to come between us. He's stalking me, Momma."

"Shut it, just shut it, all right?" She raised the diary as if she might hit her with it. "You slept with this man's friends! Gave them stars for their performances, and you expect me to believe *he's* stalking *you*?" I'd never seen her so mad at Keisha. "I never thought I'd ever say this about my own daughter, but Keisha, you're a whore."

I could see the hurt in both mother and child as their tears flowed freely. I went to Gloria and placed my arms lovingly around her shoulders.

Keisha threw her hands in the air. "I hate you, Darnel!" she screeched.

"I'm so sorry you had to go through this, Momma," I said smugly. I hugged her protectively as I heard Keisha stomping down the hall and out the door.

Once again, mission accomplished.

James
38

T.G.I.F. As a hardworking man, I'd always looked forward to my weekends, but ever since I became involved with Sandra, they were even more special. I could come home from work on Fridays knowing that she and I would have three nights and two days of uninterrupted time together. I loved every minute I spent with her. I had fallen in love with this woman. That was part of the reason I was afraid to tell her about my lung cancer.

In the time since my cancer diagnosis, I had been wrestling with a healthy dose of denial. I had the phone number of the oncologist, but I had yet to call him. Once I saw a specialist and set up a schedule for chemotherapy and radiology treatments, then my disease would be a reality—one I would have to share with Sandra. Every time I thought I had worked up the nerve to tell her what was happening inside my body, I looked at her sweet face and decided I didn't have the heart to take away her smile. So instead, I decided to wait a few weeks before making my appointment, and I was determined to enjoy every last minute of the remaining days when our relationship wouldn't be affected by cancer.

Every weekend that we'd been together, I'd given Sandra some token of my affection. It started out with a bouquet of flowers, a box of gourmet candy, or a nice bottle of wine for us to share. Having lost her father at a young age, I figured she probably wasn't accustomed to getting gifts from a man. I think that's why her face lit up every time I brought her something. It didn't matter if it was something as small as a single rose; she just seemed to love getting gifts. And I think I felt as good giving them to her as she felt receiving them. I loved to make her happy.

Lately, my giving had become a little more extravagant, moving from flowers and candy to cashmere sweaters and gold jewelry. I think subconsciously I was trying to make her as happy as possible so that those feelings might carry her through the rough times that were ahead. The way she responded, with her whole heart, body, and soul, she took my breath away—not to mention the added bonus that as the gifts got a little more expensive, the sex seemed to get more explosive. It was a win-win situation for both of us. I soaked up every moment, planning to remember them in the coming days when chemotherapy would be beating me up.

During the week, I had to hide Sandra's gifts in the trunk of my car. It wasn't that I was worried about her finding them in the house if she happened to come over. It was Jamie I was worried about. She had never liked to see me spending money on any female but her. And, truthfully, it was never much of an issue, because my heart was never in it with those other women, so my wallet wasn't opening too often anyway. But this time was different. My feelings for Sandra were genuine, and I was gladly spending money on her. I knew that eventually Jamie would find out, but she would just have to deal with it this time, because Sandra wasn't going anywhere. No one, including my daughter, was going to tear apart the relationship we were building.

Plenty of women from my past had been trying, though. After I brought Sandra to my church, word spread, and I'd had plenty of unexpected visits and phone calls from women thinking they could draw my attention away from her. But each of them left unsatisfied. In the past, I would tell a woman not to expect much more than sex from me, because I was not the relationship type. Now I was telling these women not to expect *anything* from me because I *was* in a relationship—a committed one. Needless to say, plenty of women went away unhappy.

One night, I took Sandra out to a sushi restaurant where we happened to be seated across the room from a woman I had fooled around with for a short while. The affair hadn't ended well, and she seemed determined to be a thorn in my side from that point on. This night, she was having dinner with her husband, but she still didn't waste any time coming over to our table to speak her mind.

"James Black, you oughta be ashamed of yourself for keeping this *young* woman out so late," she said, twisting up her face in disgust at the word *young*.

"Thanks for the advice, Sister Lucille. But Sandra is a grown woman and quite capable of making her own decisions."

"I'm sure she is," Sister Lucille continued, "but does her father know she's out with you?"

To Sandra's credit, she did not jump in Lucille's face the way I think Jamie might have. She remained cool, calm, and collected and let me handle the situation—which I did gladly.

"Actually, Sister Lucille, Sandra's father passed away quite a long time ago. But let me ask you something: Does your husband know you were out with me the night before your wedding anniversary last year?"

Sandra stifled a laugh. Again, I was proud of the way she was handling herself. She was confident enough that it didn't even faze her to hear me talking about a past affair. And why should it? She knew for sure I was going home with her that night.

Sister Lucille, on the other hand, was quite ruffled by my question. She looked nervously back at her husband, then quickly said, "Well, y'all enjoy your meal," and rushed away from our table.

When she was gone, Sandra lifted her cup of sake and proposed a toast. "To letting go of the past."

"And looking forward to the future," I added before downing my drink.

Now, I was looking forward to taking my beautiful date out to dinner again, but not before I presented her with another gift. We had been at the mall together recently, and I had noticed her checking out the designer purses in Saks. I returned to the store without her and picked out a midnight blue leather bag for her. I'd had it specialty wrapped and purchased a card to go with it. I'd obviously never been the mushy type, but with Sandra I found myself writing verses of love poetry inside the card. This woman just did something to me that brought out romantic tendencies I never knew I had.

When she showed up at my place, I was happy to see she

wore a formfitting dress that would look perfect with the new bag I'd bought. I couldn't wait to give it to her.

"You ready? I'm starving," she said after giving me a long, wet kiss.

"Just let me get something before we go."

When I brought the gift out from my bedroom, where I'd put it earlier, her eyes lit up in the way I'd hoped they would.

"Oooh, that's a big one. What's in it?"

I laughed at how cute she was. "It's not always the size that matters, you know," I teased.

"Maybe, but ain't no denying I'm a woman who loves a big package," she said with a seductive glance toward my crotch. My manhood immediately sprang to attention. My lungs might have been in trouble, but my equipment below was still working just fine.

"Go ahead, open it."

She tore off the paper, and her smile got even bigger when she saw the Saks logo on the box. I was looking forward to the expression I just knew would be on her face once she saw the bag I'd picked out. But her reaction was nothing like I expected.

"Oh . . . ," she said, sounding a little deflated. "It's cute. Thanks, honey." I got a lousy peck on the cheek. And even worse, she didn't even bother to take out the card and read it before she set the box down on a nearby end table.

"Okay, can we go eat now? I've been craving lobster all day."

I didn't answer her for a second, because I was still trying to decipher the unexpected response I'd gotten. Where was the giant hug and kiss I'd been anticipating? I mean, I had gotten more appreciation after the sterling silver necklace and earrings I gave her last week. This bag had cost a whole hell of a lot more.

"But I thought you'd be happy about getting a Coach bag. You don't like it?" I asked.

"Oh no," she said blandly. "It's nice. It's just that . . ." Her voice trailed off, and instead of looking happy, she looked utterly disappointed, like the kid who gets a pair of flannel pajamas for her birthday.

"It's just that what?" I couldn't imagine what was wrong with the bag. Whenever I bought Coach for Jamie, she couldn't thank me enough. But Sandra seemed totally unimpressed with my gift. "Well, it's just that what?"

"It's just that I was looking at the Gucci bags in Saks, and when I saw the box, I thought—"

"You thought I spent more than two thousand dollars on a handbag?" I asked, amazed that this five-hundred-dollar purse was suddenly something so unimpressive.

She looked confused as she said, "Yeah. Why? You don't think I'm worth it?"

"Now, Sandra, you know how special you are to me. But cut me a little slack here, will you? I need some time to get used to the idea of spending as much on a handbag as I do on my mortgage." I chuckled and tried to make my voice sound light-hearted, but it didn't stop her from pouting.

"But it's what I want."

"Hell, baby, I want a Maybach, but you don't see me being unhappy rockin' my Lex," I joked, though part of me wasn't finding this very funny. This was the first time Sandra's behavior reminded me of the spoiled tantrums Jamie sometimes threw.

"James, this is not funny to me. I don't think there's anything wrong with two people in love giving each other what they need, even if it means sacrificing once in a while. I mean, don't I always give you all the sex you can handle?" She reached out and caressed my arm. "Even when I'm really tired, don't I always take good care of you? Don't I let you bend me into any position you desire, no matter how uncomfortable? Aren't you the one who told me you've never met a woman who was so eager to give head whenever and wherever?"

As she spoke, I could feel myself growing harder and harder. And the more turned on I became, the less important that two thousand dollars felt. Oh hell, what would it hurt to give the girl what she wanted? I had no doubt that if I did, she would make sure to return the favor, and at that moment, my imagination was running wild with the possibilities.

I bent over and picked up the box that contained the Coach bag.

"How hungry are you?" I asked.

"Pretty hungry. Why?"

"'Cause I was thinking that maybe we could stop at the mall

on the way to the restaurant and exchange this bag for a Gucci. What do you think?"

"I think you're the most wonderful man in the world," she said, giving me a squeeze that let me know I had a great night to look forward to after dinner.

Jamie

39

It was the worst one week, three days, seven hours, and six minutes of my life. I felt like crap, I looked like crap, and all I could do was think about the crap going on between me and Louis. I missed him so much—despite the fact that he was a no-good, cheating son of a bitch. I'd shed more tears in these past two weeks than I had in my entire life. Throw in the fact that Sandra was over every single day playing house with Daddy, and I was a basket case. I'd been spending as much time as possible locked in my room, just to avoid looking at my father and that gold digger. And because I was in my room alone, there wasn't much to do but nap all the time. I was falling into a serious depression.

As I started drifting off to sleep once again, I heard my phone vibrating on the nightstand next to the bed. The only person calling me at this hour of the night would be Louis. He'd been blowing up my phone every night, but I'd been ignoring him. It would have been too easy for him to talk me into coming back home, as lonely as I was feeling. But now that he was calling for the hundredth time tonight, I was pissed off enough to answer just to curse him out.

"What!" I yelled into the phone.

"Jamie?" He sounded relieved to hear my voice, but I would make sure that didn't last for long.

"What?" I asked again.

"Sweetheart, please, let me explain."

"Explain what, that you're cheating on me?"

"I'm not cheating on you." He actually sounded sincere, but then so does every man who gets caught with his hands in the cookie jar and tries to talk his way out of it. I wasn't about to fall for his act.

"What about the white woman?"

Silence, then, "What white woman?"

I laughed. "The white woman my brother saw you with in Manhattan."

"Jamie, I told you Darnel was mistaken."

"So, was my dad mistaken when he caught you with a blonde at that restaurant you took me to? Can you explain that?"

From the way he hesitated, I could tell he was caught off guard. What, did he think my father wouldn't tell me about it? I did wonder why Daddy waited as long as he had to say anything, though. He didn't actually tell me until after I'd moved back home. But either way, my father let me know what he saw, so Louis was busted.

"Jamie, it's not what you think. That woman, we're not involved. I swear to God."

"I thought you didn't know that woman. I thought Darnel was mistaken." Of course, I was making the assumption that Daddy and Darnel had both seen him with the same woman, but it wasn't that far-fetched. They'd both described the same type, and I had found that light-colored hair on him a while back, so I thought it was pretty safe to say we'd all seen evidence of the same skinny white blonde.

"I . . . uh—"

"You know what, Louis?" I stopped him before he tried to come up with some lame-ass explanation. "You are full of crap."

"Jamie, I am not lying. You have to believe me."

"No, I don't. You might think I'm gonna stand by and watch you lie to me, but I've been a witness to this type of mess too many times. You're gonna have to make do with another woman, 'cause, baby, ain't nothing happening here."

"Jamie, please—"

"Bye, Louis."

"Don't hang up," I heard him pleading as I hit the END button. Just to prove that I meant business, I turned off my phone. Let him call my father's number, I thought, because Daddy would lay him out. He messed with the wrong man's daughter this time.

I felt like waking Daddy up to tell him what was going on,

but I hadn't heard Sandra leave, and the last thing I wanted was to see her ass laid up in Daddy's bed. Dammit! I tossed my cell phone on the floor next to the bed, threw the covers over my head, and tried to fall asleep.

The next morning, like every morning, I still couldn't get Louis out of my mind. I turned on the television, then flipped through the channels to find something to distract me. Daddy had already left for work. I'd stayed in my room, thumbing through the latest copy of *Essence* until I heard his car pull off. On every page there was either an article about getting over a man, keeping a man, or finding a man. I was still so confused that I didn't know which of those things I wanted to do.

The doorbell rang, but I didn't feel like getting out of bed to answer it. I picked up another magazine, but then the knocking started. Whoever was at the door was not going away. At this point, I figured it was Louis, and he was getting on my damn nerves. I ripped off the covers and hurried down stairs, prepared to give him a piece of my mind.

I was startled when I opened the door, because while I'd been expecting to see my tall, handsome ex standing there, I was greeted by the pale face of a petite blonde. This wench was standing at my door looking like a damn schoolteacher, and it took only a few seconds for me to realize who this chick was. My only question was, did she come on her own, or did Louis send her? If he did, then she was one dumb bimbo for doing whatever he said.

"Can I help you?" I placed a hand on my hip and looked her up and down.

"Are you Jamie?"

"Who wants to know?" I answered like I didn't have a clue who she was. Let her do all the work of explaining why she was at my door at nine-fifteen in the morning.

"My name is Ashley Ford. I'm a friend of Louis."

"A friend of Louis." I laughed. "I'm sure you are. You know, you have some nerve coming over here."

"Look, Jamie, you've got this all wrong. I'm not involved with Louis."

"Is that right?" These two must have really thought I was a

fool. But she was an even bigger fool than me if she was willing to come over here and deny their relationship. What kind of weak-ass woman allows herself to be kept in the second slot—or even worse, allows herself to be used as bait to get the other woman to come back? If she wasn't screwing my man, I might have felt sorry for this wench.

"He really loves you, you know."

I shifted my body, aggravated. Louis must have really put it on her, 'cause she was dumb as rocks. Ain't no way in hell I'd go to the other woman and tell her how much my man loved her.

"So I guess you two just work together, huh?"

"Something like that."

"Well, that makes sense. I'm sure he takes all his clients out to romantic restaurants."

"Look, Jamie, you really don't understand."

I stepped forward and got in her face, thinking that if my name came out her mouth one more time, I was gonna have to slap the shit outta her. But I had to give her credit; she didn't back down. It actually looked like she might do something if I took a swing at her.

"No, *you* don't understand," I snapped in her face, still trying to intimidate her. "Where I come from, you don't go to the other woman's house if you ain't ready to whip her ass. Now, I don't know how or why Louis talked you into coming here, but it's best you leave, or I can't be responsible for my actions."

She didn't say anything, but she smirked at me like she knew some secret I didn't. As far as I was concerned, that was as good as fighting words. I took a swing, but somehow I missed and landed on the ground. When I looked up at her, she was panting a little, standing in some weird karate-looking stance. For a second, I thought maybe she had put me on the ground.

"I wouldn't do that again. You're going to hurt yourself," she said, as calm as can be. This skinny white girl didn't seem the least bit scared of me, and it was really starting to piss me off.

I got up and lunged at her. She barely touched me, but I landed on the ground again, this time harder. How the fuck did she do that?

"Jamie, you need to listen to me," she said as I lay on the

ground, looking up at her. "Louis is a good guy. He really loves you."

I struggled up from the ground, but this time I kept my distance. My ass was hurting from falling so hard, but she barely looked winded. I knew she'd put me down a third time if I tried anything.

"Yeah, well, he loves three of us—me, you, and the other woman in Detroit." If I couldn't hit her, maybe I could hurt her with my words. I thought maybe I had succeeded, because when I mentioned Detroit, this funny look passed over her face.

"Oh, so you didn't know about Detroit?" I asked to make it sting a little more.

"I know all about Detroit. But I'm not Louis's woman, and he doesn't have a woman in Detroit."

"You know, you must really think I'm stupid. If you ain't his woman, then what the hell are you doing here?" I asked, getting ready to slam the door in her face.

"I'm a U.S. federal marshal assigned to protect Louis." She pulled out a badge and ID and gave it to me. The name on the badge read AGENT ASHLEY FORD. I wanted to dismiss it as a fake, but it looked real enough, and together with her surprising martial-arts skills, I was starting to wonder if she was telling the truth.

"What the heck is going on?" There was no more toughness in my tone, just a sick feeling in the pit of my stomach.

She gave it to me straight: "Louis is in the Witness Protection Program, and we think you may have alerted some people to his whereabouts."

My knees went weak as I realized she was talking about the phone call I'd made to the mystery woman in Detroit. Had I really put Louis's life in danger? Is that why he let me go so easily when I told him I was moving out? *Well, if you really want to leave, then maybe that's for the best,* he'd said. I started to cry when I realized that if this woman was telling the truth, Louis might have let me go for my own safety.

"Let's go inside so we can talk," she said.

I was too confused to protest. I followed her into my living room and sat, numb, on the couch beside her.

"He's a brave man. But in order to keep him safe, I need you to tell me a few things."

I looked at her with scared eyes, afraid of hearing how I had put my man in danger.

"Is he home? Can I see him?"

"He's not at home anymore. We had him moved when you moved out. Don't worry. Just a security precaution. And, yes, you can see him. That's why I'm here."

Darnel

40

I was sitting on a bench across from Keisha's apartment complex, waiting to see what broke-ass nigga she would drag home tonight. Believe it or not, even after the scene at her mother's house, she still hadn't realized that she had no choice but to come back to me. She wouldn't even answer my calls. So, I was gonna wait here on this bench until she came home and then get rid of whatever dude was sniffing behind her and try to talk some sense into her. It's not that I wanted to be sitting there, but I needed to make my point—whatever she did and whoever she did it with, I was gonna be watching her ass.

I was so caught up with my thoughts that I didn't see Keisha approach me from the side.

"You need to stop this, Darnel." Her brown eyes were flashing. I checked out the tight jeans and the barely there top skimming her breasts. Damn, the girl had a hot body. I could feel the blood rush to my groin. No matter how mad she made me, Keisha could still turn me on.

"What?" I asked innocently, taking a page from her playbook: unless you're caught in the act, the smart thing to do is deny everything.

"I'm sick of this shit!"

"Sick of what? I'm just sitting here on a public bench, minding my own business. You're the one who came over here and talked to me."

"No, you're sitting here on a bench across from my goddamn apartment, waiting for me. You're stalking me! You done destroyed my life. You keyed that man's car, sent pictures over the

Internet, ruined my friendships, made me lose my job, and now my parents won't even talk to me."

"And you don't think your behavior had anything to do with that?" I stood up and got in her face. "I mean, your own mother called you a whore."

"Fuck you!"

"That would be nice, but I must insist that you have an AIDS test first. You can understand that, can't you, with all these multiple partners you have and all."

"You're not going to get away with this." She turned and started walking away.

I called after her, "I'm just saying, you shouldn't blame a brother for your own foul-ass behavior. Now, if you want, we can go upstairs and talk like two rational adults. Maybe order some Chinese."

My offer made Keisha stop in her tracks. She turned around to face me and screamed, "Are you crazy? I'm not letting you in my house." She was standing there in the middle of the road, waving her arms around and screeching like a madwoman. The shit actually looked kind of funny—funny enough to be a YouTube video. I pulled out my camera phone and turned on the video function.

"This is good!" I taunted. "Keep it up and this video will go viral in no time."

She froze for a minute as she realized what I had just said. Then she really blew her top. "Oh, so you think this is funny? You wanna put me on the Internet again? Well, go right ahead, motherfucker! As a matter of fact, here's something else for you to put on there." Suddenly, she pulled her top up and shook her exposed breasts wildly.

"Keisha, stop it!" I yelled, but she just kept right on going, pulling her top off totally and posing all kinda crazy ways. People passing by in their cars were twisting their heads around to make sure they didn't miss a moment of the action.

This wasn't fun anymore. I closed my phone and walked over to her.

"Put your shirt on."

"Why?" she asked, still steaming mad. "You the one wanna play with pictures on the Internet. I might as well give you something to play with. You want to put the shit on MySpace or

YouTube or something? Go right ahead, 'cause guess what, Darnel? I don't give a damn anymore."

"Why are you acting this way?" I asked.

"Motherfucker, you know why I'm acting this way! You kept pushing me and pushing me, wouldn't let up. Well, you done put my business out there so bad, there's nothing left that could embarrass me."

"I was only trying to get you to understand how bad you were making yourself look by acting that way. I just wanted the old Keisha back."

She actually laughed out loud at that one. "Yeah, well, I sure as hell don't want you back. Matter of fact, check this out." She turned around and screamed for the whole neighborhood to hear, "This motherfucker right here's got a little-ass, two-inch dick! And he can't fuck worth a shit! I'm thinking he's probably on the down low!" With that, she spun on her heel and stomped away, giving me the finger as she left.

I headed straight for my car, trying to hide my embarrassment, thinking, *What the hell was that all about?* I never expected things to go that way. I needed a drink.

An hour and a half later, I was sitting at the bar at T.G.I. Friday's when my cell phone rang. It was Keisha.

"Since you like pictures, check your e-mail." She hung up before I could respond, and when I tried to call her back, she didn't answer. I checked my e-mail on my phone, but what she sent was an attachment, and I couldn't open it. I had to get to a computer. I threw down some cash and hustled to my car.

On the drive home, Keisha called my phone again.

"Did you like that?" she asked.

"I'm not at my computer yet."

"Oh, wait 'til you see this."

"What the fuck is going on?"

"Darnel, how come we never had this much fun?"

"What the hell are you talking about, Keisha? We had a great time."

"Yeah, but it wasn't like this."

"Like what?"

UP TO NO GOOD

"You'll see. Check your e-mail."

"Keisha, I love you."

"You know what they say, Darnel. Sometimes love just ain't enough."

"Did you take something?"

"What, now I'm a drug addict?"

"Your voice just sounds like you're fucked up."

"I guess you can say I'm getting fucked up." She laughed, and I heard some male voices joining her in the background.

"What the hell is going on? Who's over there with you?"

"Just get to a computer and you'll find out." She hung up on me.

By this time, I was doing thirty miles over the speed limit to get home to my computer. I parked my car, not sure if I remembered to lock it, and jetted up to my front door.

I turned on my computer, which took a lifetime to boot up. Any other time, the shit would load in a few seconds, but as I paced back and forth frantically waiting to see what Keisha had sent me, my laptop was taking its own sweet time. Finally, I got online and hit my mailbox. There was an e-mail from Keisha with a link to a site where users could upload their own live video.

I was afraid to click on the link, because as crazy as Keisha was acting, I had a bad feeling about what I would see. Instead of going to the site, I picked up the phone and dialed Keisha's number.

"Are you watching?" she sounded excited.

"What's wrong with you?"

"With me? You got me fired, my parents don't speak to me anymore, I lost my friends, and mostly everyone thinks I'm a whore because of you. Well, guess what, Darnel? I don't care anymore. I don't give a fuck what you, your family, my family, or anyone else thinks about me. So I'm just gonna live my life and do whatever the fuck I want. And right now, I want some dick."

Shit. The way she was acting, it looked like my whole plan had backfired.

"Keisha, you don't have to do this, you know. It doesn't matter what anyone else thinks of you. I love you. Come back to me and I'll make things right."

"Save it, Darnel. I don't have time to talk to you about this anyway. I got some partying to do. Just click on the link, you punk."

She disconnected the call. With a sick feeling in the pit of my stomach, I went to the site and nearly lost my mind when I saw the video. It was a live feed from Keisha's bedroom. She was naked in bed with three—yes, three!—dudes surrounding her. I felt like throwing up. Where the hell did she find three guys willing to do something like this so quickly? What, did she have these freaks on speed dial or something?

I was disgusted but couldn't turn my head away. It was horrifying and fascinating at the same time. How could the woman I loved have sunk so far? All three guys were on their knees on her bed, and Keisha was squatting in front of them, giving head to each of them, going from one dick to the next and back again.

Then, on the screen, I saw Keisha do the strangest thing. She stopped sucking and picked up her phone. I watched her dial, and the next thing I knew, my phone was ringing.

"Well, are you enjoying it?"

"Keisha, stop," I pleaded.

"I sent it to your daddy too. He's a pimp. He might want to join in." This time, she didn't hang up. I watched her put the phone down on the bed, the call still connected. She got back to work on all three guys. One motherfucker had the nerve to look right into the camera and smile at me.

"Keisha!" I screamed her name desperately. "Keisha!" I had to stop this shit now.

She looked down at her phone, so I know she heard me, but she didn't pick it up. She waved to me in the camera, then flipped over on her stomach so one of the dudes could take her from behind.

I couldn't stand it any longer. What the hell was wrong with her? Had she gone completely nuts?

I shut down my computer, then sat at my desk and cried.

I sat there long enough to fall asleep in a puddle of my own tears, and I didn't wake up again until my phone rang. I picked my head up off the desk and answered the call.

"Okay, my friends are gone now, so I can talk to you."

"Why are you doing this to me?" I said, my voice cracking from all the crying and wailing I'd been doing.

"Why not? I figured it's my turn. You wanna ruin my life, call me a whore, and stalk me all over the damn place? Well, I decided I'm not gonna take it anymore. You are not gonna have power over my life, Darnel. If anyone's gonna fuck up my life from this point on, it will only be me.

"And this is just the beginning. You think this shit hurt? Just wait until I start stalking you like you been doing me."

The phone went dead, and I threw it across the room.

Keisha done lost her damn mind! What the hell was I supposed to do now?

Jamie

41

I rolled over and looked out the window at the lights of New York City, which were twinkling across the river. Louis was in the bed next to me, in the New Jersey hotel room where Agent Ford had brought me to see him.

Once she told me that my phone call to Detroit might have put him in danger, I flipped out. She had all kinds of questions for me, but I told her I didn't want to talk until I saw Louis. She brought me to him and left us alone so he could explain. I hadn't left his side since.

When I first walked into the hotel room and saw Louis, no words were necessary between us. I fell into his arms and sobbed, and he held me until I calmed down. All it took was one look in his eyes before we were making love on the couch with more passion than I'd ever felt. Afterward, as I lay in his arms, he told me the whole story.

Louis was not an orphan. He was born Rashid Jensen, and he actually came from a large, close-knit black Muslim family in Detroit. He'd been forced to leave behind his parents and five siblings, as well as the successful used-car dealership he owned, when he entered witness protection. My heart broke when he told me that, because I knew how much I loved my father and brother, and I couldn't imagine how hard it must have been to leave them like he did.

But then he explained that two of his siblings were the cause of all this. His sister Khalifa and his brother Kareem had become deeply involved in a Muslim extremist group, and they had begun to cooperate with a domestic terrorist cell. The group planned on putting toxic chemicals into various water supplies around the country to kill as many Americans as possible.

Louis might never have known about his siblings' activities except that they came to him, asking him to provide the trucks and cars they would need to transport the toxins. It seems they misjudged his feelings about his country. They thought he would be loyal to his family first. Even if he said no to providing the trucks, they never expected that he would go to the authorities.

But that's exactly what Louis did. He reported what he knew to the FBI, and they convinced him to go undercover to help break up the cell. With Louis's help, the plot was thwarted, and most of the members of the cell were taken into custody.

His brother was arrested and awaiting trial, but his sister was still at large with a few other members of the group. Unfortunately, they knew that Louis had cooperated with the FBI, and now they had a contract out on his life to stop him from testifying. Louis's reward for his patriotism was leaving behind the life he knew and starting all over again with a whole new identity.

"Still, you did the right thing," I told Louis after he told me his story.

"I only did my duty. If I hadn't reported them, too many lives would have been lost, and I would have had to carry that with me forever."

"Do you ever think about contacting your family?"

He looked at me sadly. "I can never talk to them again. It would put them in too much danger."

"And the phone call I made?" I asked, feeling an overwhelming sense of guilt.

Louis reached out and squeezed my hand. "They don't know for sure who you talked to. That was my parents' number you dialed, so it could have been one of my sisters or my aunt. The problem is that we don't know who that person might have told about the call."

"So they're not sure it put you in any more danger?"

"They're still looking into things. But there's been enough Internet chatter to make them think my identity has been compromised."

I knew what that meant. "You're never going back to that house again, are you?"

He shook his head.

"I'm so sorry, Louis," I told him, tears running down my face.

"Shhh," he comforted me. "They told me to destroy all evidence of my old identity. That license never should have been around for you to find in the first place. I just needed to be reminded of the old me sometimes."

It was almost too much for me to comprehend. Not only was Louis not cheating on me, but he was also a hero. After our conversation, I'd spent four straight days trying to apologize to him. We'd made love several times a day, as if every time might be our last.

In truth, I wasn't sure if these might be our last days together. I knew that Agent Ford couldn't let us stay in this hotel room forever. Sooner or later, they would create another identity for Louis and probably move him out of New York. But I hadn't gotten up the nerve to ask what would happen to him. And, of course, that meant I had no idea what would happen to us.

When he rolled over and opened his eyes, I leaned down to give him a kiss.

"I love you."

"I love you too," he said, taking me into his arms.

"What's going to happen, Louis?"

"What do you mean?"

"Well . . . you're not safe here. Are you going to—"

He lifted my chin and kissed me deeply. "Yes, I'm going to have to move."

Tears filled my eyes instantly.

"Once this trial is over, I've got to move to another city, to another life."

I wanted to say I would miss him, but that would mean acknowledging that I might never see him again. I couldn't even bear to think it.

"I want you to be part of that life."

I looked into his eyes as if it would help me process what he'd just said. What I saw there was love. "What are you saying, Louis?"

"When I move, I want you to come with me."

"But . . . does that mean I have to leave behind Daddy and Darnel?"

"Jamie, people move away from their families every day."

I was silent for a long time, thinking about the reality of what he'd just said. Louis left behind his whole family, but that was a sacrifice he made to save thousands of lives. Could I really sacrifice my family just to be with Louis? What if I did and then it didn't work out between us? Where did that leave me?

"This is a lot to think about, Louis. I really don't know if I'm strong enough to do it. How could I just leave Daddy like that? I mean, he's my father, and you're . . . you're—"

"I want to be your husband," he said. He got out of the bed and knelt beside it. "Jamie, I want you to come with me and marry me."

"Oh, Louis," I cried, climbing out of bed and into his arms. "I love you so much. If the circumstances were any different, I'd being saying yes right now. But you understand how difficult this decision is for me, don't you?"

He stroked my hair and spoke softly. "I know it's hard. And I know you love your father and Darnel, but they're both grown men with their own lives. Darnel is young. He's going to move on and find a new woman to love, and your father will have Sandra to help him through it if you leave."

I was too numb to even get mad that he mentioned Sandra.

"You and I can start our own life together. I promise you, I can give you a good life."

I believed he would give me the best life he could, but what kind of life would it be if it came with a whole new identity?

"I need you," he said.

"Louis, please, you have to give me some time. This is not an easy decision."

"Time is not something we have. They can only let me stay here so long before it becomes too risky. I'm only here now because I'll be testifying in the next few days, so they don't have time to settle me in to my new life yet."

"If I go with you, will I ever be able to see my family?"

He shook his head. "I can talk to Agent Ford, but I don't think she'd go for it. Not at first. Not until my sister and the others are captured."

He didn't say never; he only said I couldn't see them at first. It was a small glimmer of hope. It was the only reason I didn't immediately say no.

"I love you so much," I said. "I'm just scared that love won't be enough to get us through the hard times."

"I understand," he said, looking so sad.

"It doesn't mean I won't marry you, baby. It just means I need some time to think. Can't you just give me a few days, at least until after the trial?"

"I'll talk to Agent Ford. Maybe she can hold off an extra day or two."

"Thank you, baby. I want you to understand that this doesn't mean I'm doubting my love for you. I love you with all my heart. Just let me go home for a few days and get my head straight, and then I'll give you an answer."

He wrapped me tightly in his arms, and we made love on the floor, expressing the complex emotions that, once I had time to sort through them, would either pull us apart or bring us together forever.

James

42

I stepped into the living room wearing a black button-down shirt, a pair of black slacks, my brand-new black leather blazer, and my head shaved completely bald. I figured since I was going to go bald anyway because of the chemotherapy and radiation, I might as well do it now and make it a fashion statement. With all these brothers with receding hairlines shaving their heads, bald seemed to be in.

Darnel, who'd come over from his place, had been sulking on my sofa all afternoon. He halfheartedly smirked when he saw me. I don't know what that girl Keisha had done to him since their breakup, but the boy had more mood swings than a menopausal woman.

"So, how do I look?"

"You're kidding, right?" He snickered.

"It's not too much, is it?" I ran my hand over my newly shaved head.

"Dad . . ." He hesitated. "Do you want the truth?"

"Of course I want the truth."

"Okay." He shrugged his shoulders. "You look like a damn fool. But don't worry; it seems to run in the family lately." He didn't even crack a smile. "You might wanna invest in a couple of good hats until it grows back."

"Tell me how you really feel, Darnel," I shot back at him.

"You told me you wanted the truth."

"Well, maybe not that much truth."

I walked over to the hallway mirror to see for myself. I didn't know what he was talking about. I didn't look that bad. It wasn't like my hair had been long to start with. I was just happy that I hadn't shaved my head only to discover I lacked a proper head for such a bold move. That would have been bad, finding out after the fact that my dome had a flat top or was misshapen. I hadn't even thought about those possibilities before I took out the clippers and started shaving. Before my cancer diagnosis, I would have put more thought into making such a drastic change, but being forced to consider my mortality had begun to give me a different outlook on what was really important—and hair wasn't high on the list.

"I don't know what you're talking about, son. I look like Samuel L. Jackson in the remake of *Shaft*," I joked, rubbing my hand over my head again.

"No, you look more like Isaac Hayes when he sang the original *Shaft*. All you need is the swollen lips. You want me to hit you in the mouth?"

That boy sure knew how to hurt a man's ego. "Isaac Hayes was the man back in the day," I said with a laugh.

"If you say so. What did Sandra say?"

"She hasn't seen it yet. I was hoping she'd be here soon so I could surprise her too."

The front door opened, and I assumed it was Sandra, right on time. Instead of my lady, my baby girl walked into the room. Jamie had been MIA for a few days and had left only a brief message that she needed time away. I'd never been the kind of father who checked up on his children, but it wasn't like Jamie to disappear for days at a time, so I was a little concerned. Especially since I knew she was going through changes in her relationship with Louis. Still, I resisted the urge to be an overprotective father. I figured she was working things out with Louis or taking time out with a girlfriend to get over him. She was a grown woman, so I gave her space to work through her issues. When she walked in the house looking happy, I was relieved.

"Hey, Daddy." She rushed over and gave me a hug.

"You all right?"

"Oh my God!" she shouted. "Look at your head!" She ran her hands over my bald dome.

"So, what you think?" I posed.

"I think you look cute. You remind me of Shaft." Jamie wrapped her arms around me, putting her head on my shoulder.

"Thanks, princess. I was just telling your brother the same thing." I threw a smug look in Darnel's direction.

"So where you been?" I asked.

"I went away with Louis."

"I thought you were done with that clown." Darnel, who normally would have given Louis the benefit of the doubt, surprised me.

"He's not a clown, Darnel. I love him."

Darnel just shook his head.

"But, princess, I thought you said it was over." I knew to tread lightly, but what I wanted to say was, "Ain't no way you staying with no man who hurt you."

"It was over, but then I met the blond woman. They're not messing around. They're coworkers of a sort."

I looked at her with skepticism. I'm sure she knew I thought she was being played.

"It's hard to explain, but you just have to trust me," she said.

"Yeah, but, baby, I saw them together in Long Island, and your brother saw them in Manhattan. Those two were rather cozy."

"I know what it looked like, Daddy, but like I said, you and Darnel just have to trust me. Louis is the most honest, good man I've ever been with. You always told me don't go looking unless you're prepared to find something. I found what I wanted to, but it wasn't the truth."

"You sure?" Darnel and I said in unison.

"Yep. I was the one trippin' and well, I mean, I am your daughter, and after living with you, I just thought all men cheated."

That comment hurt, but I couldn't get mad at her for speaking the truth.

"Yeah, I can't say I've been the best role model for you two."

"You certainly were interesting to watch," Jamie teased, and even Darnel laughed.

It was nice to see both of my kids laughing, especially after everything they'd both been through lately. In fact, it was just nice to see both of my kids together. We hadn't really been spending much time as a family ever since Darnel's canceled wedding. It seems we'd all become kind of wrapped up in our own worlds, and that wasn't a good thing. These difficult times were when we should be there for each other the most. As the head of the family, it was time for me to bring us all back together. With my health and future so uncertain, it would be important for Darnel and Jamie to have each other to lean on.

"Listen," I said seriously, "since I have you both here, there's something I want to talk to you about."

They stopped laughing and looked at me expectantly.

"Why don't you sit down, Jamie?"

"Now you're making me nervous, Daddy."

"Don't be nervous. I just think it's time we all sat down together as a family. I have some things I want to talk to you about."

Jamie tried to break the tension by asking, "You breaking up with Sandra?" with a mischievous grin on her face.

I didn't crack a smile. "No, we're fine, thank you very much."

"Dad, she ain't never gonna let you be happy with no woman." Darnel looked at me sympathetically.

"Shut up, Darnel," Jamie answered back.

"Stop it, both of you," I said loudly. "This is part of what I want to talk about. There are some things going on, and we need to come together as a family and support one another. We've all been drifting apart lately, and it's time we get back on track."

"Okay . . ." Jamie gave me a look that said she was confused about why I was acting this way.

It was time to just spit it out. "Jamie, Darnel . . . I guess you kids have noticed I've been a little under the weather lately."

Darnel nodded, and Jamie's expression changed. She looked scared, almost like she already knew what she was about to hear.

"Well, I went to the doctor, and I know what's wrong with me." I took a deep breath, or at least as deep as my sick lungs would allow. "I have lung cancer."

Silence hung over the room as my words registered in my children's minds. Then Jamie began to cry. She ran over and threw her arms around me.

"Daddy, no!" She fell apart, sobbing loudly.

Tears wet the corners of my eyes, but I refused to fall apart in front of my kids.

Darnel came over and grabbed my hand, and I could see that his eyes were glistening with tears too. They were both in shock. I knew how they felt. I'd felt the same way before I had had a chance to digest this information.

"But you quit smoking. How can you have lung cancer?" Darnel questioned.

"I never should have started," I told him.

"We'll get a second opinion." Darnel, like most men, wanted to fix this, and although he couldn't do anything, I was proud of him.

Jamie managed to stop sobbing long enough to say, "Daddy, you can't give up. They have all these miracles in foreign countries. We can travel and find one of those doctors."

I patted her on the back. "I have no intention of giving up. They caught it in the early stages, and there are plenty of treatments available to me."

"What kind of treatments?"

"Well, I have to go see a specialist, but Dr. Martin thinks I'll need chemotherapy and radiation."

"You haven't seen a specialist yet?" Darnel asked.

I hesitated. He was right, of course; I should have consulted with the oncologist as soon as I got the diagnosis, but how could I explain to my son that I'd been too scared to face reality?

"I'm going to call first thing tomorrow. I promise."

Jamie hugged me tightly. "Daddy, I'm gonna be here for you. I'll take care of you. I swear I will."

"Me too," Darnel offered. "I can quit my job and help you out at the office."

His words touched me deeply. I'd always wanted him to be part of my company—but I didn't want it this way.

"Look, there is no need for anybody's life to change. I'll be all right. I'm telling you I'm going to beat this."

"We're here for you however you need us, Daddy," Jamie said, and Darnel nodded his agreement.

"You two kids are my greatest gift."

We sat together in the living room for a while, talking about the road that lay ahead and gathering strength from the love we shared. I was feeling confident that my kids would help me stay positive throughout this ordeal, but then Jamie took the conversation in a whole other direction.

"I'm sorry, Daddy, but I just have to ask: Where is the great love of your life? How come she's not here?"

"Jamie!" Darnel tried to stop her, but I could have told him it was no use. Stopping Jamie from saying or doing something she wanted was like jumping in front of a runaway train.

"No, Darnel, I wanna know where she is during our father's time of need." She turned to me. "Oh, let me guess. She's shopping." Jamie stared until I gave her an answer.

I nodded my head.

"See! That wench ain't about nothing but spending money, Daddy!"

"This is hard on her too, Jamie. She was very upset when she found out."

"You told her already? Before us?"

"Sandra's his woman, Jamie," Darnel pointed out, trying to help, but calling her my woman only made Jamie roll her eyes at him.

"Don't remind me," she said.

"Sandra was with me when Dr. Martin called to check on me earlier," I explained.

"She just found out today and she's not here now? Why is she shopping instead of comforting you? Why wasn't she here when you told your children? That's what your woman's supposed to do."

"She'll be back soon."

"Daddy, don't you get it? At a time like this, she chooses to go shopping? What woman would leave her man and go to the mall when he just told her he's got cancer? She's probably trying to spend as much of your money as she can before you have to start paying medical bills."

I cringed. If she knew I'd recently put Sandra on my gold American Express card, she'd kill me quicker than cancer ever could.

"Jamie, cut him some slack," Darnel pleaded.

"This isn't about him. It's about a woman who's only after his money. You think Crystal would be shopping right now? Hell no! She'd be right here trying to shove soup down your throat and make you better."

"Leave my mother out of this."

"I'm not trying to put her down, Darnel. I'm trying to make a point."

"You're wrong about this, Jamie. Just like I don't expect you and your brother to put your lives on hold, I can't ask Sandra to do it either."

I meant what I said; I had no intention of asking Sandra to be by my side constantly, but I did regret that she was at the mall of all places. It only served to strengthen Jamie's argument. She was convinced that Sandra was with me for my money, and there was nothing I could say to change her mind. I knew Jamie disapproved of my relationship with Sandra, but I was still taken aback by the level of hatred she felt toward her.

"Well, I'm pissed because I can't believe anybody would leave you alone at a time like this. But don't worry, Daddy. I'm here for you."

"*We're* here for you," Darnel added, putting a reassuring hand on my shoulder.

"We're gonna get through this," I said as I hugged my kids, saying a silent prayer that Jamie would change her mind about Sandra. What I needed right now was for the three people I loved most to be at peace with one another.

Darnel

43

I was driving to work, thinking over the latest bombshell my family was dealing with. The bad news just kept on coming. First, my wedding was canceled due to no fault of my own, and then my sister, always the drama queen, started having problems with her man. Plus, she'd decided to make life a living hell for my father's new woman, which I totally didn't understand. I mean, Sandra was much younger than my father, but so what? If he had finally found someone who could make him stop screwing half of Queens, then I say give the girl some credit. My own mother couldn't do it, and I'd hated him for years for treating her like he did, but I'd finally learned to forgive and forget, and I wished my sister could do the same. But Jamie wouldn't let up, even now that we'd gotten the worst news of all, that my father had cancer. Sweet Jesus, what the hell was gonna happen next?

In light of this new family dilemma, I realized that I needed to move on with my life minus Keisha. Oh, I still loved her; I probably always would, but life was too short to be obsessing over a woman who didn't respect herself, let alone me. So this was it. I was through with Keisha's ass. I would spend my energy helping my dad fight this cancer, and maybe when I least expected it, I'd find Ms. Right.

"Yeah, I'm going to leave Keisha alone," I said out loud as if to affirm my new decision. "She can do whatever she wants with Tom, Dick, and Harry. Makes no difference to me."

I parked my car and started my usual daily routine. First, I'd go to Dunkin' Donuts and get a large coffee and a chocolate donut; then I'd stop by the newsstand and pick up a copy of *The*

New York Times. After that, I'd head to the office building and take the elevator up to the twenty-first floor. I'd greet everyone I passed until I was in my office, settled in my chair behind my desk.

Today, the last part of my plan was going to be a bit different. When I got to the twenty-first floor, I was going straight to my boss's office to give him my two weeks notice so I could help my dad's company while he was battling lung cancer. I headed to the front of the office building ready to visit my boss, but I came upon an unexpected detour.

Outside the front doors, I noticed a couple wrapped in each other's arms, kissing passionately, as if there weren't hundreds of office workers rushing past them on their way to work. I shook my head, thinking that these two definitely needed to get a room. I wouldn't have paid it any more attention, but as I got closer, I noticed there was something familiar about the woman. She actually reminded me of Keisha from the side. I was just about to dismiss the thought, because every woman seemed to remind me of Keisha in some way, when the woman turned around.

"Hey, Darnel."

Turns out it was Keisha! And she had a huge smile on her face when she greeted me. I can't begin to tell you how pissed off I was that she would bring some dude to my job when all my coworkers knew her and knew about what had happened at our wedding. She was obviously doing this just to torment me. But I was determined not to let her set me off. There was no better time than the present to show her that I really didn't give a damn about her anymore. I stared straight ahead, refusing to even acknowledge her presence.

"I just wanted you to meet my new man," Keisha said in a syrupy voice.

Calm down, Darnel. These two aren't worth the trouble, I thought as I stepped toward the door. I reached for the door handle. That's when the dude she was with stepped in front of the door.

"Going somewhere, Dee?" I didn't have to see his face to recognize that voice.

"Get out my way, Omar. Only reason you acting this way is because Keisha's here." I tried to step past him, but he blocked my way again.

"Nah, talk that shit now. I'm not on crutches and my back ain't turned like it was that night. So talk that shit now, punk."

We were standing eye to eye. I tried to stay cool, but the thought of the two of them together made me snap. I couldn't help it. I took a swing. If it was any other guy in front of me, I think I could have kept my temper under control, but not with Omar standing in front of me. I hated him too much.

I missed but, unfortunately, Omar didn't. I wasn't sure what he hit me with, but it was hard, and I hit the pavement like a brick.

"You snuck up on me from behind before, but try something now." Omar stood over me, looking all tough. "I told you this motherfucker wasn't shit. I don't even know what you saw in him."

"Neither do I, baby." Keisha leaned over and kissed his neck.

"You the one ain't shit, Omar. No real man would do this to one of his boys. Man, you ain't nothin' b—" I noticed a coppery taste in my mouth. I reached my hand to my lip and saw blood on my fingers.

"Did you think 'cause you some spoiled-ass bitch who ain't never had to work a hard day in your life that you the shit?" Omar sneered.

"Oh, that's what this is all about? You jealous 'cause my family gives a shit about me? What about all the things we did for you? My father practically made you part of our family, and this is how you do?"

"Your family don't give a damn about me."

"Not anymore they don't. Not after you stabbed me in the back for this whore."

He hit me again in the face. I swear his fist felt like a piece of steel. "If you ever call my girl a whore again, I'll kill you." He gave me another hard punch in the jaw.

"Omar, stop." Keisha grabbed his hand, but Omar stood his ground, still yelling at me as I wiped the blood off my face.

"What? You think I give a damn what you think? You the pussy who can't handle your business. I ain't got no problem with mine." He cupped his package and thrust his hips in Keisha's direction.

By this time, a few of my coworkers had come on the scene

and were standing by, probably afraid of getting hit if they got too close. This just pissed me off even more, the fact that now there were witnesses to my humiliation. I was always Mr. GQ Professional at work, and now these fools had come up here, getting all ghetto for everyone to see. I thought I'd been mortified at my wedding, but this was just as bad. If I hadn't already been planning to resign, I surely would have lost my job over some shit like this.

Keisha, who just a minute ago had been trying to get Omar to leave, suddenly seemed happy to have an audience to witness my shame.

"Yeah, that's my man there," she announced, flaunting a small ring on her left ring finger. "Now, what you gotta say to that? And he'll whoop your ass even worse if you ever try to mess with me again."

So now they were engaged, I thought. Omar had always been in love with her, and I guess she had finally given in and said yes. I didn't want it to bother me; I wanted to be able to say she was a worthless whore and he could have her, but it still hurt like hell that my former best friend was with the woman who was supposed to be my wife.

I charged at Omar, but he clocked me with something. I saw a flash of gold and realized what it was: He was wearing brass knuckles! I landed hard on the sidewalk.

When I looked up, I saw Jason, the security guard who worked in our building, coming toward me. "Mr. Black, whoever this man is—and I use that term loosely—he's not worth it. Don't let him make you lose your job," he said as he helped me off the ground.

He then turned to Omar. "Young man, I suggest you get off the premises before I call the police."

I watched Keisha and Omar walk away as I caught my breath and spit blood onto the sidewalk.

"Mr. Black, do you want me to call the authorities?" Jason asked, looking relieved that things hadn't gotten physical between him and Omar. Jason was one of those overweight security guards who was posted in the lobby more for show than for safety. Omar would have whipped his ass for sure.

I shook my head. "No, don't call anyone. Just help me inside so I can clean up this blood." I almost didn't recognize my own voice. It sounded empty and dead—just like I felt inside.

The small crowd dispersed, no doubt headed to their offices to stand around the watercoolers and describe the fight they'd just seen. Jason helped me into the men's room in the lobby.

I stared at my bloody reflection in the mirror and wondered how my life had turned into this nightmare. But I considered the question with an odd sort of detachment, like I was watching this happen to me from another place. Inside of me, there was no more pain, no more jealousy, and no more love. In its place was an empty pit, waiting to be filled. I stared at my face and almost didn't recognize myself. My eyes looked lifeless.

As I examined my injuries, I began to feel something new taking root inside of me. It was like a fire smoldering in the center of my being, and I knew it was only a matter of time before that spark became a raging inferno. Now I knew what pure hatred was.

James

44

"Hey, honey." Sandra came into my study wearing a tight-fitting Victoria's Secret nightgown. She was beautiful, but her eyes looked sad. It had been a hard day for all of us.

Darnel had been beaten up pretty badly by a brass knuckles–wielding Omar. They called me from his office to tell me what had happened, and although Darnel said he was fine, I insisted that he go to the hospital to be checked out. He ended up being okay, just a minor concussion along with some scrapes and bruises. His ego was hurt more seriously than his body—so much so that he didn't even want to pursue charges against Omar. I think he felt totally defeated, and I felt powerless to change that. I left him at his apartment, making him promise to call me if he changed his mind about contacting the authorities.

On top of that, Jamie had delivered some news of her own that had me worrying about both of my kids. She had rushed over from the office with me to meet Darnel at the hospital. On the way, she confided in me the true story behind Louis, the blonde, and the Witness Protection Program. She also told me that Louis had proposed. If it weren't for my cancer diagnosis, she would have seriously contemplated it.

I told her she should go with Louis, because these people in Detroit might already be on to her. If they thought she could lead them to Louis, she might be in danger. The last thing I wanted was for something to happen to my baby, and at least I'd know she was safe if she was in witness protection with Louis. But true to her stubborn nature, she insisted that she wasn't going anywhere until my cancer was gone. She felt certain that none of the people who were after Louis knew who she was. I wanted to talk to the blond agent myself to be sure, but Jamie wouldn't even tell me where Louis was. She said she didn't want me worrying when I was sick—like I could do anything but worry at this point. I have to be honest; it all seemed like a nightmare.

Once we got back from the hospital, Jamie, Darnel, and I had gone out to dinner together. We went to a local barbecue joint, hoping the loud music and cheerful crowd would distract us. And it had. By the time we came back to my house, we were all managing to tell a few jokes and laugh a little. But when we pulled up in front of the house and saw Sandra's car parked there, Jamie's mood changed instantly.

"Looks like Miss Thing finally decided to come home. Guess she reached the limit on your credit cards."

"Jamie, honey, please don't. These past few weeks have been very hard on all of us, but it doesn't give you the right to take out your frustration on Sandra."

"My anger at her has nothing to do with any of that, Daddy. She pissed me off long before I knew you had cancer."

I sighed, knowing this conversation was going nowhere. "That may be the case, but tonight, I really just need you to give it a rest."

Darnel stepped in to help. "Hey, Jamie, why don't you come back to my place tonight? We haven't hung out in a long time, and I think maybe Dad needs some privacy tonight anyway."

"I think that's a very good idea," I said before Jamie had a chance to complain.

"Fine," Jamie said, sounding annoyed. "But I'll be back first thing tomorrow morning to make you breakfast. You have to eat to keep up your strength, you know."

I chuckled. "I know, princess. And I appreciate you wanting to take care of me."

I kissed her good night and said good-bye to Darnel, then headed inside.

Sandra greeted me at the door, and just having her arms around me was a comfort. Then she led me straight to the bedroom, and I felt all the day's tension leave my body as she caressed every inch of me before we made love. Now this, I thought, was just what the doctor ordered.

Later, while she slept, I headed into my study. I'd been lying in bed, thinking about what would happen if the treatments didn't stop the cancer. I couldn't fall asleep, so instead of tossing and turning, I decided to go put some of my papers in order so that things would be easier on my kids in the event that I didn't get better. I was sitting at my desk with bank statements and retirement account information spread all around me when Sandra came in and sat on my lap.

Her eyes rested on the papers. I tried to put them back in the folder so she wouldn't ask what I was doing. I didn't want to tell her that I was preparing for the possibility of death. I'd already promised myself I would be nothing but hopeful in front of her and my kids. She didn't say anything, but I had a feeling she had already guessed what was on my mind.

"You okay?" I asked, wanting to steer the conversation away from what she'd just seen.

"Yeah, I just was thinking." I offered my lips, but she kissed me on the forehead.

"About?"

"I'm scared, James. I'm scared for you, and I'm scared for me."

"It's going to be all right. I'm going to beat this thing," I said for what felt like the millionth time. If I said it often enough, I hoped it would come true. Apparently Sandra wasn't as optimistic.

"Are you, James? How can we be sure? The doctor said you have a good chance of survival, but he didn't say it was a hundred percent." She handed me a piece of paper that I hadn't noticed she was carrying when she came in. "Here, read this."

I glanced at it. "What's this?"

"Statistics from the American Cancer Society. It says that one out of every five people with stage one lung cancer dies even when it's found early and treated."

I studied Sandra for a moment. I wasn't quite sure what she was trying to say. I could understand feeling fearful, but there seemed to be something else lying beneath her words, like she was refusing hope. Then a thought came to mind: Was she about to tell me she was leaving because she couldn't handle it?

"Sandra, I don't care what these statistics say. I'm gonna make it. *We're* going to make it."

"Are we, James? 'Cause I was planning an elaborate wedding. Are you going to be here for it? Are you going to be able to walk down that aisle with me?"

I couldn't believe what I was hearing. Sandra and I had never discussed marriage, yet here she was telling me she had already thought about the details of our wedding. Now I was even more confused. Was she telling me she was leaving, or was she trying to tell me just how deeply she loved me?

"Sandra, I'm going to be fine. And if you and I are destined to be married someday, then yeah, I'll be there," I said, trying to sound lighthearted.

She, on the other hand, was completely serious when she said, "So why don't we just do it, then?"

"Do what?"

"Let's go down to City Hall and get married tomorrow."

"Are you serious? You wanna get married tomorrow?"

"Yes. It's the only way."

"The only way for what?"

"For you to protect me."

This conversation was becoming harder to understand by the second. I moved her off my lap so I could stand up. I paced across the floor of my study and asked, "What do you need me to protect you from?"

"Your children." She stated it like the answer was obvious. "You saw what happened to James Brown's girlfriend, how she got thrown out of the house and now she's fighting to get what should have been hers. If he loved her, he should have married her."

I stopped pacing and stared at Sandra, who suddenly didn't seem like the woman I thought she was. "What are you trying to say, Sandra? How is our situation anything at all like James Brown's?"

"James, death brings out the worst in people. And Jamie already hates me. If we're married, then I don't have to fight with her."

"Fight with her about what?" I asked, though it was starting to become clear to me what she was implying.

"You don't want me to have to fight to get control of your money, do you? If we're married, then Jamie and Darnel can't try to cut me out. And while you're at it"—she pointed toward the folder full of papers I'd been trying to hide from her—"we should change the beneficiaries on your insurance policies and your retirement accounts."

"What do you know about my insurance policies?"

"Well, to be honest, I did a little snooping."

I had to struggle to keep myself from yelling at her. She had crossed way over the line, and I was getting this sick feeling that Jamie might have been more correct about her than I ever imagined.

"You had no right to go through my papers, Sandra."

"Oh, don't be silly," she said. "I just came across them by accident. It's not like I went looking for them or anything."

"You just came across them by accident? What were you doing in my desk in the first place?" Now I was yelling, and it started a coughing fit.

"Honey, calm down before you cough up a lung. It's not a big deal, you know. I mean, let's be real. With your history, can you blame me for wanting to look through your stuff? You know, to check out credit card receipts and phone bills, stuff like that. I just happened to find the statements, and I got to thinking . . ."

The truth hit me like an elephant on my chest, and suddenly it was hard to breathe. Jamie had been one hundred percent right about Sandra. How could I not have seen it?

"Why are you looking at me like that?" she asked, hands on her hips and plenty of attitude in her voice. "James, don't trip. As many women as you messed with, I would have been a fool not to snoop around."

"This is all about money to you," I said when I caught my breath. "You're worried that I might die and you won't get what you worked so hard for."

"That's not how I meant it," she said, though not very convincingly.

"Really? How did you mean it, then? No, you know what? It doesn't matter how you meant it, 'cause when I die, everything I got belongs to my kids. And not you or anyone else is going to change that."

Jamie

45

"Ding dong, the witch is dead. The wicked witch . . ." I was singing the old *Wizard of Oz* song as I cleaned Daddy's room. I still didn't know all the details, but when I got home from Darnel's this morning, Sandra was gone and so were all her things. Yes, sir, the witch was dead, and I for one couldn't have been happier.

I had spent the day scrubbing the house from top to bottom, and now that it was nearly dark, I was putting the finishing touches on Daddy's room to get rid of any last remnants of Sandra's presence.

I moved into my room, where I stripped the bed. I was about to put on the tired old flannel sheets I'd been using ever since I moved back in, but then I thought it would be nice to have the brand-new sheets and matching comforter I'd left at Louis's house. Actually, it would have been nice to have all of my stuff back. The day I moved out, I was in a huff and just packed a couple of suitcases. I never really expected to be gone but a few days. I was only trying to scare Louis into understanding just what he would be missing. But when I got home and Daddy told me about seeing him with the blonde and Darnel reminded me of seeing him in the city, my mind had been made up for good—at least until Agent Ford showed up at my door.

I sat and pondered my situation. What should I do? Should I just go over there and get my things? Honestly, I didn't even know what was still there. For all I knew, the federal agents had emptied the place by now.

I couldn't call Louis to find out, because I'd already been warned that making contact with him was too risky. When I left him at the hotel, it was with the understanding that Agent Ford would contact me when they were ready to move Louis. Until then, there was no way for me to get in touch with him without putting him in danger. I wasn't necessarily convinced that it would be all that dangerous for me. After all, I hadn't given that woman in Detroit my name or address or anything. But I wasn't about to piss off some federal agents by disobeying their instructions. I would stay away from Louis for the time being.

As I made a list in my head of all the things I'd left over there, I realized it was more than I originally thought. There were some really great shoes I wanted back and a few pieces of jewelry that, although they weren't expensive, were some of my favorites. And, more importantly, I'd left behind my photo albums. Now that I'd decided to stay with Daddy, I knew that I might never see Louis again. Those albums would be the only memories of Louis I'd have left.

I decided to go back to the house to get my things. The agents had told me not to call Louis and not to go back to the hotel without permission, but no one had specifically told me to stay away from the house we'd lived in together. What could it hurt? I grabbed my purse and headed out.

On the drive to Louis's house, I decided it might be wise to tell Agent Ford where I was going. It was possible the feds were watching the place, and I didn't want to show up there unannounced and have some agent putting me in handcuffs or something. I pulled out Agent Ford's card and dialed the number. She wasn't in, so I left a message.

I pulled up to the house, and the sight of it made me feel like crying. When Louis and I were living here, he used to always leave the porch light on for me; now the whole place was dark. I headed inside, tossed my purse on the couch, and immediately turned on all the lights as I passed through each room.

Every place I looked held a memory of my time here with Louis, but it felt so different now. The house had an echo that gave me a slight chill, and the air was stale. It used to smell like Louis's cologne, but now there was a faint odor, like unwashed clothes or something. I wanted to hurry up and gather my things so I could get out of there.

I walked into our bedroom to start packing up the rest of my clothes, but suddenly the lights went out. It startled me, but I figured it was just an issue with the circuit breaker. We'd always had problems with the electricity, because the house was older. When too many things were on at once, it tripped one of the circuits, and we'd have to turn it back on at the fuse box. Louis had taught me how to do it, so I left the bedroom and headed toward the basement.

I felt my way down the hallway and found the basement door. I went down the stairs slowly, holding on to the banister and trying not to let the whole situation freak me out. I'd done this plenty of times before, I told myself. Nothing to be scared of.

The fuse box was all the way on the opposite side of the basement, so I placed my hand against the wall and started making my way across the room, praying I didn't run into any spiderwebs. My heart was pounding by the time I reached the box, but my nervousness was nothing compared to the fear that gripped me when I heard a loud crash and glass shattering upstairs. I froze.

"I can't see anything! It's too damn dark in here."

"Just shut up and find her. That's her car out front, so she's gotta be in here. Tear this motherfucker up if you have to."

My heart leaped into my throat as I listened to the sounds of feet moving around in the house above me. Whoever was up there was pulling the place apart. I felt my way through the darkness until I found the stairwell. I opened the door to the small crawl space under the steps and climbed in, softly closing the door behind me.

I sat under those steps and started to cry. Why hadn't I taken Agent Ford's warning seriously? Now I was going to die in this house, and then who would be around to take care of Daddy? Darnel wouldn't be able to handle it by himself, especially the way he'd been acting lately. Daddy needed a woman's touch, and I was supposed to be the one to help him. Who would be there to help Daddy and Darnel?

Oh hell no, I decided in an instant. I'd never been one to lie down and give up, and I wasn't about to start now—not when my family needed me more than ever.

I pulled myself together, determined not to go down without a fight. My purse was upstairs on the couch, but my cell phone was clipped to my belt. I pulled it out and hit the SEND button to redial the last number I'd called.

Agent Ford answered the phone on the second ring.

"I just heard your message. What the hell are you thinking going back to that house?" she shouted into the phone as soon as she answered.

"I'm in the house," I whispered, trying to hold back my tears. "Somebody's upstairs."

"Shit! Where are you, Jamie?"

"Under the basement steps, but they're tearing the place apart. They're gonna find me down here." I started to sob.

"Okay, Jamie, keep it together. Stay where you are. We'll have someone out there in the next five minutes. Do not move, you hear me?"

"Tell them to hurry."

Agent Ford disconnected the call. I shut my phone and started to pray.

Lord, please don't let them find me. I don't want to die. I'm too young to die.

I repeated the prayer over and over as I listened to the footsteps above, trying to decipher where the people were in the house. Finally, a voice came from directly above.

"Shit. I can't see a damn thing. Go down to the basement and see if you can turn the lights on. This bitch is hiding in the dark, and I'm not leaving this place 'til I find her. She's gonna tell us where Rashid is even if I have to cut every finger off her hand."

A soft moan escaped my lips. I knew it was only a matter of minutes before they felt their way to the basement and found me hiding there. I started a new prayer.

God, please take care of Daddy and Darnel after I'm gone.

Tears flowed freely down my face as I prepared for my death.

And then I heard the sirens.

"Oh shit!" one of the intruders yelled. "Out the back! Hurry up!" Again there was the sound of footsteps through the house, but this time, they were heading out.

There was a brief silence upstairs, and then I heard the front door crashing open. Now there were footsteps again, but I knew I was safe. I held my breath, trying to slow my racing heart.

Still too terrified to move, I stayed crouched under the stairs until things calmed down upstairs and I heard Agent Ford calling my name. I saw the glint of a flashlight at the bottom of the door where I was hidden.

"Jamie, it's Agent Ford. You can come out now."

I opened the door and stepped out. My legs wobbled like wilted celery. "Here I am."

I was never more relieved to see another person in my life.

"Are you okay?"

I nodded, too overwhelmed to speak.

Agent Ford took my trembling hand and helped me out of the basement. "Take it slow," she said, guiding me outside and into a waiting car.

The streets were lit up from the flashing lights of all the official cars patrolling the neighborhood and surrounding the house.

"That was a close call, Jamie," Agent Ford said. I know she wanted to tell me how stupid I'd been for going back to that house, but she didn't need to. I would be beating myself up about it for the rest of my life. Daddy had always told me my stubborn streak would get me in trouble someday. I bet he never imagined how right he would turn out to be.

I was too dazed to comprehend all that was going on. "What happened?"

"They found out where Louis was living. It looks like they had the place staked out for a few days. Thank goodness you had your cell phone on you. These are some dangerous people we're dealing with."

"Did they get away?"

She nodded, then told the driver to take us away from the neighborhood.

"Where are we going?" I asked, resting my head against the seat. I was suddenly exhausted.

"Do you have your purse with you?"

"No, I left my purse in the house."

"We didn't find a purse in there when we searched the place. Was your license in there?"

"Yes." I turned to look at her with terror in my heart. "Does that mean—?"

"Yes, they know who you are. It's not safe for you."

"What are you trying to say?"

"Jamie, welcome to the Witness Protection Program."

James

46

It had been two days since I'd seen my oncologist, and I was still reeling from the news he'd given me. It was hard for me to believe, but the chemo and radiation weren't working. My cancer was now Stage 3 and was spreading fast throughout my body. The doctor had given me less than a year to live, at best.

Strangely enough, I was all right with that, as long as the kids were okay. I was still young, but I'd lived a rich life.

I'd gotten all my papers in order—I'd even made sure Jamie's share of my estate would be placed in a trust in case she ever needed it or ended up coming home. That was the part that really hurt me, the thought that I wouldn't be able to say good-bye to Jamie. Agent Ford had explained to me that she had to go into the Witness Protection Program with Louis in order to save her life. The people who were after them were unforgiving and relentless, with no concern for human life.

Deep down, I wished I could be the one to protect her, just like when she was younger and life was simpler. But fate had dealt me a different set of cards, and I had to put my trust in Louis, her new husband, to keep her safe.

Agent Ford told me they had gotten married as soon as they moved out of New York. It all seemed a bit rushed to me, but it was less complicated for the feds to create identities for them as a married couple. Besides, Agent Ford assured me that Jamie had exchanged vows of her own free will. Even if I had been able to advise her to wait, Jamie would have done just what she wanted to do. That girl had always been hardheaded, and while that part of her personality used to drive me crazy, now I was glad to see this experience hadn't changed her. It gave me some comfort knowing she would never let herself be pushed around. I believed that she was happy with Louis and would probably run to the four corners of the earth with him.

I smiled as I thought about my daughter, the one true love of my life. She'd grown into a smart, confident woman, and even though I'd been the one raising her, I had to admit she'd taught me a few things too. At no time was that more correct than when it came to her assessment of Sandra. I really thought Sandra was in love with me, but God stepped in at just the right time to show me her true intentions. I examined my conscience and finally recognized that relationship for the midlife crisis that it was. At least if I never get to see Jamie again before I die, she would know that I had finally listened to her. The morning she came home to find Sandra's things gone, she'd had the pleasure of telling me, "I told you so." Yes, my strong-willed girl would be just fine.

Darnel had shown me lately that he was headed in the right direction too. With Jamie gone, he had been coming around a lot more often to help me out. He seemed to be much less focused on his failed relationship, and he was no longer moping around drinking gallons of vodka. He seemed to be putting the past where it belonged—behind him—and his future was looking bright.

He'd practically taken over the day-to-day dealings in my office. That boy was really making his old man proud. He could charm just about any of my clients, so I knew he'd make a fortune in real estate if he chose to stick with it after my death. And I had no doubt he would go on to take good care of Crystal. I'd built a pretty good nest egg over the years, and even if I'd never given Crystal the love she deserved, I hoped that somehow she would feel it now, flowing from the devotion of the son she'd given me.

Yeah, even in times of sadness, I had a lot to be grateful about. Life had been kind to me. What more could a man ask for who had been abandoned by his mother? I had two self-reliant, well-raised children who I trusted would go on and make good lives for themselves.

I'd even decided to make peace with my mother. She was living out in St. Louis, so I got her number and called. I told her that I forgave her. There wasn't any reason to tell her about my illness. I didn't need her that way anymore. I had finally become the one thing I always believed I was—a happy man. And every night before I fell asleep, I took extra time to thank the Lord for giving me my journey. I knew Darnel and Jamie were going to be fine, and that is all a man can ask for at the end of his life.

Darnel

47

I was headed home, feeling good. Today, I'd found out two couples I had sold houses to were approved for their mortgages, and another couple made an offer on a house we had listed. So much for the real estate business being in the toilet. Not a bad day's work if I did say so myself. I was glad Dad had insisted I take the test for my real estate license when I got out of college, even though at the time I had no intentions of joining the family business. Because I was already educated in the field and had experience in sales, I was able to hit the ground running when I did step in to fill Dad's shoes while he was receiving cancer treatments.

Speaking of my father, I was going to stop by his house to check on him once I changed my clothes. Although we spoke every day, he hadn't come by the office in two days, and that just wasn't like him. No matter how ill the chemotherapy made him feel, he still managed to stop by for a short while each day. I think being in the office helped take his mind off his troubles too.

He'd been going through a depression lately with Jamie being gone. He assured me that he knew she was in good hands. He trusted that the feds would keep her safe and that Louis would treat her like the princess she'd been raised to be. But I knew her absence still left an empty place in his heart. And the chemotherapy and radiation sure didn't help, because he looked like he'd aged five years in a few months' time.

I was so worried about him that I'd asked my mother to come up and spend some time with him. I didn't want him to ever feel alone in his remaining days. She refused, telling me that she was done with him after he got together with Sandra. She had finally reached the breaking point in their decades-long relationship and promised herself she would never again leave her heart vulnerable to him. All she wanted from James Black was for him to do right by me. It was a shame, really, because I knew deep down inside he was the only man she ever really loved.

When I got home, I rushed to the mailbox like I'd done every day for the past two months, hoping that I'd find a letter or postcard from Jamie. Nothing ever came from her, but I kept hoping. My dad had told me what details he knew about how Jamie and Louis ended up in the Witness Protection Program, and I knew the chance of us hearing from her anytime soon—if ever—were slim, but part of me didn't want to believe it. I missed my pain-in-the-ass little sister a lot. I just prayed that she was okay.

Inside my house, I sat down at the kitchen table and thumbed through the mail, throwing bills and junk mail to the side. I was left with two envelopes. One was a letter from an old college friend, and the other was in a pale blue envelope with fancy writing. It appeared to be some sort of card or invitation.

I opened it up and read the contents:

You are cordially invited to the wedding of
Keisha Nia Nichols and Omar Jonathan Wilkins
On March 25th

I dropped the invitation like it was on fire, then sat at my kitchen table, stunned, for a good few minutes. Even after Omar attacked me outside my office, I'd tried to forget about him and Keisha, but deep down, I couldn't. I functioned in my day-to-day life and was doing well with the real estate business, but that was just how I appeared on the outside. Inside, that hatred was still smoldering in the pit of my stomach. I thought about them every day, especially since they seemed obsessed with sending me reminders of how they'd betrayed me. Over the past two months, they had e-mailed me pictures of themselves doing all the things Keisha and I used to do, like going to Times Square, having dinner at City Island, going down to Atlantic City, and, of course, having sex. It was like they were trying to provoke me into doing something I shouldn't. But I was determined not to let them get to me.

It was hard work, but every time I heard from the two love-birds, I managed to suppress my anger. Yeah, sure, I cursed them out when they called me at three and four o'clock in the morning, but eventually I changed my number and my e-mail address. I'd tried to remain focused on positive energy so that I could stay strong for my father and help him keep his business afloat. With Jamie gone, I had to shoulder all the responsibility, and I wanted to step up to the plate like a man. I couldn't let Keisha and Omar distract me. When they taunted me and flaunted their relationship during their late-night phone calls, the pain would gnaw at me until I wanted to rip my heart out, but I always found a way to bury it deep down inside. The only thing that really made it bearable was that I promised myself that once my father was better, I would get them back. I didn't know yet how I would do it, but one day I would have my revenge.

I thought that my payback would come sometime far in the future, but this wedding invitation was the final straw, and I was no longer able to control my rage. Not after this. Not after seeing that the date they set for their wedding was exactly one year to the day after Keisha was supposed to become my wife. They'd been screwing for years, but they'd only been a couple for a few months, and yet they were already setting a wedding date. I couldn't believe how sick this was. They had obviously chosen this hurried date just to hurt me—as if they hadn't already done enough damage. Well, they'd been trying to get a reaction out of me for months, and now they'd get one for sure. They'd be sorry they ever messed with me.

I walked over to the living room and poured myself a glass of Grey Goose vodka, gulping it down like ice water. It did nothing to put out the fire of hatred that was burning in the pit of my stomach. For months now, they'd been treating me like I was a piece of shit that had no feelings. Well, contrary to popular belief, I did have feelings, and they'd all been transformed into one big tornado of rage that was getting ready to touch down on both of them. I should have killed them both when I had had a chance.

I finished off another glass of Grey Goose, adrenaline coursing through my body. I couldn't think clearly. As I drained half the bottle of vodka, I just kept seeing images of them going down the aisle, laughing at me the whole time. I started pacing across the living room floor, growing more enraged with each step. Before I could calm myself down, I was back in my car, driving over to Keisha's place to confront them.

I parked right in front of the building. I knew that I should go home or at least call somebody, but I just couldn't stop moving to think. I stepped around to the back alley so I could see if the lights were on in the apartment. The only room lit was the kitchen. I felt my pulse jumping out of my body as I broke out in a cold sweat.

"Walk away, man." I heard the voice and barely recognized it as my own. A part of me knew they weren't worth it; those two dirt bags deserved each other, and I should just keep stepping and let them have each other. But I couldn't. My wounded heart wouldn't let me. My rage propelled me forward.

I crept up the fire escape. It was a hot night, and even from the street, I could see that the bedroom window was open. I peeked inside, and in the dim light coming from the street, I saw Omar and Keisha fast asleep. She was pressed up against him, and his arm was over her back. They were both butt naked. From the way the covers were strewn about on the floor, it looked like they'd done some wild screwing before they fell asleep.

"Calm down, man." I tried to steady my breathing.

My heart was pounding out of my chest. I watched Keisha move, throwing her leg on top of his. I could see all of them—more than I ever wanted to see of their bodies. I stared at Omar's dick, the one thing that made him special in Keisha's eyes. She was right; it was huge. Even soft, it was bigger than mine erect.

My head filled with Keisha's voice, taunting me: *And, yes, he did have a bigger dick, and he wasn't afraid to use it. And guess what? I could handle it. I liked it.*

I hadn't forgotten how she boasted to me that day. What man could ever forget the day his manhood was taken from him? And it made the insult that much more offensive that she was comparing me to my best friend. I felt like ripping his dick off and shoving it down her throat.

That's when the thought came to me, fueled by my burning

desire for both of them to suffer the way they'd made me suffer: That damn thing had to go. Without Omar's huge package to satisfy that whore, what would he and Keisha really have? Talk about sweet revenge.

My racing heart pumped Grey Goose through my veins as I climbed in the bedroom window and slid into the living room. Before I realized it, I was standing in the kitchen, staring at the Wüsthof knives that I'd bought when we moved in. I took a large butcher knife out, then stepped away from the counter.

"You are not going to cut that man's penis off," I said out loud.

When I was little, my mother always told me I talked to myself. But then she would say that it was okay as long as I didn't answer myself—because if I did, I was crazy.

"Oh yes, I am going to cut his penis off," I answered myself.

I felt myself moving, walking back into the bedroom, but at the same time, it was like I was watching myself from across the room. I felt split in two.

I headed toward the window, thinking clearly for a moment and realizing it was time to get out of there. But before I got a foot out, I glanced back at my two enemies, sleeping peacefully. Keisha and Omar had taken advantage of my kindness. I chose to love them all those years, and this was how they repaid me. This was what they thought of my life.

I was in more pain than even the night before I was supposed to get married. That was a shock, but this was worse, because I realized that not only did they know they were hurting me, but they got off on the idea of how miserable I was.

Yeah, they probably called me stupid and naïve as they were screwing like wild animals. They probably made fun of everything that was important to me.

I watched their chests rise and fall with each slow, peaceful breath they took. They were probably dreaming of their next plot to torment me. Everything inside me froze. I just wanted this madness to be over.

I crept back over to the bed and stood over Omar, raising the knife above my head and imagining what it would be like to bring it down between his legs. At that moment, I saw Keisha's eyes flicker, though they remained closed. She was sleeping, her mouth in the shape of a smile, all pleasure as she rolled over and wrapped her arms around Omar.

That slight movement was enough to bring me back to my senses. I realized I had to get out of there before I did something stupid. Unfortunately, Keisha's movement had woken Omar.

"What the fuck?" he mumbled as his eyes opened and he saw me standing there. He threw his arm out to swing at me, and as I moved to defend myself, I lost my balance and fell toward Omar. The knife pierced his chest.

Oh dear God, what the fuck did I just do?

"Uuuh." Omar gasped when I pulled out the knife. Confusion and panic gripped me. It was as if Omar was no longer real, no longer human. I was unable to form a thought; all I wanted to do was take back what had just happened. But somehow, when Omar moved, I knew that I had to finish what I had started. Letting him live would mean the end of my life as I knew it. My father was sick, and there was no one else to take care of him; I couldn't risk Omar telling the police that I'd stabbed him. It would mean certain jail time.

Closing my eyes, I plunged the knife in once more. This time, he stopped moving.

I opened my eyes and saw Keisha next to him, awake, her face covered in blood spatter and her eyes wide with fear. "Oh my God, you killed him," she said in a horrified whisper. "You killed him."

"I didn't mean to. It was an accident," I tried to explain, but from the look on her face and the way she was shaking her head and mumbling to herself, I knew she didn't believe me.

Stabbing Keisha was harder than stabbing Omar, but I knew I had to do it before she could scream. Besides, she'd never keep her mouth shut. When I pulled the weapon from her body, there was no need to stab her a second time. She was gone.

I fell back onto the floor, dropping the knife by my side. The entire room was spinning, and I couldn't catch my breath. I struggled to comprehend what had just happened, because it didn't seem real. It was as if the pieces of myself that had splintered were just coming back together. Maybe I was just waking up from a bad dream. I looked around the room and saw that the walls Keisha and I had painted a beautiful sea green were now speckled with deep red. Everywhere I looked, I saw the same red. And now, finally, I was calm. I just wanted to close my eyes and rest.

"Oh my God!" The neurons in my brain started firing again, and I realized that my clothes were painted red with the blood of two people I had once loved dearly. I looked at the two lifeless bodies on the bed, then down at the knife lying beside me.

"What have I done?"

A river of tears flowed from my eyes. I loved this woman. And even though he'd betrayed me, I still loved Omar. They'd hurt me deeply, but I had never really closed off that part of my heart that still loved them. And now they were dead by my hands. I wanted to die, too, to have this be over. I was so tired of hurting, of gnawing myself raw with thoughts of their betrayal.

I raised the knife high in the air but then dropped it from my trembling hands. I couldn't do what I wanted to do.

I had to call someone. I found my phone buried in my pocket, and I dialed the one person I needed.

"Dad . . ."

James

48

My cell phone was ringing, and by the time I crossed the living room to pick it up off the coffee table, my chest was heaving. I picked up the phone and checked the caller ID while I caught my breath.

I was happy to see Darnel's number displayed on the screen. He'd been working his butt off over at the office lately, and I had been wanting to talk to him so I could tell him how proud I was. Plus, my health was declining steadily now, and it was time I finally told him about the doctor's prognosis.

"Hey, son," I answered.

"Dad . . . I need you to come over here." His voice was thick with panic, sounding almost like it had when he was a child and he would call me to come save him from one of Crystal's spankings.

"What, son? What is it? Are you all right?"

"Yes . . . no, I'm not really sure. I just need you to come here. Right now."

I was wrong. His voice sounded worse, much more scared than he'd ever sounded as a child. Hearing him so distraught set off some sort of primitive instinct inside of me. Suddenly, my adrenaline was rushing, and I was ready to take on whatever was necessary to protect my son.

"Where are you, son?"

"I'm over at Keisha's."

"What?" I caught myself and tried to speak in an even tone. I didn't mean to raise my voice, but there was no logical reason for him to be at her house. "What are you doing there?"

"I just need you to come over here right away."

I decided to stop questioning. My son needed me, and that was all that mattered. "I'll be right over."

The moment I hung up, a wave of dread came over me. My mind sifted through the possibilities: *Maybe he went over there and tore the place up. What if she came home and now the cops were there? Or what if he set fire to the place?* Any one of those scenarios meant plenty of trouble for Darnel. I tried to take my thoughts in another direction. *Maybe they ran off and eloped and now he's having second thoughts.* That could be more easily solved, I decided. But deep in my heart, I knew that none of those explanations could account for the chilling tone in Darnel's voice. No, something worse had happened.

Gripped with fear, I climbed into my car and took the longest drive of my life. When I finally pulled up in front of Keisha's apartment, I heaved a deep sigh and walked on trembling legs to the front door. Each step I took up to her second-floor apartment was accompanied by a burning pain in my chest. I ignored it as best I could, focusing only on Darnel's panicked plea, which still echoed in my head: *I just need you to come here.*

I rang the doorbell. Slowly, the door creaked open, and there stood Darnel, looking like he was in some sort of trance. I stepped inside the dimly lit living room, and my nose was assaulted by a strange metallic smell. As my eyes adjusted to the light, I realized that Darnel's shirt and pants were covered in blood.

"Oh my God! Son, what's wrong with you? What happened to you? Who did this to you?" As I spoke, I was examining him, looking for the source of the bleeding. I struggled to comprehend what could have happened. Could Keisha have done this? Or maybe she had a new man who had come by and caught Darnel here.

Darnel still hadn't moved, still hadn't spoken.

"You okay?" I was about to pull out my cell phone and call the police, but he reached out a hand to stop me.

"Dad, I'm all right." His voice sounded surprisingly measured, calm.

"What the hell happened? What's all this blood on your clothes?"

Tears began to flow down his expressionless face. "I just snapped," he told me in a hoarse whisper. "I couldn't take it anymore. I didn't mean to do it, Dad. I swear. I love them both so much."

"Who are you talking about? What did you do?" I grabbed his shoulders and shook him. I was so afraid, and all I wanted was for my son to come out of this trance and tell me everything was fine.

"Omar and Keisha."

"What happened to them?"

"I killed them."

He said the words that I had been afraid of hearing. From the sound of his voice on the phone to the sight of his bloody clothing, my subconscious mind had already pieced together the truth. But only now as he spoke it out loud did I feel my whole world come crashing down around me.

"They're dead, Dad. I don't know what came over me. I lost it."

I watched as Darnel, my son who had grown into such a fine young man, fell apart and cried like a baby. "Daddy, please help me."

I wanted to pull him into my arms and cry right along with him, but he needed my strength right now more than ever.

"Where are they?" I asked.

Darnel turned around and pointed to the back of the apartment. "In there."

I walked to the bedroom, still praying that this was some horrible nightmare or practical joke. But the grisly scene that greeted me when I looked into the bedroom shattered any last hope of that. I had to hold my mouth to stop from regurgitating at the sight of Keisha and Omar, lying naked in a congealed river of their own blood. It was splattered all over the flowered sheets, the carpet, and the wall. A huge butcher knife, still wet, glistened on the floor next to the bed. Now I could identify the putrid stench I'd noticed when I first entered the apartment. It was the smell of fresh blood and death.

I turned back toward the living room where Darnel stood motionless.

"What the . . . ? Who . . . ? Darnel, how did this happen?"

My boy couldn't have done this. He didn't have the heart. "Who did this?" I demanded, my mind screaming for him to tell me it was someone other than him.

"I did," Darnel said simply. He looked down at his bloody hands, shaking his head as though he, too, couldn't believe what he'd done. "I'm sorry, Daddy."

"Okay, we need to call a lawyer." I fought to stay rational against the panic rising inside me. "This was an accident, right? You didn't mean to kill those people." I couldn't even say their names. Omar and Keisha had been coming to my house for as long as I could remember. Those corpses on the bed bore no resemblance to the lively, happy young people I had once known, before the wedding was canceled and Darnel's life came apart at the seams.

"This was an accident, right, Darnel?"

"Yes. I didn't mean to do it. But they're never going to believe it, Daddy."

The image of Darnel actually wielding the knife and committing this brutal act nearly brought me to my knees. I reached out and grabbed the couch before I fell. It was becoming more difficult to get a deep breath, but I forced myself not to give in to the wave of blackness threatening to overtake me. I concentrated on my breathing until I got it under control enough to speak.

"Jesus Christ, what would make you come over here?"

"They sent me a wedding invitation. . . . They were getting married the same day me and Keisha were supposed to. They just pushed me too far." He sat down on the sofa and buried his face in his bloody hands.

I sat next to my son, no longer able to hold back my tears. I cried right along with him. It was a long while before he spoke again, and when he did, his voice sounded stronger, like he'd somehow come to terms with what he'd done.

"Dad, we need to call the police."

I looked at him, not willing to agree to what he was saying. "No."

"We just have to face facts. My life is over. I'm going to jail, Dad."

It was an image familiar to too many black families: another young black man, sitting in prison for the rest of his life. Except this wasn't just some statistic; this was my son. I couldn't bring myself to accept that as a possibility.

The first thought I had was to send him away to Europe. Then I would have one child hiding in witness protection and another on the run for the rest of his life. Not an ideal situation, but better than the alternative. But then I remembered the biggest difference between Jamie and Darnel: Darnel had a mother who would want to know where he was. There was no way he could disappear without having to tell Crystal why he was going. Even worse than the thought of Darnel going to jail was the thought of him having to tell his mother he'd murdered two people. I would never let that happen.

I thought about Crystal, who had sacrificed so much over the years. I had never given her the true commitment she longed for, and it had cost her heart dearly. Yet she had never kept my son from me. She had raised him to be a good, honest young man who had made me so proud over the years. I had to believe that these murders were not his true nature. This was a crime of passion, not one that he would repeat if given the chance to remain free. And that's when I knew what I had to do. I owed it to Crystal to do right by our son.

"Dad, we've got to call the police. It's over." Darnel went to pick up the phone.

"Put the phone down, son," I ordered, feeling that my decision was right.

He turned to me for an explanation. "Go wash your hands in the sink and don't touch anything but the soap." He did as he was told, and when he returned, I said, "Take off your shirt."

He just stared at me.

"Goddammit, take off your shirt, now!" I felt my strength returning tenfold. There was no turning back now.

Darnel looked baffled, but as I stepped toward him, he unbuttoned the bloody shirt.

"Give it to me."

He did as he was told. I took off my own clean shirt and handed it to him.

"Put this on."

"Dad, what are you doing?"

"I'm trying to save your life. Now, put it on."

With my clean shirt on, he no longer looked like the zombie who'd opened the door for me. Save for a few blood spatters that needed to be wiped off his face, he almost looked like the successful young son who'd been running my business the past few months. That alone was enough for me to trust that I was doing the right thing. I was making it possible for him to put this all behind him.

"Now give me your pants."

"Dad . . ."

"Look, boy. Just do what I tell you. Take off your pants."

An expression came over Darnel's face as he realized what I was planning. "Dad, no! I can't let you do this!"

"Look, Darnel, you're my son and I love you. I know I didn't always live up to my responsibilities as a father, but—"

"No, Dad, you're wrong. You were always there for me whenever I needed you. Mom and I never went hungry. I did this, not you."

"Your mother and you deserved much better, son. True, I supported you financially, but I failed as a father when it came to what really matters. I spent so much time up to no good, chasing physical thrills and running away from the love that your mother offered. I showed you the worst example of how to deal with love, and now I take the blame for what that did to you. Maybe if I had opened my heart and married your mother years ago, we'd all be in a different place right now."

A single tear rolled down to Darnel's chin. "You can't do this, Dad."

"I have to do this, Darnel. I owe it to you and your mother."

He shook his head.

I pleaded with him to understand. "You've got your whole life ahead of you. Mine's almost over anyway. My cancer's spreading. The doctors have already given me a death sentence. I'll be gone in a year. I don't know if I'll ever get to see Jamie again either. I have nothing left to lose, but you have *everything* to lose if you stay here. Now, please, take off the pants and give them to me."

Looking defeated and helpless, Darnel finished undressing and handed me his things.

"Now listen to me, Darnel," I said as I made the switch into his bloody pants and shoes. "This is what I want you to do. Get out of here, go home, and take a good shower; then drive down to your mother's. Before you get to her house, take the car to a detailing place and have it cleaned from top to bottom. Whatever you do, don't tell anyone what went on here. Ever."

He nodded but said nothing. I could only hope that he was comprehending everything I said to him. His freedom would depend on it.

"I want you to go on and live a good life. Make me proud of you. Fall in love with the right woman and have yourself some babies. Tell your mother I'm sorry and that I love her very much."

"Dad, are you—"

"Yes, I'm sure. This is the only way. Now get out of here."

Darnel stepped toward me, and although I longed to hug my son one more time, I backed away. "Don't touch me. I don't want any blood on your clothes."

"I love you, Dad," he cried, and those words meant everything to me.

"I love you, too, son. I always have."

"You don't have to do this," he tried one more time.

"Yes, I do. You would do the same for your son." I tried to smile as I motioned for him to leave. "I love you. Now get the hell out of here and make me proud."

With that, Darnel walked out. I didn't move until I saw him get in his car and drive away.

I made a final sweep through the apartment to be sure all evidence of Darnel's presence was erased. I was wearing Darnel's shoes, but just to be safe, I trampled over the bloody footprint I found until it was nothing but a red smear. I wiped all the surfaces in the apartment—doorknobs, furniture, countertops, and windowsills—any place Darnel might have touched. Back in the bedroom, I picked up the knife and wiped Darnel's fingerprints off of it; then, fighting back the nausea, I laid my hand in a pool of blood to place my own bloody prints on the knife.

Next, I delicately lifted Keisha's nude body and wrapped it in the Oriental rug that lay on the bedroom floor. I wanted the police to think I had tried to hide my crime at first. The more guilty I looked, the less likely they would be to do a thorough crime scene investigation.

Last, I said a quick prayer. "Lord, please help me pull this off. Let my son go on and live a good life. I've had a good life, and I thank you, Lord. I just need you to help me one more time."

Satisfied, I picked up the phone and dialed 911. An operator answered.

"Emergency operator. How may I help you?"

I took a deep, calming breath before I spoke. "My name is James Black. I've just murdered two people."

My son was safe and his life would go on. I had no regrets. I was at peace.

UP TO NO GOOD

CARL WEBER

ABOUT THIS GUIDE

The following questions are designed to facilitate discussion in and among reading groups.

Discussion Questions

1. In the opening scene, did you expect the woman who busted in on James and Crystal to be one of James's lovers? And when you found out it was his daughter, did you think her reaction was justified?

2. Did Darnel go overboard when he attacked Omar and Keisha in his hotel room the night before his wedding? If so, how should he have behaved?

3. Have you ever gone back to a man or woman after they cheated on you? If so, what were your reasons?

4. Should Darnel have searched for Keisha's diary, or would he have been better off never knowing the truth about her cheating?

5. Have you ever met a playboy like James? Was James as bad as his reputation?

6. Did Jamie get on your nerves the way she interfered in her father's and her brother's lives? What would you do if you had such a meddling family member?

7. Did you believe that Louis was telling the truth from the beginning? Or, did you think he was sleeping with the blond?

8. Who was your favorite character? And who did you like the least?

9. Have you ever been like Crystal? Is there a man or woman in your life that you would always sleep with, even if you were in another relationship?

10. What would you do if your parent started dating one of your friends?

11. Did you feel that Sandra was a gold digger from the very start?

12. Were you surprised that Jamie went into witness protection? If she'd had a choice, do you think she would have stayed home with James, or gone to be with Louis?

13. Could you have done what James did for one of your children?

14. Did James help or hurt Darnel by taking the blame? Do you think Darnel was a bad person?

15. If Carl Weber were to write an epilogue, what would you like to see happen to James, Darnel, and Jamie? Do you think it's possible for these three to have a happily-ever-after?

Don't miss the exciting follow-up to Carl Weber's
SOMETHING ON THE SIDE,

BIG GIRLS DO CRY

Coming in February 2010 from Dafina Books.

Prologue

The taxi pulled into the circular driveway, rolling to a stop in front of the expensive double oak doors of the large brick colonial. Roscoe, the driver, a forty-something-year-old dark-skinned man, placed the car in park and turned toward the woman in the backseat.

He liked the way she looked. She was just his type of woman, thick and pretty like a chocolate bar, with large, melon-sized breasts. Yes sir, Roscoe loved a woman with some meat on her bones. He had even thought about asking for her number or perhaps offering to show her around the ATL when she first entered his cab at the airport. Over the years, Roscoe had bedded many a lonely female passenger after picking them up at Atlanta's airport. All it usually took was some small talk and an invitation to one of ATL's bars for a drink. But this sister spent most of the ride on her cell phone, probably talking to some insecure boyfriend or husband back home who was afraid her fine ass would wind up with a Southern charmer like him. Now that they had reached her final destination, he would have to make his move quick.

"That'll be forty dollars, ma'am." He smiled, revealing a mouth full of gold teeth.

Tammy, a woman in her late thirties, didn't notice his unattractive smile or his country accent, things that would have surely caught her attention if she weren't already preoccupied with looking at the house they'd just pulled in front of. She would never admit it to anyone back home, but a twinge of jealousy swept through her body as she stared at the house. The large colonial was at least twice the size of her Jamaica Estates home back in New York, and compared to her tiny yard, this house appeared to be on an acre of land, maybe two.

This has to be the wrong address.

"Are you sure we're at the right house?" she asked without moving her head. She was still trying to process what she saw before her.

"Yes, ma'am, you said four Peach Pie Lane in Stone Mountain, didn't you?"

Tammy glanced at the paper in her hand, then looked at the large number four on the house. "Yes, that's what I said."

"Then this is where you want to be. Do you want some help with your bags?"

She reached in her purse. "How much do I owe you?"

"Forty dollars. I usually charge fifty, but havin' a pretty woman such as yourself in my cab, I feel like I owe you. Maybe I could show you around town before you leave. My name's Roscoe."

Tammy rolled her eyes and shook her head, preparing to put this homely country fool in his place. But before she could reply, she saw someone come out of the house. A big, shapely, light-skinned woman, not quite as large as Tammy, came running toward the taxi. That's when Tammy knew there was definitely no mistake; she was at the right address. But how the hell did her best friend Egypt get a house like this?

Tammy handed the driver a fifty dollar bill then stepped out of the car without asking for change.

Egypt threw her arms around Tammy's neck and pulled her in closely. "Tammy, girl, I missed you something awful." Egypt placed a huge red lipstick kiss on her cheek.

Tammy smiled at Egypt when she let her go. She'd missed her friend too. "Girl, you moving on up, aren't you?" They turned their gazes toward the house.

"You think? Come on in and let me show you inside." Egypt was grinning from ear to ear. "You can leave her bags by the front door," she instructed a disappointed Roscoe.

Tammy nodded and followed her friend. Yes, she wanted to see her house. She wanted to see if the inside looked anything like the outside, and even more importantly, she wanted to know how Egypt and her soon-to-be husband Rashid could afford such a nice house when they earned far less than Tammy and her husband did. Did someone hit the lottery and not tell her?

Tammy and Egypt had known each other for almost thirty years and had been best friends since they met back in elementary school. But even best friends could have rivalries. As close as they were, the two of them had played a one-upmanship game when it came to material things, like clothes, men, houses and such since they were teenagers. Tammy had been winning this competition handily for the past ten years, thanks to her marriage to her successful husband, Tim, but as she walked into the flawlessly decorated foyer of Egypt's house, for the first time she was afraid that the tides had changed.

As she followed behind her friend from room to room, she was so amazed that she barely noticed the people sitting in the large family room until Egypt shouted out, "B.G.B.C. in the house!" and the people in the room all stood in unison and echoed, "B.G.B.C. in the house!"

Tammy couldn't help but blush. She smiled at Egypt, who gave her a thumbs-up. Tammy could feel tears welling up in her eyes, and she experienced a sudden rush of pride. One of her dreams had actually become a reality: She was witnessing the first meeting of the new Atlanta chapter of the Big Girls Book Club, a group Tammy had founded in New York five years ago. Now that Egypt had moved to Atlanta, she was starting her own branch of the book club. Looking around the room at those in attendance, Tammy was happy to see that the requirements for membership in the group seemed to be the same; not one person in the room was smaller than a size 14.

Meet the members of the Big Girls Book Club in

SOMETHING ON THE SIDE

Available now wherever books are sold.

1

Tammy

I love my life.

I love my life. I love my marriage. I love my husband. I love my kids. I love my BMW, and I love my house. Oh, did I say I love my life? Well, if I didn't, I love my life. I really love my life.

I stepped out of my BMW X3, then opened the back driver-side door and picked up four trays of food lying on a towel on the backseat. I had only about twenty minutes before the girls would be over for our book club meeting, but I'd already dropped off my two kids, Michael and Lisa, at the sitter, so they weren't going to be a problem. Now all I had to do was to arrange the food and get my husband out of the house. The food was easy, thanks to Poor Freddy's Rib Shack over on Linden Boulevard in South Jamaica. I merely had to remove the tops of the trays from the ribs, collard greens, candied yams, and maca-roni and cheese, pull out a couple bottles of wine from the fridge, and voilà, dinner is served. My husband was another thing entirely. He was going to need my personal attention be-fore he left the house.

I entered my house and placed the food on the island in the kitchen, then looked around the room with admiration. We'd been living in our Jamaica Estates home for more than a year now, and I still couldn't believe how beautiful it was. My kitchen had black granite countertops, stainless-steel appliances, and handcrafted cherrywood cabinets. It looked like something out of a home-remodeling magazine, and so did the rest of our house. By the way, did I say I love my life? God, do I love my life and the man who provides it for me.

Speaking of the man who provides for me, I headed down the hall to the room we called our den. This room was my husband's sanctuary—mainly because of the fifty-two-inch plasma television hanging on the wall and the nine hundred and some odd channels DIRECTV provided. I walked into the den, and there he was, the love of my life, my husband, Tim. By most women's standards, Tim wasn't all that on the outside. He was short and skinny, only five-eight, one hundred and forty pounds, with a dark brown complexion. Don't get me wrong—my husband wasn't a bad-looking man at all. He just wasn't the type of man who would stop a sister dead in her tracks when he walked by. To truly see Tim's beauty, you have to look within him, because his beauty was his intellect, his courteousness, and his uncanny ability to make people feel good about themselves. Tim was just a very special man, with a magnetic personality, and it only took a few minutes in his presence for everyone who'd ever met him to see it.

Tim smiled as he stood up to greet me. "Hey, sexy," he whispered, staring at me as if I were a celebrity and he were a star-struck fan. "Damn, baby, your hair looks great."

I blushed, swaying my head from side to side to show off my new three-hundred-fifty-dollar weave. I walked farther into the room. When I was close enough, Tim wrapped his thin arms around my full-figured waist. Our lips met, and he squeezed me tightly. A warm feeling flooded my body as his tongue entered my mouth. Just like the first time we'd ever kissed, my body felt like it was melting in his arms. I loved the way Tim kissed me. His kisses always made me feel wanted. When Tim kissed me, I felt like I was the sexiest woman on the planet.

When we broke our kiss, Tim glanced at his watch. "Baby, I could kiss you all night, but if I'm not mistaken, your book club meeting is getting ready to start, isn't it?"

I sighed to show my annoyance, then nodded my head. "Yeah, they'll be here in about ten, fifteen minutes."

"Well, I better get outta here, then. You girls don't need me around here getting in your hair. My virgin ears might overhear something they're not supposed to, and the next thing you know,

I'll be traumatized for the rest of my life. You wouldn't want that on your conscience, would you?" He chuckled.

"Hell no, not if you put it that way. 'Cause, honey, I am not going to raise two kids by myself, so you need to make yourself a plate and get the heck outta here." He laughed at me, then kissed me gently on the lips.

"Aw-ight, you don't have to get indignant. I'm going," he teased.

"Where're you headed anyway?" I asked. A smart wife always knew where her man was.

"Well, I was thinking about going down to Benny's Bar to watch the game, but my boy Willie Martin called and said they were looking for a fourth person to play spades over at his house, so I decided to head over there. You know how I love playing spades," Tim said with a big grin. "Besides, like I said before, I know you girls need your privacy."

Tim was considerate like that. Whenever we'd have our girls' night, he'd always go bowling or go to a bar with his friends until I'd call him to let him know that our little gathering was over. He always took my feelings into account and gave me space. I loved him for that, especially after hearing so many horror stories from my friends about the jealous way other men acted.

Tim was a good man, probably a better man than I deserved, which is why I loved him more than I loved myself. And believe it or not, that was a tall order for a smart and sexy egomaniac like myself. But at the same time, my momma didn't raise no fool. Although I loved and even trusted Tim, I didn't love or trust his whorish friends or those hoochies who hung around the bars and bowling alleys he frequented. So, before I let him leave the house, I always made sure I took care of my business in one way or another. And that was just what I was about to do when I reached for his fly—take care of my business.

"What're you doing?" He glanced at my hand but showed no sign of protest. "Your friends are gonna be here any minute, you know."

"Well, my friends are gonna have to wait. I got something to do," I said matter-of-factly. "Besides, this ain't gonna take but a minute. Momma got skills . . . or have you forgotten since last night?"

He shrugged his shoulders and said with a smirk, "Hey, I'm from Missouri, the Show Me State, so I don't remember shit. You got to show me, baby."

I cocked my head to the right, looking up at him. "Is that right? You don't remember shit, huh? Well, don't worry, 'cause I'm about to show you, and trust me, this time you're not going to forget a damn thing." I pulled down his pants and then his boxers. Out sprang Momma's love handle. Mmm, mmm, mmm, I've got to say, for a short, skinny man, my husband sure was packing. I looked down at it, then smiled. "Mmm, chocolate. I love chocolate." And on that note, I fell to my knees, let my bag slide off my shoulder, and got to work trying to find out how many licks it took to get to the center of my husband's Tootsie Pop.

About five minutes later, my mission was accomplished. I'd revived my husband's memory of exactly who I was and what I could do. Tim was grinning from ear to ear as he pulled up his pants—and not a minute too soon, because just as I reached for my bag to reapply my lipstick, the doorbell rang. The first thought that came to my mind was that it was probably my mother. She was always on time, while the other members of my book club were usually fashionably late. I don't know who came up with the phrase "CP time," but whoever it was sure knew what the hell they were talking about. You couldn't get six black people to all show up on time if you were handing out hundred-dollar bills.

Tim finished buckling his pants, then went up front to answer the door. I finished reapplying my makeup, then followed him. Just as I suspected, it was my mother ringing the bell. My mother wasn't an official member of our book club, but she never missed a meeting or a chance to take home a week's worth of leftovers for my brother and stepdad after the meeting was over. Truth is, the only reason she wasn't an official member of our book club was because she was too cheap to pay the twenty-dollar-a-month dues for the food and wine we served at each meeting. I loved my mom, but she was one cheap-ass woman.

My mother hadn't even gotten comfortable on the sofa when, surprisingly, the doorbell rang again. Once again, Tim answered the door while I fixed four plates of food for him and his card-playing friends. Walking through the door were the Conner sisters—my best friend Egypt and her older sister Isis. Egypt and I had been best friends since the third grade. She was probably the only woman I trusted in the world. That's why sometime before she left, I needed to ask her a very personal favor, probably the biggest favor I'd ever asked anyone.

Egypt and Isis were followed five minutes later by the two ladies I considered to be the life of any book club meeting, my very spirited and passionate Delta Sigma Theta line sister Nikki and her crazy-ass roommate, Tiny. My husband let them in on his way out to his spades game. As soon as the door was closed and Tim was out of sight, Tiny started yelling, "BGBC in the house," then cupped her ear, waiting for our reply.

We didn't disappoint her, as a chorus of "BGBC in the house!" was shouted back at her. BGBC were the initials of our book club and stood for *Big Girls Book Club*. We had one rule and one rule only: If you're not at least a size 14, you can't be a member. You could be an honorary member, but not a member. It wasn't personal; it was just something we big girls needed to do for us. Anyway, we'd never really had to exclude anyone from our club. I didn't know too many sisters over thirty-five who were under a size 14. And the ones who I did know were usually so stuck-up I wouldn't have wanted them in my house anyway.

About fifteen minutes later, my cousin and our final member, hot-to-trot Coco Brown, showed up wearing an all-white, form-fitting outfit I wouldn't have been caught dead in. I know I sound like I'm hatin', but that's only because I am. I couldn't stand the tight shit Coco wore. And the thing I hated the most about her outfits was that she actually looked cute in them. Coco was a big girl just like the rest of us, but her overly attractive face and curvy figure made her look like Toccara, the plus-size model from that show *America's Next Top Model.* Not that I looked bad. Hell, you couldn't tell me I wasn't cute. And I could dress my ass off too. It's just that the way I carried my weight made me look more like my girl MóNique from *The Parkers.* I was a more sophisticated big girl.

Taking all that into account, some of my dislike for Coco had nothing to do with her clothes or her looks. It had to do with the

fact that she was a whore. That's right, I said it. She was a whore—
an admitted ho, at that. Coco had been screwing brothers for
money and gifts since we were teenagers. And to make matters
worse, she especially liked to mess around with married men. Oh,
and trust me, she didn't really care whose husband she messed
with as long as she got what she wanted. Now, if it was up to
me, she wouldn't even be in the book club, but the girls all seemed
to like her phony behind, and she met our size requirement, so I
was SOL on that. I will say this, though: If I ever catch that woman
trying to put the moves on my husband, cousin or not, she is
gonna have some problems. And the first problem she was gonna
have was getting my size 14 shoe out of the crack of her fat ass.

As soon as Coco entered the room, she seemed to be trying to
take over the meeting before it even got started. She was stirring
everybody up, talking about the book and asking a whole bunch
of questions before I could even start the meeting. And when she
and Isis started talking about the sex scenes in the book, I put an
abrupt end to their conversation.

"Hold up. Y'all know we don't start no meeting this way." I
wasn't yelling, but I had definitely raised my voice. "Coco, you
need to sit your tail down so we can start this meeting properly."

Coco rolled her eyes at me and frowned, waving her hand at
Nikki, who had already made herself a plate, asking her to slide
over. Once Nikki moved, Coco sat down. Now all eyes were on
me like they should be. I was the book club president, and this
was my show, not Coco's—or anybody else's, for that matter.
But she still had something to say.

"Please, Tammy, you should've got this meeting started the
minute I walked in the door, because this book was off the damn
chain." Coco high-fived Nikki.

"I know the book was good, Coco. I chose it, didn't I?" I
know I probably sounded a little arrogant, but I couldn't help it.
Ever since we were kids, Coco was always trying to take over
shit and get all the attention. "Well, once again, here we are. Before I ask my momma to open the meeting with a prayer, I just
hope everyone enjoyed this month's selection as much as my
husband and I did."

Egypt raised her eyebrows, then said, "Wait a minute. Tim
read this book?"

"No, but he got a lot of pleasure out of the fact that I did. Can you say chapter twenty-three?" I had to turn away from them I was blushing so bad.

"You go, girl," Isis said with a laugh. "I ain't mad at you."

"Let me find out you an undercover freak," Coco added.

"What can I tell you? The story did things to me. It was an extremely erotic read." Everybody was smiling and nodding their heads.

"It's about to be a helluva lot more erotic in here if you get to the point and start the meeting," Coco interjected, then turned to my mom. "I don't mean no disrespect, Mrs. Turner, but we're about to get our sex talk on."

"Well, then let's bow our heads, 'cause this prayer is about the only Christian thing we're going to talk about tonight. Forget chapter twenty-three. Can you say chapters four and seven?" my mother said devilishly, right before she bowed her head to begin our prayer. From that point on, I knew it was gonna be one hell of a meeting, and Tim would appreciate it later when he came home and found me more than ready for round number two.

GREAT BOOKS, GREAT SAVINGS!

When You Visit Our Website:
www.kensingtonbooks.com
You Can Save Money Off The Retail Price
Of Any Book You Purchase!

* **All Your Favorite Kensington Authors**
* **New Releases & Timeless Classics**
* **Overnight Shipping Available**
* **eBooks Available For Many Titles**
* **All Major Credit Cards Accepted**

Visit Us Today To Start Saving!
www.kensingtonbooks.com

All Orders Are Subject To Availability.
Shipping and Handling Charges Apply.
Offers and Prices Subject To Change Without Notice.